CORPORATE RULES

ALSO BY DENNIS CARR

Coastal Confessions
The Eight Vital Signs (Nonfiction)

CORPORATE RULES
- A NOVEL -

DENNIS CARR

CORPORATE RULES. © 2014 by Dennis Carr. All rights reserved. No part of this book may be reproduced in any manner whatsoever without written permission except in the case of brief quotations embodied in critical articles and reviews.

Published by MedEcon Analytics, LLC

THIRD EDITION

Cover design by Kristin Webster

Author photograph by Scott Quady

Editorial assistance by Cheryl Carr

ISBN 978-0-9881-8641-5

This is a work of fiction. Characters, corporations, institutions and organizations in this novel are the product of the author's imagination, or if real, are used fictitiously without any intent to describe their actual conduct. However, references that are documented in footnotes are accurate.

The Age of Chivalry is gone; that of sophisters, economists, and calculators has succeeded.

—*EDMUND BURKE*

American Medical Researcher Killed in Fiery Plane Crash

ZURICH, SWITZERLAND - Dr. William Mallory died yesterday in a plane crash near the Swiss/French border. Mallory was aboard a private aircraft that went down with two crew members. The crash was reported to have occurred sometime after 10 P.M. last evening. Investigators have offered no indication as to the cause of the tragedy, but Swiss aviation officials are currently investigating the crash site.

Document searches report that Mallory was a prominent research scientist who holds numerous biotechnology and pharmaceutical patents. Believed to be in Switzerland on business, a flight plan indicates that Mallory was en route to his home in Atlanta, Georgia at the time of the crash. Eyewitness accounts report that the jet was a French-made Falcon 50 and rumored to be owned by Zuritech, a Swiss biotech venture. Mallory is survived by his ex-wife and two children.

Prologue

ANAHEIM, CALIFORNIA
WEDNESDAY, JULY 24
9 P.M. PDT

Roberto Perez barreled through the double-doors like the building was on fire. The doors slammed against the second floor entrance and exploded into a hailstorm of glass. In the chaos, he lost his balance, managing to regain his footing only after tumbling down half a flight of stairs. Without thinking, he leaped over the handrail into darkness, instantly wishing he hadn't—he felt pain like needles pricking away at his jeans. Then something sharp snagged his leg, followed by a ripping sound that trailed his descent. Branches snapped under his weight, finally spitting him out headfirst onto a walkway. Instinctively, his hands went out as a shield, and the concrete sheared into his palms like a cheese grater. His body hit the ground in a dry-heave, followed by a rattling like BB's on the sidewalk.

Gasping for breath, Roberto cocked his head for a look back. Beneath a stand of hollies, a lighted sign read: *Anaheim Cardiology Clinic*. A wave of nausea hit him, intensified by throbbing in his head. He drew a hand up to his face and watched as blood soaked into a patch of white powder. The hand was shaking. Scrambling to his knees, he began to pat the ground, searching until he found one of the pills. It was as tiny as a pebble and smooth to the touch. Wrapping it in his fingers, he resumed the search, recovering three more.

On the landing above, Roberto heard footsteps in the broken glass. He panicked and fumbled the pills again, hyperventilating until he noticed one had stuck to his palm. Stuffing it in a shirt pocket, he cut his eyes up at the stairs. The backlighting cast shadows across the man's face, but the silhouette was unmistakable.

"Move and you die," the man shouted, raising a pistol.

Roberto sprang to his feet and slipped, this time going down on his chin. He screamed, and then crawled on hands and knees until he regained his footing. There was an empty parking lot out front, but he knew he would be a sitting duck out there. Instead, he limped down the walkway to the end of the building. His leg felt like it was on fire as he picked up speed, rounding the corner and plowing into a patch of dense landscaping. He blazed his way through to an alley, then slowed to check over his shoulder. There was no one following. A little further down, the alley dumped into a street where a truck blew its horn, swerving to avoid him. Changing course, he crossed the street and made for a Honda parked on the next block.

The door was stuck, and Roberto had to wrestle with the handle before climbing in and gripping the steering wheel. The pressure burned his palms as he sank deep into the vinyl seats. Still shaking, he let go of the wheel and drew a hand across his chest. Then he said a prayer. *God, make him go away.* A bead of sweat trickled down his forehead, and a scene unfolded as he covered his eyes. The image was in his mind, but as vivid as if he were watching it on a movie screen.

Roberto was standing in the clinic's waiting room earlier that day studying a bulletin board. He scanned the room, examining the faces. One or two patients called out his name, but he silenced them by pressing a finger to his lips. Then he eased over to a reception window to inspect a stack of brochures. The Coke-bottle glass slid open, and a woman in uniform leaned out.

"Mr. Perez, I'll have to ask you to leave," she said, cradling a telephone on her shoulder.

"I'm sorry," was all Roberto said.

The glass shut.

Footsteps on the street brought Roberto back to the present. He peeked through his fingers and spotted the man from the clinic standing beneath a street light. He studied the traffic in both directions, and then headed back into the alley. Roberto pressed his fingers tight once again, wondering if coming here had been a mistake.

Roberto had been born in Mexico forty-three years ago. It was only recently that he had dropped the "o" from his name in the hope of making himself sound all-American. The patients in the clinic understood and obliged by calling him Bob, a sign that his rebirth was taking hold. And despite recent events, his ambitions had persevered, driven by the same instincts that had motivated him years ago to smuggle his sixty-seven year old mother into the country.

In Mexico, the missionary doctors had diagnosed her with a heart condition. The prognosis was certain: premature death if untreated. Unfortunately, they had limited resources and lacked the necessary medications. Then a friend from Naucalpan told him about a new pharmaceutical being produced in the plant where he worked. Word had leaked out that the miracle drug was being developed for patients in the

US. Out of sympathy, he had given Roberto hope, but more importantly an address where treatment was rumored to be available across the border.

Roberto had known of people who had made the trek north to America, most never to be seen again. The prospect had frightened him, especially knowing they had broken the law. But that was before his mother's condition had deteriorated. Once the Grim Reaper's shadow appeared, the risk seemed trivial, and soon her life was all that mattered. That was over four years ago.

Today at the clinic, he had spotted patients who were enrolled in the clinical study. He had kept track of dozens that continued to receive free medications, most learning about the study two years earlier in a *La Opinión* ad. A handful admitted to being paid to take pills, simply for answering questions during office visits. It was the same story they had given his mother when she arrived, along with the promise of the best medical care in Los Angeles. At the time, the decision was a no-brainer.

In the reception area last week, Roberto overheard a conversation behind the window about an upcoming meeting at the UCLA Medical Center. He wasn't interested at first, but then a doctor mentioned the magic word. *ZuriMax*. It was the drug Maria Perez had taken for years as a participant in the clinical trial. Roberto didn't know if there would be answers at the meeting, but he owed it to his mother to find out.

Back in the car, Roberto wiped away a tear and popped open the glove box. He pulled out a pair of rosary beads and kissed them before extracting a business card. He checked the street one last time and started the engine.

The address was only a few blocks away, and as he pulled in, the strip shopping center reminded him of his childhood. A patchwork of neon graffiti had been scribbled across the front, leaving few traces of the original paint. He located the suite number and went inside.

There was no receptionist, only plastic chairs in front of what remained of a cubicle partition. He peeked around the partition and spotted a man at a metal desk midway down the wall. The room was narrow with mirrors running full-length on both sides, perhaps a hair salon in its heyday. The man lifted a cigarette, taking his time as Roberto locked eyes with him.

"What do you want, Padre?"

Roberto stood speechless, staring at the man. He resembled a character he'd once seen in a black and white movie, complete with stained necktie. Roberto looked over his shoulder, checking to see if the man was addressing someone behind him. When he saw no one, he eased toward the desk, catching his own reflection in one of the mirrors. An uncertain pair of eyes stared back at him as he reached for a side chair.

"Not so fast," the man said, holding up a hand. He blew smoke into the air. "State your business."

Roberto lowered his eyes, and then bowed. "Are you Mr. Anthony Harkins?"

"What if I am?"

Roberto pulled out the business card. "I need information, *por favor*—please."

"I'm a lawyer, not the Chamber of Commerce," Harkins said. "What kind of . . ." He paused mid-sentence to take a drag on the cigarette. "Do you have money?"

"Yes, yes," Roberto said. "I have money for you to find the doctor meeting."

"A doctor meeting? You sure as hell don't look like a doctor. Why do you need to find this meeting?"

"Please, a doctor treated my mother. She was ill and participating in a clinical trial. Then she died while taking their new drug. The doctor is attending a meeting at the UCLA Medical Center," Roberto said. "I have one hundred and fifty dollars." He stuffed his hand in a pocket.

"You say she died from taking a drug?" Harkins said. He sorted through a drawer and pulled out a pad, noticing blood on Roberto's chin and jeans for the first time. "You're not thinking of stalking this doctor, are you?"

Roberto extracted a wad of bills, and after a moment of silence, looked up shaking his head. He stepped forward and dropped the money on the desk. "One hundred and fifty dollars." Fumbling with his shirt pocket, he pulled out a pill and set it next to the money, pointing. "ZuriMax."

"What's your name, Padre?" Harkins leaned forward and poked the pill with his pen. It was white and chalky.

"Robert Perez."

"Tell me what you know about this meeting: the participants, the agenda . . . and is your mother going to be there?" Harkins hesitated, and then slapped his forehead. "Of course not, she's dead." He reached for the bills and peeled them apart, counting. The money had traces of blood.

"The doctors are meeting on Friday," Roberto said.

"Got it. Can you spell the name of the drug for me?" Harkins wrote as Roberto struggled with the letters. "Take a seat out front, and I'll see what I can do." Harkins reached behind the desk for a telephone directory. "And fill out one of those cards on the clipboard." Roberto hurried out as Harkins picked up the phone and dialed.

"Yes, I'm scheduled for a meeting at the center on Friday, only my assistant misplaced the time and room number," Harkins said into the phone. "That's right, Friday . . . ZuriMax . . . yeah."

A moment later, Harkins appeared in the waiting area. "There you go, my friend." He offered Roberto a slip of paper. "What do you know about this drug?"

"I don't understand," Roberto said, handing over a clipboard.

"There may be grounds for a settlement, especially if your mother died from negligence. These pharmaceutical companies aren't exactly Saint Peter when it comes to liability. And to be honest, the phrase *clinical trial* doesn't suggest tried and true treatment, if you know what I mean. I'd be happy to look into the matter, if you're agreeable to my terms."

"You wish to help me?"

"That depends. Do you have a green card?"

Roberto closed his eyes.

"It might interest you to know, I do immigration work as well," Harkins said. He checked the address and phone number on the clipboard as Roberto suddenly seemed anxious to leave. Harkins held up the money. "We'll just call this a retainer."

Outside, a Mercedes van cruised by the front of the shopping center, slowing when Roberto stepped out of Harkins's office. It turned as he started across the parking lot and eased past him. Approaching his car, the van pulled into the adjoining space, forcing Roberto to squeeze by. Digging out his keys, he was reaching for the door handle when a blow struck him from behind. His knees buckled, and he fell against the car. Before he could react, someone grabbed his hair and hauled him into the van. Duct tape was slapped across his mouth, and then he was forced facedown while his wrists and ankles were bound.

Once secured, Roberto was rolled onto his side. The man from the clinic looked down at him and smiled, popping Roberto on the cheek. "Good news, you're going home . . ."

Chapter 1

ATLANTA, GEORGIA
MONDAY, AUGUST 22
7 P.M. EDT

Cal Hunter studied his reflection in the window. It might have been a premonition or his mind playing tricks, but regardless, an uncertain image stared back at him. Deep within, something stirred, and he looked outside, where the cloudy evening had already begun to cast shadows beneath the trees. He blinked, and then returned to his reflection in the foreground.

Success is about results, not egos. The thought lingered in his mind.

It was a truth he understood well. He'd had his share of success, probably more than most. But at the moment, it was a distraction.

It must be the butterflies.

There was a knock at the door, and his assistant, Sheri, stepped inside. "The crew is ready to prep you," she said. "Is it okay to send them in?"

Cal glanced sideways at her. "Sure," he said. "And Sheri, make sure the lobby is in Bristol condition like we discussed." He straightened the collar of his knit polo, and then lifted his jacket by the lapels, letting it fall naturally onto his shoulders.

"The florist just finished up, Herr Kommandant," Sheri said in a mock accent.

Cal gave her an irritated look, just as two collegiate types bounced through the doorway sporting carefree attitudes.

"Remember what I told you," Cal said, pointing a finger. "The corporate guys aren't going to think it's funny when you accidentally let one of those slip. And you know how I like to say—"

"Chill out," Sheri said, rolling her eyes. "I know all of your little sayings, and you're putting way too much pressure on yourself. You're going to do fine."

"I'll chill after this is over," Cal said. He checked out the duo that had just landed in his office.

"You must be Cal?" the girl said. "I'm Jamie, and this is T-Rex. I'm here to do your makeup, and T-Rex is going to wire you for sound." Jamie crossed the room to a conference table where she dumped the contents of a shoulder bag. Then she walked over and held out a hand. "Ah, you executive types. Have you been to the beach?"

Cal shook her hand. "What gave it away?"

"Your skin," Jamie said. "It's got that fun-in-the-sun glow." She stepped closer, well inside of his comfort zone. "Someplace exotic, I hope."

"Sailing in the Virgin Islands," Cal said. He took in Jamie's distressed ensemble, hoping he hadn't come across uppity, worse yet—old. "We were celebrating the new job."

"Wow. This office is awesome," Jamie said, beaming as she looked around. Two glass walls overlooked the Chattahoochee River, and the other two were covered in grass cloth. "I hear it's nice down there."

Cal followed her gaze to the far end of the office to his teak desk. An oversized watercolor of a sailboat hung on the wall behind it. "How's that?"

"The Caribbean," she said, raising her nose to within inches of his. "By the way, you have nice features. A narrow nose and sharp jaw—no spare baggage for those nasty little shadows." She cradled his face in her hands and took a lingering look before letting go. Grabbing a makeup brush, she swirled it inside a plastic container. "I'll bet your wife gets lost in those baby blues—"

"Ahem," T-Rex interrupted. "If you don't mind, while Jamie dreams of bearing your children, I'll set the wireless mic for you." He slipped in behind Cal mouthing the words, "baby blues", directly in Jamie's line of sight. "Dr. Hunter, I'm about to attach a transmitter to your belt, so don't think I'm trying to get into your pants." T-Rex delivered the line like he had used it once too often.

Cal laughed. "That reminds me of the joke about a doctor who always smiled when he gave his patients prostate exams."

"Seriously?" Jamie chimed in. "My doctor smiles a lot. But hey, who says a guy can't enjoy his work." She dusted Cal's cheek with makeup. "So what's with the big production?"

Cal looked up at the ceiling, trying to dislodge a mental image of Jamie's last remark.

"We're launching a new drug to treat hypertension and elevated cholesterol."

"Cool," Jamie said. "What's hypertension?"

"It's what your doctor gets when he puts you on the examining table," T-Rex said, shaking his head.

Jamie shot him a pissed look.

"It's commonly referred to as high blood pressure," Cal said.

"Yeah, that's what I thought," Jamie said, leveling a fiery stare at T-Rex. "Something you won't have to worry about as long as we're working together."

Jamie turned to Cal and reached up to straighten his collar. The smile flipped on like a switch. She checked a button on his shirt, and then ran her hands down the lapels of his jacket. Leaning closer, she fluffed the sides of his dark hair with her fingers. "Let's see, I'd say you're forty-five years old, six-one, and a hundred and eighty pounds?"

"Not bad," Cal said, taking a half step back. "So what can you tell me about the reporter?"

"Paula Ritchie, she's the greatest," Jamie said. "You'll just love her."

T-Rex stepped around Cal and clipped a microphone to his lapel. "Especially, if you're into high maintenance chicks," T-Rex said. "All done. Nice meeting you, Dr. Hunter."

"Yes, likewise," Cal said.

"That's a wrap," Jamie said, checking her watch. "Paula will be ready for you in, let's say, three minutes." She gathered up her bag and spun around to leave. The bag slipped out of her hands and landed on the floor. Cal turned in time to catch her squatting down. A tattoo appeared above the waist of her jeans, centered on her lower back. Jamie smiled over her shoulder, and then took off after T-Rex through the doorway.

Cal shook his head and turned to the window, ignoring Sheri who had witnessed the entire operation from the doorway.

"Shall I call Kate and tell her to expect your baby blues home late tonight?"

"Just another day in the salt mines, Sheri," Cal said. "Anyway, bribery isn't your suit. That's why I brought you along for this little adventure."

"Salt mines? You just spent the last ten days in the Caribbean."

"You're conveniently forgetting about my first three weeks on the job, a cross country tour of the largest clinics in our ZuriMax trial."

"Yeah, like wining and dining doctors at five star restaurants is roughing it."

"Any way you look at it, sixteen hour days on the road is real work. Did you send the follow-up letters?" Cal said.

"All thirty-six," Sheri said.

"Now, if you don't mind, I could use a moment alone." Cal focused on the window, catching a glimpse of Sheri sticking her tongue out as she closed the door. He tested a side profile, gauging his best angle for the interview.

With the office quiet again, Cal retreated to his earlier thoughts. *Three minutes before my debut is bad timing.* It was true he'd already had his fifteen minutes of fame, but that was another time and place. And of course, the stakes were higher this time. And riskier. Only he now had the credentials to deliver. He was at the top of his game. At least that's how the world would see it after tonight's interview. Cal gave himself a thumbs-up in the window, and then headed for the lobby.

Paula Ritchie sat in a chair with Jamie and T-Rex hovering over her. Cal inspected the lobby, and then walked over.

"Paula, I'm Cal Hunter."

"Such a pleasure to meet you, Dr. Hunter," Paula said, her smile putting the Cheshire cat to shame.

"Cal, please."

"Since you've already looked over the questions, we'll do a sound check and dive straight in," Paula said.

"I need you both over here," T-Rex called out, directing them to the center of the lobby.

"We really appreciate the exclusive," Paula said. "My bureau chief spoke to your assistant and agreed to the other media representatives joining us for the facility tour after the interview. Did you have any—"

"That's a wrap," T-Rex said. "Ten seconds."

Paula raised an eyebrow, and then positioned herself next to Cal, smiling again as the camera started rolling. "Good evening. I'm WNGA reporter, Paula Ritchie, on location tonight to take a look at an industry that touches millions of lives. According to the most recent data, pharmaceuticals are an enormous $320 billion industry in the United States with profits that are the envy of every segment of our economy. Tonight we're going to hear about one of the most profitable areas of this business. I'm referring to the treatment of cardiovascular disease, a leading cause of death in our nation. Although the pharmaceutical industry claims to be struggling to replace older drugs that are going off patent, some estimates put the cost of all forms of treatment for coronary disease at $110 billion annually. Tonight, I'm standing on the campus of one of the hottest biopharmaceutical companies in the nation, and it's right here in our own backyard. The name of the company is Zuritech, and I'm here with their recently appointed US CEO, Dr. Calvin Hunter III. Dr. Hunter, can you start by telling us a little bit about Zuritech?"

"Good evening, Paula, and welcome to our US headquarters," Cal said. "Zuritech Corporation is a wholly owned subsidiary of the Swiss biotech company, Zuritech AG. Although it isn't a household name here in the States, the parent company is based in Zurich and has been around in Europe for over fifteen years. More recently, Zuritech has been focused on developing new therapeutic treatments, primarily concentrating on major health concerns around the world, and of course, the reason the company is making important news tonight."

"Important news, indeed. Please tell us about this promising new drug. I understand it will be Zuritech's first entry into the US market and scheduled to be available in a few months."

"Paula, it's an exciting new medication called ZuriMax. The drug is currently in phase III clinical trials, and upon FDA approval is expected to be a major breakthrough for individuals suffering from hypertension and elevated cholesterol. As I'm sure most of your listeners are aware, these medical conditions afflict millions of people across the nation and are considered to be leading causes of heart attacks and strokes. Estimates of high cholesterol alone are at unhealthy levels for those of us nineteen years of age and older. Zuritech has developed a drug that will not only provide greater patient convenience, but has the advantage of being more affordable when compared to traditional treatments. You see, doctors typically prescribe two separate drugs for these conditions. ZuriMax will not only make it easier for a patient to follow doctor's orders by taking a single tablet each day, but at the same time will save them hundreds of dollars each year. These factors are especially important to senior citizens who often find it difficult to take their daily medications, not to mention the challenge of paying for them."

"I believe I've heard there is an additional benefit. Can you comment on that?" Paula said.

"For years now, millions of Americans have been advised to take a daily aspirin as a precautionary measure against heart attacks. I'm pleased to report that those same properties have been formulated into ZuriMax. So for individuals taking the drug, there may be a third benefit and cost savings."

"Wow, this could be the greatest development since penicillin," Paula said. "What can you tell us about the campus? Was the drug developed here?"

"That's correct, Paula. The campus sits on forty-five acres in Technology Park on the north side of Atlanta. The research laboratories were constructed four years ago and have been dedicated exclusively to the development of ZuriMax. We employ over a hundred scientists who are currently working on the final stages of the drug's approval. The building we're standing in was completed earlier this year and will be our US headquarters for the executive, administrative, and sales staff. Since I'm the first non-research executive to be hired, my initial focus as CEO will be to put together a US team that will be responsible for launching ZuriMax."

"So you're all alone in this beautiful building?" Paula said, glancing around the lobby.

"Pretty much, except for my assistant, but we begin the hiring process next week," Cal said.

"Looking beyond the US, will the drug be sold in other parts of the world?"

"The goal is to first launch ZuriMax in the US, and then follow on with approvals in Europe, Japan, and the rest of the world," Cal said.

"Why have you chosen to launch first in the US? I mean, it's great news, but you said the company has always operated in Europe."

"As you may know, the US represents roughly half of the global market for pharmaceuticals. So you can appreciate the fact that it makes good business sense. But there is something else unique about ZuriMax. It is the first drug to be marketed by the company that was actually developed in the US. The active pharmaceutical ingredients, known in the industry as APIs, are the result of research conducted at the University of Rochester."

"So this leading edge American technology will eventually benefit millions around the world," Paula said. "Now, tell us a little bit about yourself. I believe you earned dual degrees, an MD and MBA from Northwestern University. And I also understand you are somewhat of a veteran pharmaceutical executive and have held prominent positions at VistaBio, possibly even instrumental in launching their blockbuster cholesterol drug. Why have you decided to leave one of the industry titans and start over with this new venture?"

"VistaBio is a great American company, and I was fortunate to be a part of many exciting opportunities there. You mentioned their blockbuster cholesterol drug—many people were instrumental in its success, so I wouldn't want to accept personal responsibility for a well-executed team effort. But I did leave the company to join Zuritech, primarily to be involved in what I believe will become one of the great pharmaceutical achievements of our lifetime. ZuriMax is a medical breakthrough that will improve the quality of life for millions facing coronary disease, and for many it will prove to be a life-saving discovery. As you've mentioned, I have a combination medical/business background. In fact, I worked in biotech venture capital before joining VistaBio. So you might say I have a track record in emerging biotechnologies."

"Well, we look forward to coming back to your beautiful campus after ZuriMax is approved for a follow-on report," Paula said. "Thank you for taking time to speak with us tonight." Paula turned directly into the camera. "This is Paula Ritchie reporting from Atlanta."

"We're off," T-Rex said, drawing a finger across his throat.

Cal let out a breath and stepped away from the lights. A small crowd was collecting in the lobby. He turned to Paula. "So how did I do?"

"You were perfect," she said. "You've clearly done interviews before."

"Well, a few."

"It looks like our band of media representatives has arrived," Paula said. "If it's okay with you, I'll take care of a few things, and then join the group for the tour."

Cal waited as T-Rex removed the microphone, noticing a striking woman watching him from across the set. When T-Rex finished, Cal walked over.

"Welcome, I'm Cal Hunter. The tour will begin in a few minutes."

The young lady smiled. "It's tempting, but I'm a bit jet lagged," she said, and then paused. When he didn't respond, she gave Cal the once-over. "I had no idea the hiring process started next week."

There was an awkward silence following her comment.

"I'm sorry," Cal said. "Did I miss something?"

She looked Cal in the eyes. "You don't know who I am, do you?"

"No, but apparently I can't say the same about you," Cal said. He checked the crowd over his shoulder. "If you'll excuse me, I have people waiting."

"Then perhaps I should be direct," she said.

Cal cut his eyes at her.

The young lady extended a hand. "I'm Singh Lee, your new chief financial officer."

Chapter 2

AL BASRAH, IRAQ
TUESDAY, AUGUST 23
7 P.M. AST

The Boeing 747 floated down the glide path as gently as a soaring seagull. There was a slight headwind, but no air traffic or holding pattern, not another plane in the sky.

"ORMM tower, this is FDX221. We have a fix and are on final," Captain Robert Fine said into the headset, adjusting a pair of aviators perched on his nose. He rolled his head to check on his co-pilot, Harris Taylor.

"FDX221 cleared on 171, standing by," the tower responded.

Taylor gripped a clipboard, running his finger down a checklist.

Fine glanced over his left shoulder, fixing his eyes on the port wing until the landing lights lit up. Somewhere in the bowels of the giant bird hydraulics engaged the landing gear. He turned to give Taylor a thumbs-up, but he was engrossed in the instrument panel.

Taylor checked the horizontal situation indicator, and then tapped the glass for good measure. "HSI in the crosshairs, wind 10 knots southeast, and visibility 100 percent," he said.

"Lenny, you copy back there?" Fine said into his headset.

There was a crackle. "Roger that. Final check complete, and I'm headed for the jump seat."

"Is there food in the galley?" Fine said.

"Big negative on that," Lenny said. "This bird wasn't scheduled to depart Newark until tomorrow morning, which by my calculations has now come and gone in the Eastern Time Zone. Looks like we'll have to go native."

"Afraid not," Fine said.

"No problem, Chief. We're on layover, right?" Lenny said.

"Not if I can help it," Fine said, looking ahead. He spotted the airstrip rising out of the sand like a mirage, and then looked west. The sun radiated across the desert like an oil painting he'd once seen, half buried in silky smooth sand dunes. Then his co-pilot suddenly jolted him.

"Abort, abort!" Taylor screamed.

Fine jumped, nearly ripping off his headset. He cut his eyes over at Taylor, who now sat there stunned.

"The Lord is my shepherd . . ." Taylor began to chant.

"What's going on?" Lenny said in the headset.

Fine rechecked the altimeter–five hundred feet. HSI remained in the crosshairs. He made another visual. The aircraft was perfectly aligned on the runway. He leaned forward for a better view to starboard.

"He leads me beside quiet waters . . ."

"You're not going to believe this," Fine said.

"Should I buckle in or what?" Lenny said.

"We've got a bunch of camels charging out of the desert," Fine said.

"Even though I walk through the valley of the shadow of death . . ."

"Taylor's never seen a camel?" Lenny said.

"Not like these," Fine said.

"No copy on that, Captain," Lenny said.

"It's a band of Arabian Knights, and they're headed toward the runway."

"I can't see a thing from back here," Lenny said.

"They're waving AK47s—"

"Holy—"

There was a jolt that drowned Lenny out as the wheels touched down. The reverse-thrusters kicked in, then abated once they had slowed to taxiing speed.

"Speak to me, Captain," Lenny said.

"Stand by," Fine said. He scanned the runway as the tower came over the headset with instructions.

"If you keep the engines running, I'll dump the goods," Lenny said, once they had stopped. "Then we can get out of here."

"Amen," Taylor said.

"Lenny, meet us in the cargo hold," Fine said. He opened a console and retrieved a pistol, slipping it into his flight jacket.

Minutes later, a pair of military transports raced across the tarmac as Fine, Taylor, and Lenny marched single file down a ramp at the rear of the jet. A tempest of dry air swept across the airstrip.

"Let me handle this," Fine said, stepping off.

Taylor did a three-sixty, like he was expecting to be surrounded at any moment.

"There's a fence around the perimeter," Fine said, pointing into the darkness.

A man in an Adidas wind suit hopped out of a transport as it rolled to a stop. There was a grinding noise, and it started backing toward the cargo bay.

"Why'd you park us way out here?" Fine yelled to the man, straining to be heard above the engines.

"You're with Federal Express?" the man said, pulling a collar tight around his neck.

Fine cocked his thumb at a FedEx logo on the aircraft's tail. "I ain't the Avon lady."

"Captain Fine, I presume?" the man said.

Fine gestured to the terminal. "We need to get inside."

"The fence won't hold them," Taylor shouted from the ramp.

"The airport closed as soon as you landed," the man said.

"I didn't catch your name," Fine said, stepping in closer.

"Martin," the man said. "Is everything on board?"

"What's going on?" Fine said. "The airport's closed?"

"Not to worry." Martin turned to a second truck backing up. "It happens frequently in this part of the world."

"Listen, I don't know who you are, but I got halfway over the pond, and they rerouted us from Baghdad to Al Basrah. Now, I'm standing in a closed airport with a band of armed soldiers circling the gates."

"Captain, it's for your own protection. There's been an Al Qaeda cell reported in the area," Martin said.

"I think I got the picture," Fine said. "Get this cargo off my aircraft, and we're outta here."

"Once again, the airport is closed. But if I may beg your assistance in loading—"

"I fly these birds. I don't handle cargo," Fine interrupted. "Besides, we haven't eaten."

"Help me, and I'll see that you get a hot meal and safe place to spend the night."

"This is all wrong," Fine said, glancing over his shoulder. *Who charters a 747 with a dozen pallets aboard?*

"We're wasting time, Captain," Martin said. "The winds will only get worse with nightfall."

After loading the cargo, Martin positioned the flight crew in one of the transports behind a row of the pallets, unfurling a canvas flap over the tailgate once they were situated. In the distance, an exchange of gunfire pierced the darkness.

"You'll be safe back here, but please stay low," Martin said.

"Tell me you're not taking us to Baghdad in the back of a truck," Fine said.

"As you wish," Martin said, closing the flap.

Fine drifted off to sleep and didn't perk up until he heard the transport's brakes squeal. He checked his watch as the vehicle shifted in reverse. Once they had stopped, Martin appeared and rolled up the flap, then left without a word.

Fine hopped out with the others, stretching and taking notice of a tanker floating at a lighted port facility down the hill. He strained for a better look and could just make out a partially sunken ship in the distance. A pair of forklifts pulled up and swung into action at the rear of the transports.

Fifty yards away, a helicopter set down, and Fine turned to spot Martin at the truck cab. He slung a leather satchel over his shoulder and started for the chopper.

"Wait here," Fine said to Lenny. He sprinted after Martin, catching up to him just as they were within striking distance of the blades.

Both men had to shield their eyes from the sand.

"Where do you think you're going?" Fine called out.

"My associate, Christoph, will take care of you from here," Martin said.

"They're loading the shipment on a boat. It was slated for Bagdad."

Martin smiled. "*Danke*, my dear Captain," he said, climbing into the cockpit. The blades accelerated to a whine.

Fine sprinted out of harm's way, taking a last look as the helicopter lifted into the darkness. It banked, and he caught the reflection of a cross on the rear fuselage, then it was gone.

When he returned to the transports, the forklifts were already down at the ship.

"Captain Fine, we'll be taking leave now," a man in a bomber jacket said, hopping out of the second transport. "Do you and your men need anything before I go?"

"Are you Christoph?" Fine said.

"At your service."

"We were told there would be food and bunks," Fine said. Just then, Taylor and Lenny walked up.

"Over there," Christoph said, pointing to a building.

There was a rust-covered sign in Arabic, and beneath it Fine made out, "UmQasser Port Administration".

"Is the facility secure?" Taylor said.

"Who's taking us back to the airport?" Fine said, shouldering Taylor's question.

"The transport will drop you off in the morning," Christoph said, starting to back away. "But tonight you are safe, as long as you remain within the compound."

"That's it?" Fine called out.

Christoph was now thirty feet away.

"Hey," Christoph shouted. "Have you seen Elvis lately?"

"What?" Fine said, raising his hands.

"You know. FedEx—Memphis—Elvis—hunka, hunka, burning love," Christoph mimicked, rocking his hips.

Taylor and Lenny started laughing.

Fine shook his head, catching a glimpse of a flag on the stern of the ship. It bore the same cross he had seen on the helicopter. He yelled back to Christoph, "Who are you, Red Cross?"

"You must be color-blind, Captain."

"Where are you taking the drugs?" Fine said.

"To America, but you didn't hear it from me."

"Why are you taking them back to the US?"

Christoph didn't respond, only turned and sprinted for the dock.

"Is it me or is this the twilight zone?" Lenny said.

"Unbelievable," Fine said. "Our lives are in the hands of an Elvis impersonator."

Chapter 3

**ATLANTA, GEORGIA
MONDAY, AUGUST 22
8 P.M. EDT**

A dozen media representatives had gathered in the lobby by the time Cal kicked things off, "Good evening and a warm welcome to each of you. For those who may have missed the interview, my name is Cal Hunter, US CEO of Zuritech. It is a pleasure to be conducting the tour this evening. And now if you'll join me, we'll get started."

The group followed Cal across the lobby, where only minutes ago he had been standing with Paula Ritchie in front of a TV camera. As they passed by, a dusting of golden light illuminated an over-sized floral arrangement sitting on a table in the center of the room. Cal proceeded to a plate glass window at the rear of the lobby, allowing the group to form a semicircle around him.

"My assistant, Sheri, is handing out media packages that contain all of the pertinent information about the company, including recent press releases. While she's finishing up, I would like to give you some background on the facility and point out a few of the architectural features you will see repeated throughout the tour. First, you will notice that the architects have taken great pains to create a feeling that the building is an extension of the surrounding ecology," Cal said. "All structures on campus are one story and constructed with materials harvested from the site. If you look closely at the floor, you'll find hardwood that was milled from displaced vegetation. And wherever you see stone such as in the floors or the fireplace hearth to my right, it's all local."

"They appear to be polished," a woman said, admiring the hearth.

"Those were extracted from the Chattahoochee River which runs about forty yards behind the building. You can thank Mother Nature for their beauty," Cal said. "Stones with sharper features came from the excavation. Once again, none of the materials have been processed due to efforts to harmonize with the natural habitat. You will notice that the finishes on the floors, doors, and beamed ceilings have all been color-matched with the hardwoods indigenous to the campus, down to the hues in the moss."

"Dr. Hunter, why has Zuritech taken such elaborate measures with the facility? It's beautiful and clearly expensive, but what does all of this have to do with developing drugs?" a reporter asked.

Cal stepped toward the man. "That's an excellent question. Who do you represent?"

"The *Atlanta Business Chronicle*."

"I'm sure you realize that the Europeans are trendsetters as it relates to the green movement. Zuritech believes in good corporate citizenship when it comes to the environment. But there is something else. We believe just as strongly in our most valuable resource, human capital. Our associates devote extraordinary amounts of time and energy to developing breakthrough pharmaceuticals. Since we ask them to invest long hours to expedite these life-changing drugs to market, we believe it is important to provide not only a comfortable workspace, but an environment that facilitates the creative process."

"I wouldn't mind giving up my cubicle for this," the reporter said, drawing laughter from the group.

"So you can relate to what I'm saying. Over your shoulders you'll notice a couple of hallways. For time's sake, we won't go into these areas, but there are meeting and conference rooms down the far one. All feature state of the art videoconferencing equipment and wireless networks. The hall directly to my right leads to the executive offices. Now, if you'll follow me."

Cal led the group across the lobby and down a short corridor. As it opened up into a cavernous room, everyone gasped.

"This is the employee lounge. As you can see, we've maintained a consistent theme. There's a fireplace for ambiance, and the bar provides refreshments for employees, free of charge—"

"Do you serve alcohol?" someone asked.

"Only on special occasions," Cal said. "Everyone is expected to be on their A-game while on the job. There's a small theatre over to my right. Many of our associates enjoy coming out to watch ballgames and movies with their families. The room is wired with digital surround sound, and you'll also notice we have air hockey, foosball, and a pool table in the rear. If you go down the hallway next to the bar, you'll find a three lane bowling alley and fitness room, fully equipped with lockers, showers, and sauna. And before anyone asks—no, the showers are not coed."

"Do you have any evidence that all of these perks actually yield more productive employees?" a reporter asked.

"Not specifically, but I point to early adopters to validate the concept. Companies like Google and SAS Institute come to mind. Both have successfully created unique corporate environments, and as you all know, have done quite well in their respective industries," Cal said. "If you'll step this way, we'll head out the rear door."

The door opened into a glass-enclosed breezeway, and Cal led the group across to a cozy lobby, complete with reception desk and fireplace. A Persian rug centered the room with sofas and armchairs scattered around it. Cal stood next to a crackling fire, waiting for everyone to squeeze in.

"I've already explained the high expectations we have of our employees—a relentless commitment to deliver novel drugs. You will also recall that we are owned by a Swiss parent company that is located ten hours away." Cal turned and pointed to a young girl poised behind the reception desk. "This is the lobby of Hotel Zuritech."

Several members of the group whispered amongst themselves.

"We have a twelve room mini hotel designed to accommodate international visitors as well as our research personnel who occasionally need a nap while on extended shifts."

"Isn't this a bit over the top? Why don't your visitors stay at the Holiday Inn like the rest of us?" Paula said.

"As you may have heard, the Swiss are sticklers for detail. In our particular case, security and secrecy are critical to the projects housed on campus," Cal said. "We are all aware of the unfortunate conditions in the world today: terrorists, kidnappers, corporate espionage, and I could go on. Zuritech is committed to protecting the wellbeing of personnel, but also our proprietary research. The attention to security will become obvious throughout the tour, especially when we visit the adjoining research facility."

"So that explains the security guards at the front gate," Paula said.

"That's correct. And they are all military trained by a renowned Swiss agency. If there are no further questions, we'll head next door for the final phase of the tour. I had hoped to take you down to the river for a look at the recreation area, but I'm afraid the darkness won't afford a good view."

Cal directed the group down a hallway to the main lobby. He then ushered them out the front door and down a lighted walkway lined with trees and natural flora. They followed it to the entrance of a nondescript building that was only partially visible in the nighttime shadows. Inside they were greeted by a guard.

"Here's a bit of humor for you," Cal said as everyone huddled around. "The research facility you're standing in has been affectionately nicknamed Beta Hut by the staff. It's rumored that the name originated when it was the only building within miles of this location. The story goes that the scientists felt as if they were conducting experiments on beta compounds in a remote jungle bordered by the river, so it became known as Beta Hut. By association, the administration building next door is now referred to as Alpha Hut."

Cal stepped over to a desk. "To comply with FDA regulations, each of you is required to sign in. You will then be issued a security badge, and once we enter the glass doors to my right, one of our scientists will conduct the tour."

Thirty minutes later, Cal gathered the group on the walkway in front of Alpha Hut. "That concludes this evening's tour. Are there any final questions?"

"How much did you spend on the campus?"

"Roughly a hundred million," Cal said.

Someone let out a whistle.

"I know what you're thinking, but laboratory space is pricey," Cal said.

"How do we apply for a job?"

"I'm with her," another reporter said. The group broke into laughter.

"Send me your resumes. I'm sure we'll want to hire you all," Cal said. "It's been a pleasure having you on campus, and I look forward to your next visit. As I'm sure you've noticed, you can't see the main road from here. Please follow the signs up to the gate and drive safely."

Cal directed the group to a parking area, and with a final wave, reentered the lobby. Pulling out his iPhone, he headed down the hallway to the executive suites, remembering he had sent Sheri home earlier.

"Kate, it's me," Cal said into the phone. "Yeah, still here . . . it went fine. I'm going to take care of a few things, and then I'll be on my way." When he reached his office, the door was ajar. "Listen, I'll see you when I get home."

Cal nudged the door open, noticing the soft glow of recessed lighting around the perimeter of the room. Slipping inside, he spotted china laid out on his conference table with a single red candle burning in the center. Just then one of the chairs swiveled, revealing a lone visitor facing the window. A woman with shoulder-length hair sat with her back to him, sipping wine.

"Can I help you?" Cal said, approaching the table.

Singh Lee turned and smiled, holding up her glass.

"I hope you don't mind," she said.

Chapter 4

WASHINGTON, DC
MONDAY, AUGUST 22
9 P.M. EDT

Silverware clinked against gold-rimmed china that had been carefully arranged at one end of the dining room table. Three men sat like royalty beneath a lofty ceiling feasting on roasted game hen, butternut squash, and grilled asparagus. The table shimmered, stretching across the room like an airport runway. Its patina basked beneath a golden chandelier that had been dimmed for the occasion.

"You'll want to let that breathe a bit longer," the secretary said, raising his fork. He sat at the head of the table.

A pudgy man sat to his left in a navy suit, examining the label on a wine bottle before setting it down.

"You haven't mentioned the review board's position on the proposal," the secretary said, turning to the third man who wore gray. His hair was speckled like a fine herringbone fabric, giving the impression it had been accessorized to the suit.

"The IRB has been nothing but supportive, Mr. Secretary," the man said. He spoke slowly to soften his accent.

"I take it there have been no dissenting opinions?" the secretary said, gesturing once again with the fork.

"That would be a correct interpretation," the man responded.

"But let's not fool ourselves—"

"I'll see to the agency's position as long as you assure me you'll stay the course," the secretary said, cutting short the pudgy man. He maintained eye contact with the man in gray. "Need I remind you of the price of failure?"

"But of course not," the man said. The wrinkles on his forehead hinted concern, but it quickly dissipated.

"Well then, gentlemen, we have a plan. But allow me to remind you, I'm staking my future, and yours, on the prospect that the American people will rally behind a renewed sense of leadership to this national crisis," the secretary said.

"We couldn't agree more, Mr. Secretary," the pudgy man said. He patted a napkin to his mouth.

The secretary smiled, and then swept his eyes to a portrait hanging over a white marble fireplace. They lingered, prompting the other men to follow suit.

"The man was a genius and a fine leader, but perhaps not his finest rendering," the secretary said.

"You have a keen eye, Mr. Secretary," the man in gray said. "The American people are indeed hopeful. And in due time they will recognize that a new portrait is unfolding before them."

"Tonight is a turning point," the pudgy man said. "I'd like to propose a toast."

Instead of engaging, the secretary rose from his chair and walked over to the fireplace. His guests poured wine as he studied an inscription chiseled in the marble beneath the portrait. "I pray heaven to bestow the best of blessings on this house and all that shall hereafter inhabit it," he read. "May none but honest and wise men rule under this roof." The secretary lingered for a moment, and then retraced his steps to the table, tossing down his napkin.

"My dear friend," the secretary said, planting a hand on the shoulder of the pudgy man. "My dear, dear friend." He turned and walked away.

The two men sat in silence as the secretary crossed the room, his profile casting a shadow on the white oak paneling. He exited through a paneled door that closed behind him.

"I'll be damned," the pudgy man said, coming out of his seat. He leaned across the table and extended a hand.

The other man held back. "Is the secretary trustworthy in such matters?" he said, slowly lifting his eyes.

"Do you have any idea where you're sitting?"

"So I have your assurances?"

"Lawrence and I go way—"

"Do I have your word?" the man in gray interrupted.

"I delivered exactly as promised."

The man in gray shifted his eyes.

"The problem is half-solved," the pudgy man said. "It's up to you now—so make sure your team doesn't screw the pooch."

"Leave my people to me."

"Do we have a deal?"

"I have a long flight home, but I will see to the contract amendments in the morning."

"That's all I need to hear," the pudgy man said. Satisfied with the response, he headed over to the mantel for a closer look at the inscription.

"I am somewhat familiar with your country's history."

"Thomas Jefferson conducted business in this very room. Doesn't that give you a strange feeling?"

"Yes . . . one of your national heroes. So you wish to give me a civics lesson?"

"Tonight has that 'giant leap for mankind' feeling to it, at least it does for me."

"But of course," the man in gray said. "And maybe one day you will be famous. I remain cautious about your fraternity brother, but I must confess he is a gracious host." He extracted a pair of Cuban Espléndidos from his jacket, carefully snipping off the ends. He offered one to his companion.

"Are you sure we can smoke those in here?"

"Perhaps you should look it up in your history book," the man in gray said. He lifted a silver bell from the table. "And now we must drink to our success."

Chapter 5

ATLANTA, GEORGIA
MONDAY, AUGUST 22
9 P.M. EDT

Cal circled the conference table to a leather chair directly across from Singh Lee. There were two place settings at the table, complete with tea cups, chopsticks, and silverware. He recognized the monogrammed china which had been taken from the boardroom. A steaming teapot sat next to the candle in the center of the table.

"You don't approve," Singh Lee said, pausing. There was only silence. "When I spoke to you earlier, you looked famished, so I decided to pick up dinner. Sheri loaned me your car." She set down her wine glass and stood up.

As she brushed past, Cal noticed she was no longer wearing the business suit from earlier in the evening, but a short black dress and heels, both accentuating her dark hair. Singh Lee walked matter-of-factly, stopping in front of a credenza where she picked up a bottle of wine.

"I had hoped for a view of the river," she said, raising her eyes to the window. She stepped back, and then returned with the wine. "I understand it's beautiful down there."

Cal's eyes swept over to the credenza where takeout containers had been laid out. "I'm surprised Sheri didn't check with me," he said, now looking directly into Singh Lee's eyes.

"I asked her not to interrupt the tour. Anyway, she said your wife wasn't expecting you."

"Is Singh Lee your full name, or is there a surname?" Cal said, changing the subject.

"Actually, I dropped my last name after the divorce, mostly for personal reasons. May I serve you dinner?" Singh Lee said, gesturing toward the credenza. "We also have wine." She leaned in next to Cal, setting the bottle on the table.

Cal waited for her to step back, and then checked his watch. "You and I have business to discuss," he said, lifting a plate off the table. Then he motioned for Singh Lee to lead the way.

Once they were seated, Singh Lee poured the wine. Upon closer examination, Cal said, "That's an exceptional cabernet."

"Yes it is," Singh Lee said. "I'm impressed that you recognize the vintage. But perhaps I'm being a bit presumptuous—"

"Do you have a resume with you?" Cal interrupted.

"I'm afraid not, but I'll e-mail it to you when I return to my room."

"So you're not local?" Cal said.

"That's correct," Singh Lee said, pausing for a taste of soup. "Would it help if I told you a little about myself?"

"To get things started, yes," Cal said.

"I come from a long line of naturalized Chinese-Americans. I was born in San Francisco, earned an undergraduate degree at Cal Tech and my MBA at Stanford. After grad school, I went to work for Kleiner Perkins and focused on biotech startups. That's where I met my former husband who talked me into buying a Napa vineyard. I pulled together a business plan and financing while he handled operations."

"Did you work on any biotechs I'd recognize?" Cal said.

"Emdeon, Corixa, Questcor, Celedon—shall I continue?"

"That gives me the big picture. In light of your career path, I take it you've remained current on emerging technologies?"

"I've been out of the market a few years, but keep abreast of the promising biopharmaceutical companies," Singh Lee said. "What do you think of the wine?"

"It's quite rare, actually. How did you come by it?" Cal said, reaching over to inspect the label again.

"I have a minority interest in the vineyard."

"You're a shareholder in Tigerlily?"

"Guilty as charged," Singh Lee said, shrugging her shoulders. "Along with my former husband. But as it turns out, he's somewhat of a fanatic, and I had to divorce him so he could devote himself to his first love. After all was said and done, I walked away with a quarter of the equity, control of seventy-five cases a year, and unfortunately, my share of the debt." Singh Lee swirled her glass.

"There are only three hundred cases produced annually," Cal said. "We're drinking a five hundred dollar bottle of wine."

"But you'll be happy to know it's not going on my expense account," Singh Lee said, holding out her glass for another pour. "That's the CFO in me speaking."

"Right . . . which brings us to Zuritech and your interest in the chief financial officer appointment. There are half a dozen resumes on my desk, and I'm certain yours isn't among them," Cal said. He poured wine into their glasses.

"I'm afraid I can't help with the internal politics, but I can tell you that while I was divorcing my husband, I contacted my former boss at Kleiner Perkins. As it turns out, he assisted Martin Zeiss on a deal last year."

"So you're connected to our global CFO?"

"Precisely. Martin interviewed me, and I was hired on the spot."

"And when did this take place?"

"I flew to Zurich three weeks ago," Singh Lee said. "So you're serious, no one told you?"

"No, but I intend to get to the bottom of it, starting with Nicolai von Weir. Communication is essential if we're going to successfully launch ZuriMax in the coming months," Cal said. "Did you meet Nick as well?"

"Chairman and CEO of Zuritech AG," Singh Lee said. "Do you hate me? I mean, this is terribly awkward. While I was waiting for you, I thought about catching the red-eye for the Coast."

"There's nothing more we can do tonight, but I'll speak to Nick and figure out where we go from here," Cal said. "In the interim, proceed with whatever assignments Martin has you working on."

Chapter 6

SANTA BARBARA, CALIFORNIA
MONDAY, AUGUST 22
6 P.M. PDT

Jana Cruz kicked back in her cubicle with a three inch binder on her lap. The heels of her jogging shoes rested on a work surface, and a pair of earbuds sat nestled in her ears. She flipped pages as her feet kept tempo with the music. Feeling a tap on the shoulder, she ignored the interruption long enough to finish the page she was reading. When she was done, she dropped her feet to the floor, pulling out the earbuds.

"What's up, boss?" she said. A guy in his late-twenties stood in the doorway.

"How are you coming with the SOPs?"

"About thirty minutes further along than the last time you asked," Jana said, rolling her eyes. *My God, this guy acts like he just graduated from junior high.*

Billy Danforth leaned against the cubicle, smiling and acting weird, like maybe he was about to ask her to the prom. "That's cool," he said. "We've never worked together, but just ask anyone, I always look out for my team. I'm available if you need anything. Anything at all."

"Yeah, I've heard you're sweet like that," Jana said. She looked away, tempted to stick a finger down her throat. "How long have you been doing this?"

Billy flexed his shoulders and leaned into the partition. "Five years at Bioscene. I was with another CRO before that."

"And what made you join a clinical research organization instead of signing up with Big Pharma or the medical profession?"

"I saw the handwriting on the wall. Went to USC, you know?" His head bobbed like he expected this tidbit to elevate his stature. "Yeah, I figured Big Pharma had the fix in to outsource all of their clinical trials early on. Being a scientist, I wanted to be where the action was." He began to rub his shoulders against the partition.

"And living in Santa Barbara's not such a bad gig, either," Jana said.

"I plan to be an equity player within, oh, five years. But if it doesn't happen here, there are plenty of hot startups around." Billy gave a tug at the Bioscene logo on his shirt, and then let it snap back into place.

Jana twisted her head so Billy wouldn't see she was holding back a snicker. She put a hand over her mouth and leaned forward in her chair. "I gotta go to the bathroom."

Billy seemed oblivious to her announcement and didn't budge from the doorway. "Any questions so far about the project or Bioscene? I meet weekly with the execs and can get answers for anything you want to know."

Jana dropped back into the chair and grabbed the binder. "Have you read this stuff?"

"It's on my to-do list. What's up?"

"I reviewed the standard operating procedures for the clinical trial—"

"SOPs—that's one of my strong suits," Billy interrupted.

"I've worked on a number of projects, but these are different," Jana said.

Billy crossed his arms, all serious now. "How so?"

Jana flipped pages. "Well, first of all, I noticed we've been using Bioscene's clinical management system to track the ZuriMax trial in the field, but Zuritech intends to have us manually enter the data into their system."

"That's right," Billy said. "It's stated in the contract. They plan to do their own data analysis."

"I understand, but shouldn't we validate the data in our system, and then upload it to theirs?"

Billy kicked off the cubicle. "Come with me," he said. Jana followed him to a bank of workstations in an open area across the room. "These computers are wired directly into Zuritech's server. As soon as we have the site data from the doctors, we'll input it into Zuritech's system for a final wrap on the project."

"But what about data integrity, our proprietary method—"

"The secret sauce," Billy interrupted.

"What?"

"Our patented data validation process. I call it the secret sauce. Other than the US Patent Office, only the FDA has seen our secret recipe."

Jana clinched her jaws as she took a breath. "Okay, all I'm saying is, that's part of the value we offer our clients. Why are they skipping the secret sauce?"

"Jeez Louise," Billy said. "Don't get so paranoid. Zuritech has their own proprietary methodology. That's all."

"Yeah, but are you sure it's in the contract?" Jana said. "We could enter errors into their system. I mean, we're bound to make mistakes."

"Gotcha. To err is human, and to really foul things up requires a computer."

"Come on, Billy."

"Why don't I read the SOPs and give you my professional opinion? How about over dinner tonight?"

"One other thing," Jana said, ignoring his advance. She hoisted the binder, rustling through more pages until she found one that was dog-eared. "They're using our clinical management process and forms, right? Well in the manual, it says they've designated Alpha 127 as a practitioner field, but there's no documentation on acceptable values or how it's used in the study. What's a practitioner field?"

"Chill out babe." Billy grinned.

"Chill out, my ass," Jana said, drawing a finger at Billy. "Call me that one more time, and I'll light yours on fire."

"I said I'll take a look. What else do you want me to do?" He paused. "And I'm sorry, you're not a babe."

"USC grad, right," Jana said. "But seriously, aren't you concerned about gaps in the procedures? I don't want the FDA coming down on Bioscene because of bad data."

"Listen, these Zuritech guys have been around for a long time—"

"But not in the US," Jan interrupted.

"They've been in the global market for years. And they're big boys who understand what it takes to get a drug approved," Billy said. "So they have a process, and if Bioscene wants to do business with them, we've got to be flexible."

"But what about the FDA? Bioscene's potentially liable for the quality of the data."

"Then I say we're protected by the contract. We've agreed to do it their way, and that means they accept liability."

"Have you ever known a pharma company to take this approach?" Jana said.

"I've seen a lot of things, just not this particular one."

"So you appreciate my concerns?"

"What can I say? These guys are control freaks. They don't want their data being leaked to competitors. Big deal," Billy said, holding up his hands. "Hey, it's their dime, and if they want to keep us at arm's length on details—"

"Such as the practitioner field?"

"That's right. Only don't get too relaxed about all of this. I've seen clients create special fields that were designed to validate the integrity of the CRO process. Alpha 127 could be a validation on us. And you didn't hear it from me, but I have it on good authority that Zuritech has a dual feed."

"Meaning?"

"They've already received the data directly from the clinics. Our entire process is nothing but a quality control measure."

"I've never heard of anyone going to that extreme," Jana said.

"Me either. But it's costing them a bundle, so don't get all gushy on me, thinking this is an easy project," Billy said, leaning in next to Jana. "These guys are paying top dollar to get the job done fast. In fact, there's a bonus in it for Bioscene if we hit their deadline." Billy lowered his voice. "And I am responsible for divvying it up."

Chapter 7

**ATLANTA, GEORGIA
TUESDAY, AUGUST 23
1:55 A.M. EDT**

Fried rice and sesame chicken littered the floor as two bodies skidded across the credenza, plowing takeout containers in their path. In a fit of panting, neither noticed the plopping sounds, much less the mess. Cal's hand glided over bits of rice clinging to the front of Singh Lee's dress. Under labored breath, he glanced up into a window at his reflection. A shard of chicken clung to his hair. Singh Lee wrapped her arms around his neck and pulled him down on top of her. Their lips met as she toyed with his tucked polo.

Cal jerked, lifting his head. "No, this is—"

"Shhhh," Singh Lee said.

A hand grasped Cal from behind and shook him. He turned, and to his horror, Kate appeared over his shoulder staring directly down at him. Ripping himself free, he couldn't bring himself to make eye contact. Instead, he stood up in shock, looking down at Singh Lee sprawled out amongst the Chinese takeout.

Cal ran both hands through his hair. "It was the wine," he said to Kate. He expected her to come unhinged, but instead she shook him again.

"Cal—Cal."

Cal stretched his neck for another look over his shoulder. Kate's face reappeared, this time out of the darkness. He closed his eyes, contemplating a plea of insanity.

"What?" Cal moaned, rubbing his eyes.

"Your phone is ringing," Kate said. Her voice sounded tired, not hysterical.

Cal's breath was raspy as he glimpsed at the nightstand. The clock displayed 2:03 A.M. "My phone?" he said, settling back into the pillow. "It's down in the office. You couldn't possibly—"

"It's been ringing off and on since 1:30," Kate said, nudging him again. "You better go see who it is."

Cal rustled free from the covers and grabbed a t-shirt. He waddled out of the bedroom, combing his hand through a tangle of hair. At the end of the hallway, he passed through the kitchen and dining room into a foyer. On the far side of the foyer, he stepped into his office, which was dark except for a computer monitor. He plopped down at his desk and turned on a lamp.

The light shrouded the room in a glow that was warmed by mahogany paneling. Next to the monitor sat his iPhone nestled in a docking station. He lifted the phone and touched the screen.

Kate couldn't possibly hear the phone from the bedroom.

The phone's call log showed four missed calls. Pressing the screen again, he noticed that the originating numbers had been blocked, and the words, "Private Number", appeared next to each call. Another thought struck him, and he touched the mail icon. He waited as an e-mail downloaded. It was a message from Singh Lee with a resume attached. He yawned and scratched his head, reaching for the lamp. The phone suddenly went off, and he nearly dropped it.

The screen lit up with the message, "Private Number Calling", as it rang. The time above it read: *2:10*. Cal raised the phone to his ear, hearing only static at first.

"Hello? Is this Dr. Calvin Hunter?" a female voice said.

Cal swiveled in his chair. "This is Cal Hunter. Who's calling?"

"Please hold for Dr. von Weir," the woman said. There was a click.

A recording came on the line that sounded like a commercial, only it was in German.

"Calvin," a voice finally said. There was a rushing sound in the background, like wind blowing. "This is Nicolai. How are you?"

"What's the matter, Nick?"

"Listen, I just watched a video of last night's interview in Atlanta. I wanted to be the first to congratulate you on a job well done. This is precisely the press coverage we need at the moment."

"I'm glad you're pleased—"

"Our PR man is preparing copies of the newscast for the wire services."

"That's great, but tell him to be careful. The FDA takes a tight stance on media, especially for unapproved drugs."

"We've covered all that. The lawyers have reviewed the press release, and it's fine," Nicolai said. "Your Food and Drug Administration will have no issues."

"Are you sure your guys understand US marketing regulations?" Cal said. "The FDA has an entire organization for policing promotional activity, the Office of Prescription Drug Promotion. OPDP for short."

"But of course, Calvin. You should not worry. Our legal department is small, but otherwise well respected in the industry. Thomas Jacobs held a top spot at Merck's operation in Belgium before we hired him away."

"Good to hear," Cal said, dropping his forehead into an open palm.

"You'll be happy to know we have just hired an attorney for the US team. He's joining us from Quasar Biotech and will be on board within a matter of days."

"Nick, hold on," Cal said, tightening his grip on the phone. "You're hiring a guy from Quasar? They're under SEC investigation. I just read about it in *The Wall Street Journal*. There are subpoenas—"

"Calvin, my dear Calvin," Nicolai interrupted. "Nathan assures me they are nothing but frivolous allegations."

"Nathan—who's Nathan?" Cal said. He opened a desk drawer and pulled out a pad.

"Nathan Friedman is the comrade we're hiring—"

"Listen, Nick. I had no idea you were hiring US executives. I've scheduled interviews with some of the best attorneys in the industry. And I'm talking about brass from Big Pharma. We shouldn't settle—"

"That is why I must trust Thomas's opinion on the matter."

"But that's not the point. I'm flying in candidates from all over the country next week." Cal jotted down Nathan Friedman's name. "We're mounting a massive US product launch, one that you've hired me to lead. Last night I found out that a chief financial officer has been hired."

"Yes, yes, yes. I understand what you're saying. Martin had every intention of calling," Nicolai said. "Only he did not wish to distract you from the TV interview."

"Nick, all I'm saying is we have to talk. If the strategy has changed, I need to be in the loop. How am I supposed to pull off a multi-billion dollar launch if I keep getting surprises?"

"It's late, and you're tired. Please do not misinterpret any of these actions. We're merely trying to help. You have more than enough on your plate, and we wish to ensure your success. As you recall, we discussed a matrix organization when we hired you, and nothing has changed. The US executives report to you with dotted-line responsibilities back to Zurich. We are a global enterprise, now."

"I understand, but the people we hire must fit my leadership style," Cal said, jotting Quasar Biotech on the pad.

"A value we all share," Nicolai said. "Last year we spent seven hundred thousand francs for McKinsey & Company to identify best practices. And as a result, we appointed you to lead the US. How's that for a good fit, as you call it?"

"I've engaged McKinsey on many occasions, and they've never advised hiring an executive who hasn't interviewed with his or her prospective manager," Cal said. "Maybe I should cancel the interviews until we iron out the process."

"Calvin, is there a problem with Singh Lee?"

"That's exactly my point. I don't know." Cal ran a hand through his hair at the mention of Singh Lee. Checking the time on the phone, he realized he had been dreaming about her only twenty minutes ago. "I just met her last night. We're supposed to talk tomorrow—I mean, later this morning."

"Excellent. If you don't like her, tell Martin to deal with it," Nicolai said. "With the winds blowing as they are in Washington, we must move fast. You can appreciate the investment we're making in the US, so I expect nothing less than a flawless launch from your team. And I don't have to remind you how success in the States will impact Zuritech's future. Hundreds of employees, millions of patients, and some very important investors are counting on you, Calvin."

Chapter 8

**ATLANTA, GEORGIA
TUESDAY, AUGUST 23
7 A.M. EDT**

Hardwoods concealed most of the building as Cal pulled into a spot on the Alpha Hut side of the parking lot. As he got out of his car, he spotted a Mercedes SL that he'd never seen before. The red exterior offered a sharp contrast to his Range Rover's ebony finish. He headed inside.

Sheri greeted Cal as he passed through her open workspace, an area just outside of his office. "Good morning, blue eyes," she said. "Will there be any coeds dropping by this morning?"

"Remind me to discuss my visitor policy and loaning car keys to people I don't know later," Cal said. "Who owns the Mercedes outside?"

"Actually, what I meant was, you look like you could use an espresso," Sheri said, quickly changing her tone. "There weren't any cars in the lot when I arrived. Why don't I grab us a coffee, and you can go powder your nose before we dive into today's agenda?"

Cal finally smiled. "Keep it up, and you'll be working the midnight shift like I did last night," he said, heading into his office. Once inside, he called over his shoulder, "But good morning, just the same."

Cal set his leather satchel behind the desk and flipped on his computer. He glanced over to the desk phone where a message light was blinking. Sitting down, he logged onto the computer and clicked a desktop icon. He then logged into a second layer of security to access Zuritech's IBM Notes system. An electronic inbox popped up, and he scanned down a string of e-mails from Nick. Without opening any of them, he got up and walked out of the office.

"Sheri, I'll be . . ." Cal paused mid-sentence when he noticed Sheri wasn't at her desk. He proceeded down the hallway, then turned and crossed a breezeway, checking the first doorway he came to. There was a light on, so he stepped inside. Looking around, he noticed a laptop computer sitting on the desk. Across the room, the windows framed the Chattahoochee River flowing in the distance. He headed back down the hallway and into the lobby.

"Have you seen Singh Lee this morning?" Cal said to Sheri as their paths crossed in the lobby.

"Check the employee lounge," Sheri said, scrunching her nose. "And I forgot your coffee. Do you mind?"

Cal entered the lounge and spotted Singh Lee standing next to the bar stirring a cup of tea. She removed a teabag and set it on the saucer, then looked up.

"You're up early," Cal said, eyeing her grey plaid suit. *Brooks Brothers*. "In case you didn't get the message, we're business casual on campus."

"So I hear. But you're forgetting, I'm still interviewing—sort of," she said. "Tea?"

"Sheri suggested something a bit stronger." Cal pulled a cup and saucer out of a cabinet and fiddled with a knob on the coffee machine.

"I received an e-mail from Martin Zeiss this morning. He asked me to help with the quarterly presentation on Thursday," Singh Lee said. "After reviewing the PowerPoint templates he sent over, I realized I needed systems access. Apparently, Zuritech maintains all of its financials in SAP, so I pulled a few strings and got set up. If it's okay with you, I'll take a first pass at the slides, and then sit down with you later this morning."

"A meeting on Thursday?" Cal said, setting down his cup. "Are you sure?" He pulled out his phone and checked the calendar.

"I just confirmed it with Sheri," Singh Lee said, "Martin organized it before I was on board, so I'm just hearing about it this morning."

"That makes two of us," Cal said, motioning for Singh Lee to follow him. "So it's a video meeting?"

"No, it's in Zurich," she said, balancing her cup as she hurried to catch up to Cal. "Eight o'clock on Thursday."

Back in the executive suite, Cal slowed at Sheri's desk and said, "Would you check availability on tonight's Delta flight to Zurich?" Then he continued into the office.

Singh Lee shrugged as she slipped past Sheri, and then trailed inside behind Cal.

"There's one more thing—"

"This is crazy," Cal said, interrupting Singh Lee. He set down the coffee and dropped into his chair, quickly retreating to his e-mail. There was an electronic invitation that Nick had forwarded from Martin with a message at the top: *See you Thursday*. The document had a 2:45 A.M. timestamp. Cal glanced up at Sheri as she entered the office. "What's the word from Delta?"

Sheri hesitated, looking over at Singh Lee. "You're not going to like this," Sheri said.

Cal sat with a puzzled look on his face.

"Would either of you care to explain what's going on?" Cal said.

"Martin suggested we take the corporate jet," Singh Lee said, her eyebrows lifting.

Following an awkward silence, Sheri said, "Is Avery Messinger aware of the meeting?" She sat down at the conference table.

"His name was on the invitation, but you may want to confirm it with him," Singh Lee said.

"Avery's already in Zurich working on the global research strategy. He can take care of himself. Is there anyone else?" Cal said.

"The agenda covers R&D, financials, and a business update. So I'd say, between the three of us, we should be able to handle it," Singh Lee said.

"If you don't need me for anything else, I'll be at my desk," Sheri said, getting up to leave. "The midnight shift will be here before you know it."

Cal seemed to miss the humor as his eyes followed her across the room. "Work with Singh Lee to pull together the presentation. You can use my slides from last week's board of directors update," Cal said, leaning back in his chair. Singh Lee turned for the door. "Singh Lee, can we have a moment?"

"I'll only be a minute," Singh Lee said to Sheri.

Sheri left the office, closing the door behind her.

"Please sit down," Cal said. "Martin is sending over a jet to fly the two of us to a meeting?"

"I'm as surprised as you," Singh Lee said. "Like I told you, I found out this morning."

"Martin beat me up last week for proposing an additional half million in product samples. Now, he's out buying jets?"

"Cal, settle down."

"Did you hear what I just said?"

CORPORATE RULES 53

"The jet is here in the States," Singh Lee said, stiffening her back. She suddenly remembered her tea and took a sip.

"What are you talking about?" Cal said, coming out of his chair.

"Don't shoot the messenger, okay? There are expenses for a new Gulfstream on the books," Singh Lee said. "I stumbled across them while I was familiarizing myself with SAP this morning."

Cal stopped in front of a window and looked out. Then he turned. "I reviewed the financials last week . . . there was no jet. We're talking about fifty million dollars."

"Fifty-six to be exact. That's what caught my attention. It's a G550, crème-de-la-crème," Singh Lee said rolling her last words in a French accent. "Only you wouldn't have found it on the Zuritech books, if that's where you were looking. The transaction was booked in a US subsidiary. You have to run consolidated financials to see it."

"You're telling me there are additional US companies I haven't reviewed?"

"If you say so," Singh Lee said. "Whoever's been pulling together the financials for you must have provided only the pharmaceutical company reporting. SAP requires a bit of tweaking to pick up all companies within a geographic region."

"Wait a minute," Cal said, working his way over to the credenza. He sat on the edge. "We have organizational controls in place. Martin can't buy a jet in the US, at least not without my approval. A transaction of this size requires my signature."

Singh Lee put down her teacup and headed over to the conference table and sat down, facing Cal. She leaned forward with her hands clasped together. "I'm not one to speculate, but the transaction I saw in the system was fairly complex. In addition to an aviation company, there's a second subsidiary that appears to be some type of trading business."

"Please tell me Martin isn't taking risks with company funds," Cal said. The thought creased furrows into his forehead.

"The dollar has been weak for the past few months. It's possible he's hedging currency contracts," Singh Lee said. "If it's true, he could have used trading profits to acquire the jet. To be quite honest, it's more complicated than that. He didn't actually purchase the aircraft. He leased it using an off balance sheet financing arrangement with an option to purchase at a later date . . . a pretty tax savvy maneuver, if you ask me."

"Wait a minute," Cal said, shaking his head. "How certain are you about all of this?" He didn't wait for a response. "Are there other transactions?"

"Point well taken. I haven't had time to check any of this thoroughly, so perhaps we should table the discussion until I do a little research." There was silence. "Listen, I'm only trying to help. How was I to know you didn't know about the jet?" Singh Lee said. "But let me tell you what I do know. I found a security deposit for a hangar at an airport called Briscoe Field. Based on experience, I can assure you there'll be additional expenses for a flight crew, operating costs, and maintenance."

"And the trading company?"

"Sometimes companies set up shell corporations for special activities," Singh Lee said. "But in this case, it's not clear what generated the cash. The transactions aren't exactly transparent."

"The US doesn't have a product on the market, which means there are no profits to invest in a subsidiary," Cal said, sliding into a chair next to Singh Lee.

"Just because the trading company is a US subsidiary doesn't mean the investments originated in the US," Singh Lee said. "I can't explain where the cash came from, at least not yet."

Cal sat silent for a moment with a troubled look on his face. "I don't like it," he said. "But you are right about one thing. Whatever's going on is clearly unrelated to the pharmaceutical business." Cal popped out of the chair. "When it comes to offshore bank accounts, Martin had better know what he's doing."

"I can investigate, if that helps."

"No, we've wasted enough time. Go help Sheri with the presentation," Cal said, pausing. "By the way, is that your Mercedes in the parking lot?"

"How do you like it?" Singh Lee said, getting up to leave. "Martin had it delivered last night."

Chapter 9

**NEW YORK, NEW YORK
WEDNESDAY, AUGUST 24
11 A.M. EDT**

The elevator doors opened on the 47th floor of the Fifth Avenue high-rise, and Christoph stepped out into the lobby, yawning. He buttoned his jacket as he made his way over to a receptionist.

"I have an eleven o'clock with Harold Bennett," Christoph said to the young lady. He surveyed the mahogany and steel decor, taking it all in as the receptionist worked a switchboard behind the counter.

"Thank you," she said into a headset. She glanced up and smiled. "And your name, sir?"

"Christopher Smith."

After an exchange over the headset, she pointed down a hallway. "It's the last conference room on the right."

Moments later, an assistant stopped by with coffee as Christoph extracted a tablet computer from his bag and booted up. After loading a presentation, he positioned himself near the head of the conference table.

Harold Bennett arrived a few minutes later, offering a handshake and a business card. The card had a raised VistaBio logo and an obscure title: *Director, Special Marketing*

Projects. With the pleasantries out of the way, Bennett settled into the power seat and leaned in for a look at Christoph's screen.

"First of all, thank you for your time this morning," Christoph said. "I know you must be busy, so if you don't mind, I'll skip the window dressing and jump straight into the presentation. Someone of your stature will quickly grasp the implications of the Rx Freedom Project."

"We've got about thirty minutes," Bennett said, checking his watch.

"And please, call me Chris. I'm a pharma veteran, so formalities aren't necessary."

"Excellent. What's your background?"

"Most recently—J & J. I held several executive positions in New Brunswick before serving as country head in Italy. Four years later, I rotated through a series of senior marketing positions, finally opting for early retirement."

"Retirement, no way," Bennett said. "But regardless, I have nothing but high regard for Johnson & Johnson."

"Kind words, thank you," Christoph said. "So what do you say we take a look at potential synergies between our organizations?"

Christoph touched the screen, and the slide show began.

"As you can see, I am founder and president of the Rx Freedom Project, or RFP for short. Our mission is to promote health, charity, and American values to regions of the world where closed door policies have historically prevailed. As you can see, there are many examples of a rapidly changing global scene: the former Soviet Union, Eastern Europe, and the Middle East, just to name a few." Christoph advanced the slide. "A number of established agencies deal with hunger, shelter, education, and even vaccines, but few are focused on pharmaceuticals."

"Just so there's no misunderstanding, VistaBio operates in some of those regions," Bennett said.

"An excellent observation, but not a stumbling block. You see, RFP's footprint prioritizes regions based on US State Department initiatives. We continually search for opportunities that align with our charitable missions, focusing primarily on geopolitical areas that have been hostile to American businesses. From the beginning, I designed the model to not only parallel State Department policies, but also to tailor our strategy to the needs of each and every donor. For example, VistaBio can carve out a specific geography, and RFP will ensure that donated pharmaceuticals go only into those countries. From a tactical standpoint, you never have to worry about cannibalization of products."

"The State Department adds a unique angle to your operation," Bennett said. "How about confidentiality?"

"We're happy to a sign a nondisclosure agreement, and yes, the program has been recognized by the industry as media savvy, not only for RFP, but also for our sponsors. Wherever freedom emerges around the world, you can be certain that RFP will have a foot in the door. And since the initial exposure is through charitable endeavors, a sponsor like VistaBio doesn't have to worry about the media throwing you under the bus."

"So what exactly do you want from VistaBio?"

"Three things. First, I'm looking for product donations—"

"Hold on," Bennett interrupted. "That opens up immediate regulatory concerns."

Christoph scrolled ahead and stopped on a slide entitled, "Legal Structure".

"RFP is registered as a Section 501(c) charitable organization in accordance with Internal Revenue Service guidelines, meaning VistaBio contributions are tax deductible. But just to be clear, we hold a US Drug Enforcement Agency license which grants us the right to receive and distribute pharmaceuticals."

"Excellent. So you've cleared the first hurdle," Bennett said.

"Your point is well taken. Now prepare to be blown away." Christoph advanced to a slide displaying half a dozen photographs. "This is our DEA inspected facility in New Jersey. As you can see, the warehouse is situated next to Newark International Airport. We've placed our operation in an Urban Enterprise Zone, which I don't have to tell you, draws considerable attention from the press and government for reasons such as employment, investment and community revitalization. These photos give you a feel for our hundred thousand square foot facility."

Christoph paged through more slides, allowing Bennett to read headlines from Newark newspapers praising the Rx Freedom Project.

"You said there were three things," Bennett said, checking his watch again.

"I like the way you think," Christoph said. "Secondly, we are seeking cash donations to support operational costs. As you may have gleaned from the slides, we utilize the funds for shipping, warehousing, laborers, equipment, computers, supplies, and contract production."

"What about overhead? Things like executive salaries?" Bennett said.

"RFP is a charitable cause not only for our partners, but for me as well. I draw no salary or benefits and utilize only part-time labor in the warehouse."

"You mentioned contract production. What's that about?" Bennett said.

"A perfect lead into my third and final point," Christoph said. "I believe you'll find this interesting. Knowing the industry as I do, I've developed a new means for business and charity to cooperate, creating a distinct win/win scenario. As we're both aware, pharmaceutical companies own production facilities that operate at varying levels of capacity. Oftentimes, they find themselves in seasonal periods of excess capacity, which we insiders know drives up production costs."

"We're challenged daily about forecasts, mostly from the manufacturing organization," Bennett said.

"I knew you would understand. What I intend to do, once RFP has sufficient cash on hand, is purchase excess production capacity from our partners. This means companies like VistaBio will gain efficiencies by fully utilizing their production lines, which as you realize, lowers cost. RFP wins by acquiring pharmaceuticals at a nominal price, further supporting our mission overseas."

"Are you sure that's legal?"

"One hundred percent," Christoph said.

Bennett snickered. "Those manufacturing guys are a pain. My boss is going to love this idea."

"We also accept dated inventory, as long as it's within reason," Christoph said. "Now if you don't mind, I'll wrap up and get you out of here." Christoph scrolled through more slides.

"Just a second," Bennett said. "What's that?"

"This is a recent drop in Iraq," Christoph said. "So far we've provided only limited assistance due to product constraints. In fact, I just returned from there."

"Whoa. You guys live on the edge."

Christoph moved on to the next slide. "We're currently working with the American Red Cross, Salvation Army, and State Department, as I mentioned earlier. And we're also seeking certification as a United Way Agency. If I'm not mistaken, VistaBio is a major contributor."

"That's right."

"Initially, RFP will focus on drugs that treat heart disease: cholesterol and hypertension medications."

"VistaBio owns those categories," Bennett said.

"Exactly. LipidRx is a blockbuster." Christoph punched the screen. "I'm calling on every major pharmaceutical company in the United States to support our efforts. At the moment, I'm looking for strategic sponsors to champion the initial drug categories. You're my first stop, but I'll be contacting Pfizer, Merck, GlaxoSmithKline, and Johnson & Johnson next week." Christoph advanced to a picture of an American flag with fireworks exploding in the background.

"Chris," Bennett said, coming out of his seat. "Is there any chance you could hold that sponsorship until I get back to you?"

"What's on your mind?" Christoph said, tossing a business card on the table.

Bennett stepped forward and snapped up the card. "I've got a feeling you can forget about the rest of those guys."

Chapter 10

ZURICH, SWITZERLAND
THURSDAY, AUGUST 25
6 A.M. CEST

Cal arrived early and stood in the doorway with a cup of espresso, checking out the setup in the empty meeting room. Tables covered in white linen stretched across the room in a U-shaped pattern with bottles of water set out every few feet. In a corner, baskets of pastries overflowed next to an arrangement of silver coffee carafes. At the rear, French doors had been opened up to showcase Hotel Belvoir's sweeping view of Lake Zurich in the valley below.

Hoping to shake his jet lag, Cal crossed the room and exited onto a stone terrace. The lake stretched as far as he could see, just above the tree line. A breeze stirred, and he took a deep breath, trying to forget the restless night he had just spent on an undersized mattress. The air had a bite to it, inviting him to enjoy the lake view and sip coffee, replaying the previous night's arrival.

Upon landing at the *Flughafen* Zurich on the company jet, he and Singh Lee had been greeted by a pair of chauffeurs. Neither was fluent in English, but it didn't seem to matter as the chauffeurs conversed between themselves in Swiss-German. They loaded the two of them and their baggage efficiently, dividing everything between two cars. Afterwards, the chauffeurs secured their passports and boarded the plane with a customs official. Moments later, Cal and Singh Lee were whisked away in separate limousines, and that was the last he had seen of her. When he arrived at the hotel, he found an agenda packet in his room, indicating that the executive, finance, and R&D meetings were being held in different locations.

Cal set his coffee on a stone fence that bordered the terrace, suddenly aware he didn't have Singh Lee's or Avery's cell numbers. Pulling out his iPhone, he fired an e-mail to Sheri requesting a contact list. He started to dial Kate when the phone rang.

"Sheri," Cal said, pressing the phone to his ear. All he heard were gasps. "What's the matter?"

"There's been a fire," she said. Her voice sounded distressed.

"Okay, take a few breaths and calm down." Cal checked the time on his phone. It read 6:30 local time, which meant 12:30 A.M. in Atlanta.

"It's Beta Hut," Sheri said. "I received a call twenty minutes ago. You and Avery are out of town, so I had to come. Somebody has to be here."

Cal pulled the phone away and checked his call log. "No one has tried to contact me."

"I'm pulling up to the front gate."

Cal listened as a guard greeted Sheri, confirming that the facility was on alert. Then he heard a warning about going inside. Sheri cut the man off, reminding him of her twenty-four hour access. The car's engine accelerated.

"What an idiot," Sheri said. "Cal, I'm pulling into the parking lot, and there's no sign of a fire truck." A car door opened, followed by rapid footsteps. Then there was a beep and the swish of a door opening. "I'm inside Beta Hut. I'll call you back."

Ten minutes later, Sheri telephoned again.

"There's been an incident in the lab," Sheri said. "Chemicals either spilled or boiled over, eating through a wall into an electrical circuit that started a fire, but they're telling me it was contained. I'm sitting in a conference room with a security guard and haven't seen any smoke in the area." The tone in her voice was approaching normal. "I have you on speakerphone, so I'll let the guard brief you on the status."

"This is Cal Hunter. Can you tell me your name?" He paused, detecting sirens wailing in the background.

"Yes, this is Kurt Handle."

"Kurt," Cal said, "Are you the one who contacted Sheri?"

"No," Sheri cut in. "Karl Spears called me."

"We didn't wish to upset anyone," Kurt said. "An experiment in the lab exploded, and the chemicals melted through electrical wires causing a circuit to blow."

"How extensive is the damage?" Cal said.

"The lab is not so bad since the sprinklers stopped the fire," Kurt said. "But the computer room is on the other side of the wall, and I'm afraid the news is not good in there. The fire reached the file server."

"The sprinklers didn't activate in the computer room?" Cal said.

"They haven't been installed. I understand that a special system is required," Kurt said. "But I was able to get inside and put out the fire with a handheld extinguisher."

"Do you know if the fire shut down the computer networks?" Cal said. He was now pacing the terrace.

"Someone shut them down, but only in Beta Hut. Alpha Hut was not impacted. The initial word is that the server contained, let's see, clinical data. That's it," Kurt said.

Cal ran a hand through his hair. "Kurt, you're saying the fire damaged the ZuriMax server?"

"Yes. That is correct, Dr. Hunter. It was completely destroyed."

"Sheri, what's your assessment?" Cal said.

"I haven't seen the computer room," Sheri said. "Do you want me to go inside?"

"Dr. Hunter, there are toxic fumes. You can probably hear the alarms going off in the lab," Kurt said. "We must wait for the air to clear."

"Cal, we haven't hired any computer techs yet," Sheri said. "If it's okay with you, I'll call our contractor, Chase. He does the desktop installations, and maybe he can determine if the server can be saved."

"Great idea," Cal said. "But first talk to Avery and brief him on what's going on."

"I'll do it first thing in the morning and get back to you," Sheri said.

"Avery should have a disaster recovery plan in place," Cal said. "It's standard procedure to back up critical files offsite. He'll want to replace the server immediately. Otherwise, we can forget about the upcoming FDA submission."

Chapter 11

ZURICH, SWITZERLAND
THURSDAY, AUGUST 25
8 P.M. CEST

With Nicolai chairing the CEO meeting all day, Cal had to wait until they were on a shuttle headed for dinner to discuss the implications of the fire. To his surprise, Nicolai showed little reaction, seemingly unfazed by the possibility of a delay in the ZuriMax submission.

After dinner, the group sipped wine in a private dining room while Nicolai rolled out his latest corporate initiative. Boston Consulting Group would be assisting Zuritech in securing a spot on Fortune's list of "100 Best Companies to Work For". The announcement jump-started a festive mood that carried the evening until Nicolai closed with a champagne toast. As the attendees prepared to leave, Nicolai and Cal headed to the bar.

"Thank you for remaining behind," Nicolai said to Cal as they pulled up stools. The room had a Swiss chalet décor, bristling with a lively crowd that pressed in all around them. Nicolai waved to the others who were filing out the door to catch the shuttle back to the hotel.

"So what do you think of the Gulfstream?" Nicolai said, pausing for Cal's reaction. "But what is this look?"

"I'm not accustomed to flying in such a manner," Cal said.

"And what is this manner you speak of?"

"Big private jets, like Gulfstreams."

Nicolai held up a hand and snapped his fingers. A bartender appeared. "Two Dunkle Perles," Nicolai said, turning back to Cal. "I am delighted to have you at the helm of our US organization. As you can appreciate, the board shares my sentiments and wishes to provide every tool necessary to assure your success." The bartender clunked down two foaming steins. "But let us turn to another matter—the ZuriMax submission. I spoke to Avery, and he has every confidence that our setback is temporary. He believes the FDA filing has not been jeopardized or delayed, for that matter. But of course, the CEOs all anxiously await the US launch. And that is why I laid out the strategy so clearly today. We are destined to become a global player, but it is not possible without success in the US."

"I couldn't agree more," Cal said.

"We must maintain our momentum by encouraging our associates to remain focused. I am thinking of putting a plaque on every desk with the inscription, 'Achieve Top 5 Ranking in the Global Pharmaceutical Market within 10 Years'." Nicolai held out his hands for Cal's response.

"You realize the clinical data may have been destroyed today? That means we'll have to restore and revalidate the files," Cal said, looking away. A man down the bar caught his attention. There was something odd about the way he cut his eyes. He wore a wrinkled overcoat. *Was he eavesdropping?* Cal ignored the thought and turned to Nicolai. "Don't get me wrong. The plaque is a nice gesture, but only if we're walking the talk."

"But of course," Nicolai said. "And to your first point, Avery has given his word that the data will be recovered without disruption. But there is another matter. As I see the situation, your FDA allows themselves a twelve month window for new drug approvals. They do not seem to appreciate the concept that time is money, as the accountants say."

Cal shook his head as he reached for a stein. He slid it closer, trailing a stream of foam across the bar. "Everyone in the industry wrestles with the FDA. Unfortunately, they're a force we can't control—"

"But what if we filed an orphan drug submission?" Nicolai interrupted.

"I don't see how it's relevant, but if that were possible, it would cut the approval time in half," Cal said, giving Nicolai a look. "Avery has never mentioned an expedited review. Besides, the parameters would have to be in the current protocol."

"Avery has identified a genetic disorder that interests your FDA," Nicolai said. "In fact, he plans to look for patients in the clinical trial with this unfortunate disease."

"Orphan drug status applies to conditions where fewer than two hundred thousand patients are diagnosed each year. Avery has something?"

"He's very confident."

"If he's right, and that's a big *if*, we would have to move the launch forward six months in order to reap any benefits," Cal said, raising an eyebrow. "But that's a problem I would welcome."

"My sentiments exactly," Nicolai said. "It puts us on the market sooner and accelerates our plans for the rest of the world."

"Are you prepared to handle the funding?" Cal said. "We'll need to hire a thousand sales representatives, ramp up production, put on inventories—not to mention headquarters staff. And we'll have to do it fast."

"The financial arrangements are not your worry. It is a matter for Martin and Singh Lee to handle. But if we are to pull this off, I must take care of my CEO." Nicolai patted Cal on the shoulder. "You will be happy to hear more good news in this regard, my dear Calvin."

"Hold on, Nick. An expedited review isn't a given at this stage. In fact, I'd say the odds are against us. I would advise caution. Have Avery review the data, and then develop a plan if warranted," Cal said. "He has to prove that he has patients with the condition simply to get to first base with the FDA. With material issues like this, I prefer to under promise and over deliver, especially if we intend to involve the board. I'm scheduled to meet with Albert Jensen at Johns Hopkins next week. I'd like to see what he thinks about the idea."

"But of course, Calvin. I understand," Nicolai said, hefting his beer stein. "In the meantime, the board has agreed to a change in your contract, a sweetener for expedited approval. If ZuriMax is approved within six months of FDA submission, you will be granted an additional five hundred thousand stock options." Nicolai elevated the stein in anticipation of a toast.

Cal stared down at the bar, thinking. Then he lifted his beer, clanking it against Nicolai's. "*Danke schoen*," he said.

Fifteen minutes later, Nicolai sped away in the back of a limo as Cal headed over to Bahnhofstrasse to catch a cab. The streets in Old Town were dimly lit, but brimming with pedestrians moving in all directions. He picked up his stride as he turned a corner in the direction of Lake Zurich. Two blocks down, he came to an intersection and paused, waiting for a break in the traffic. Someone bumped into him.

"*Excusez-moi*," Cal heard over his shoulder. He turned and did a double-take. It was the man from the bar. He stepped up next to Cal and looked him in the eyes.

The accent didn't fit. Cal's mind processed the pronunciation. *French?*

"We need to talk," the man said.

"You were in the restaurant," Cal said, realizing the man had switched to English. He entered the intersection with the man falling in behind him. Cal turned the words over in his mind, and for some reason the accent troubled him. He pulled out his cell phone. "Back off or I'll call the police."

"I need some information about ZuriMax," the man said.

Cal stopped in the middle of the street. A steady stream of pedestrians side-stepped them as he took another look at the man's outfit. His collar was turned up, and he wore a fedora.

"Who are you?" Cal said. A horned blasted, and he had to jump for the curb to avoid a passing car. Looking up, he spotted two Swiss soldiers coming his way.

When Cal turned back, the man was gone.

Chapter 12

ATLANTA, GEORGIA
MONDAY, AUGUST 29
7 A.M. EDT

Sheri spotted Cal in the parking lot, dragging as he got out of his car. By the time he reached her office, she had a cup of coffee waiting.

"You read my mind," Cal said, taking the cup. "Do you have any news on the fire, this morning?"

"Well, as you know, Avery's team worked all weekend. They've reported minimal damage in the lab, but I was a bit surprised when they passed on Chase helping out with the computer room," Sheri said. "Within the hour, they expect to have a new server up and running."

"Let's keep our fingers crossed," Cal said. "What else do we have on tap for today?"

"As requested, Singh Lee will join you in about five minutes. You've got lunch with the Georgia Biomedical Partnership, and then at one o'clock an R&D update over in Beta Hut." Sheri paused. "Someone named Dr. Timothy Warren left a phone number, and Karl Spears has been trying to reach you, but no message."

"You're running like a fine Swiss watch this morning," Cal said. "How was the weekend?" He continued into his office with Sheri trailing behind.

"It was supposed to be a three-dayer until you started leaving all of those voicemails on Friday. I thought you were on a flight?"

"The Gulfstream has a satellite phone, and I had a lot on my mind," Cal said. "Why didn't you tell me Singh Lee was staying over in Switzerland?"

"I didn't find out until Thursday evening. She asked me to make arrangements for a return flight on Saturday. That's all I know," Sheri said. "And by the way, when you synch your iPhone, you'll have the latest company directory." She looked out into the hallway. "And here's your first appointment."

Singh Lee passed Sheri in the doorway and slipped into the office, making a direct line for the conference table. Her hair was pulled back, and the navy slacks and oxford blouse she was wearing added a formal air to her arrival.

"You seem fully recovered from the trip," Singh Lee said. She settled into a chair and opened a laptop computer, flexing her eyes open.

Cal grabbed a stack of papers off his desk and joined her. "How was the meeting in Zurich?"

"Unbelievable. Only we met at a place called the Steigenberger Hotel in Davos. The train ride through the Alps was postcard perfect. And you'll be happy to know I picked up a few pointers on international accounting. Martin has nothing but good things to say about the progress here in the States and made it clear that the US will be setting the bar for the rest of the world."

"Nothing like a little backdoor pressure," Cal said. "Any time to hit the slopes?"

Singh Lee diverted her eyes to the window. "I needed a break," she said, attempting a smile. "The meeting ended Thursday, but I stayed over an extra day for just that reason."

"That's great," Cal said, taking a sip of coffee. "Listen, our discussion during the flight over helped quite a bit. My agenda is pretty tight in the coming weeks, but we'll schedule regular meetings to ensure we're on the same page." He set the coffee down, and then flipped through the papers. "Now, about the financials you provided for my presentation. I noticed that the figures are the same as my last board presentation. As you recall, we discussed consolidating the US results—"

"The numbers are fine," Singh Lee interrupted. "Martin confirmed we were to present only the Zuritech Corporation financials at the meeting. The board of directors wants you focused on the pharmaceutical business, and Martin has concerns that it will only confuse everyone by including the aviation and trading companies in your presentations."

"Then Nick didn't get the message. He drilled me in Zurich on this very point—in front of the global CEOs, no less," Cal said. "He asked if the figures were consolidated, and naturally I told him they were. But on the flight home, I compared the reports and—"

"I presented the same financials in Davos," Singh Lee said. "I assume you would agree that we should report consistent data to Nicolai and Martin?"

"That goes without saying. Everyone needs to read from the same script. I have no intention of misleading anyone on US performance."

"Point taken," Singh Lee said. "I'll address the matter one last time with Martin and follow up with you. I have to speak to him about revising the forecast, anyway."

Cal lowered his eyebrows. "Why would you revise the forecast?"

"We need projections for the expedited FDA review—"

"Hold on," Cal interrupted. "Avery agreed to look into the orphan indication only last week. It's a bit premature for forecasts, wouldn't you say?"

"If that were true, I'd agree," Singh Lee said. "But Martin mentioned it during my interview weeks ago." Her eyes lowered to the laptop as she began to type. "I'll discuss the timeline with him."

"Good. I plan to take it up with Avery this afternoon," Cal said. "And one last thing regarding the financials, I found an error in last month's ZuriMax development expenses."

Singh Lee's eyes peeked over the top of the laptop. "How so?"

Cal left his seat and walked over to the door. "Sheri, can you bring in the Bioscene file?" He returned to the conference table and sat down, facing Singh Lee. "I authorized a million dollar payment to our contract research organization last month. The summary ledgers report only seven hundred and fifty thousand."

"Maybe we didn't owe the full amount. Is it possible you overpaid the previous bill?" Singh Lee said.

"The payment was executed on the fifteenth of the month," Sheri called out from the door. "I faxed a request to accounting a week earlier."

"No need to get defensive, I'm not blaming you," Cal said to Sheri. "Check the previous payment. I believe it was three months earlier." He came out of the chair and headed over to his desk, pulling out a binder.

"I want to make sure I understand the process," Singh Lee said. "You fax the bills to accounting in Zurich?" She looked to Sheri for confirmation.

"That's right," Sheri said, stepping into the office. "Cal, the previous payment was made on April 15th for the same amount." She closed the folder.

Cal flipped in the binder. "Payments are handled out of a centralized services group in Switzerland that reports to Martin. We fax over signed requests, and they execute payments out of our US operating account." He paused and ran his finger down a page. "Here it is again. The April payment was made before I came on board, but the ledger reports seven hundred and fifty thousand. The books are misstated by half a million dollars for these two transactions alone." He looked up, still thinking.

"I'll do some research," Singh Lee said. "It's surprising to see errors of this nature, especially in a Swiss organization."

"I don't like it—"

"Let me handle it," Singh Lee interrupted. She turned to Sheri. "If you don't mind, I'll need to borrow the folder."

"While you're at it, print copies of the aviation and trading financial statements," Cal said. "Do these companies have names?"

"Zurich Aviation Corporation, or Aviation for short. And Trading—"

"For Zuritech Trading Corporation," Cal said, completing her sentence. "Run year-to-date financials, just in case Nick presses me again."

Chapter 13

ATLANTA, GEORGIA
MONDAY, AUGUST 29
1 P.M. EDT

Cal swiped his security badge at the Beta Hut entrance and waved to the guard behind a glass partition as he passed through the lobby. In the back corner, he used the badge a second time to access a stairway that took him down to an underground office area. The space was decorated in natural décor, like Alpha Hut. Rows of cubicles sat in the center of the room, surrounded by offices with name plaques, all ending in "PhD".

Cal slowed as he passed Avery's office, checking to make sure he wasn't inside. Then he headed to the next doorway into a conference room. Avery looked up from the far end of a granite conference table where he was feeding paper into a shredder. He wore a green polo shirt and sported a Van Dyke that was chestnut-colored, like his hair. Just above him, an oversized flat screen bounced through scenes of exotic waterfalls, smoking volcanoes, and sandy white beaches. The calming sounds of nature filled the room in surround sound.

"Good to have you back, Avery," Cal said above the crashing waves. He took another look at the screen and sat down.

Avery managed a smile as he finished up, carefully folding a paper in his hand. "So how long were you in Zurich?"

"Off and on for three months," Avery said, slapping the paper down. "There's no place like home."

"By the way, I had lunch with the brass at the Biomedical Partnership. Apparently, the local universities have a fine crop of graduate students looking for internships next summer." Avery stood up and crossed the room in Cal's direction. "You may want to give them a call."

Avery pulled out a smartphone and typed. "Excuse me while I get the team," he said, slipping past Cal.

Glancing over his shoulder, Cal slid out of the chair and made his way over to where Avery had been sitting. A broken pencil lay splintered in the carpet. He leaned over the shredder and noticed cuttings overflowing onto the carpet. After checking the door, Cal reached for the sheet on the table and unfolded it. He recognized the shape. It was a bell-shaped curve, only one side was skewed, giving it a lopsided effect. There was an exchange of voices outside, and Cal pushed the sheet aside, returning to his seat in time to be greeted by a half-dozen men and women filing into the room.

Avery came in last and closed the door. He pulled a remote from his pocket and pressed a button. The scenery on the flat screen was replaced by a presentation. "It's good to see everyone," Avery said. "As you all know, this week marks the end of the ZuriMax phase III clinical trial. I am happy to report that we are now ready to move into our post-trial activities. To highlight the occasion, our esteemed CEO, Dr. Cal Hunter, has taken the time to join us for this significant milestone." He extended a hand in Cal's direction as heads bobbed around the table. "I have asked Dr. Summers to begin with a review for Dr. Hunter's benefit."

A young woman in a lab coat rose and moved to the front of the room. "Thank you, Dr. Messinger," Summers said. She brushed strands of blonde bangs out of her eyes and focused on the screen.

"I'd like to begin with an update on the current market. As you can see from the first slide, there are presently dozens of branded and generic medications on the market indicated for the treatment of elevated cholesterol. Many claim to reduce low density lipoprotein, better known as LDL, which we all know is bad cholesterol. A few have proven to boost high density lipoprotein, HDL, which has demonstrated benefits, especially at levels of sixty milligrams or more in the bloodstream. VistaBio, the producer of torvastatin calcium, better known by its trade name, LipidRx, has overtaken Pfizer's Lipitor, which has gone generic after dominating cholesterol therapies for years. Slide please.

"Similarly, there are currently a host of hypertension drugs on the market. Top medications in this category include beta-blockers, ace inhibitors, and calcium channel blockers. IMS reports quite a variety of drugs being prescribed, both old and new. In this case, the prevalence of so many choices is unfortunate, adding complexity to an already difficult treatment regimen. Typically, new hypertension patients are prescribed a single drug therapy, but often experience sustained symptoms over time, prompting physicians to prescribe in a grab bag fashion until they get the condition under control. And as you can imagine, patients faced with combined symptoms of elevated cholesterol and hypertension often deal with drug therapies that are quite complex and financially inhibitive. It is estimated that patients with a two prescription regimen are now spending four thousand dollars a year for branded drugs. Clearly, a lower cost solution is needed, but also one that can provide improved patient compliance." Summers signaled for the next slide.

"If I may break in at this point," Cal said. "This is an excellent introduction, but as you may know, I am familiar with the US market. If you don't mind, I'd like to focus our limited time on the ZuriMax update."

Summers turned to Cal, her face expressionless. "But of course, Dr. Hunter," she said. "Advance the slide, please." She paused as one of her associates scrolled through the slide deck.

"Here we are," Summers said. "The ZuriMax phase III clinical trial is a double-masked study with three thousand patients. The US-based study was initiated twenty-four months ago with two clinical endpoints. The ZuriMax protocol targeted a thirty percent decrease in cholesterol and a one stage drop in blood pressure relative to the control group. Although we're not seeking an indication, we are collecting data to validate that our formulation delivers the same benefits as low dosage aspirin. There's no question that a triple combo efficacy will redefine prescribing habits across the country."

"Why didn't you go for the third indication?" Cal said.

"The dual claim already adds significant complexity to the study, but we believe it is sufficient to differentiate our product from existing therapies," Summers said.

"What about the other combination drugs on the market?" Cal said.

"None of them have anything approaching our Z-Pulse technology," Summers said. "And we believe a third indication would have slowed the trial, especially if the FDA required additional legs to the study. Instead, we chose to simply measure the effects of the drug, which will allow the statistical results to be published for the scientific community. Naturally, the data will find its way into medical literature where physicians can evaluate it and form their own opinions."

"So tell me how it's going, Dr. Summers?" Cal said. "I realize the code hasn't been broken at this point, but do you have anecdotal comments from the participating clinics?"

"To be quite honest, there's somewhat of a debate among ourselves, Dr. Hunter," Summers said. "We're hearing rumors that certain clinics have experienced attrition rates that are higher than customary for studies of this nature. If true, it could indicate a statistical deviation from previous trials with both statins and hypertension compounds."

"How significant is the difference?" Cal said. He paused to look around the room, noticing a few scientists squirming in their chairs. "Karl, would you like to comment?" Cal turned to Karl Spears. Although brilliant, Karl looked more like Elvis Costello than a scientist.

"Yes, thank you for the lovely introduction, Cal," Karl said, adjusting a pair of black-framed glasses. He reclined in his chair. "One might have predicted minor elevations in attrition rates versus prior phase III trials as it relates to individuals on existing treatments. After all, our drug is a combo therapy and may trigger responses in less drug tolerant segments of the population. We all know Merck had problems with their Enhance trial."

"That's a different type of combo therapy," Cal said. "What are the ZuriMax estimates?"

"It's all speculative since we haven't tapped into the data, but we're thinking roughly twelve percent attrition based on conversations with the clinics," Karl said. "That compares to a two percent norm in the cholesterol subset and two-point-seven percent in the hypertension group. Since we're dealing with a double blind study, my colleagues argue that neither the physicians nor the patients know who has received which treatment."

"So they're suggesting the attrition may be related to the control group," Cal said. "Then why are you concerned, Karl?"

"Precisely," Summers said, taking aim at Karl. "We shouldn't speculate in the absence of hard data."

Karl laughed and folded his hands behind his head, fanning out his elbows. "Go ahead and kick me, but we all know we're losing valuable time playing this little suck-up game, or whatever you want to call it. The fact is—attrition is inconsistent with previous studies conducted on similar control groups. Your defense defies logic." Karl locked eyes with Summers.

"The control group is taking a placebo," Cal said, studying Karl's face.

Karl smirked at Summers. "Bingo. We're comparing ZuriMax to a sugar pill—"

"Which is standard practice," Summers interrupted.

"That's true," Cal said. "Big Pharma takes this path on all new drugs, even when there are existing therapies to use as benchmarks. What's the plan once we're on the market?"

"Phase IV studies are already on the drawing board," Summers said. "After we're commercially viable, we'll compare ZuriMax to the leading drugs. As you so eloquently pointed out, it's done all the time."

"Does anyone have a theory about the patients who've left the study? Maybe there's a compliance issue," Cal said. "I've just returned from a tour of east coast clinics, and there was no mention of attrition in the centers I visited."

"Well, I guess that settles it," Karl said. "But I'm telling you, twelve percent is roughly three to four hundred patients. That's enough to make me nervous. No, scratch that—a conscientious objector. As for your tour, Cal, I've always believed physicians are reluctant to tell a CEO what to do with his drug, especially when he's paying them to participate in the study. I wouldn't bite that hand."

"What do we know about adverse drug reactions?" Cal said, ignoring Karl's last comment.

"Reported ADRs have been consistent with existing therapies: headache, diarrhea, upset stomach, and muscle aches," Summers said. "There's no indication of a health risk, not even anecdotally to use your words, Dr. Hunter."

"Let's keep in mind, the attrition is only a rumor at this stage. We'll have to wait for the data," Avery said. "Dr. Spears, do you have any further comments?"

Spears leaned forward with his elbows on the table. He glanced over at Cal, and then up at the slide. After a moment of hesitation, he turned to Avery. Then he faded back to Cal and shook his head, settling back into the chair.

"Next steps," Summers said, as the slide advanced. "After the data is unmasked, preliminary statistics will be generated in-house. We'll run all FDA required analyses and combine them with the clinical package currently being assembled by our team. Once submitted, we'll await FDA follow-up, a panel recommendation, and final approval. With any luck, we'll be on the market in twelve months."

The screen went blank.

Not wasting any time, Avery stood. "Thank you all for your time." He pressed a button, and a tropical sunrise beamed onto the flat screen. He hurried to the door and directed the scientists outside.

"Avery," Cal said, watching as he returned for the paper. "You left out the update on the fire. What's the status of the data recovery?"

"Can't you see how nervous these guys are? I'm doing my best to keep everyone motivated," Avery said. "Bioscene has been working around the clock and will be ready to transmit as soon as we complete the wiring on our end."

"So you're confident the incident won't delay the FDA filing?"

"If you want proof, the new server's sitting in the computer room," Avery said. "While you're at it, take a look at the old one. It resembles an oversized lump of coal."

"Maybe later," Cal said. "I'm also curious about your conversation with Nick last week. He mentioned you had an idea about an orphan drug indication, possibly expediting the approval. There was no mention of it in the presentation." He swiveled his chair to face Avery.

"I thought I just explained that. Scientists have tendencies to get worked up over project milestones, especially when they involve novel compounds like ZuriMax." Avery raised a hand, gesturing in the direction of his departed staff. "I prefer to foster as little debate as possible, at least until there's more to go on."

"So it's true. You want to file an expedited review, and then follow on with the broader indications."

Avery rose from his chair and closed the door, crossing to the far end of the room where an image of a waterfall cascaded into an aqua-blue tidal pool. "I suppose we can speak in confidence—"

"Seriously?" Cal said. "I've got a product launch to execute, and you think, just maybe, we should talk about this?"

"I'm being cautious, that's all," Avery said. "Nicolai pressed me for options. He said if we wait for a normal FDA review, it will cost the company billions. So I offered an alternative."

"What exactly?" Cal rose from his chair and found the remote. He hit the power button, and the room fell silent.

"Actually, Dr. Jensen developed the original theory," Avery said, staring up at the blank screen. "I spoke with him at a scientific convention a few months ago."

"Albert Jensen of Johns Hopkins?"

"You know him?" Avery said. "Of course you do, you launched LipidRx."

"I'm meeting with him next week about serving as our ZuriMax spokesperson," Cal said.

"He has my vote," Avery said. "Anyway, the doctors at Johns Hopkins have studied statins as a combination therapy for a number of therapeutic treatments. Dr. Jensen has been a pioneer in the effort. He now believes ZuriMax may represent a breakthrough for a rare form of restenosis."

"Restenosis, what's so special?" Cal said.

"As you know, it's not uncommon to see a narrowing of the coronary arteries post-angioplasty," Avery said. "It's believed to be caused by clotting or tissue growth inside the arterial walls. Jensen thinks he's identified a gene that stimulates the response in a select group of patients."

"Which is great news, but aren't you forgetting one thing?" Cal said. "You have to conduct a clinical trial to show efficacy. Designing a study will take longer than getting the original drug approval."

"That's true, but only if you're starting from scratch," Avery said. "I had my doubts at first, but Jensen convinced me that our existing patient population contains an adequate sample of the bad gene. Once we crack the code on our study, he believes the combination of his ongoing research and data from our clinics will support a fast-track approval."

"It'll take months to convince the FDA to look at his hypothesis," Cal said. He sat down on the edge of the conference table.

"Evidently, he's already engaged an FDA reviewer, one who has an interest in his theory. Jensen thinks the guy has enough muscle to champion an expedited review."

"So you've potentially got support," Cal said, looking down at the floor. "Scientifically speaking, do you have enough confidence in his theory to move the ZuriMax launch forward six months?" He raised his head, awaiting Avery's response.

"We're talking billions of dollars, Cal. Just think of what that means to the company, not to mention our careers. I say we get outside of the box on this one." He paused. "Why are you looking at me that way?"

"It's nothing," Cal said, smiling. "I was just thinking about the patients."

"Let me offer a bit of advice. We both know what's at stake here. Nicolai is serious about introducing ZuriMax into the US market posthaste, so if you're about to challenge the expedited review, I'd be careful." Avery rubbed his hands down his face. "If you haven't figured it out, the boys in Switzerland are as aggressive as hell."

Chapter 14

**CHULA VISTA, CALIFORNIA
TUESDAY, AUGUST 30
2 A.M. PDT**

The automatic doors at the Chula Vista Medical Center emergency room rattled like a train coming down the tracks as they parted for a team of EMTs wheeling in a gurney. Outside, an ambulance's strobes lit up the night, splashing streaks of red across the walls in the admissions area. A man was strapped onto the gurney covered in white linen with only his mop of graying hair and leathery complexion exposed. An EMT pressed her fingers to the patient's neck while another steered, clutching an IV bag in his free hand. As they scrambled down a hallway, staffers in scrubs parted to give way. A little further in, an on-call physician appeared from a doorway and fell into stride alongside the EMTs.

The physician's tousled hair suggested it had been a rough night. He extracted a penlight from his scrubs and used a thumb to open one of the patient's eyelids as they wheeled into an empty cubical.

"Vitals?" the physician called out.

"He's in cardiac arrest," an EMT said, reaching out to hook the IV to a pole. The gurney was still moving. "His pulse flat-lined when we were loading him."

The EMT pressed a wheel brake, and the gurney lurched to a stop. An amber-colored bottle broke free from the linens and bounced across the tile floor.

"Were there any responses en route?" the physician said, still focused on the patient.

"We initiated chest compressions along with assisted breathing."

"For how long?" the physician said, not waiting for a response. He yelled over a shoulder, "I need assistance over here, stat," then turned to the EMT. "Okay, let's get the blood work rolling and a tube in him. Point-five milligrams of epinephrine." There was an agitated look on the physician's face as a nurse sprinted in. "Where the hell is everybody?"

"They're on the way," the nurse said, spinning around to a supply cabinet.

"What else do we know?" the physician said to the EMT. The other EMT released the patient restraints and prepared a hypodermic needle.

"It was a 9-1-1 call by a driver on the 805. They reported a crosser that collapsed on the side of the road."

"Have you observed changes to his condition since your first visual?"

"He was in and out of consciousness when we arrived on the scene. He didn't appear to speak English, but kept repeating a name that sounded like Max somebody. That's all we got," the EMT said.

"Were there others with him?"

"The dispatcher reported a group of them running down the expressway, but we never got a visual on anyone."

"Identification?" the physician said, now working a stethoscope across the man's chest. "Do you think his name is Max?"

The nurse reappeared and wedged past the doctor and EMT. Sliding a defibrillator across a counter on the back wall, she plugged it into an outlet with one hand while reaching over and loosening the man's shirt with the other. She tore open a plastic bag and poured the contents on a surgical tray.

"No ID," the EMT said, kneeling down. He searched the floor.

The physician switched on the penlight for another look at the man's pupil. It was fully dilated. Just then the defibrillator shrilled.

"Charged," the nurse yelled. She grabbed a packet of contact gel and tore it open, coating the patient's chest. "Ready when you are, Doctor."

They physician switched off the penlight and stood silent for a moment.

"Ready," the nurse repeated.

The physician exhaled.

"Doctor, we're ready."

Turning away, the physician said, "Close the bag. This one's just run his last Hail Mary."

The nurse glared at the doctor, but he was standing with his back toward her. She looked down at the patient.

"We've got an Rx bottle with a white tablet inside." The EMT stood up and shook the bottle. A pill dropped out into his hand. "There are no markings."

"He probably picked it up across the border," the physician said. "He's got all the classic signs of coronary disease. Put him down as a myocardial infarction. And you can forget about whatever's in that bottle."

"Apparently, Mr. José Rodriguez," the EMT said, studying the label. He slipped the tablet back inside and handed it to the nurse.

"Do you want the lab to take a look at this, Doctor?" the nurse said. She reached over and lifted a clipboard off the counter and began scribbling.

"All indications are we've got an uninsured patient who is likely an illegal," the physician said. "Send him downstairs, and notify the police. Mr. Rodriguez is out of our jurisdiction now."

Chapter 15

**BALTIMORE, MARYLAND
FRIDAY, SEPTEMBER 2
10 A.M. EDT**

The Gulfstream banked, and then descended into Baltimore/Washington International Airport. A limo met Cal at the Signature Flight hangar and whisked him off to Dr. Albert Jensen's office in the Johns Hopkins medical complex. Upon arrival, he was escorted down a hallway where he had to dodge patients and staff flowing in and out of an endless maze of examining rooms. At the end of the hall he was shown into a paneled office.

Cal noted the impressive furnishings as he made his way over to an armchair. Before he could settle in, Jensen huffed in through the doorway.

"Albert Jensen," he said.

Cal stepped forward and grasped Jensen's meaty hand. "Cal Hunter," he said. "Thank you for working me in on such a busy day."

"Nonsense, this is typical," Jensen said. "I limit office hours to three days a week, but I have six associates in the practice. There's also the support staff: a psychologist, three nurses, and six medical technicians. The operation practically runs itself."

"Impressive," Cal said. "I take it you spend your time on special cases."

"That's right—mostly surgery," Jensen said. "The staff handles the pre- and post-op care."

"And the other two days—golf?"

Jensen laughed. "I'm afraid not. I do a lot of lectures and conferences. With these managed care weasels turning the profession into a bureaucracy, most of us physicians have diversified. We're all scrambling to find ways to make up for the lost revenue the insurance companies are sucking out of our practices. You wouldn't believe the sidelines my associates are getting into these days: real estate, automobile dealerships, mini-warehouses. One opened a Dunkin' Donuts last month. Can you believe that? Where'd you go to medical school?"

"Northwestern. I completed my residency at the Mayo Clinic in Jacksonville while I was working on an MBA. I've remained focused on the business side of medicine for most of my career. In fact, you and I met once when I was working at VistaBio."

"You're a damn genius. I'm seeing a lot of that these days. Some of the brightest graduates are jumping straight into biotech and venture capital," Jensen said. "I look at these pharma megadeals, especially after a ten hour day of surgery, and realize I'm in the wrong line of business."

"Well, I'm fascinated by how you've managed to impact the profession. You must get great satisfaction in knowing that you're helping physicians understand the latest in cardiology care," Cal said. He scanned the wall behind Jensen's desk where there was an arrangement of degrees, certificates, and framed magazine articles. "I read your recent interview in *Time*. And now that I think about it, I've seen you quoted in *The Wall Street Journal* as well. You're somewhat of an icon in the press, which is one of the reasons Zuritech has an interest in you."

Jensen smiled and leaned back in his chair. "I don't mind admitting that I'm plugged-in to the right people. In fact, your soon-to-be competitors have approached me on numerous occasions. I was top-runner for the Lipitor spokesperson a few years back, but Pfizer moved just a little too slow for my tastes."

"A man in your position can appreciate what it will take to make ZuriMax the next breakthrough in cardiology—a blockbuster."

"A billion dollars in sales," Jensen said, whistling. "I like the sound of that."

"At full stride, we'll hit twenty billion," Cal said. He allowed time for the statement to sink in. "This is the opportunity you've been waiting for. The company has plans for a national campaign. We will establish a presence at the top conferences, consumer advertising—"

"Does that include television spots?" Jensen interrupted.

"TV, radio, newspaper, and Internet. We will also sponsor continuing education for physicians and free medications for indigents."

"Sounds pretty media savvy," Jensen said, shaking a finger at Cal. "What about the international markets?"

Cal smiled. "As you know, Zuritech is Swiss owned. ZuriMax will be the company's first global brand, and naturally US success will open the door for further expansion. Are you interested in speaking overseas?"

"Does a dog have fleas?" Jensen said. "I'm a contributor to three international journals. There's promising research going on outside the US, and I intend to remain on the leading edge. I'm hands-down the best fit for ZuriMax, so tell me what's on your mind."

"Well, as you may recall from our telephone conversation, Zuritech is looking for a spokesperson with a stellar reputation and stage presence. Ideally, we want an individual who has worn many hats: experience as a practitioner, respected by peers, someone at the pinnacle of his or her career—those sorts of things. But we also need someone with a public persona. ZuriMax will be a game-changer, but we're up against a tidal wave of promotional spending by Big Pharma. Naturally, we'll have to be creative."

"That's exactly my way of thinking," Jensen said. "I don't know if you've heard, but I've already tested ZuriMax for restenosis, and it looks very promising. We're talking about a condition researchers have been trying to crack for decades. Can you imagine the media coverage if we release a story like that? When I mentioned it to ol' von Weir, his eyes lit up like a Roman candle, especially after I explained about expedited reviews."

"Which I'd like to hear more about, but I understand you have to be in surgery in a few minutes," Cal said, checking the time on his iPhone. "If you don't mind, I would like to discuss terms for a business arrangement."

"Fire away." Jensen sank back in his chair.

"First of all, I'm putting together an advisory panel comprised of the top cardiologists in the country. We're meeting in a couple of weeks, here in Washington. In fact, I believe we've booked the Willard InterContinental."

"Done," Jensen said. "And I'll take care of my own accommodations." He leaned forward and winked. "You may want to check out the Thomas Jefferson Suite. What else?"

"It's late notice, but how would you feel about serving as chairperson? I've already put together an agenda, so all you would have to do is preside over the discussions."

Jensen pulled out a business card and slid it across the desk. "E-mail the agenda to that address tonight. I'll do the chairman gig for ten thousand a day plus expenses."

Cal nodded approvingly. "And we're sponsoring a presentation at next month's American Academy of Cardiology. Do you think you could handle that if Avery Messinger offers his assistance? I believe you know Avery?"

"We've spoken a couple of times."

"Perhaps the two of you can get together and develop a ZuriMax strategy for the Academy. We're sponsoring a dinner on the opening night with fifty of the leading specialists in the US. It's a perfect opportunity for you to say a few words about ZuriMax," Cal said. "By then, we'll both know if we're happy with the relationship and can hammer out the details of a contract."

"We should have preliminary numbers from the clinical trial by then," Jensen said. "I say we dazzle them with a few scientific observations while they sip after-dinner cognacs." He climbed out of his seat and stared out a window behind his desk. "So let's make it ten thousand a day plus expenses for the Academy. I believe the meeting's at the Grand Wailea on Maui. I'd prefer that both payments go directly to my clinic in the form of unrestricted grants. Assuming it all works out, we're talking two hundred thousand in grants over the next year. And travel expenses, of course. For that, I'll give you ten public appearances and the right to quote me in promotional pieces. I suggest a first right of refusal on a contract renewal for a term of say—five years."

Cal cocked his head. "Twenty thousand per appearance. That's quite generous of you."

"As you can see, I want this drug to succeed. But more importantly, I'm looking to make a difference in the lives of patients suffering from coronary disease. That's the big win for me," Jensen said, turning to a framed picture near the window.

Cal followed his gaze to a photo of Jensen reeling in a marlin from the transom of a sleek cabin cruiser. A man was standing next to Jensen, but his profile was washed out by the sun. Cal checked the time and slid out of his seat.

"Dr. Jensen, thank you for your time. I'll have the agenda sent over tonight and start the paperwork for the first two grants."

"Just one more thing," Jensen said. "If it's not too much to ask, I'd like you to jet me and the missus to Maui in that Gulfstream of yours."

Chapter 16

**ATLANTA, GEORGIA
MONDAY, SEPTEMBER 5
8 A.M. EDT**

Sheri was pissed by the time she reached Cal on his cell phone. He was on the speakerphone in his car and had to turn it down while she launched into a tirade.

". . . he claims to be the new chief legal counsel, and at first, I thought he was kidding. But now I'm this close to strangling—"

"Sheri," Cal interrupted. "Repeat after me . . . I love my job."

Still annoyed, she continued, "He's using compliments to try and pump me for information. He just adores my auburn hair and—"

"Okay, okay. Listen up," Cal said. "He's for real."

"But when did you? . . . he's not . . ." Sheri exhaled.

"Where is he right now?"

"Sitting in your office. I offered him coffee, but I don't think it's going to hold him much longer."

"Take him down to an empty office, maybe the one across from Singh Lee. Give him time to put together a list of office needs and settle in. Then send him over to security for a badge. Afterwards, make lunch reservations for the two of us."

"Is there anything else you haven't told me?" Sheri said, stretching for a peek into Cal's office. She cupped a hand around the mouthpiece. "This one's a real jackass."

"Need I remind you . . . you let the last stranger into my office and gave her my car keys? So let's call it even," Cal said.

"That's your excuse?"

"It's the best I can come up with under the circumstances," Cal said. "I'll give you the details later."

Cal slid into a booth at Alexander's directly across from Nathan Friedman. The waiter seemed tense, hovering nearby while he kept tabs on a growing line at the restaurant's entrance.

"So Nathan, Nick didn't tell me much about you," Cal said. "How did you come to have an interest in Zuritech?"

"Call me Nate, please. You know the industry, as well as I do, Cal. It's large in many aspects, but quite the fish bowl once you've been around awhile." Nate took a sip of water. "I tend to stay abreast of industry news, never too busy to entertain new opportunities. But actually, it was Martin Zeiss who suggested I might be a good fit. One thing led to another, and here I am."

"And you met Martin—how?" Cal said.

"Through a mutual VC friend. Like I said, it's a small world."

"The venture capitalists apparently love us," Cal said.

Nate's eyes twitched as he set down his glass. He smiled, and then leaned forward, folding his hands on the tabletop.

"So I'm sure you've heard the Zuritech story," Cal said. "Perhaps our time would be best spent discussing legal priorities and milestones prior to product launch. I could use your help in reviewing a couple of non-compete agreements for prospective sales and marketing candidates."

"Where are they currently employed?" Nate said.

"One is at Pfizer, the other, Merck."

"Hundred percent," Nate said. "There'll be wailing and gnashing of teeth, but that's typical in dealing with those guys. Anyway, back to your point on priorities. From a legal standpoint, we should focus on the New Drug Application. We have to make sure the NDA package is buttoned up and perfectly aligned with FDA requirements. Let's certify that there's nothing missing from day one. Once we cross that bridge, it's critical that we monitor for any lawsuits being filed."

"You think there's a chance we'll be sued?"

Nate laughed, and then slid back in his seat. "We're not exactly filing new chemical entities here. Have you read the University of Rochester patents? Come on. I mean, they're creative, but never underestimate your opponents. Big Pharma's not the type to turn the other cheek, not when it's their party we're crashing."

"That's true, but Rochester holds composition patents on the ZuriMax active pharmaceutical ingredients. You believe someone's going to challenge the formulations?"

"You're missing my point. These guys don't let anyone play in their multi-billion dollar sandbox without slinging a little mud," Nate said. "We'll do the same if a competitor launches a product similar to ZuriMax. What you do is petition the court for an injunction, regardless of the merit. For only a few hundred thousand in legal fees, all competitive launches will be put on hold. And that, my friend, buys you a license to make out like a bandit while the other guys scream bloody murder. If you play your cards right, you eventually settle out of court, possibly stiff-arming the competitors into a royalty stream. Yes, life is incestuous in the fishbowl, but insanely legal."

"So you're suggesting a contingency plan, just in case the FDA approval is delayed. That means we need to be prepared to deal with potential fallout over the next year," Cal said.

"Six months. And no, the FDA can proceed with litigation pending," Nate said, lowering his voice. He leaned in closer. "Of course, even if they grant an approval, there's a chance the court will attempt to keep us off the market pending a trial. But that's why Nicolai hired me to develop a legal strategy."

The waiter arrived with their sandwiches.

"Schedule a follow-up meeting so we can discuss responses to potential legal delays," Cal said. "We're going to spend a bundle in the coming months, so we'd better work on Plan B, just in case your scenario comes into play."

Nate reached for his sandwich. "Check the box, and move on, Cal. We already have a silver bullet. It's called an orphan drug claim. Let the big dogs scream infringement on their intellectual property, if they like. But word has already leaked out about our clinical trial. There's not a cardiologist in the country that hasn't heard about ZuriMax's broader indications. The problem is, the competition has no defense against our restenosis claim, and it would be suicide for them to fight us on it. People die from this condition. The press would crush them. We'd see to it."

"So you're suggesting we launch based on the limited claim, knowing full well it will be prescribed for broader use?"

"All legal, by the way," Nate said, eyeing the sandwich, "as long as our sales force promotes only the restenosis story. Of course, Dr. Jensen will be able to tout the broader benefits from the podium. The average physician already knows that ZuriMax is in the same drug class as the leading medications. They're even under pressure from their patients to do something about drug costs. Who are we to tell a doctor how to prescribe? At the end of the day, those suffering from restenosis will benefit, your early stage heart disease patients win, the public saves millions of dollars, and our Zuritech stock soars into the stratosphere. The lame walk, the blind see, and well, you know the rest."

"You believe the expedited review has merit?" Cal said. "And just to be clear, you're okay with Jensen promoting both uses of the drug?"

"Absolutely. Only we don't call it promotion. He's presenting scientific data to his peers. And by the way, if you have Jensen's contract, I'll be happy to look it over."

"Who told you the data supports the restenosis claim?" Cal said.

"Can you imagine what happens if they pull the trigger on a US spinoff?" Nate said, ignoring Cal's question.

"Wait, Nick wants to sell the company?"

"Who cares? We're all going to be rich."

"Nate, who told you about the restenosis claim?"

"Avery Messinger," Nate said. He took a bite of sandwich and looked up. "Bon appétit."

Chapter 17

ATLANTA, GEORGIA
TUESDAY, SEPTEMBER 6
10 A.M. EDT

Cal buttoned his jacket as he stepped up to the podium, checking out a gold banner over the stage that read: *Georgia Tech Research Institute*. He glanced up into the ceiling before looking out across the auditorium at a sea of faces as he waited for the applause to subside.

"Thank you for such a warm welcome to the Georgia Biomedical Partnership," Cal said into a microphone. "Zuritech is proud to be part of an expanding biotechnology industry in Georgia. As many of you may know, we have made significant investments in both people and facilities here in the Atlanta area. Since taking on the job of Zuritech CEO, I have been asked a host of questions, perhaps the most frequent being, 'Why has Zuritech located its US headquarters so far away from the heart of the pharmaceutical industry?' And naturally, they're referring to the Garden State of New Jersey. For me the answer is simple, and only a PhD in bioinformatics would overlook the obvious. I tell them, it's the weather, stupid."

The crowd roared amidst a thunderous applause.

"Although the state of Georgia cannot take credit for the weather, it has taken great strides in developing an infrastructure for biotechnology and pharmaceutical companies. From the construction of university laboratories to recruiting industry professionals and rolling out programs designed to encourage entrepreneurship in the field, Zuritech and many others are here today as a result of the positive outlook for our industry in Georgia. So Zuritech is proud to be a part of this community, and we're looking forward to an expanding presence both in the United States and abroad."

More applause interceded.

"Today, I'm pleased to announce the completion of the ZuriMax phase III clinical trial, a drug which is destined to become the gold standard in hypertension/cholesterol lowering medications. The study included three thousand patients and was designed to demonstrate how Americans suffering from coronary disease, the leading cause of death in our country today, will benefit from this new drug."

Cal paused as applause once again filled the auditorium.

"Over the coming weeks, Zuritech will file a New Drug Application, seeking FDA approval for dual indications. We believe the trial will prove that ZuriMax is both safe and efficacious in managing cholesterol and hypertension in patients. Our staff intends to work diligently over the next year to expedite the approval, supporting the FDA in every way possible to ensure a speedy market introduction. Not only will ZuriMax save lives across the United States, but it will become a beacon to the rest of the world as to how US technology and know-how can improve the conditions of mankind. Thank you, and I look forward to Zuritech's participation in this worthy organization."

The audience rose for a final ovation.

The chairwoman climbed the stage and stood next to Cal. "If you will take your seats, we have time for Dr. Hunter to answer a few questions."

A hand went up in the front of the auditorium, and a wireless microphone was rushed over.

"Dr. Hunter, early reports indicate that your drug has been successful in patients suffering from high cholesterol and hypertension, but what about those suffering from just one of these conditions?"

"That's an excellent question," Cal said. "One well-guarded secret about ZuriMax is its ability to control the release of actives in the formulation. We've accomplished this through our patented Z-Pulse technology that responds to individual blood chemistry. This allows us to safely deliver a one-size-fits-all combination drug without adverse effects. The amount of drug released into the bloodstream is dosed precisely to the patient's need."

The auditorium hummed with conversation before a spattering of applause. By the time the room had settled down, the microphone was positioned in front of another man.

"Dr. Hunter, what are Zuritech's plans after the launch of this initial product? Do you foresee moving into additional therapeutic categories?"

"Our focus on ZuriMax hasn't allowed time to make noise about much else. But to answer your question, ZuriMax is our flagship product and will be followed by a host of additional brands. Without giving away our strategy, we intend to move into additional chronic conditions, and have indeed engaged in early stage licensing and research along these lines."

A hand went up in a back corner of the auditorium, and Cal paused as the microphone made its way across the room. In the aisle, he noticed a WNGA camera and Paula Ritchie standing next to it. The microphone stopped at a scholarly looking man.

"Yes, Dr. Hunter. Can you comment on the growing domestic unrest over the price disparities between the US and the rest of the developed world?"

Cal smiled, and then leaned into the microphone. "I can't speak for the industry as a whole, but ZuriMax will be a money-saving medication for millions who are currently taking multiple prescriptions. Zuritech is very proud of this fact. We intend to be good corporate citizens by introducing our product at a price that will provide relief to many Americans who are living on fixed incomes. And of course, we have plans to launch an indigent program as well."

Cal started to back away from the podium when the man grabbed the microphone. "So are you saying ZuriMax will be marketed at an equivalent price in other countries?"

"I'm afraid, I can't answer that question," Cal said. The crowd stirred. "Not that I wish to avoid the issue, but as CEO of the US business, I have no control over pricing in the international markets. For now, I can assure you US patients will save money if they are currently on dual-branded therapies."

The chairwoman stepped forward. "We have time for one more question." A hand went up in the back of the auditorium.

"Dr. Hunter, can you address rumored setbacks to gaining FDA approval?" The woman looked down at her hands and continued. "And can you remark on reports that ZuriMax may have undisclosed side effects?"

Cal spotted a man in an overcoat behind the woman. The crowd grew silent as he hesitated, watching the man exit through a rear door.

"I'm sorry," Cal said. "What types of side effects are you referring to?"

"Uh . . . death."

Cal shifted his weight before taking his eyes off of the door.

"I'm sorry, I can't comment on rumors, as you call them." Cal stepped away from the podium, switching places with the chairwoman on stage.

"Thank you all for coming today. We look forward to seeing you next month," she said as the audience stirred to their feet.

Cal hurried off the stage and pushed through the crowd. He made his way to the back of the auditorium and slipped through a set of doors into an atrium.

"Hello, Dr. Hunter," someone said. Cal turned to a well-dressed woman. "I'm Dr. Janice Spencer, FDA director for the Atlanta District."

"A pleasant surprise," Cal said. His eyes darted over Spencer's shoulder. "I've been looking forward to meeting you."

"Congratulations on your progress. I can hardly wait to tour your research facility," she said. "Dr. Mallory invited me to the groundbreaking ceremony, but I haven't seen the campus since it was put into service."

"Dr. Mallory?" Cal said, focusing his attention back to Spencer. "You mean, Dr. Messinger—Avery Messinger."

"Actually, I'm referring to Dr. Messinger's predecessor. It's hard to believe it's been six years," she said. "Dr. Mallory was truly excited about ZuriMax's prospects. It's unfortunate that he died at such an early age."

Cal started to respond, but caught sight of the attendee who had thrown the bombshell inside. Much closer now, she looked young. "If you'll excuse me, Dr. Spencer, I will speak to Dr. Messinger about a tour."

Cal rushed out of the building after the girl.

"Excuse me," Cal called out as he stepped into the sunshine. He raised a hand to his brow, squinting as she turned and smiled once she recognized him.

"Dr. Hunter," she said. "I loved your speech."

"Thank you," Cal said. "May I ask you a question? First, your name, and then how you came to hear these rumors?"

"Wait, you've got it wrong," she said.

"But didn't you—"

"You said you had a question, as in . . . one question. You thought you'd slip that second one past me, didn't you?" she said with her eyes teasing.

"Maybe you'll forgive me this once," Cal said, smiling.

She held out a hand. "I'm Holly Thompson, a student here at Georgia Tech. I have a friend who's working on your clinical trial. She told me I should check out your speech."

"A friend?" Cal said. "Did she put you up to this?"

"Jana? No, she had nothing to do with it."

"What did she tell you?"

"Oh, you mean the side effects. She didn't—I mean—I have a confession. Actually, the whole thing was kinda weird." Holly raised her eyebrows.

"You mentioned deaths."

"That's what it said," Holly said.

"I'm not following you."

"You see, I was standing in the back of the auditorium minding my own business when this guy came up." Holly flipped a strand of hair out of her eyes, and then slipped her hand into a pocket. "He offered me twenty dollars to read the questions off a sticky note." She pulled out a twenty and unfolded it. A yellow note was attached. She handed it to Cal.

"And that's all you know?" Cal said, studying the note.

Holly nodded.

"He was wearing a tan overcoat, right?"

She continued to nod.

"Did he have a French accent?"

She stopped. "For someone who wants to ask a girl a question, you sure talk a lot, Dr. Hunter," Holly said. She scrunched her nose and pointed to a dormitory over the treetops. "Most of us college students live on fixed incomes, like the people you mentioned in your speech. An extra twenty comes in handy every now and then." She took the bill from Cal, and then turned on her heels. "Nice talking, but I've got to go to class."

"Thank you," Cal called after her. "And good luck with your studies."

Holly looked back over her shoulder. "Thanks," she said, spinning around and walking backwards. "By the way, I'm a bioinformatics major. And no, the man didn't have an accent."

Chapter 18

SANTA BARBARA, CALIFORNIA
TUESDAY, SEPTEMBER 6
9 P.M. PDT

A foldout table sat in the middle of the floor covered in pizza boxes and water bottles. Billy lounged in a chair with his feet propped up next to a workstation, finishing off a slice of pizza. Jana checked her watch and bounced out of her seat.

"Where are these guys?" Jana said. She snapped up an empty bottle and lobbed it across the room. It hit the rim of a trash can, and then rattled around inside.

"They didn't give a specific delivery time," Billy said.

"Then why did you send the others home? What happens when an avalanche of paperwork arrives, and I'm the only one here?"

"Chill out babe, I've got a plan."

Jana's cheeks turned red. She balled her fists and leaped at Billy. "What did I say would happen if you called me that again?"

Billy drew his hands to his face, dropping his pizza on the floor.

"Light my ass on fire. You didn't say anything about hitting me."

She grabbed one of his shoes and shoved it off the workstation. His feet went airborne, but he managed to grab an armrest to keep from falling headfirst into the pizza.

"Yeah, well you'll be lucky if they find enough DNA to identify you," Jana said. She kicked his chair.

Just then a door opened at the far end of the office, and a man in black strolled in carrying a Bankers Box. He looked around, eventually locking eyes on Billy and Jana. Crossing the room, he swung the box from side to side effortlessly before plopping it down on the table. He extracted an electronic clipboard from his jacket.

"You guys with Bioscene?" Not waiting for a response, he tapped the screen with a stylus. "I'm looking for William Danforth."

"That's me," Billy said, pushing up from the chair. "There's a loading dock around back, if you want to pull your truck around."

"Just the one box," the man said, working the stylus.

"The delivery is from Zuritech?" Billy said.

"That's right."

"We're expecting a truckload," Billy said.

"Well, it ain't happening tonight, professor," the man said, now scribbling on the screen. "I need to see some ID, and then a signature."

"Does Zuritech know you're running late?"

The man held out the clipboard and pressed the stylus into Billy's chest.

"Who's your little sidekick here?" the man said, smiling. "Mind if I see your ID, darling?"

Jana fingered a security badge clipped to her jeans, drawing a smile from the man. She felt a chill as his eyes lingered.

Billy signed the clipboard and pulled out his badge.

"Where's the rest of the stuff?" Billy said. "And which delivery service are you with, anyway?"

"The other *stuff*, as you call it, is in process," the man said. He stepped closer to Billy, taller by a head. "I work for Zuritech. Would you like a comment form so you can rate my service?"

"That—um—won't be necessary," Billy said, stepping back. He glanced over at Jana, and then down at the floor.

The man turned and walked gorilla-like for the door.

"I get a lot of that," the man said without looking back. "And by the way, you're cute." He opened the door and disappeared.

Jana eased over to the box and popped off the lid, looking inside. "There are barely any forms in this box."

"I'm speechless," Billy said.

"You're a wimp."

"I didn't see you making any demands to that—Mike Tyson."

"Do you have a Zuritech contact you can call?"

"Did you hear what he said, *cute*? Was he talking to you or me?" Billy said, falling back into his chair.

"You said the ZuriMax data entry had to be finished tonight." Jana checked her watch again. "It's after nine o'clock, and we've got zip. The data usually starts trickling in from the sites immediately. It's been a week."

"I told you, this company handles things differently—"

"You said they were control freaks. Where is the data?"

"Zuritech procedures clearly state they are responsible for collecting the data and delivering it to us," Billy said.

"We've got a week's worth of data entry if six of us work full-time on the project." Jana pulled a form from the box and looked it over. Then she grabbed a handful and started flipping through them.

"I'll take it up with my boss in the morning," Billy said.

"I'd get him on the phone, right now."

"It's unprofessional to kick issues upstairs before evaluating the options."

"Political jerk-wad," Jana said, looking up. "And your mysterious practitioner alpha field is populated on a bunch of these."

"That thug looked more like a mercenary than a delivery guy," Billy said. "And I think he had a pistol under his jacket."

"My hero," Jana said with a smirk. She returned to the forms.

Billy sprang out of the chair and headed for his office.

"Give it a rest," Billy said.

"This alpha field might as well be coded in Mandarin."

"Enter everything you've got in the morning. I'll run down the rest, but count on all-nighters until this project is done."

"Whatever," Jana said. "I think I'll stick around and get started tonight."

"A hundred thousand in bonuses down the crapper," Billy said.

Chapter 19

**MIAMI, FLORIDA
WEDNESDAY, SEPTEMBER 7
7 A.M. EDT**

Grace and Art Marigold shuffled up to the guard shack with Grace in the lead. The white clapboard siding stood out in sharp contrast to the green shutters and terracotta roof. A man in uniform stood just outside the doorway where Grace was now sizing him up.

"You the captain?" Grace said.

"No ma'am, port security."

Grace lowered her eyes to a pistol attached to the man's belt. She turned to Art. "A nice looking man," she said.

The Marigolds crossed a gangplank, exchanging comments about the breeze blowing in from Biscayne Bay. Both clung to a handrail, with Grace clutching a pocketbook in her free hand as she looked back every few seconds to check on Art. She had now lost count, but Art repeated a question he had been asking since they left the house.

"Did you get the money, Gracie?"

"Don't you remember stopping at the bank?" Grace said.

Art didn't answer.

They stepped onto the ship's deck, and a man in white greeted them, leading the way across the starboard deck.

Inside, the main cabin was laid out like a ferry with rows of seating spanning the interior, separated by aisles on each side of a center section. A noisy throng comprised mostly of senior citizens filled the seats. The steward had to circle the cabin before finding a spot for the Marigolds. They quietly sat down.

Minutes later, the boat steamed out to sea.

Once underway, a projection screen lowered from the ceiling at the front, and a woman's voice blasted through speakers set around the periphery of the cabin. The young blonde on the screen welcomed the passengers aboard and announced that a free breakfast buffet would soon be available on the upper deck. Grace joined a swarm that lifted out of their seats and funneled into a double stairway at the rear of the cabin.

The blonde continued, "Upon mooring alongside the *Rx Freedom*, we ask that you form lines at the designated exits indicated by the overhead signs. Simply find the exit that includes the first letter of your last name. You will be required to present a valid US prescription for one of the medications posted on the marquee when you came aboard. All transactions are payable in cash only. Should you need assistance at any time during the voyage, licensed nurses are stationed on the rear deck for your convenience. While aboard the *Rx Freedom*, you will have the opportunity to speak with a doctor regarding medical questions. Please have your prescriptions ready prior to boarding. Finally, the breakfast buffet is now open. You will find an assortment of juices, fruit, pastries, coffee, and bagels. Thank you for choosing to sail with us today, and we hope you will sit back and enjoy the voyage."

"Did you get the money, Gracie?" Art said when Gracie returned.

Grace ignored the question and sat down next to Art, handing him a cup of coffee. She slipped the pocketbook off her shoulder and opened it, pulling out two bagels wrapped in napkins. "They were out of cinnamon rolls, so I had to settle for these," she said.

Art set down the coffee, taking a bagel. He attempted to pull off a piece. When the effort failed, he stuck it between his teeth and managed to get a mouthful. He chewed, and then took a sip of coffee.

"Did you get the money, Gracie?" Art said. He looked outside at the ocean, positioning the bagel for another bite.

Grace straightened her dress. "Eat your breakfast, and we'll walk around on deck later." She leaned a shoulder into Art. "They're putting in a shuffleboard court up top next to the buffet."

"Nice," Art said. "And they're showing one of those sitcoms you like. What's it called?"

"*Golden Girls*," Grace said. "But that's next month."

"*Golden . . . Curls?*" Art said, as if dumbfounded. He wiped his mouth with the napkin. "Did you get the money, Gracie?"

"GIRLS," Grace said in a raised voice. "It's called *Golden Girls*." She set down her coffee and bagel, then stood up. "Do you want to go out on deck?"

"No, I'll just stay and watch the *Golden*—um—the show," Art said. His eyes followed as Grace worked her way down the aisle. "Did you get the money, Gracie?" He called out, but she didn't hear.

At 0900 the *American Dream* sat off the Miami coast alongside the *Rx Freedom*, a freighter twice her length. A section of the cargo hold below deck had been converted into a makeshift service area. There were tables set up around the cabin with lines forming in front of each. Grace and Art stepped up to a table with a sign that read: *LIPIDRX*.

A lady in a lab coat sitting behind a computer said, "Prescription, please."

Grace unclasped her pocketbook as Art looked on. She dug for a moment, finally pulling out a pill bottle and handing it to the lady.

"Do you have a prescription?" the lady said. She turned the bottle over in her hand, examining the label.

"Last month, they told us we had two more refills," Grace said. "It's supposed to say so on the bottle." She leaned over the table while Art hunched over, looking down into Grace's pocketbook.

"You have to get up pretty early in the morning to put one past you, Mrs. Marigold," the lady said, smiling. "It says you have two refills. The prescription is for Mr. Marigold?"

"Present," Art said, straightening up.

Grace tugged the strap of her pocketbook and dropped it on the table. She dug inside until she found Art's identification card and a twenty dollar bill. After she slid them across the table, the lady started typing on the computer. A printer beneath the table buzzed to life as she reached down and retrieved a freshly printed label and a bottle of pills. She affixed the label to the bottle.

"And that will be twenty dollars," the lady said. She scooped up the cash and placed it in a metal box. "Do you have any questions?"

"I get one more refill, right?" Art said, watching Grace drop the pills in her pocketbook.

"That's correct, Mr. Marigold. And after that, we have a doctor aboard who can write a new prescription for you. Of course, you're always free to go to your regular doctor back in Miami."

"Fort Lauderdale," Art corrected. He focused on the lady with his one good eye. "How much does he charge?"

"The office visits are free, but if you have any conditions other than elevated cholesterol or hypertension, we ask that you see your personal physician."

"How on earth do you do it?" Art said. "That prescription costs one hundred and fifty dollars at the drug store. And it doesn't include the doctor visit."

"The *Rx Freedom* is here to help people like you and Mrs. Marigold," she said. "Most senior citizens are struggling to make ends meet, and prescription medications don't make it any easier. We want to do our part to help."

"Which way for this one?" Grace said. She held out a prescription.

"That one is over there," the lady said. "You and Mr. Marigold have a wonderful day. We'll see you next month."

"Canadians don't pay a hundred and fifty for a prescription, at least that's what they're saying on CNN," Art said. A devilish look spread across his face, and he leaned in closer. "Say, you got any of that Viagra?" He flexed his eyebrows.

"That's for old people, Mr. Marigold," the lady said with a laugh.

"Ha, you got it figured out, don't you kitten?" Art said as Grace took him by the arm. "Did you get the money, Gracie?"

Chapter 20

ATLANTA, GEORGIA
THURSDAY, SEPTEMBER 8
2 P.M. EDT

Cal wrapped up a video conference with Nicolai and swung by the employee lounge for coffee before heading to his office. He stopped off at Sheri's desk.

"Check to see if Singh Lee is available," Cal said.

"I have her on standby," Sheri said, dialing her desk phone.

Cal waited for her to hang up. "I e-mailed you a 'Dear John' draft for the job applicants that didn't make the cut. Proof it, and then forward the originals to me for signature. I'd like to schedule second interviews with my two finalists next Friday at the Willard."

"You're heading up to the advisory panel early?" Sheri said. "I don't have it on your calendar."

"Work your magic with the arrangements. And make sure there's a sitting area for the interviews, but nothing fancy."

"Is 8:00 A.M. early enough?" Sheri said. "Oh, and are you taking your Gulfstream?"

"Eight is perfect, and it's not my Gulfstream. While we're on the subject, did you mention the jet to Dr. Jensen?"

"Come on, it was a joke. And in what universe do you think I'd be talking behind your back?"

Singh Lee walked up.

"I'll be with you in a minute," Cal said to Singh Lee, returning to Sheri. "I need you to look into a legal matter. Talk to Nate, and find out if FDA regulations allow us to fly Dr. Jensen on the Gulfstream to the Academy."

Singh Lee disappeared into Cal's office as Sheri jotted on a notepad.

"Anything else?"

"What do you know about the groundbreaking for this campus?"

"Not much, but I can double-check the media package."

"Put on your investigator's hat, and see if you can pinpoint a date. Maybe there's a building permit in the files. Someone mentioned that construction started six years ago, but I'm certain it was more like four," Cal said, starting for his office.

"One more thing," Sheri said. "Security called about setting up your home computer for company e-mail. You requested it a week or so ago. They need to get into your house this afternoon."

"Call Kate. She'll handle it."

Cal slipped into his office where Singh Lee was already seated at the conference table. "I need an update on the issues we discussed last week."

"Where would you like to start?"

"How about any conversations you've had with Martin regarding the consolidated financials?" Cal slipped over to his desk and sat down. "I have to take care of a few things, but I'm listening."

"We played phone tag for a while, but I spoke to him yesterday. Martin confirmed we're only to report Zuritech Corporation financial statements."

"So no Aviation or Trading? What about Nick's comments?"

"Well, Martin said it was his fault," Singh Lee said. "He promised to clear it up, so you needn't worry."

"Regardless, I'd like a look at the financials for both. Do you have them?"

"I'm working on it, but there seems to be a system problem."

"The computer systems aren't working?" Cal said.

"My security access has stopped working, but only for those two companies."

"Anything I can do to help?"

"I mentioned it to Martin, and he was unaware of any problems. He gave me a contact in Zurich," Singh Lee said. "I left a message, but I'm waiting on a callback."

"How about the clinical trial expenses?"

"That one is a bit more interesting."

"Go on," Cal said, leaning around his computer for a look at Singh Lee.

"I received an e-mail response from the global R&D controller in Zurich. He's certain the expenses are correct on our books."

"How do you spend a million dollars and record only seven hundred and fifty thousand?" Cal said, turning back to the computer.

"The missing quarter of a million was booked in Switzerland. It has something to do with a technology transfer."

"Would you care to explain?"

"He only gave me the highlights, so I'm charting it out on the whiteboard in my office. I'm still trying to understand it myself."

Sheri poked her head into Cal's office.

"Sorry to interrupt, but your marketing candidate is on the line and needs to speak to you. She says it's important," Sheri said.

"Tell her, I'll be just a moment." Cal turned to Singh Lee. "You've struck out on all of the assignments from last week."

Singh Lee rolled her eyes. "I wouldn't put it like that. What more would you like me to do?"

"You don't have to solve them all at once, but at least show some progress."

"I'll start with the clinical trial expenses, if you don't have an issue with that," Singh Lee said, leveling her eyes on Cal.

Cal picked up the telephone receiver. "I can't do my job and yours. Now if you'll excuse me, I've got to take this call."

Chapter 21

SANTA BARBARA, CALIFORNIA
FRIDAY, SEPTEMBER 9
11 P.M. PDT

Three days had passed since Billy's encounter with the delivery guy. Jana sat alone at one of the Zuritech computers in the corner of the office, staring at the screen. She tapped on the display.

"There's no reporting function in this system," Jana said. Frustrated, she clicked the mouse randomly, up and down the screen. "Wait a minute. I know this software. The front-end looks a little different, but I've seen this before." She studied the keyboard, and then pressed the "F5" key. A menu popped up.

"So there you are," Jana said. She made a selection, and a flood of green characters filled the display, glowing against a dark background. "So much for state-of-the-art, you bunch of control freaks." She glanced over her shoulder at the empty work area, and then turned back to the computer, dragging the mouse across the screen until the entire electronic report had been highlighted. Opening a spreadsheet she pasted the data into it before tabbing down the rows and stopping at the last entry. *Row forty-three.*

"I knew it," Jana said. After comparing the data to her input sheets, she typed an e-mail with a copy to her home account, attaching the spreadsheet. Once it was sent, she shut down the computer and rolled back in her chair, grabbing a handful of papers.

Next to the copy machine, Jana picked up a FedEx envelope and stuffed the papers inside. She addressed the envelope and dropped it in an outgoing mail bin. Making a sweep of the office area, she checked to make sure no one was around, and then headed for her cubicle.

Dialing on her office telephone, a voicemail greeting picked up on the other end. When it ended, she said, "Hi, it's Jana in La-La land. Sorry to call so late. You're probably asleep by now, but when you get a chance take a look at the spreadsheet I just e-mailed."

Jana paused, standing up and peering over the top of her cubicle. She sat back down. "The spreadsheet contains fifty patients I entered into the clinical trial system. I guess I should say forty-three since seven of the patients seem to have evaporated into thin air. They were there until I hit the batch submit function. Since you're a systems geek, I was hoping you might have an idea about what's going on. You're the best when it comes to debugging. Anyhow, this probably sounds like gibberish at two o'clock in the morning, so call me when you can." She started to hang up, and then held the receiver back up to her mouth. "Call me at the apartment. Love ya."

Jana hung up and immediately slapped the work surface. *I forgot to tell her about the FedEx.* She reached for the receiver and jumped as someone pounded on the outside door. She could have sworn it was a hammer. Before she could think, the door slammed open. She dropped to her knees and scrambled to get out. The commotion was only twenty-five feet away, but a row of cubicles blocked her view. She rose into a crouching position and made a run for it, distancing herself from the invasion. At the end of her cubicle pod, she rounded the corner into the next aisle and dove headfirst under a work surface. Wheeling a chair between her and the doorway, she heard voices.

"Where is she?" a man said. "Check the bathroom."

Jana thought she recognized the voice.

"No one in the ladies room," another man said after a brief delay.

There was movement all around the office.

"Over here," the first man said. "The monitor's still warm. Go ahead and disconnect it. It's going with us."

Jana heard footsteps moving closer.

"Which one's her office?" the first man called out. "Wait a minute, here it is."

The desk chair rattled across the floor, and then she felt the wall move. Jana's back bounced off the partition, and it dawned on her that she was in a cubicle that adjoined hers. She felt another bump, and then heard wires being ripped out of the wall.

"I've got her computer," the first man said. "Where the hell did she go?" Cubicle bins opened and slammed shut. Then picture frames crashed to the floor.

"Hey, Boscoe," the second voice called out from across the room. "There's a loading dock out back. I think Goldie Locks may have skipped out on us."

"Find her, and you get to make the delivery to Mexico," Boscoe said.

Jana heard one set of footsteps moving away, but the other still in her cubicle.

"I hate frigging blondes," Boscoe said.

The door to the loading docked bumped open. "Are you coming, Boscoe?"

Boscoe hefted a chair over his head and slammed it against the cubicle partition. On the other side, Jana drew up into a ball.

The second man hurried over. "What happened?"

Boscoe pointed to the work surface. A purse and keys sat next to a stack of binders. "Check the other side," he said, then raised his voice. "You can come out now."

Jana heard a metallic click.

"Be a good little girl," the second man said, heading around to the next aisle.

Jana squeezed her eyes shut.

"Don't underestimate her," Boscoe said, his voice trailing behind the other man.

"Boscoe, over here."

Jana opened her eyes and looked up as the chair was pulled free. Two men stared down at her. One was the Zuritech delivery man.

"I knew she was trouble the first time I laid eyes on her," Boscoe said.

Chapter 22

ATLANTA, GEORGIA
SATURDAY, SEPTEMBER 10
8 A.M. EDT

Kate leaned across the kitchen counter and adjusted a television so it was viewable in the breakfast room. She grabbed her toast and coffee as she rounded the corner, dropping into a chair next to Cal who was already seated at the table. She hopped up and grabbed a napkin and slid back into the chair.

"Anyone ever tell you, you're about as much fun as Sleeping Beauty when your head hits the pillow at night?" Kate said.

Cal lowered a newspaper and reached for a mug. He drained his coffee, setting it back down. "That's why she was so beautiful. She was a sound sleeper."

"And she didn't have an exhausting job in the pharmaceutical industry."

"True," Cal said, folding the newspaper and tossing it aside. "Then again, she did have that pesky curse hanging over her."

"At least, she didn't snore."

"I don't snore."

"Never mind, let's start over," Kate said, reaching for the TV remote. "Good morning, Sunshine."

"You're not getting out of this one," Cal said, leaning closer. His nose brushed hers just before he snapped up his mug and headed for the kitchen. "Not a good subject for you, is it my love?"

"I've only been accused of snoring by one bedmate," Kate said.

"You've only got one bedmate."

"That's debatable," Kate said, pointing the remote at the TV.

"So in addition to snoring, you're now going on record as being a floozy?" Cal said as he returned to his seat.

"Floozy?" Kate said in a burst of laughter. "Oh where, oh where, could you have learned this term? Medical school?" She flipped through the channels.

"Actually, I picked it up when I was an undergrad. Back then, I was quite partial to floozies."

"Maybe we can go to the mall later, and you can spot a few for me." Kate covered her mouth to keep from losing it.

"You're changing the subject. Now, about this other bedmate of yours," Cal said, closing one eye.

"I don't snore, either," Kate said, moving closer.

"I have a recording on my iPhone."

"We were talking about bedmates," Kate said. "What if I told you I had been sleeping with only half a man these past few weeks?" She closed an eye to match Cal's.

"Then I'd say he must be something else because you look like one satisfied woman to me."

Kate lowered her coffee cup and kissed Cal on the lips. "Are you quite done?"

"No," Cal said, kissing her back. He tossed back in his chair and fluffed the newspaper, raising it between them.

"Well?"

"Well what?" Cal said from behind the paper.

"What was it you wanted to say?"

Cal peeked over the top. "I forget."

"Cal?"

"Good morning, Sleeping Beauty," Cal said, smiling.

Kate squinted, and then leaned back and perched her feet on the chair. "So I thought we'd barbeque out on the deck tonight. Do you have plans for today?"

"I reserve Saturdays for my wife when I'm in town."

"There's a new chick flick at the Regal."

"Sign me up," Cal said. "But I want extra credit."

"I hate to tell you this, but the computer in your office has gone nuts ever since they hooked up that thing-a-ma-bob."

"Who did the work?"

"A couple of Zuritech guys," Kate said. "And why are you asking me? They work for you."

"Not the IT department. We use contractors."

"You're the boss, but I don't think so."

"I'm the boss?" Cal did a double-take at the television, and then fumbled for the remote.

"They had Zuritech logos on their shirts. Pretty Egyptian cotton polos," Kate said.

Cal turned up the television.

"One of them had a cute name for the other. What was it?" Kate said. "Might have been Roscoe or something—"

"Hold on," Cal said.

"In the news this morning, Secretary of Health and Human Services, Lawrence Baker, announced he will endorse a private charity that distributes pharmaceuticals to developing regions around the world."

The broadcast flipped from a reporter to Baker standing behind a podium.

"Today, I am happy to announce that the United States will be spreading goodwill around the globe as we witness the launch of an innovative charity. The organization is appropriately named the Rx Freedom Project and will be based out of Newark, New Jersey. Their mission is to work alongside US State Department efforts to showcase American goodwill to countries where freedom has been merely a mirage on the western horizon. The Rx Freedom Project will utilize private funding and pharmaceutical company donations of prescription drugs to target millions who are oppressed by unfortunate political circumstances. Although the initiatives are being executed out of the private sector, they have the heart-felt blessing of the president and his administration. Godspeed to the men and women invested in this noble cause. Thank you."

The picture flipped back to the reporter standing in front of a sprawling building.

"The secretary made the announcement this morning while attending a breakfast sponsored by the Pharmaceutical Research and Producers Association here in Washington. He also said that while many lives will be touched by the lifesaving drugs, millions will experience firsthand the outpouring of charity that is possible in a free society. Reporting from Washington—"

Cal pressed the remote and muted the volume.

"Maybe Zuritech should hook up with those guys," Kate said. "It looks like free publicity."

"We don't have FDA approval, so there's nothing to donate," Cal said, rubbing the stubble on his chin. He glanced out the window.

"Anyway, I was saying you might want to take a look at the computer because it's acting weird."

"What's it doing, snoring?" Cal said.

"Ha-ha. No, it's sluggish, and last night while you were resting peacefully, I heard its little hard drive whirring like it was processing or something."

"I do blockbuster drugs, not computers," Cal said, getting up from the table.

"Then you may want to call your techs. Come to think of it, I saw a van like theirs out at the street when I came home yesterday. Maybe they already know about the problem."

"I'll get Sheri on it," Cal said. He slipped around behind Kate's chair and wrapped his arms around her.

"What is this, an apology?"

"Did I do something wrong?" Cal said.

"You worked way too much this week."

"I'm taking you to a chick flick, remember?"

"And that's supposed to take care of everything?" Kate said.

"What did you have in mind?"

"I don't know. I haven't made up the bed yet."

"I'm not doing housework," Cal said, smiling.

Chapter 23

**ATLANTA, GEORGIA
WEDNESDAY, SEPTEMBER 14
9 A.M. EDT**

Cal sat in his office, tapping his fingertips on the conference table. Just when he decided to get up, Singh Lee slipped through the doorway with her laptop. She paused to close the door with her foot before rushing over to join him. Dropping into a chair next to Cal, she brushed back her hair as she opened the computer.

Cal took a second look, remembering the outfit she wore the first night they met. The scent of perfume hung in the air.

"Okay, let's see what you've got," Cal said.

Singh Lee rolled her chair closer, adjusting the laptop for a better view. "Sorry it's taken almost a week, but I've had several conversations with Martin. I'm glad you're into finance, otherwise this might be difficult."

"It's been a few years."

"I'll simplify as much as possible," Singh Lee said. "Let's start with the expenses you questioned on the financial ledger. As I mentioned last time, they are impacted by a technology transfer agreement that was put in place before you joined the company. In ZuriMax's case, the company has executed a strategy that places ownership of all inventions, patents, and intellectual property in the Swiss entity."

"The Swiss entity?" Cal said.

"I'll use the Swiss to refer to Zuritech AG, our Swiss parent company. For simplicity, I'll refer to Zuritech, Inc. as the US."

"So Zuritech intends to own ZuriMax in Switzerland, even though it was invented in the United States and being developed by Avery's team here in Atlanta?"

"That's correct," Singh Lee said.

"The University of Rochester licensed the drug rights to the US. Are we allowed to transfer ownership?"

"That's an excellent question. I reviewed the contract, and we are free to sublicense to our affiliates. Of course, the Swiss have to abide by the original terms of the agreement."

"I see where this is going," Cal said, focusing on the screen for the first time. "You're telling me the Swiss are going to purchase the ZuriMax rights from the US."

"Correct again, only it's already happened." Singh Lee pointed to a flow chart. "It was part of the original US funding."

"This may show my ignorance, but if the Swiss own the product, why aren't they paying for the clinical trial?"

"The short answer is, they are," Singh Lee said, scrolling to another slide. "But the precise answer is a little more complex. "Basically, the Swiss now own the rights to ZuriMax, but they have contracted the US to carry out the development work."

"You're saying they intend to pay Avery and his staff to turn ZuriMax into a commercial product?"

"Actually, they've been paying for quite some time. And they've agreed to continue until ZuriMax is approved by the FDA," Singh Lee said.

"I'm missing something. The financials indicate that the US is paying the bills."

"Let me explain it this way," Singh Lee said, pushing her hair back. "The accountants in Switzerland have reviewed all R&D expenditures here in the States."

"Does that include Beta Hut?"

Singh Lee's hair brushed Cal's shoulder as she leaned closer. "It includes Beta Hut, Bioscene, and all R&D expenses currently being handled by the US. But here's the key, the Swiss finance guys have determined that only twenty-five percent of the costs are related to ZuriMax ownership."

"How can they say that? Everything we're doing in Beta Hut is connected to ZuriMax. It's the only product being developed over there."

"Just hear me out," Singh Lee said. She reached out and rested a hand on Cal's arm.

"This is getting complicated."

"That's why you hired me," Singh Lee said, smiling. "Okay, presently the Swiss pay the US as a subcontractor to develop ZuriMax. The contract calls for the US to handle all activities associated with regulatory approval." She trained her focus on Cal and waited until he nodded. "But it doesn't imply they will pay for anything outside of that scope."

"You'd better get to the punch line," Cal said, shaking his head.

"The Swiss will reimburse only for specific services. All other Beta Hut expenses are the US's responsibility."

"So I reassert my case. Beta Hut and Bioscene are working only on ZuriMax."

"But look at it this way, Cal. Beta Hut isn't fully utilized. In fact, the ZuriMax development team occupies only a small portion of the building. Seventy-five percent of Beta Hut's capacity is idle."

"Let's assume for a minute that the Swiss didn't direct the construction of Beta Hut, which we both know isn't true. What about Bioscene? They're only working on the ZuriMax clinical trial. How do you explain that?"

"A portion of the activities associated with the trial are going to be used by the marketing team to support the US launch."

"But you said they own the product."

"They've also contracted the US to distribute ZuriMax. This means we will market, advertise, and do whatever it takes to make the product commercially available. Bioscene's activities will provide promotional value when it comes time to sell to doctors and consumers, especially the clinical data."

"So as US distributor, I am responsible for all costs related to ZuriMax marketing?" Cal said.

"Try not to think of it as us and them. We're all the same company. The behind-the-scenes accounting is nothing more than a tax maneuver."

Cal caught another whiff of Singh Lee's perfume before turning to her. She was playing with one of her earrings. "You're confident the Swiss finance guys can vouch for all of this?" he said.

"I've been assured there is a complete analysis with supporting data."

"What do the Swiss get out of this?" Cal said. "They're paying a portion of the expenses, but the structure doesn't generate ZuriMax sales outside the US. We've done nothing but shift expenses into Switzerland."

"I warned you it was complex. We're not done yet," Singh Lee said. "As owner, the Swiss have the right to charge the US a royalty for granting a distribution license."

"They're selling back a portion of the rights they bought from us in the first place," Cal said. He perked up, like a light bulb had just turned on.

"As long as they've done their homework, it's all legal. You may find this next detail interesting. The Swiss also hold the manufacturing rights."

"Which production facility do they plan to use?"

"Naucalpan," Singh Lee said.

"Which means they're using a low cost operation," Cal said. "What's the markup? We have local profit targets to hit."

"Martin hasn't given me final figures, but I can make a pretty good guess."

"I thought you preferred not to speculate."

"Things seem to be improving between us, so I'll go out on a limb this once," Singh Lee said. "Forty percent."

"Forty percent of what?"

"Sales. But that includes royalties and product cost."

Cal whistled. "That's billions."

"Not a bad return on investment, wouldn't you say?"

"I have another word for it. A bottle of ZuriMax will cost around, let's say, two dollars to manufacture. We'll sell it for one hundred and fifty. At forty percent, the Swiss will make sixty dollars."

"And the US keeps the remaining ninety dollars."

"You know better than that. We'll spend another forty percent on marketing and sales activities. Then we'll lay out another fifteen percent for R&D, even though we'll never own what comes from it. According to my calculations, that leaves five percent in US profit. Seven-fifty. Forty percent of that goes to Uncle Sam, netting four dollars and fifty cents."

"Your finance skills seem to be intact," Singh Lee said.

"It's all a tax game. What's the going rate in Switzerland?"

"Ten, maybe eleven percent."

"And just think, people's eyes glaze over at the mention of bean counters. The Swiss laid out a few million on ZuriMax, but they'll transfer billions in profits out of the country," Cal said. "And they'll reap enormous tax savings by shifting ownership to Switzerland."

"It's all legal," Singh Lee said. "The research agreements are in place."

"But just to be sure, we'll bring in an outside auditor at the end of the year. I don't intend to be in the hot seat when the IRS catches wind of this."

"That makes two of us," Singh Lee said.

"Then we're in agreement," Cal said, pushing back from the table. "But you still owe me financial reports for Aviation and Trading. And I want you to e-mail a copy of the material you just covered so I can review it before Nick and Martin arrive next week."

"Understood," Singh Lee said. She closed the computer and stood up as Cal headed for his desk. "So we're good, right?"

Cal stopped and studied the floor for a moment. "Just stay on top of things, and keep me informed." He finally smiled. "And while you're at it, don't forget to have a personal life."

Singh Lee hugged the laptop. "I like it when you smile."

Chapter 24

ATLANTA, GEORGIA
THURSDAY, SEPTEMBER 15
2 A.M. EDT

Boscoe cleared Beta Hut security and marched down a hallway on the main level to a secure door where Kurt Handle was waiting. The walls and floor had shiny finishes, illuminated by overhead lighting that produced a sterile feeling. Boscoe entered a code into the keypad mounted next to the door. There was a buzz, and they slipped inside.

Automatic sensors triggered on lights, revealing a shoulder-high rack filled with humming electronics that ran the breadth of the room. Negotiating their way to the back, the men rounded one end of the rack and headed to a second keypad hidden in the corner. Punching in another code, Boscoe opened a door, drawing an immediate gasp from Kurt who stared into an abyss of glowing monitors.

They're watching us, Kurt thought. He cleared his mind and tried to focus.

"Okay, listen up, 'cause I'm only running through this once," Boscoe said. Motion detectors turned on the lights as they entered the doorway. "We refer to this room as mission control. As you are about to find out, we have embedded monitoring devices around the campus."

The men walked up to a bank of consoles set up just below three rows of monitors mounted on the back wall.

"These are all live?"

"Bear with me, kid." Boscoe pointed to a series of plaques below the monitors. "Working your way across, you will note our strategic positions in Alpha Hut. Those are on the top row: the lobby, boardroom, employee lounge, and Dr. Hunter's office."

"Nice. And the second row is Beta Hut. There's the lobby, downstairs conference room, Dr. Messinger's office . . . where's that one?" Kurt said, pointing to a monitor on the end.

"That's the computer room we just passed through. Now, the third row is a work in progress." Boscoe moved forward and tapped a monitor.

"I don't recognize that one, either," Kurt said.

Boscoe turned and shifted his weight, studying Kurt's eyes as he spoke. "You've got those Swiss cheese brains, kid. It's the office in Dr. Hunter's residence. I installed it last week. We've also wired microphones on the main level of the house." He gestured to a pair of headphones lying on a console. "You listen in over there."

Boscoe headed over to a piece of equipment on an adjacent wall.

"These devices store video. We have capacity to maintain feeds from all locations for one week. After that, the disk loops and overwrites the previous material."

"Do the storage devices require maintenance?" Kurt said.

"Just make sure the green lights remain lit at all times."

"No problem," Kurt said. "Any concerns about air handling?"

"HVAC is controlled by the computers next door." Boscoe lifted a boot and stomped. "We've got raised-panel flooring to pipe in cool air. You shouldn't worry unless the computer room shuts down."

"Who's been cleared for access?"

"It's in the notebook over there. But after today, only the two of us are authorized to enter mission control. Now listen up, if anyone types a random code into the keypad outside this door, all systems go into lockdown. Once that happens, it takes my personal intervention to bring the systems back up. So be careful when you enter."

"We've always monitored the grounds up at the guard shack. Is there backup monitoring here?" Kurt said.

"Let the gate handle the outdoor areas, including the deck down by the river."

"What about the computer networks?"

"They're controlled in Switzerland. They'll notify me if anything needs investigating."

"You mentioned a special project," Kurt said.

"I like your spunk," Boscoe said, pointing to the monitors again. "As you can see, we presently have five units not in service. The last four, you can forget about. But the first one, here, I need a camera installed tonight."

Boscoe walked over to a shelf and retrieved a device with a pair of dangling wires.

"Now that's impressive technology," Kurt said, reaching out. "I've read about these."

"Excellent. We'll put that knowledge to work."

"Will I be issued a firearm?" Kurt said, cutting his eyes to a pistol peeping from beneath Boscoe's jacket.

"In due time," Boscoe said. He pulled back his lapel, revealing a Zuritech logo on his shirt. "I run a tight ship, kid. And we're all gonna look professional. I'm issuing shirts to all US based security personnel, so go ahead and grab one out of the box over there."

Kurt walked over and pulled out a shirt. "What are my official hours?"

"2200 to 0600," Boscoe said. "Come have a seat, and I'll sketch out the camera installation."

"Where will I be installing it?"

"Hotel Zuritech—room seven."

"I see," Kurt said. A bead of sweat popped out on his brow. He took a hard look at Boscoe. "I thought security personnel were all Swiss?"

"Then you thought wrong."

"They didn't tell me much about you," Kurt said.

Boscoe smiled. "Perfect."

Chapter 25

**WASHINGTON, DC
FRIDAY, SEPTEMBER 16
3 P.M. EDT**

Cal wrapped up his last interview, and then decided to take a break and tour the Willard InterContinental. Afterwards, he stopped off for coffee before returning to his room and dialing the office.

"I was wondering when I'd hear from you," Sheri said on the other end. "Is everything okay in DC?"

"Couldn't be better," Cal said. "The early check-in worked perfectly. What time is your flight?"

"I'm headed out as soon as we hang up."

"You're going to love this place."

"I can't wait. I have a few logistics to take care of when I arrive," Sheri said. "Do you have dinner plans?"

"I'm afraid so, a working dinner with Avery. But do yourself a favor, and try the Occidental Grill or the bistro. You won't go wrong either way. The hotel service is superb."

"Thanks for the tip."

"Sheri, I'm running late for a call with Nate, and he's not answering his phone. Could you see if you can rouse him for me?"

"Just one thing first," Sheri said. "A young lady called the office twice this morning. I asked if there was anything I could do to assist her, but she was pretty tight-lipped. She finally said to tell you Holly called."

"No last name?"

"Wasn't that the cute little college intern? The one with the—"

"That would be Jamie," Cal interrupted.

"There're so many bachelorettes showing up unannounced, it's hard to keep track."

"If she calls back, find out what she wants," Cal said. "But right now, I need Nate on the line."

"See you soon, blue eyes."

Cal held the line.

"Cal," Nate answered. "How is Washington?"

"You'd never know there was a debt crisis from the looks of this place."

"Listen, I've got a four o'clock call so I'll jump straight into our agenda," Nate said. "First, the non-competes you sent over for your job candidates. They're both pretty solid contracts, but I have an idea about how to get around them."

"I'm all ears," Cal said.

"Even though they're currently employed at different companies, my plan should work for both. Remember how I told you Big Pharma operates like a pack of overbred poodles? Well, these non-competes are virtually identical. Before Zuritech makes offers, both candidates will need to resign from their current positions and exercise their vested stock options."

"Then we'll be in the clear—legally speaking?"

"They'll probably be sued."

"That doesn't have a good ring to it."

"Listen, these guys have to face reality. There will be legal threats no matter where they go. But it's not as bad as it sounds. Both non-competes are conditioned upon compensation in the form of ongoing option grants. As soon as their employers cut them from the plans, they'll be free to pursue opportunities elsewhere."

"What if the companies decide otherwise?"

"Then you may have to delay hiring, but your candidates will be in the money, so to speak. After the plan period passes, they'll opt out, and you'll be free to move forward."

"How long of a delay are we talking?"

"Well, the plans run on a calendar year basis, so I'd say you're looking at a worst case of three months. But mind you, it's more likely they'll be terminated immediately, seeing how Zuritech is an emerging competitor. Once they walk away from their stock, they'll expect you to cover any losses. We'll need to draft language in the employment agreements to accommodate sign-on bonuses."

"I'm familiar with the routine. Keep the contracts handy. I'll talk to both candidates and get back to you," Cal said. "Next topic—"

"Signatory rights. You wanted to know who is accountable for corporate decisions in the States."

"For all legal entities," Cal said.

"Based on the board resolutions, Zuritech Corporation falls under your responsibility. The board of directors has given you complete discretion, with the exception of a few non-operational areas."

"Let's step through them," Cal said.

"It's pretty simple. Avery is responsible for all early stage activities, such as the ZuriMax clinical trial and FDA approval. From that point forward, you're on the hook for marketing and distribution."

"Why the distinction?"

"Avery has control of the R&D process. As such, he's accountable for making new products available to the US business. In contrast, you're to ensure that only FDA certified products enter the market. It takes both roles to be successful, which naturally means you'll both hang if anything goes wrong. It's a pretty standard check and balance process for the company's protection."

"That may explain Avery's stress," Cal said, mostly to himself.

"A good organizational structure keeps the heat on the right people. I've got two minutes. What else?"

"Subsidiaries of Zuritech Corporation," Cal said. "Who has signature authority on those?"

"It's funny you should mention subsidiaries. I had to dig a bit to find the paperwork."

"As in, someone didn't want you to find it?"

"Don't be silly," Nate said. "This is a startup company. One of my jobs is to organize the legal files."

"What do the corporate papers say about my responsibilities for these entities?"

"Did you sign anything?"

"Maybe we should be clear about the subsidiaries in question. I'm specifically interested in Zuritech Aviation Corporation and Zuritech Trading Corporation."

"Right," Nate said after a pause. "I'm checking the files now."

"What do you know about them?"

"Excuse me, did you say you *did* or *did not* sign for them?"

"I did not," Cal said.

"I believe these are paper companies—the kind accountants set up for tax purposes. If you didn't sign on the dotted line, I'd leave it to them to worry over."

"And if you were in my shoes, you would be comfortable with the arrangement?"

"It's precisely the way I'd do it. The Swiss are masters of detail," Nate said. "I apologize, but I've got to run, Cal. Call me if you need anything else."

Cal hung up and noticed an envelope resting under the door to his suite. He slid off the sofa and retrieved it. It was addressed to him on hotel stationery. The note inside read: *Meet me tomorrow at 10 P.M.* with a location specified at the National Mall.

Cal reached for the door, opened it, and leaned out into the hallway. It was quiet in both directions.

* * *

Avery leaned back in his chair, animated as he spoke. "The data is being revalidated as we speak."

Cal took a sip of his wine. "You're looking better than last time I saw you."

"There's nothing like seeing your life's work flash before your eyes to send the old heart into arrhythmia. Say, I've been dying to know if Albert Jensen signed on as spokesperson."

"Sign, sealed, and delivered. He's going to be a tremendous asset."

"I suppose we'll see him in action tomorrow," Avery said. "What did he say about fast-tracking ZuriMax?"

"He's convinced it's the way to go and a publicity win for the FDA."

"I told you so," Avery said.

"Find some time to hook up with him during the meeting. Now that you've got the data re-queued—"

"I know, I know. Time is of the essence. You can save your breath. Did you agree to the new timeline?"

"Not officially," Cal said, setting down his glass. "How about you?"

"Like I've got a free will in all of this. You'll know soon enough if ZuriMax is working because I'll be the first patient taking it." Avery drained his glass, and then set it down on the table, staring at it as if it might refill itself.

"By the way, do you know anything about a former head of R&D?"

"Mallory," Avery said, not bothering to look up.

"I've never heard his name mentioned."

"He was my predecessor. What can I say?"

"Do you know his story?"

"He died in a plane crash returning from Europe," Avery said. "It's the kind of news that can eighty-six a company's stock, especially when it involves an executive who is vital to the company's future."

"What was he working on back then? I was under the impression that ZuriMax development started when you came on board."

"He negotiated the University of Rochester contract. Let's see, I believe he worked with a guy named Warren. Their agreement was the genesis of the entire project."

"Is there a reason it's been kept under wraps?"

"Frankly, I'm not sure that's true, but it's not rocket science. He worked on the early research, now he's dead," Avery said. "And thanks for reminding me. That'll keep me awake tonight in this hotel named after a damn rat."

"My apologies," Cal said, looking around for a waiter. "I'll buy you another drink."

Chapter 26

WASHINGTON, DC
SATURDAY, SEPTEMBER 17
1 P.M. EDT

The Willard's Old World charm has a way of setting guests adrift in its guilt-edge decorum. If the advisory panel doctors were impressed, there was little evidence in their demeanor. During an early morning break, an argument broke out over the origins of the ballroom's crystal chandeliers, whereby a steward later confirmed their European heritage. At lunch, someone reported spotting Henry Kissinger strolling down Peacock Alley, only to be trumped by a Hillary Clinton sighting.

The doctors wandered in from lunch, now at home in the five thousand square foot ballroom. Their seating arrangements had been carefully laid out at the front, where each had a personal workstation that was comfortably spaced from the others. The desks were equipped with Internet-ready computers and accessorized with fresh cut flowers, desk sets, and leather chairs. A brass triangle sat on the front edge of each, engraved with the doctor's name and a Zuritech logo.

"Welcome back," Cal said from a podium. He stood in front of an oversized monitor mounted in the millwork behind him. With the push of a button, an agenda popped up.

"During lunch, many of you were kind enough to offer comments regarding Ernst & Young's presentation this morning. I trust everyone learned something about the latest trends in cardiology, specifically as they relate to the expanding role of pharmaceuticals in this market." Cal glanced over his shoulder, and then back to the audience. "And of course, we were also entertained by the wit and brilliance of Dr. Albert Jensen. We're honored to have Dr. Jensen serve as our first chairperson for this advisory panel. Before we proceed, are there any questions or comments related to the morning session?"

A hand went up.

"Yes," Cal said.

"I'd like a copy of the presentation," a physician said.

Cal pointed over the doctors' heads to where Sheri was seated at a computer. "The presentation will be e-mailed to each of you shortly. As a reminder, the analysis presented was based on IMS figures. If you're not aware, IMS represents the gold standard in pharmaceutical data. Zuritech has made a considerable investment in this type of information to help shape our understanding of the cardiology marketplace. It will allow us to track future utilization back to physicians and know precisely who is prescribing ZuriMax. As advisors, you will have access to periodic updates."

"This is wonderful intelligence for us docs," Jensen said from his workstation.

The others nodded in agreement.

"If there are no additional questions, I'll turn the floor over to Dr. Jensen for a discussion on ZuriMax opportunities. I hope each of you will speak your mind and make this afternoon's session a spirited one."

The group applauded as Dr. Jensen sprang to the podium.

"Gentlemen, you are here because you are all top guns!" Jensen bellowed, pressing a remote. *Danger Zone* pounded through speakers around the ballroom as the floor began to vibrate. He bounced his head to the beat. "That's right. You are the Mavericks of cardiology." Jensen advanced to a photo of Tom Cruise leaning against a motorcycle with Kelly McGillis on his arm. "And as you all know, Tom always gets the girl."

The doctors let out catcalls as Cal headed to the back where Sheri was seated. Avery slipped out a side door as Cal sat down.

Up front, the room thundered with applause as Jensen did a little dance before throttling the music.

"Did anyone check in early yesterday?" Cal said, leaning next to Sheri.

"As far as I know, you're the only one."

"How are we doing for this evening's events? Did everyone confirm?"

"Except for Dr. Jensen. He says he has to prepare for tomorrow's session," Sheri said. "Is anything wrong?"

"No, but I need Avery to host the river cruise."

"And you want me to tell everyone . . . what?" Sheri said, looking him in the eyes.

"Something came up unexpectedly," Cal said, turning his attention up front to Jensen.

". . . frankly, I'm honored to be in the presence of such brilliance," Jensen said. "If a bomb went off in this building right now, the future of cardiology would be set back ten years. Take a look at the accomplishments of those sitting here." He turned to the monitor. "One hundred and twenty-three articles published in medical journals; two collaborators on physiology textbooks; grants from the National Institutes of Health; awards from the AMA too numerous to mention; an advisor to the US Surgeon General; forty-seven patents; seven tenured professors; three past presidents of the American Academy of Cardiology; current president of the American Academy of Cardiology; a Rhodes Scholar; dozens of past and present seats on pharmaceutical and biotech boards; medical advisor for a James Patterson novel. We're talking about the Academy Awards of cardiology." He laughed, and then pointed to Sheri. "If Steven Spielberg calls, tell him I'll have to get back to him." The doctors roared. "Now, let's do what we do best, and get down to business."

By four o'clock, Jensen had produced a "Top Gun" list summarizing their discussion. The flipchart overflowed with ideas organized around the theme of making ZuriMax a blockbuster drug. He smiled at his audience, who beamed back as he wrapped up by inviting Sheri to the podium to lay out plans for the evening.

"I'll make this brief," Sheri said. "We have dinner reservations for seven o'clock at The Oceanaire's Barracuda Room, so I ask each of you to be in the hotel lobby at six-thirty to catch the shuttle. Dress for the event is jacket, but no tie. After dinner, we have a chartered moonlight cruise on the Potomac. We will return to the hotel beforehand in case anyone wishes to change clothes for the event. The river can be cool at night.

"Until our departure, there are amenities here at the hotel to help you relax. There's the Elizabeth Arden Red Door Spa offering a wide range of activities. It's rumored that Kelly McGillis will be making a surprise appearance this afternoon." Sheri waited as cheers sounded off around the room. "If you would like to visit the spa, please see me for scheduling. There's also a fitness room, complete with Olympic-sized swimming pool and workout equipment. And of course, there's the Round Robin Bar serving a fine selection of heart-healthy wines for those preferring a more congenial form of relaxation. Please direct the hotel staff to book charges to the Zuritech master account, including cocktails at the lounge. If there are no questions, I'll see each of you in the lobby at six-thirty."

* * *

By the time they had returned from dinner and preparing to depart again, Cal manned the front walkway, using the occasion to speak to the doctors as they loaded onto the shuttle. Once everyone was accounted for, he checked his watch.

"Sorry to hear you can't make the cruise," Avery said, stepping up.

"Thanks for standing in," Cal said. "Sheri's at your disposal if you need anything. I'll see you in the morning."

"Cheers," Avery said, climbing aboard.

Cal stood on the sidewalk until the shuttle's tail lights disappeared into the night, and then hailed a cab. Within minutes he was dropped at an intersection, taking his first glimpse of the National Mall. He stood in the grass for a moment, captivated by the glow of the Washington Monument. It towered above him like a mirage against the night sky. When voices finally broke the solitude, he remembered he had come for a reason and started walking. He headed down the Mall toward Capitol Hill with the monument's presence fading behind him.

The sidewalk was mostly empty as he continued his course. Moments later, he spotted a string of benches, and then someone seated at one alone. From that point forward, each step became a drumbeat as he drew closer, the rhythm of his heels keeping pace with his pounding heart. The lighting was dim, but the person on the bench was reading a newspaper. Cal stopped and checked the area, but saw no one else around.

Then he advanced, taking shorter steps now. The face was hidden behind the paper.

Cal's footsteps seemed to be of interest. The man lowered the newspaper and peeked over the top, pretending to study the Capitol in the distance. He puffed on a cigarette, like he might be passing time. After a glance in Cal's direction, he turned away. Cal detected familiarity as he approached the bench, and then noted the newspaper's banner: *Los Angeles Times*.

The man folded the paper and took a drag on his cigarette, flicking it to the ground. Tiny sparks bounced across the sidewalk, and then faded.

"Have a seat, Dr. Hunter."

Cal maintained his distance, now recognizing the overcoat, but not the greasy hair. The resemblance hit him, only the man in Zurich had been wearing a hat. He was clean-shaven, but the light cast shadows on his face.

"You're an American," Cal said.

The man looked away.

"Who are you?" Cal said.

"The question of the night, Dr. Hunter." The man looked directly ahead, but not at Cal. "Only, I predict you'll be the one asking yourself that question before the night is over. To be quite honest, I've lost quite a bit of sleep wondering who you are . . . a man of character? . . . or perhaps one of them?"

"One of who?" Cal said. He ran a hand across the back of the bench before sitting down. "You'd better explain why you're following me."

"So you're a thinking man? I like that," the man said, pulling out another cigarette. His hand swept the air. "It gives me hope. I have a good feeling about you, Dr. Hunter. You strike me as someone predisposed to, I don't know, truth and justice. Let's call it the American way."

"You didn't answer my question," Cal said, taking a harder look. "What's your name?" The man sat silent, and Cal stood up. "Very well."

"Nobody's holding a gun to your head," the man said. "But before you go, I'm curious. How much do you know about your company and this new drug, ZuriMax?" He perched the cigarette between his lips and lit up.

"Okay, so you know I work for Zuritech," Cal said after a brief hesitation. "What are you looking for?"

"You're based in the US and pretty new to the job," the man said, turning to Cal and studying his face for the first time. "What's your take on the clinical trial?"

"Look, what's your interest in all of this?"

"Call me a human gadfly," the man said, releasing a stream of smoke. "But I prefer to think of myself as the common man's hero."

Cal shifted, rubbing a hand across his chin. "I think we're done here." He turned to leave.

"People are dead, Dr. Hunter," the man said. "Does that mean anything to you?"

Cal stopped, but hesitated before facing the man again. "In case you haven't noticed, people die all the time. What's this got to do with me?"

"These people were in your clinical trial," he said. "How's that for starters?"

"Patients on medications, like ZuriMax, often have serious health conditions. They die from coronary disease, even ones taking part in clinical trials."

"But you've got protocols to follow. If patients are having what you guys call adverse drug reactions, then you pull the plug. Just like Merck did with Vioxx."

"It's not the same. We're conducting a clinical trial. Our drug isn't on the market, and anyway, you can't compare ZuriMax to Vioxx." Cal started to walk away.

"My name is Harkins. Anthony Harkins, esquire," the man called out.

Cal froze in place, making a slow turn. "A lawyer?"

"As in class action lawsuit, my friend," Harkins said. "I was hoping you might be one of those rare executives with a moral compass."

"You are aware that there are no deaths in the trial—"

"No reported deaths," Harkins corrected. "I've got dead clients who would state otherwise. That is, if they could speak."

"Where's the evidence?" Cal said, making his way back to the bench. "You're an attorney. Give me a reason to listen."

Harkins flipped out a business card and handed it over. The address was in California. Cal shook his head as Harkins planted the newspaper in his stomach.

"Page 17," Harkins said. "Do a little homework."

Cal took the paper. "This is your evidence?" he said, holding it up.

"Are you familiar with an outfit called the Anaheim Cardiology Clinic?" Harkins said.

The date on the newspaper caught Cal's eye. He took one last look at Harkins and walked off.

Chapter 27

WASHINGTON, DC
SUNDAY, SEPTEMBER 18
11 A.M. EDT

A mosaic of flip charts covered the walls in the Willard ballroom. For the last hour, Jensen's "Top Gun" list had been arranged and re-arranged before settling into the final hierarchy. Jensen paced back and forth up front, admiring his handiwork. He stopped next to a chart.

"I believe it's time to recap the top three priorities, just to be sure we're all on the same page," Jensen said. "Are you guys with me?"

Everyone nodded.

"Top priority, *numero uno* . . . the Big Kahuna," Jensen said, rapping his knuckles against the chart. "We're all in agreement. Zuritech should invest considerable resources to obtain preferred status on the leading managed care formularies. This means a period of intense negotiation lies ahead. Big Pharma has top billing at the moment, and they're not about to stand down while Zuritech robs the cradle." He faced the audience. "Cal, do you have any questions?"

"It's been a while since I've been directly involved with managed care organizations," Cal said. "Do you have suggestions for networking our way into the top MCOs?"

Jensen resumed pacing. "You'll first want a cost/benefit analysis to determine your walk-away position. The purchasing agents at the MCOs are compensated for delivering discounts off WAC, but never lose sight of the fact that we're dealing with the big enchilada, here."

"What's a WAC?" one of the doctors said.

"WAC stands for wholesale acquisition cost," Jensen said. "And remember, these guys represent millions of patients, so it's important that we win their hearts." He paused for a second, laughing at himself until the others caught on.

Cal came forward, addressing the audience as he joined Jensen. "I've just made a job offer to a sales executive who will head up our field activities, including MCOs. These accounts will have his full attention. And I'm wrapping up a second offer for a marketing vice president. She'll be in charge of educational literature and compiling outcomes data."

"Cal," a doctor called out from his seat. "You'll want to personally participate in the initial sales calls alongside of your vice president. We're talking about the Walmarts of drug distribution. They command attention."

"And you'll want to focus your sales message on cost savings, emphasizing discounts and patient outcomes. They'll quickly grasp the fact that converting patients to a combination drug like ZuriMax translates into big bucks," another doctor said. "Remember, you're dealing with businessmen. Always show them the bottom line."

"And let's not forget the restenosis indication," Jensen said. "If you can prevent angioplasty cases from lapsing into secondary procedures, that's icing on the cake. It's sure to get their attention."

"Everyone in the room writes prescriptions for these plans," someone said. "We all have inside contacts that may help cut through the red tape."

"And once you get preferred status, MCOs will see to it that doctors write prescriptions for your meds. I've got bruises to prove it. Most physicians prefer not to wake the eight hundred pound gorilla." Jensen rubbed his posterior, prompting laughter from the audience.

"Perhaps each of you can provide a list of contacts for the top ten MCOs," Cal said.

"Everyone e-mail your contacts to Sheri before leaving today," Jensen said, making a note on a chart before proceeding. "Okay, number two. Zuritech must roll out a national program to ensure share of voice with the opinion leaders in cardiology." He smiled. "This begins with the physicians in this room. As we are well aware, doctors are required to attend continuing education on an annual basis. I know for a fact that we can score big by positioning ZuriMax in the various curriculums on coronary disease."

A doctor shifted in his chair. "Between us, I'd say we have the clout to not only saturate cardiology specialists with the ZuriMax message, but a sizeable share of general practitioners as well."

"And it doesn't hurt to conduct training in a strategic location, such as a golf course or beach," another physician said. "Hawaii always works for me."

"Avery is responsible for rolling out training modules to promote the science behind ZuriMax," Cal said, turning to Avery. "We'll have plenty of data once the clinical results are compiled. Our new marketing executive will assist in weaving the ZuriMax message into our courses for optimum impact."

"And while we're waiting for the clinical results, I suggest we appoint someone from the advisory panel to orchestrate a plan of attack in this area," Jensen said.

The doctors chimed-in their agreement.

"I'll discuss my recommendation with you after the meeting," Cal said. "And Avery will serve as point of contact within Zuritech."

"Priority three," Jensen said. "We must support the practitioners in the field: provide them with literature, food for their staff, and whatever else it takes." He leaned forward with a hand beside his mouth, like he was telling a secret. "Loyalty has a price. If the staff warms up to your sales representative, it's a direct path to the doctor's heart."

"What about ZuriMax samples?" a doctor said.

"Fast and furious," Jensen said. "We're dealing with a chronic medication, which means we want doctors putting as many patients as possible on ZuriMax. And samples are the key. Once patients try it, they're more likely to have their prescriptions filled."

"Patient loyalty has a price as well," another physician said. "My staff constantly hears complaints about the cost of office visits. We've found that providing free product samples to patients helps minimize the issue. You may want to err on the side of over-sampling, Cal."

Murmuring broke out across the room.

"In my previous experience with cholesterol medications, it's common to start with a ratio of, say, four samples for each prescription a doctor writes," Cal said. "Then as the product gains momentum, you lower the ratio. Once the drug plateaus, you shift into a two-to-one ratio. It's costly to implement, but necessary in order to win new patients."

"You can pinpoint prescriptions to that level?" a doctor said.

"We know every physician's prescribing habits," Cal said.

"By name?" someone interrupted.

"By name, address, and state license number," Cal said.

"So if you're writing prescriptions for the competition, watch out. We know which ones and how many you're writing," Jensen said. "If a doctor hasn't demonstrated loyalty to ZuriMax, then he'll lose his supply of samples. And as we've already heard, they make patients much nicer people."

"Bunch of troublemakers," a doctor said, laughing.

The room fell silent.

"Are you referring to the pharmaceutical companies or the patients?" Avery called out from the back of the room.

"What do you think?" the physician shouted.

The doctors came unleashed.

Cal took the floor. "I'll have my executives on board soon," he said. "And I'll make sure each of you has the opportunity to meet them at the Academy."

"It's noon, and we've committed to having you guys out of here by lunch time," Jensen said. "So if there are no further comments, I'd like to offer heartfelt thanks for your participation on the panel. We're planning a follow-up meeting at the Academy in Maui next month. Since it will be a working meeting, Zuritech has agreed to pay for travel, hotel, conference registration, meals, and entertainment."

"And don't forget to bring your spouse or significant other," Sheri called out from the back.

The doctors applauded.

"Thank you, Dr. Jensen," Cal said. "I want to personally express my appreciation for a job well done this weekend. We value the time and counsel each of you has provided, and as a token of our sentiments, Sheri has arranged to have the workstations shipped to your homes. And we hope the Zuritech jackets will be worn with pride. I understand they came in handy on the river cruise last night." The doctors broke into a round of applause. "Above all, thank you for your contributions to the field of cardiology. I will see you in Maui."

Chapter 28

ATLANTA, GEORGIA
MONDAY, SEPTEMBER 19
10 A.M. EDT

There was a tap on the door, and Cal looked up from his desk as it inched open. A tentative nose poked in.

"Please, don't be mad," Sheri said, shielding herself with the door.

"What's gotten into you?" Cal said.

"I know it's Monday, and you're swamped after your trip, but I couldn't bear to leave her out at the gate." Sheri leaned on the jamb with a "sad puppy" face.

"This must be a doozy," Cal said.

"Remember last week when I told you someone named Holly called the office?" Sheri stepped inside, and at the same time reached out into the hall. "I'm sorry if it wasn't the right thing to do, but I think you should speak with her." She gave a tug.

A young blonde stumbled in, speechless as she entered the unfamiliar surroundings. She froze next to the doorway with a pair of bloodshot eyes. The t-shirt and jeans were wrinkled, like they had been slept in.

"Hi," Holly said, fanning a hand full circle. She cleared her throat. "Remember me?"

"Holly?" Cal said, coming out of his chair.

"That's me, Holly Thompson."

"Are you okay?" Cal said. He couldn't remember if it was her normal look. "Can we get you coffee or something to eat?"

"Water would be great," Holly said.

"I'll be right back," Sheri said. She grabbed Cal's coffee cup and disappeared.

"Have a seat," Cal said. He joined Holly at the conference table, offering her a chair.

Holly sat down with her eyes darting between the tabletop and Cal.

"Thanks for seeing me," Holly said. She twisted a ribbon of hair around her finger. "I wasn't sure you'd remember."

"Of course, I do. Bioinformatics, right?"

Holly smiled. Just then, Sheri returned with coffee and water.

"Anything else?" Sheri said.

"Why don't you join us," Cal said. "Holly attended my speech at the Georgia Biomedical Partnership meeting a couple of weeks ago."

"Sorry if I was short with you last week," Sheri said, patting Holly's shoulder before sitting down. "It's my job to keep the wolves away."

"No problem," Holly said. She lifted a hand from her lap and placed a FedEx envelope on the table.

"So what can we do for you?" Cal said.

"In case you haven't noticed, I'm a little freaked at the moment. But I'm not nut-so or anything," Holly said. "It's just . . . I don't have anywhere else to go."

"Take your time. We're listening," Cal said.

Holly unscrewed the cap from the water bottle and sipped. Then she fidgeted with the envelope. "By any chance, do you know someone named Jana Cruz?"

"I believe you mentioned her name when we met," Cal said.
"She works for Bioscene."

"Bioscene, I know," Cal said.

"This is so weird," Holly said. "Jana is a friend of mine out in Santa Barbara. She works with companies conducting clinical trials—"

"Bioscene is working on ZuriMax," Cal interrupted. His face tightened. "Your friend, Jana—she didn't disclose confidential information, did she?"

"Oh no," Holly said. Her eyes locked onto Cal's. "She wouldn't do anything like that. At least, not intentionally."

"Does this involve the man who gave you the money?"

"I'm not sure," Holly said, shaking her head. Then she stared out the window. "All I know is, I can't go back to my dorm. It probably sounds crazy, but you're the only person I could think of that might be able to help." Her eyes began to well up.

"You're with friends now," Cal said, cutting his eyes to Sheri. "Holly, clearly something has frightened you. Can you tell me about Jana?"

"She left a voicemail two Fridays ago," Holly said. "She said she was sending an e-mail. I received it, but it didn't make sense."

"What was it?" Sheri said.

"It was a spreadsheet with patient names from a clinical trial she was working on. There were forty-three names in the file, but she claimed there were supposed to be fifty. She said seven names had disappeared."

"What did she mean?" Cal said.

"I wasn't sure, so I tried to call her. She didn't return the call, and I tried again the next day."

"Can you show me the spreadsheet?" Cal said.

"It's gone," Holly said. She fingered the water bottle. "After my classes on Monday, I went to the dorm, and someone had broken into my mailbox in the lobby. When I got upstairs, they had been in my room. The place looked like a bomb went off. All of my stuff was thrown everywhere, and my laptop was gone. The spreadsheet was on the laptop."

"And you think this has something to do with Jana?" Cal said.

"In a weird way, yeah."

"Have you heard from Jana since then?" Sheri said.

"That's the freaky part. It's not like her at all. After the break-in, I was afraid to stay in my room, so I sacked out with a friend for a few nights. But she needed her space over the weekend, so I stayed in a hotel."

"You poor thing," Sheri said. "I hope you called the police."

"They filed a report. But last week, I noticed a couple of suspicious-looking guys hanging out at the dorm. They were way too old to be in school." Holly rolled her eyes.

"Why do you think the break-in is linked to Jana?" Cal said.

Holly reached out for the FedEx envelope. "Because of this."

"What is it?" Cal said.

"It's what they're after," Holly said. "The dorm manager gave it to me on Friday. It wouldn't fit in my mailbox, so it sat behind the front desk all week."

Holly reached inside and pulled out a handful of papers, sliding them over to Cal.

He studied the top sheet. "This is patient documentation for the ZuriMax trial. She shouldn't have sent this."

"I didn't ask her to," Holly said. "In fact, she didn't mention it in her message, just the spreadsheet."

"She may have broken the law by disclosing this type of information," Cal said. "The guys in your dorm could be government officials."

"Can they just come in and nuke my room when I don't have any idea of what's going on?" Holly said. "I haven't done anything wrong, and Jana wouldn't either unless something serious was happening."

"Then she should have gone to the police," Sheri said.

"I studied those over the weekend," Holly said, looking from Sheri to the stack of papers.

"Like I said, they're patient records," Cal said.

"Jana's voicemail said seven patients had disappeared from the clinical management system. I can't be sure, but I don't remember those names from the spreadsheet."

"So you believe these patients are missing from the ZuriMax clinical records. Is that what you're suggesting?" Cal said.

"Yes, that's it exactly," Holly said.

"Should we call Avery to see if he knows anything?" Sheri said.

"He told me everything has been recovered," Cal said. "Holly, do you know anyone Jana worked with that we could contact?"

"I don't think that's a good idea," Holly said.

"And why is that?" Cal said.

"Dr. Hunter, you're welcome to look at what they did to my room," Holly said. "If that doesn't convince you, then take a closer look at those patients. They're the reason Jana is missing."

Maria Sanchez Perez

Maria Perez of Orange County was pronounced dead at UCLA Medical Center on Monday. According to her son, Roberto Perez, Ms. Perez was a native of Mexico and most recently resided in Orange County. Cause of death is unknown, but Mr. Perez indicated that his mother had been involved in a research study testing a new drug treatment for heart disease. He also told the Coroner's Office that he had brought his mother to the United States in hopes of finding a cure for her condition, but reported it had deteriorated over past weeks. Due to Ms. Perez's immigration status, her remains will be returned to Mexico for burial.

Chapter 29

ATLANTA, GEORGIA
TUESDAY, SEPTEMBER 20
11 P.M. EDT

Cal sat alone in his office at home, refolding the *Los Angeles Times* before dropping it into a briefcase on the floor. He had read the obituary at least a dozen times since Anthony Harkins had shoved it at him in Washington.

Cal knew that Harkins's accusations about people being dead were unfounded. Lawyers were notorious for firing shots across the bow as a means of putting their opponents on the defensive. The newspaper was hardly evidence. In fact, ZuriMax wasn't even mentioned. And for good reason. Harkins had apparently overlooked a key fact. The date on the paper predated the ZuriMax clinical trial, which meant it was unrelated to Maria Perez's death.

"Damn lawyers," Cal said out loud.

"Are you coming to bed or do you intend to stay up all night cursing in your PJs?"

Cal cut his eyes to the doorway where Kate appeared in a flimsy, thigh-length tank top.

"Sometimes I think you just sit around scheming of ways to undermine my ability to make a living," Cal said.

"There are times when a girl likes to believe she doesn't have to keep her own derrière warm in bed."

Kate spun in the doorway, lifting the back of her shirt as she scooted away.

"Damn women," Cal said, running a hand through his hair.

Cal turned to his computer and clicked a Google icon. He typed and waited as a string of information filled the screen. He read halfway down and selected a line. A notice appeared for a patent application filed by Dr. William Mallory almost ten years ago. Cal scrolled down and found a schematic of a chemical composition with references to the discovery of a controlled release mechanism for pharmaceutical agents. *The Z-Pulse technology.* He backed up to the Google list and found a number of hits for drug research and patent filings. Near the bottom of the screen, another item caught his attention. He selected it and read:

American Medical Researcher Killed in Fiery Plane Crash

ZURICH, SWITZERLAND - Dr. William Mallory died yesterday in a plane crash near the Swiss/French border. Mallory was aboard a private aircraft that went down with two crew members. The crash was reported to have occurred sometime after 10 P.M. last evening. Investigators have offered no indication as to the cause of the tragedy, but Swiss aviation officials are currently investigating the crash site.

Document searches report that Mallory was a prominent research scientist who holds numerous biotechnology and pharmaceutical patents. Believed to be in Switzerland on business, a flight plan indicates that Mallory was en route to his home in Atlanta, Georgia at the time of the crash. Eyewitness accounts report that the jet was a French-made Falcon 50 and rumored to be owned by Zuritech, a Swiss biotech venture. Mallory is survived by his ex-wife and two children.

Cal rubbed his eyes, allowing time for the information to sink in.

"People are dead," he said out loud. *What possible connection could either of the stories have with the ZuriMax clinical study?*

Cal reached out and slid a business card across the desk. He pressed it between his fingers, flicking it back and forth against his chin. Then he grabbed his iPhone. As he dialed, he remembered Kate's knack for hearing things in the office. He hopped up and walked into the foyer.

"Harkins here," the voice answered.

"You've got five minutes to convince me," Cal said into the phone. "So make it good." He opened the basement door and closed it behind him, flipping on a light.

"Who is this?" Harkins said.

"First condition, this conversation is off the record. And no lawsuits until I'm convinced of the facts," Cal said as he descended the stairs. He turned on another light. "Otherwise, we're done."

"Well-well-well, Dr. Hunter," Harkins said. "You know I can't promise that. I've got clients."

"What's your hurry?" Cal said. "They're all dead."

"Let me put it to you this way," Harkins said. "Either you help me, or you can go down with the ship like the rest of your Zuritech cronies. It's your choice."

The line went silent.

"That's not the way we're going to play this," Cal said. "You need my help, especially if you want evidence."

Cal heard noise on the other end, like a garbage truck emptying a dumpster.

"How long do I have to wait?" Harkins said.

"Until we can prove the law has been broken."

"Would it make a difference if I told you I'm looking into another death?"

"Only if you can connect it to ZuriMax."

"There's another case down south of here similar to Maria Perez," Harkins said. "Did you read the obit?"

"It only proves my point."

"Roberto swears his mother took ZuriMax."

"That's impossible," Cal said. "The clinical trial started two years ago."

"Ever heard of the Anaheim Cardiology Clinic?" Harkins said.

"You asked me that in Washington," Cal said.

"So I take it, the answer is *no*?"

"I want to talk to your client."

"That may be a problem," Harkins said.

"Listen, this isn't going to work if—"

"Roberto is missing," Harkins interrupted.

"So you're telling me, you have nothing."

"He disappeared right after he told me about the drug. In fact, I followed you to Switzerland to see if I could find some answers."

"Have you tried immigration?"

"I already checked."

"Then he changed his mind. It was a scam from the beginning."

"That boy loved his mother like the Virgin Mary."

"But he's an illegal," Cal said.

"It was part of the deal. I promised to fix that right after I settled the case for his mother."

"You've got nothing," Cal repeated.

"You don't believe that or you wouldn't be spouting things like, *off the record.*"

"What are you doing in the office at this hour, anyway?"

"My clients don't exactly keep bankers' hours," Harkins said. "Not everyone's from the land of Oz."

Cal walked over to a pool table. He reached into a corner pocket and rolled a ball across the table.

"Listen, I need a favor," Cal said. The ball came back, and he rolled it again.

"I'm listening."

"I want you to check something for me."

"Shoot."

"But it's off the record."

"I'm starting to like you, Dr. Hunter."

Chapter 30

**ATLANTA, GEORGIA
WEDNESDAY, SEPTEMBER 21
7 A.M. EDT**

Starbucks was hopping when Sheri slipped through the entrance. She searched the nooks and crannies in the seating area, finally spotting Cal behind a *Wall Street Journal*. A cup and saucer sat on a table next to his chair.

"I was hoping you'd take me out sometime, but more on the order of Veni Vidi Vici," Sheri said.

"You'd love to tell Kate that story, wouldn't you?" Cal said.

"Actually, no."

"Precisely."

"She'd grind me up like a coffee bean the second she caught me in your personal space. Correction, make that *her* personal space," Sheri said. She sat down in a chair next to Cal's.

"That woman's better than Homeland Security," Cal said. "Did you bring the list?"

Sheri slipped an oversized bag off her shoulder and unzipped it. "By the way, Dr. Timothy Warren called again this morning. He left a callback number a few weeks ago."

"Who is he?"

"I thought he was someone you knew."

"Never heard of him," Cal said.

"He won't leave a message."

"Next time he calls, do your job," Cal said. "Now, the list."

"There are over two thousand names," Sheri said, pulling out a folder.

"And how did you get it?"

"I've been trained on the clinical data system, just in case extra hands are needed."

"But do they know you accessed the data?"

"Only if someone is looking really close. I have my own logon."

"How current is the information?" Cal said.

Sheri opened the folder and glanced inside. "It's real time data . . . as of this morning."

Cal grabbed a leather briefcase and extracted a sheet of paper. "Tell me how it's sorted."

"Cal," Sheri said. She waited for him to look up. "Is there something you'd like to tell me?"

"Can we take it up later?"

"We're slammed at the office. Nick and Martin are flying in tomorrow, and here we are sitting in a coffee shop with you looking like you've had too many lattes."

"Not a bad characterization," Cal said. He dropped the paper in his lap and picked up his coffee, somewhat contemplative as he set it back down. "Do you trust me?"

Sheri's eyes twitched. "Oh boy."

"Don't get excited. It's a simple question."

"Last time you said that to me, you resigned from Vista-Bio."

"I did that?" Cal said.

"Totally, and you made me wait, even though I knew something gargantuan was about to happen."

"This is a little different."

"How different?" Sheri said.

"Let's say, it's for your own good."

"Does it have anything to do with new employees showing up without being interviewed?"

"Not exactly, but that is suspicious—"

"Or college co-eds dropping in with confidential information? Or clinical trial payments not adding up?" Sheri toyed with the folder, staring at Cal.

"Try not to worry," Cal said. "I promise to fill you in as soon as I've convinced myself."

"Where is Holly?"

"She's staying at the house for a few days, but keep that to yourself. Kate's helping her deal with the situation."

Sheri looked down in her lap. "Okay, I'll wait. But remember your promise."

"Always," Cal said, smiling. "Tell me about the list."

"I sorted it by last name."

"Then let's start with this one." Cal lifted the sheet from his lap. "Maria Perez."

Sheri dug into the stack and began leafing through it before stopping on a page. "There's an Alberto Perez at the El Paso Cardiology Group."

"We're looking for Maria."

"There's Alberto, and then the next name is Omar. He's at the Arizona Heart Clinic."

Cal called out seven more names, and each time, Sheri found no match.

"You're certain about the data?" Cal said.

"Do you care to spill the beans now?" Sheri closed the folder.

"At least it confirms Avery has restored the data."

"That's good, right?"

"But it doesn't explain why these names aren't in the database." Cal held up the sheet.

"Wait a minute. That's the information Holly brought to your office, isn't it?" Sheri said, counting on her fingers. "There were only seven missing names. You just read off eight."

Cal didn't look at her. "We need the spreadsheet."

"Any luck with contacting Holly's friend?" Sheri said.

"Just voicemail."

"So where does that leave us?"

"On another topic. Have you found anything on the groundbreaking?"

"I'm still working on it, but that question makes me nervous as well."

"Bear with me."

"What if someone asks about all of these projects I'm working on?"

"Like who?" Cal said.

"Let's say Avery wants to know why I printed the report."

"Tell him it was for me."

"And how about the inquiries into clinical trial expenses?"

"Refer him to Singh Lee."

"And what if I want to resign?"

"Then I'll sic Kate on you." Cal smiled.

Chapter 31

**ATLANTA, GEORGIA
THURSDAY, SEPTEMBER 22
2 P.M. EDT**

Cal walked out of his office, deep in thought.

"Good luck with the meeting," Sheri said as he passed her desk.

When he reached the lobby, Cal continued to the front hallway, and then down to the boardroom.

"Good afternoon, gentlemen," Cal said, closing the door behind him.

Nicolai and Martin were seated directly across from each other at the conference table. They rose as Cal entered.

"So good to see you," Nicolai said.

Cal gripped Nicolai's hand as Martin offered a greeting. The men returned to their seats, and Cal joined them.

Cal glanced down to the end of the table where Singh Lee and Avery were seated next to a screen extending from the ceiling. He started to speak when Nicolai broke in.

"I understand you have been in negotiations this morning," Nicolai said. "I trust you have good news."

Singh Lee looked away as Cal turned to Nicolai.

"I expect to have responses by tomorrow," Cal said.

"You have moved with admirable speed," Martin said. "Congratulations."

"Thank you," Cal said. "But I think we'll all feel better once we have product to sell."

Nicolai leered as Singh Lee and Avery sat silent, removed from the exchange.

"Nevertheless, we will celebrate your success at dinner tonight," Nicolai said.

"I am also waiting for Nate to confirm that there are no legal obstacles with Pfizer or Merck," Cal said. "I've asked him to join us for dinner."

"Excellent. We'll put pressure on him then," Nicolai said. "Shall we begin?"

Cal pressed a remote, and an agenda popped up on the screen. "To kick things off, I've asked Avery to provide an update on the clinical trial. Afterwards, he will entertain questions over dinner here in the boardroom," Cal said. "Then Singh Lee will present the latest financials, followed by a discussion of any outstanding business issues. Avery, would you like to get started?"

"I'm happy to report that the ZuriMax clinical trial has officially ended," Avery said. He retrieved the remote from Cal and activated a display of virtual fireworks, complete with sound effects that filled the room.

Nicolai and Martin rose in place and applauded. Singh Lee's eyes locked in on Cal for a moment, and then she stood and joined in.

"Yet another reason to celebrate at dinner," Nicolai said above the noise.

Avery muted the fireworks.

"Singh Lee," Martin said. "Would you be so kind as to arrange a case of your precious Tigerlily for dinner tonight?" His hand brushed the air in a shooing motion.

Singh Lee hesitated, but then rose from her seat, smoothing the pleats in her skirt. Her eyes darted around the room before she slipped out without a word.

"Nicolai, if I may impose upon you and Martin to join me in Beta Hut after tonight's meeting, I would like you to address the research team, personally. It would certainly be a morale booster," Avery said.

"But of course," Nicolai said.

"Perfect." Avery clicked the remote as he turned to the screen. "With the trial complete, we turn to our next milestone, the analysis phase of the project."

"First, can you tell us how much the fire cost?" Martin said.

Avery stuttered, surprised by the question. "The latest estimate was around forty thousand dollars. Singh Lee can confirm the figures when she returns."

"I understand the data has now been restored," Cal said. "Is the system operational?"

"Fully," Avery said. "And there's backup data stored offsite."

"Excellent, but please move on," Nicolai said.

"The research team has been divided into shifts to accelerate the second phase of the project. Beginning tonight, we will have scientists on campus 24/7 until the analysis is complete. Hotel Zuritech has been booked for the duration," Avery said.

"Then perhaps I should give up my room for tonight," Cal said.

"Nonsense, Calvin. This is a special occasion," Nicolai said.

"Avery, can you brief us on findings so far?" Martin said, wasting no time.

"The analysis is only beginning," Avery said. "We will have to be patient while the biostatisticians run their models."

"Do you have a final tally on the number of patients in the study?" Cal said.

"The figure stands somewhere between twenty-five and twenty-six hundred."

"The original study called for three thousand," Cal said.

"Yes, that was our target population. But as you know, actual patient recruitment always varies."

"Will the FDA require an explanation for the variance?" Cal said.

"These are mere formalities," Nicolai said, looking from Cal to Avery. "What is your latest thinking on the expedited review?" He snapped his fingers. "What is the name of the condition again?"

Avery shifted his weight, staring back at the slide before pressing the remote. The screen went blank. "If we're to pull this off, we must familiarize ourselves with the terminology. The condition is called restenosis," he said, looking over at Nicolai and instantly wishing he'd shown restraint. His voice softened. "It's characterized by a narrowing of arterial walls post-angioplasty. Our interest centers on a gene-specific form that affects only a small group of patients."

"Do we know if there is sufficient data to analyze the condition?" Cal said.

"In my last conversation with Albert Jensen, he assured me the data will be irrefutable," Avery said. "With that type of endorsement, ZuriMax may soon be viewed as a medical miracle. Cal, I seem to recall your reporter friend referred to it as the greatest breakthrough since penicillin."

"But if I understand you correctly, Dr. Jensen doesn't have the data. How can he make such a claim?" Cal said.

"He's spoken to a number of doctors conducting the study. He believes their experience mirrors his own laboratory findings at Johns Hopkins," Avery said.

Cal rose from his seat and headed over to a credenza for a bottled water before returning to his seat. As he sat down, Singh Lee reentered the room.

"You have something you wish to say, Calvin?" Nicolai said.

"Simply stated, the scientific data will speak for itself, so let's not get ahead of ourselves."

"Are you saying you don't trust Dr. Jensen?" Avery said.

"This particular form of restenosis is extremely rare. We're talking about a few hundred patients in the entire country," Cal said. "I'm surprised such a diverse group of cardiologists can identify the condition. Most of them have probably never seen it." Cal turned to Avery.

"Dr. Jensen collaborates with the brightest physicians in the country. Do you think he would put his reputation on the line if he didn't know what he was doing? You're talking career suicide," Avery said.

"I just want to be sure everyone understands the situation," Cal said.

"Gentlemen, please forgive me for introducing such a delicate matter," Nicolai said. "But as you realize, the board has already revised their expectations. Need I remind you of what an early launch means to Zuritech, not to mention the wellbeing of those sitting in this room? Let's not waste time squabbling over straw men."

"Nick, I've made offers to two of the finest executives in the industry. I'll be ready to market ZuriMax, but I hope we aren't being overly optimistic," Cal said.

Nicolai's eyes drifted over to Cal before locking onto Avery. Nicolai waited.

"Dr. Jensen has arranged a meeting with the FDA next week," Avery said. "Cal, why don't you join us? That way you can see firsthand how they respond to our proposal."

Chapter 32

**NEWARK, NEW JERSEY
THURSDAY, SEPTEMBER 22
4 P.M. EDT**

Halogen lighting buzzed from the rafters, casting a grayish glow on the floor fifty feet below where the coolness had set in like a morning fog. The warehouse basked in an eerie stillness as Boscoe examined rows of pallets stacked in the center of the building. They made only a small footprint in the expanse surrounding them. He turned when he heard a steady clicking that originated from a back corner. First noticing only a forklift, he spotted a man coming out of a doorway, marching in his direction.

"Hard hat area," Christoph yelled with a hand cupped to the side of his mouth. His voice echoed as he waved an orange hat and headed over.

Christoph planted the hard hat in Boscoe's stomach, and then turned his attention to the pallets. They appeared to be undisturbed.

"Are these all the goods?" Boscoe said.

"What do you think?"

"You really want to know?" Boscoe tossed the hard hat aside. "'Listen to me, you little—"

"Please," Christoph interrupted. "I've got semis en route with thirty-six hundred pallets aboard. Things are about to get crazy in here."

"Where's the hired help?"

Christoph checked his watch. "The core teams are on the semis. The rest will clock in shortly."

"I'll audit the delivery process when they arrive. Afterwards, I'd like to take a look at the personnel files," Boscoe said. "And I'll need access to the security equipment in the communications room."

"It's more like a closet."

"I know exactly what it's like. I installed it," Boscoe said. "The hardware's now wired into Atlanta, and it better be as I left it."

"You told me—"

"How long has this . . ." Boscoe paused, squinting at a label through the shrink-wrap, ". . . LipidRx been on the premises?"

"Since last night."

"I'll verify that on the security feed. How about inbound inventory?"

Christoph's face twisted in disbelief. "What about it?"

"What's your estimated turnaround?"

Christoph motioned for Boscoe to follow him. Once back at the doorway where he had emerged earlier, Christoph lifted a clipboard hanging on the wall and scanned the top sheet.

"Eleven tonight."

"Twenty-three hundred hours," Boscoe said. "What's on board?"

"The same drug, LipidRx."

I instructed you to computerize the manifests last time I was here," Boscoe said, snatching the clipboard from Christoph.

"I know, I know." Christoph raised his hands in defense. "There hasn't been time to train anyone on the computer. Paper will have to do for now."

At the rear of the building, a corrugated door rattled to life, rising like a curtain from the warehouse floor. Christoph paused as three semis pulled up outside. A man hopped out of one and made a direct line for the forklift. He climbed aboard and started the engine.

"Come with me," Christoph shouted over the forklift.

Boscoe followed along as they climbed a stairway to the second floor and opened a door into an office. Three of the walls were covered in faux mahogany paneling. The fourth was a sheet of glass, offering a view of the warehouse below.

Boscoe headed for a metal desk in front of the glass wall, plopping down in a vinyl chair. He swiveled over for a better look at the workers.

Christoph rustled through a file cabinet, extracting a stack of folders. He dropped them on the desk.

"Rule number one—don't leave manifests in an unsecure area," Boscoe said. He pointed beyond the glass. "Anyone can waltz in that loading dock and acquire an ass-load of intelligence from those clipboards.

"The computerized process will be up and running next week," Christoph said.

"Shred the originals, and have the chaff incinerated." Boscoe held up two fingers. "Number two—the loading dock remotes never leave the building."

"But the teams handle shipments while I'm out making calls on prospective partners."

"Correction. Retrieve the remotes and destroy them," Boscoe said, still staring out the glass. "I can't even begin to imagine what these lowlifes are thinking. For all you know, one of them might be living next door to an FDA inspector."

"Doesn't that responsibility fall under security . . . as in background checks?"

"Nuke the remotes," Boscoe said, slamming a fist on the desktop. "And don't tell me how to do my job."

Christoph stepped back from the desk. "Those are the personnel files," he said, pointing.

"Now tell me where the LipidRx is headed."

"It's on the clipboard."

"You don't hear well, Christoph," Boscoe said, smirking. "And does anyone buy that Christopher Smith alias? Now that's a frigging security risk, if you ask me."

"You were the one who told me to never use my real name stateside," Christoph said. He picked up the clipboard, running a finger down it. "The first shipment is bound for Miami."

"Give me the number of cases and mode of transportation."

"Forty-five thousand cases on FedEx," Christoph said, flipping the page. "Then forty-five thousand to the other sites: New York, Los Angeles, and San Francisco. All will be shipped by FedEx."

"In the future, allocate shipments across different carriers. Logistics intelligence should never reside with a single vendor."

"Got it," Christoph said.

"You did a dry run to the new sites like we discussed?"

"It went off like clockwork."

Boscoe gazed into the ceiling, silent for a spell. "What about the residual?" His eyes leveled on Christoph.

"Residual? I'm not familiar with the term."

"By my estimates, there'll be thousands of cases remaining in the warehouse."

"The rest is earmarked for overseas clinics," Christoph said.

"Ship it tonight, and make sure it diverts to Miami. I understand the operations down there are at full throttle."

"But we're finalizing negotiations with the State Department on a relief project."

"Then do your job and secure more product. I want this stuff out of here tonight. How's the cash flow?" Boscoe said, just as his cell phone rang. "Hang on." He swiveled so that his back was toward Christoph. "Okay, fire . . . those were his exact words? . . . people are dead? . . . okay . . . two nights ago? Check to see if Switzerland intercepted anything on the network. Right . . . and keep tabs on his office. Nice work, son." He hung up and spun around.

"In terms of cash flow, are you referring to contributions or receipts?" Christoph said.

"I want to know everything, down to the size of the boxers you're wearing."

Christoph shook his head, trying to stay focused. "Our partners have ramped up cash contributions quickly, and there will be more once they verify the press coverage. That's the reason the State Department initiative is so important. I have to hold inventory," Christoph said.

"How about receipts from operations?"

"Couriered by sea and deposited in the Grand Cayman account."

"So you've got millions of dollars floating around on the water at any given time," Boscoe said. "Sounds risky."

"I was told to keep the money in international waters."

"Time is money, Christoph. Of course, you're the MBA, so what do I know? You might want to consider air freighting the cash." Boscoe scratched his head and leaned back in the chair.

Christoph stretched for a view of the loading dock. "I need to get downstairs and inspect the shipment."

"Remember what I said about the inventory," Boscoe said.

"Next week."

Boscoe leaned forward and picked up the folders. "Not another pallet spends the night in the warehouse until you get rid of the paper."

"Got it," Christoph said, scrambling for the door.

"And Christoph—"

"I said . . . I've got it."

Christoph disappeared down the stairwell.

"Smile, 'cause you're on *Candid Camera*," Boscoe said.

Chapter 33

ATLANTA, GEORGIA
FRIDAY, SEPTEMBER 23
1:25 A.M. EDT

A bottle of Tigerlily dangled from Cal's hand as he crossed the Alpha Hut lobby, looking over his shoulder. Avery waved goodnight as he ushered Nicolai and Martin out the front entrance.

"Pleasant dreams, my dear Calvin," Nicolai called out. "We will offer your warmest wishes to the comrades in Beta Hut."

With that pronouncement, the three men exited, leaving Cal behind with only his bottle of wine. He headed for the Hotel Zuritech breezeway.

There was a crackle in the fireplace as Cal passed through the hotel lobby and continued down a hallway that housed the suites. At the door to his room, he checked to make sure he had the right one. *Seven.* He pinched the bridge of his nose, certain he hadn't overindulged. After a wave of dizziness passed, he switched the bottle to the other hand and dug into his pocket, removing a plastic key card.

The card slipped effortlessly into the slot, but the door wouldn't budge. Cal looked up and scanned the empty hall, then glanced at his watch. It was 1:30 A.M. "What am I doing here?" he said out loud before looking down at the door handle.

The key card sat snugly in the slot, but there was a red light flashing. He plucked the key out and held it up, drawing it to within inches of his nose. When it came into focus, he noticed a black arrow pointing upward.

Cal studied the arrow, and then looked up at the ceiling. His eyes returned to the key card as he bent over, setting the bottle next to the door. Then with his free hand, he rotated the card until the arrow pointed downward. He steadied himself with the other hand.

A green light flashed this time, and the handle turned. Cal retrieved the wine and stepped inside.

The sitting area was dark except for a small lamp next to the sofa. He looked for a light switch, but gave up and passed through the bedroom into a bathroom. There he found a switch on the wall.

Cal set the bottle next to the sink as a light came on over the vanity. When he looked into the mirror, a pair of bloodshot eyes stared back. Turning on the tap, he splashed water on his face and reached for a toothbrush, loosening his belt. When the buckle clanked on the tile floor, he stepped out of his pants.

Taking a closer look in the mirror, he unbuttoned his shirt, allowing it to slip off his shoulders onto the floor. With a foot, he guided the shirt into the corner next to his pants and finished brushing his teeth. He rinsed and returned to the mirror.

His eyes seemed faded. Squinting up into the light, he closed them. Despite his best efforts, Nick and Martin had managed to skirt a discussion about the aviation and trading subsidiaries throughout dinner. Nate and Singh Lee had joined in the overall celebratory mood, but remained tight-lipped as well. Hoping to clear his mind, Cal opened his eyes to find the Tigerlily bottle staring back at him.

He raised a hand and used his fingers to count. "That can't be," he said. The words came out syrupy, so he counted again in his head. *Eleven bottles of wine? I need to . . . lie down.*

Cal switched off the light and eased through the doorway into the bedroom. *But I only had three glasses.* He bumped into the bed, barely able to make it out in the darkness. Feeling with his hand, he found a crease, yawned, and slipped between the covers. He buried his face in the pillow as a mental fog descended upon him. His thoughts turned to Kate, sparking a twinge in his muscles as he dreamed of snuggling next to her.

Drifting in and out of consciousness, Cal pulled the pillow tight to his face. He couldn't shake a feeling that she was with him. He could almost feel her hands gliding down the contours of his back, gently kneading the muscles.

A shiver coursed through him, shooting all the way down to his toes. Then he felt the skin on his back tighten as fingernails raised goosebumps up and down his spine. Her breath was on his neck. A nibble on the earlobe. Cal felt his body responding. It all seemed real as he rolled onto his side in the darkness, reaching out to snuggle her. She felt good. Her toes were slightly chilled and her legs silky smooth. He drew a hand upward, and she cozied up against his chest. Her lips brushed his, and he kissed her, tasting sweetness.

Cal ran a hand down her back, stopping to caress the warmth of her derrière, as she liked to call it. She pressed closer.

Another wave of lightheadedness hit him, and the bed felt as if it was moving. When it passed, his mind backtracked. *Her lips taste like . . . Tigerlily? A warm derrière?* Cal opened and closed his eyes, attempting to adjust to the darkness. As he opened them a second time, he could only make out one of her eyes. A strand of dark hair was draped across the other. Cal pushed up on his knees, sending the sheets sliding down his back.

He stumbled off the bed and grabbed his pillow. On top of the nightstand, he found a lamp and flipped it on. Steadying himself, he yelled, "Get out."

Moving slowly, she tugged on the sheets as she sat up. Her eyes were full of betrayal in the lamp's glow, but then they moistened.

"Don't even try that with me," Cal said.

She sat speechless on the bed staring up at Cal. A tear slipped down her cheek.

"As of this moment, you're . . ." Cal paused, sorting his thoughts. ". . . you're fired."

Singh Lee raised her head, and a tear hit the sheets, leaving a charcoal stain.

Chapter 34

**ATLANTA, GEORGIA
FRIDAY, SEPTEMBER 23
8 A.M. EDT**

The Range Rover skidded to a stop in front of Starbucks, and Cal hopped out before the engine stopped running. He set his shoulder into the front door, nearly swiping a patron who was leaving. Inside, he checked the seating area, and then zeroed in on a leather chair in the corner.

"Never, and I mean never, come to the office again," Cal said, thrusting a finger in Harkins's face.

"Nice to see you, Padre—"

"Go to hell." Cal stood in place with his chest heaving. His clothes hung loosely, like they'd been slept in.

"We've got enough problems without dragging fire and brimstone into the fray," Harkins said. "Why don't you have a seat?"

Nearby patrons stopped their conversations to witness Cal's next move. He remained silent for a time as the sounds of a hissing espresso machine wafted over from the counter, then dropped into a chair next to Harkins. "From now on, use the telephone."

"Hey, relax. Look, I bought coffee." Harkins picked up a cup and handed it to Cal.

"I don't like surprises." Cal calmed himself by taking a sip.

"I'm a bit slow, but I got the message," Harkins said. "So what's this style you're wearing . . . last night's wardrobe?"

"If I were you, I'd get straight to the point." Cal looked down, attempting to smooth the wrinkles in his shirt.

"I come bearing news. And you just might want to show a little appreciation for the wear and tear I'm putting on my body for security purposes," Harkins said.

"Do you realize the risk you took by showing up at the campus?"

"First of all, I had to see the place. And I'd say you're on the money. There are some pretty intense security cameras at the front gate, not to mention armed guards. It's clearly your call, but it might be dangerous exchanging telephone calls in a facility that tight," Harkins said.

Cal sat silent for a moment. "You think the telephones are bugged?"

"It wouldn't surprise me. By the way, do you see any familiar faces in here?"

Cal checked the line at the counter and shook his head.

"I drove up to Santa Barbara and visited Jana Cruz's apartment, just like we discussed. The complex wasn't exactly the Ritz-Carlton, but I'd say she was doing okay by California standards. Anyway, the front door had been jimmied."

"Did you call the police?" Cal said.

"Eventually." Harkins reached into his blazer and pulled out a cigarette. He rolled it between his lips without lighting up. "Seeing how the door was already open, I went in for a look around. The place reminded me of a fraternity house after a party. Only difference is, I don't think anyone was having any fun when this thing went down."

"Meaning . . . someone broke in?"

"You're a fast learner, Padre. The place was tossed like a garden salad," Harkins said.

"By any chance, did you happen to find an answering machine?"

"No such luck. But I did notice that her computer had been removed. The wall jacks were dangling, like they had been ripped out. There was a makeshift desk in the living room, and if I were a betting man, I'd say they were searching for something. It was destroyed."

"And the girl?"

"Wherever she went, she didn't pack for the trip. All her personal belongings were there. I spoke to the apartment manager, and he hasn't seen her for two weeks. In fact, the rent's past due."

"But you called the police?"

"I called a buddy down in San Diego and asked him to take care of the logistics. It's not prudent to go public with this sort of thing at the moment."

"But the manager saw you. What if he identifies you as being at the scene of the crime?"

"We pinky swore, remember? You said I couldn't go public. If I go down, we both have some explaining to do." Harkins shifted the cigarette to the other side of his mouth.

"That's not going to happen. I wasn't there."

"Harkins stood up and extended a hand to Cal, pasting a cordial expression on his face. "Good afternoon, sir. My name is Dr. Calvin Hunter, and I was wondering if you might tell me the whereabouts of the occupant of unit B-3, Ms. Jana Cruz?"

"You gave the manager my name?" Cal said.

"Now, tell me how she measures into our investigation." Harkins sat down.

"That's confidential," Cal said, noticing stares from the patrons. This time they were following the bouncing cigarette in Harkins's mouth.

"And so is what I'm about to tell you, but we're entering into a new phase of our courtship," Harkins said.

"Drop the gumshoe and get to the point," Cal said.

Harkins laughed, and the cigarette dropped into his lap. "I'm afraid I left the trench coat at home, but I appreciate the sense of humor. Now don't react too quickly, just listen. The way I see it, I should take you on as a client. Call me crazy, but I've decided you're not a party to whatever's going on, which means you need representation."

"For what?" Cal said.

"Zuritech has irreparably violated unspecified terms in your employment contract."

"Which terms?"

"The ones stating that the company cannot enter into illegal activities beyond your knowledge that might jeopardize your future career."

"How do you know it's in my contract?"

"Trust me," Harkins said.

"You're thinking this can ruin me?"

"Only if you're lucky enough to live through it," Harkins said. "Remember, people are dead. How about it?"

Cal reached for his cup, looking out the window. "It appears Jana Cruz may have been working with the ZuriMax clinical data. Not as a Zuritech employee, but with an outside CRO, a contract research organization."

"But how about the drug? Did she handle ZuriMax?"

"It doesn't work that way," Cal said. "None of this has been verified, but I believe she was working with patient data coming in from the clinics."

"And what makes you think such a thing?"

Cal turned to Harkins and gave him the once-over, like he was undecided.

"It's okay. Attorney-client privilege," Harkins said.

Cal set down the coffee. "She sent a report to a friend here in Atlanta," Cal said. "It was the girl you bribed down at Georgia Tech."

"You don't say. Do you know this girl?"

"I thought maybe you did," Cal said.

"Never seen her before."

"I spoke to her after my presentation to find out about you."

"And she told you this?"

Cal pulled back and sank into the sofa. "Not exactly. She showed up at my office earlier this week."

"Now it's starting to make sense," Harkins said. "Did you know Jana was missing when you called me?"

"No."

"But you suspected?"

"Holly, the girl at Georgia Tech, couldn't get in touch with Jana. She was worried," Cal said.

"And where is Holly right now?"

"We'll get to that. You had something you wanted to tell me."

"Never be fooled by the wardrobe, I always say," Harkins said, poking at Cal's outfit again. "You've got a sharp noodle there, Doc. My cop buddy gave me a courtesy call. Another stiff showed up in Chula Vista, a José Rodriguez. I went down, and guess what I found?"

Harkins reached inside his blazer and produced a folded paper. He opened it and handed it to Cal.

"It's a photocopy of a pill."

"The crime lab pegged the ingredients as identical to the ones in your ZuriMax," Harkins said. "Only thing is, it doesn't have the required FDA markings."

"Was the patient enrolled in the clinical trial?"

"That's what I'm hoping you can tell me."

Chapter 35

**ATLANTA, GEORGIA
FRIDAY, SEPTEMBER 23
3 P.M. EDT**

Cal slipped out of a back entrance and descended a stone walkway that hugged the contour of the hill behind Alpha Hut. Near the riverbank, he negotiated a tree lined path to a wooden deck, where the Chattahoochee bubbled underfoot as it swirled between beams supporting the structure. Beyond the deck, whitewater frothed among hundreds of boulders peeking out of the river.

Pausing for a moment, Cal inhaled the scents of the river as he watched mist floating above the water's surface. Something moved behind him, and he turned to spot Singh Lee hovering in a back corner, away from the river. He took another glimpse at the surrounding beauty and made his way over to her.

"Be very careful," Cal said directly. He gestured up the hill. "Sheri's watching from my office."

"She's not alone," Singh Lee said, pointing overhead.

Cal turned to a lamppost behind them and scaled it with his eyes. A light was mounted on top, and beneath it was a small black box.

"When I was briefed on the arrangements for last night, they mentioned a video feed from your room," Singh Lee said.

"So you're telling me there's a camera up there?" Cal said. He stepped to one side, leaning against the railing.

"I don't think they can see us at this angle," Singh Lee said.

Cal cut his eyes back to Alpha Hut. "I had no idea they taught this type of negotiating skill at Kleiner Perkins. What do you want from me?"

"Listen, Cal. You have every right to fire me," Singh Lee said.

"I already have."

"If you don't trust me, I understand. It's obvious that I sold out when Martin hired me. You may not believe it, but I was nervous walking in unannounced and declaring myself CFO. But no one told me they intended to go this far with their plans. They waited to set the hook, and by that time, it was too late to back out."

"You're responsible for your actions, including what you did last night."

"I'm not making excuses, but here's the truth," Singh Lee said. "After my divorce, I had to get my career back on track. It was a matter of survival. When Zuritech threw money at me, it seemed like the perfect opportunity."

"And this makes you feel better, how? This is one screwed-up . . ." Cal didn't finish the sentence.

Singh Lee moved closer and gripped the railing. When she looked up this time, tears were in her eyes. "You're right, okay? So don't expect me to disagree. I want to fix it. Maybe that's not possible, but I want to try."

"Before or after I fire you again?"

"If you've made up your mind, then just say so. That way, I can at least claim I made an effort."

Cal pushed off the railing and crossed the deck to the river. After a few minutes, he returned, rubbing a hand across the back of his neck.

"Here's the deal. One misstep and you're out of here," Cal said.

Singh Lee nodded as she wiped away tears.

"And we start right now," Cal said. "Who put you up to this?"

"Martin, but I don't think he's working alone."

"So you're suggesting Nick is involved," Cal said. "What are they after?"

"I'd rather not speculate," Singh Lee said. Her voice wavered, like she didn't know whether to laugh or cry.

"I need options, and the only way to create them is to have better information."

"There's something else you should know," Singh Lee said. "Last night's video didn't exactly go as planned, but it does prove one thing. You don't trust me anymore."

"So your cover's blown. Maybe that will buy time to figure out what they're up to."

"Cal," Singh Lee said, waiting for him to look at her. "Suppose they thought I still had leverage over you. It might work to our advantage."

"Tell me why it matters."

"For one thing, I have access to Martin."

"And how does that help?" Cal said.

"Well, they've already seen how you reacted on the video. So I have to convince Martin that I blackmailed you, maybe by threatening to go to your wife," Singh Lee said. "Once I smooth things over, we can figure out how to get what you need from him."

"If you're right about the video, they've already got enough to send my marriage and career over the brink," Cal said. "What do you know about the security setup?"

"Nothing, really."

Cal tensed up, like he was still deciding whether to believe her. "They've kept you at arm's length, which means we're clueless about their plans."

"Exactly. But it also implies they're less threatened by what happened last night."

"Don't be so sure," Cal said. "It means you're expendable."

"But—"

"You'll tell them I had second thoughts about what I said last night. I set up this morning's meeting to offer you a truce in exchange for certain indiscretions."

"Wait a minute. What about your wife?"

"So now you're concerned about my wife? Your job is to sell Martin on the new arrangement, a strict kiss-and-no-tell policy."

"And you're going to let them video us doing . . . what?"

"People flirt in the office all the time, but affairs take place in the shadows. Of course, you'll have to make a believer out of Martin."

"That could be difficult," Singh Lee said.

"Tell me about it, I just looked into the river, and there wasn't a reflection," Cal said.

"What do you mean?"

"We've got work to do." Cal gripped the railing and looked over at Singh Lee.

"So you're going to trust me?" Singh Lee said.

"That or I can hire someone else for the job," Cal said, facing her.

Cal reached out and touched Singh Lee's arm.

"I'll walk out, and you'll never see me again. I promise," Singh Lee said.

"One more thing," Cal said.

Pressing her body up to Cal's, Singh Lee looped her arms around his waist and rested her head on his chest. Cal looked up at his office, and then raised his eyes to the black box overhead. He placed a hand on Singh Lee's shoulder.

"Let's try this over by the river," Cal said.

* * *

The men sat around the boardroom conference table, sipping coffee from monogramed china. Hoping to slip into the meeting quietly, Cal walked onto center stage, instead.

"My dear, Calvin. We were getting worried," Nicolai said. "Martin and I have a flight to catch."

"Perhaps you had too much wine—"

"Avery, get coffee for him," Nicolai said, cutting Martin short. "I wish to review our action plan."

Cal dropped into a chair.

"We've just completed a conference call with Dr. Jensen, who sends his regards," Nicolai said. "He believes your FDA will be most agreeable to reviewing the ZuriMax data for our restenosis claim. I want you to be present at the meeting next week."

"Albert has already compiled the findings from his research for the FDA," Avery said, setting a cup in front of Cal. "I'll provide an update on the clinical trial."

"I want your assurance that you have a strategy for the expedited launch," Nicolai said. "You must drive home this point at the meeting."

What are you up to? Cal glanced at Nicolai, and then turned to Avery. "If I have Avery's commitment, I will see to the commercial operations," Cal said, cutting his eyes back to Nicolai.

Avery nodded. "I have already scheduled weekly conference calls to review the status with all stakeholders."

"I will have acceptances from my VP candidates today. Once they're on board, I'll lay out a game plan," Cal said. "Timelines on launch spending will be pulled forward accordingly."

"But of course, Calvin," Nicolai said. "Martin and Singh Lee are at your service."

Cal bristled at the suggestion, but then had a thought. "Now that you mention it, Singh Lee is having problems with the financial systems. I'm sending her to Zurich next week to resolve them."

Martin looked down at the table. "This is entirely unnecessary," he said. "Let's not waste valuable time."

Cal studied Martin's eyes as they retreated to Nicolai for support. Martin's bearing hardened as he refocused on Cal.

"I'm afraid not, Martin. This is a deal-breaker. There will be no revised forecast until we have workable systems," Cal said.

Martin snapped at Nicolai in German, initiating an exchange that ended with the two of them staring at one another in silence.

"She'll be in your office on Monday," Cal said.

Chapter 36

**ATLANTA, GEORGIA
SUNDAY, SEPTEMBER 25
2 P.M. EDT**

The mainsail luffed just enough to make a popping sound, a sign that the wind had shifted. Checking the instruments, Cal looked up into an expanse of white canvas set against the crisp blue sky. He adjusted the boat's bearing, tightening a bit on the mainsheet. The sail snapped to, and he rechecked the instruments.

"No you don't," Cal said to Kate who was stretched out in the cockpit next to him.

"Oh, but I do," Kate said. She propped a foot on the helm, smiling from behind a pair of Costas.

"I brought her along so we could settle this today."

"How far would you say it is from here to the bow," Kate said, pointing ahead.

"Forty feet."

"That's precisely how far apart we are on this particular issue."

"Why would I tell you about the video, and then hold out on you?"

"I—want—to—see—it," Kate said, slowly.

"If it's any consolation, I haven't seen it, either."

"She's a—"

"Not so loud," Cal said. "They're down in the galley."

"She's an oriental Barbie doll—"

"Kate, it was a setup. It's not the real her, and for heaven's sake, you know it's not the real me."

"So it wasn't really you between those sheets?"

"Come on, why are you doing this?"

"I want to see the video."

"And then what, solitary confinement?"

"I was thinking more like taking a boat hook and whacking the head off that little—"

"Here they come, so do us all a favor and stay away from sharp objects."

Singh Lee and Holly climbed up the companionway steps, each carrying plastic tumblers which they deposited on a pop-out table in the cockpit. Singh Lee disappeared down the companionway again.

"This is an awesome boat, Dr. Hunter," Holly said.

"She's our little getaway," Cal said.

"It's bigger than my dorm room down below," Holly said, stepping aside as Singh Lee returned and laid out a tray of cheese and crackers.

"She's a solid ride," Singh Lee said. "Shoal or deep water keel?"

"That's what I'd like to know," Kate said.

Cal cut his eyes at Kate and checked the mainsail again. "She draws five feet. Lake Lanier isn't right for deep water keels."

"Sailing was THE thing at Kleiner Per—kins," Singh Lee said, catching herself. Cal's eyes hid behind a pair of sunglasses, but she felt a visual singe.

Cal reached over and piled cheese on a cracker, popping it into his mouth. He chewed, reached for a tumbler, and then hoisted it head high. "Cheers."

The others grabbed drinks and raised them.

Singh Lee unzipped her windbreaker. As she kicked back in her seat, the wind grabbed the loose ends of her jacket, exposing a black swimsuit top.

"Hmm, what kind of wine is this?" Holly said.

"Yellow Tail," Singh Lee said, making a face. She tucked a loose strand of hair behind her ear.

"Exactly," Kate said, raising her tumbler in Singh Lee's direction. "Nice firm body."

"Kate," Cal said.

"You mean, nice full body," Singh Lee said.

"That's it. A full-bodied shiraz," Kate said. She turned to Cal and stuck out her tongue.

"I hope you don't mind. I peeked inside the old box on the chart table," Holly said. "There's some kind of brass thing inside."

"It's an antique sextant," Cal said. Out of the corner of his eye, he noticed Kate's eyes peeping over the top of her sunglasses. "Jon Browning, a friend of mine in Savannah, bought an old beach house on Tybee Island. When he was cleaning out the attic, he found the sextant and asked the previous homeowners about it. They claimed it had been in the house for decades, originally the property of a drifter named Walker. To his misfortune, Walker was mysteriously murdered offshore at the Cockspur Island Lighthouse. When Jon heard I'd bought *Coastal Confessions*, he sent the sextant as a boat-warming gift . . . sort of an old sea tale to season a new boat."

"What's it used for?" Holly said.

"It's a navigation instrument," Cal said. He grabbed another piece of cheese.

"You line it up on the stars for your position," Kate said.

"But you've got GPS aboard," Singh Lee said.

"That's right, but getting lost isn't an issue on the lake," Cal said. "Jon swears there's a smidgen of Walker's ghost inhabiting the sextant. I've decided he only stirs when there's a full moon."

"Are you serious, Dr. Hunter?" Holly said, gathering her knees under her chin. She wrapped them in her arms and hugged tight.

"Please, call me Cal," he said, taking a bearing across the starboard bow. "Preparing to jibe. Is everyone ready? Jibe-ho."

The boat passed through the wind as Kate scrambled to uncleat the jib. Holly and Singh Lee sank lower in their seats and ducked as the boom passed overhead. Once the sails were set on the port side, Cal adjusted the mainsail, and Kate secured the jib.

"Beautifully done," Singh Lee said.

"Kate, you're on deck," Cal said. "It's time to discuss our special situation." He slid aside, allowing Kate to take the helm.

"Wow, you're a sailor too, Ms. Hunter," Holly said, scooting forward as Cal squeezed in next to her.

Singh Lee popped out of her seat and switched to the opposite side of the cockpit.

"It's okay to call her Kate," Cal said.

"As in, Cal and Kate," Kate said, lobbing the comment in Singh Lee's direction.

"You're super, Ms. Hunter . . . I mean, Kate," Holly said.

Singh Lee studied Kate as she eased the mainsheet. When Kate looked her way, Singh Lee feigned a smile and wrapped the loose ends of her windbreaker around her waist.

"Holly, you're moving out of the house tonight," Cal said.

Holly shot up straight, speechless. After a few seconds, she reached for her wine, palming the tumbler in both hands. "I'll ... pack up as soon as we get back."

"Cal, don't scare her like that," Kate said.

"You're bunking aboard *Coastal Confessions* until further notice," Cal said.

"Doing what?" Holly said.

"I'm afraid I have some bad news," Cal said. "Now don't be frightened, but I've confirmed that Jana is missing. I had her apartment checked, and it's been ransacked, just like your dorm room. Until we know more, we can't take any chances. It's best if you stay under the radar while we sort things out."

"So I was right. What else did you find out?" Holly said.

"We reported the break-in to the police, but she's disappeared into thin air, at least for the moment," Cal said.

"Who's *we*?" Kate said, glaring at Singh Lee.

Singh Lee swiped hair out of her eyes. "Who's Jana?"

"Jana is not your concern, unless Martin or Nick mentions the name to you," Cal said, turning to Kate. "As for *we*, you'll find out next weekend."

Singh Lee lowered her head for a look under the mainsail. "Cruiser to starboard," she called out.

"Let me know if it doesn't stand down," Kate said.

"Kate will check in on you daily," Cal said to Holly. "You'll communicate to her by cell phone only. We'll lay in provisions for you, including a new laptop. And I'll show you how to access WI-FI at the marina."

"Cruiser bearing off," Singh Lee said.

Cal's iPhone rang, and he checked the caller ID. He climbed out of his seat and slipped below deck.

"What made you think of checking the building permit?" Sheri said without a greeting as Cal answered.

"Someone mentioned the groundbreaking, only I thought they had the date wrong," Cal said. He passed through the salon into the forward cabin and sat on a bunk. "What did you find?"

"You tell me. The permit for Beta Hut goes back six and a half years."

"Do the files indicate who was in charge of the project?"

"No, but I can keep digging," Sheri said. "I uncovered a purchase requisition signed by a guy named William Mallory. And by the way, you may want to visit the file room in Beta Hut. There's some strange stuff over here."

"You found the building permit in Beta Hut?" Cal said. He craned his head for a view into the salon.

"That's where I am now," Sheri said. "I had no idea all of these old files were here."

"Sheri listen, I don't want you alone in the office until further notice," Cal said. "Is there anyone else around?"

"Yeah, but it's okay. I came in to help with the FDA submission."

"Stay clear of those files unless you talk to me first," Cal said. "Did you book the flight?"

"Tomorrow evening," Sheri said.

Cal ended the call and headed back up top. He checked the sails before finding a seat. The crew sat quietly in the cockpit, sipping wine and enjoying the warm afternoon sun.

"I have an assignment for you," Cal said, turning to Singh Lee. "I'm sending you to Switzerland."

Breaking free from her thoughts, Singh Lee said, "What did you say?"

"You're confirmed on tomorrow's flight to Zurich. I'll fill you in later. Right now, we should head for home," Cal said, turning to Kate.

Holly emptied her tumbler and bounced out of her seat. A couple of steps down the companionway, she caught a glimpse of the sextant and reversed course, climbing back into the cockpit. "Does anyone know if it's a full moon tonight?"

Cal laughed as Singh Lee climbed out of her seat, slipping the windbreaker off her shoulders.

"What do you say we catch a few rays on the forward deck?" Singh Lee said to Holly, dropping her shorts and climbing out of the cockpit.

"Super," Holly said, wiggling out of clothes until there was nothing left but a white bikini. She fell in behind Singh Lee, glancing back at Cal. "I could get used to this."

"Oh, dear God," Kate said.

Cal's gaze followed along as the two found their sea legs, bobbing all the way up to the bow. "What's the word I'm looking for?" He took a seat next to Kate.

Kate stood up and peeled off her sunglasses. She watched in silence as Singh Lee stretched out her arms and raised up on her toes, spinning full circle in place.

"I want to see that video," Kate said.

"No, you don't," Cal said.

Kate stomped her foot. "I can't compete with that."

"Who's asking?" Cal said. He wrapped an arm around Kate and pulled her into his lap. Then he kissed her on the nose.

Chapter 37

SILVER SPRINGS, MARYLAND
TUESDAY, SEPTEMBER 27
11 A.M. EDT

Avery paced the perimeter of the conference room, slowing at the rear where there was a window overlooking an atrium. He ignored the view and started another lap, passing by two posters. One had the heading, "Protecting the Public Health", and a second, "Advancing the Public Health". Loosening his tie, he avoided Cal, who was staring at a wall clock baring an FDA logo. The second hand sounded like a ticking time bomb by the time Albert Jensen burst through the door.

"Where have you been?" Avery said. "We were scheduled to begin an hour ago."

"You can thank me later," Jensen said, turning to a man entering behind him. "Gentlemen, I'd like you to meet Dr. Raji Patel."

After introductions, Avery kicked off the discussion as everyone settled in around a conference table. "Dr. Patel, we're happy to report that our ZuriMax submission is progressing nicely. In fact, we are here today to update you on our collaboration with Dr. Jensen. As he may have told you, we now believe an orphan drug designation is in the public interest."

"Dr. Jensen has just briefed me on his restenosis theory," Dr. Patel said. "If memory serves me correctly, the incidence of restenosis exceeds the threshold for cases per year. Naturally, this would preclude ZuriMax from being considered for orphan drug status, but I will nonetheless check the data."

"Dr. Jensen, perhaps you can recap our position for Dr. Patel," Avery said. He gripped the armrests on his chair as Jensen took the reins.

"Your recollection is correct as it relates to all forms of the condition. But as I mentioned earlier, my research has focused on a subset of restenosis caused by a specific gene. Our findings indicate that this particular genetically-induced form occurs in less than a hundred thousand cases per year."

"And how do you know this gene does not play a role in the broader patient population?" Dr. Patel said.

"Simply stated, the majority of our restenosis patients have not responded to the ZuriMax regimen. After examining the blood work for hundreds of patients, our researchers have concluded that the responders all have this unique gene in common," Jensen said.

"Which also means your ZuriMax hypothesis is founded upon a rather limited sample," Dr. Patel said.

"Not exactly," Jensen said. "In the past few months, a broader base of research has surfaced that suggests statins are effective on restenosis."

"I'm familiar with the findings," Dr. Patel said.

"We believe the ZuriMax combo therapy has a unique mechanism of action not found in single therapy statins. Our results demonstrate a one hundred percent correlation between the gene and patients being treated with ZuriMax," Jensen said.

"Impressive," Dr. Patel said. "Can you tell me more about this gene?"

"I'm afraid that's under wraps at the moment," Jensen said. "Once I file the patent application, you'll be the first to know."

"Then allow me to inquire how many patients participated in your study," Dr. Patel said.

"We're tapping into the ZuriMax data as we speak," Avery said on cue. "The trial included three thousand patients, which will be more than sufficient to validate Dr. Jensen's earlier laboratory work."

"Dr. Messinger, a request of this nature not only requires adherence to our policies, but use of limited resources to fast-track your application. This comes at the expense of competing projects, so naturally we depend on credible data to advance such discussions. There are opportunity costs to consider."

Avery hesitated, giving Cal an opening.

"Dr. Patel, you have expressed familiarity with the published research in this area," Cal said. "Have you taken a look at Dr. Jensen's preliminary work with ZuriMax?"

"Seven patients," Jensen blurted out, like he was tossing out a hot potato.

"I am confused," Dr. Patel said, turning to Jensen. "This meeting is unprecedented."

"And you may want to step back and ask yourself, *why*?" Jensen said. "It is entirely possible that our research could one day lead to treatments for all forms of restenosis. On a cost basis alone, the benefits to our healthcare system are enormous."

"But you're asking me to devote a project team to your drug for the next six months," Dr. Patel said. He ran both hands down his face, and then looked over at Cal. "And you want me to do this based on a sample of seven patients?"

"Seven patients that represent a one hundred percent success rate," Jensen said. "It is impossible to get this type of outcome unless you have a breakthrough."

"And we're about to corroborate the findings with the ZuriMax clinical data," Avery said.

Dr. Patel flipped open a notebook and made notes. "You have indicated that your clinical trial has three thousand patients."

"That's correct," Avery said. "You'll have the data within a week."

"Let's make sure we're on the same page," Cal said. "If we do the math, there'll be ten to fifteen additional restenosis cases."

Dr. Patel dropped his pen.

"More like . . . thirty," Avery said.

"And I'm willing to bet a box of Cuban cigars there'll be a one hundred percent cure rate in our targeted population," Jensen said.

"Do you have sufficient blood work to identify the patients?" Dr. Patel said.

"It was covered in the clinical protocol," Avery said. "All we have to do is slice the data."

"Dr. Jensen, have you published your initial findings?" Dr. Patel said.

"I've prepared a draft, but I'm holding out for the additional patients," Jensen said.

"Can you make it available to my staff for comment?" Dr. Patel said.

Jensen leaned back in his chair, and then rocked forward onto his feet. "Dr. Patel, may I have a word with you in private?"

Without looking back, Jensen opened the door and marched out into the hallway. Dr. Patel hesitated, studying the pad. Then he grabbed his pen and left.

Chapter 38

ZURICH, SWITZERLAND
TUESDAY, SEPTEMBER 27
10 P.M. CEST

Singh Lee heard footsteps approaching from down the hall and held her breath. Inside the wiring closet, the air felt statically charged, heightened by a humming that permeated the darkness. A bead of perspiration ran down her forehead, and she tried to mentally block the distractions, but to no avail. Working by penlight, she started typing on a keyboard. Her fingers moved swiftly, pausing only when waiting for the computer to respond. The footsteps outside drew closer, prompting her to dim the monitor.

There was a beep, and a stream of data filled the display. When it stopped, the curser rested at the bottom, blinking. "Yes," Singh Lee said under her breath. She plugged in a USB drive and scrolled to the top of the data, selecting the first line. More records appeared, and she read frantically. Moving the curser to a highlighted field, she pressed a key that released torrents of information. The light on the USB drive flashed.

Wiping her forehead, she navigated back to the first screen. With a click of the mouse, she selected a second line, quickly scanning details that looked similar to the first. Halfway down, she focused on a twenty-two digit field, reciting it in her head.

There was a tap on the door, and then a sliver of light broke through as a man forced his way inside, pushing Singh Lee aside.

He grabbed the keyboard and typed. The screen unleashed reams of bright green data that disappeared faster than Singh Lee could read. After several waves, the monitor went blank except for a pulsating red message. Even though it was displayed in German, Singh Lee could tell the warning was serious.

The man took a breath and closed his eyes. Sweat dripped onto the keyboard as he raised a finger. When he let it drop, the display flashed like a strobe light until there was nothing left but a blinking cursor.

"You must come," he said, grabbing Singh Lee by the hand.

Singh Lee unplugged the USB and followed the man down two flights of stairs that dumped into an empty hallway. He took Singh Lee by the arm as he negotiated a couple of turns, finally pushing her into an office not much bigger than the wiring closet. Checking up and down the hallway, he locked the door behind them.

"Listen to me," he said, turning. "We will never speak of this again."

Singh Lee followed his eyes as they darted around the room. The walls were barren, but the desk was cluttered. "What did you just do?"

"I trust you have what you need," he said, taking a seat at the desk.

"You covered my tracks, didn't you?"

"I had to make sure the system remembers nothing." He stretched his hand across the desk to where a bottle of Tigerlily sat like a gleaming silo. "It was the only way."

Singh Lee leaned forward. When he didn't look up, she smiled. "Thank you."

"I warned them about Atlanta, and they treated me like some kind of . . . *dummkopf*. They think they know better, so now we will see."

"They called you an idiot?" Singh Lee said, leaning against the desktop. "I've heard you called a lot of things, but not that."

"I take it, this wine is good?" he said, lifting the bottle.

"What's this about Atlanta?" Singh Lee said.

"The fire, of course."

* * *

Singh Lee knocked, and the door inched open to her touch.

"*Entré*, please," a voice called out.

Singh Lee walked into the office where Martin was seated behind his desk. "You are late, my dear. I had no choice but to start without you." Tipping a champagne flute, he finished it off. "Lucky for you, there is another bottle."

Martin lifted an ice bucket and stopped off to lock the door before plopping down on a leather sofa across the room.

"My apologies," Singh Lee said. She strolled toward him, stepping over an empty bottle in the process. "It must be later than I thought." Removing her shoes, she slid onto the sofa and folded a leg underneath her as she snuggled up next to Martin.

Martin produced a fresh glass and hoisted a bottle of champagne from the ice bucket. As he poured, dribbles streamed into his lap. "I watched your performance, and I must say Cal Hunter is becoming a risk. Of course, Nate Friedman . . ." Martin paused, looking down at the puddle on his trousers. "Would you mind?"

"Allow me," Singh Lee said. She took the bottle and set it in the ice bucket, grabbing a napkin for his lap. "You're a bit flush."

Singh Lee helped Martin out of his jacket while he juggled the glass. She tossed the jacket on the floor and returned to her spot on the sofa, rubbing a hand across his chest. "So tell me about Nate Friedman."

"Cal hasn't filed the paperwork for your termination," Martin said. He fumbled with the glass before taking a sip. "We're not sure what it means."

"*We*?" Singh Lee said.

"*Oui*," Martin said, directly in her face.

"Then you haven't heard."

Martin's head bobbed, like he was having trouble holding it up. "I watched the video." He lowered his voice. "That was some . . ." His words trailed off as his eyes worked their way down to her toenails. He reached out and wrapped a hand around her foot.

"And what does Nicolai think?" Singh Lee said.

"You're a very naughty girl," Martin said. "I watched it four times."

"Martin, it worked. Cal has the hots for me."

"Hots?" Martin said, spilling champagne. "Don't be silly. He loves that woman."

"Careful," Singh Lee said, steadying his hand. "Wait, what woman?"

"Katherine, the charming wife, of course. We have him right where we . . ."

Singh Lee brushed her lips across Martin's ear and kissed. "Martin, who is *we*?"

"Do you want to know who has the hots for you?" Martin reached over and toyed with Singh Lee's collar. "I want you to . . ." He leaned forward in an attempt to get up.

Singh Lee took him by the shoulders and eased him back onto the sofa. Martin's head flopped back against the cushion. She placed a cheek against his.

"Martin, who is *we*?" Singh Lee said, running her hand down his chest.

Martin's head rolled onto Singh Lee's shoulder.

"So much for discussing the systems problem," Singh Lee said. She shook him, but he didn't stir.

Looking down, Singh Lee traced a finger along Martin's belt to a security badge and snapped it loose.

Chapter 39

WASHINGTON, DC
WEDNESDAY, SEPTEMBER 28
3 P.M. EDT

Suits filled the stately room on Capitol Hill, where postures and attitudes dripped with power. A cherry table awaited Secretary Lawrence Baker and his entourage as they filed down an aisle. He took a seat in front of a microphone while a dozen rank-and-file staffers positioned themselves to his left and right. By the time they had settled in, a gavel pounded, and Baker's name was announced over the public address system.

"Secretary Baker, if you're ready, we would like to begin," the chairman announced.

Baker looked up at the esteemed group seated twenty feet away, perched stoically in an elevated area resembling a choir loft. "I believe we're ready, Mr. Chairman," Baker said.

"Very well, then. I'd like to welcome you to this special session of the Joint Economic Committee. I speak for all of the distinguished representatives before you in stating that your testimony to these proceedings is of utmost importance in light of the present healthcare crisis. Indeed, our nation anxiously awaits your considered opinion as it relates to matters at hand," the chairman said.

"I'm honored to be here," Baker said, leaning into the microphone.

"Mr. Secretary, as you're aware, the recession has created a temporary diversion regarding what many believe to be a more debilitating national crisis, that is the runaway medical costs in these United States," the chairman said. "Our most recent data suggests that fifteen percent of the nation lacks healthcare coverage, Medicare rolls are swelling to record levels, Medicaid entitlements are crushing state budgets, and as always, medical inflation continues to outpace that of the overall economy. You may indeed call this crisis a flaw in the fabric of our nation, if not a plague upon our great land. Mr. Secretary, I would like to grant you the favor of any opening remarks you may wish to make before we begin."

"Thank you, Mr. Chairman and distinguished members of the Joint Economic Committee. As you have so noted, it appears that the medical industry continues to struggle with the notion of delivering affordable healthcare. On many fronts, this failure has frustrated those who view these services as a human right. The call by many for universal healthcare on the heels of the Affordable Care Act, for better or for worse, brings to mind the well-known mantra, 'to each according to his need'. While I view this objective as evidence of a most noble spirit, I fail to believe that a solution can or will be fulfilled by that great institution known as the US Congress. Thank you, Mr. Chairman."

Bodies stirred in the loft.

"Mr. Secretary, are you suggesting that the $900 billion we appropriated for your department last year is a waste of taxpayer money?" The chairman's response silenced the commotion around him. Not waiting for an answer, he turned and exchanged words with an aide over his shoulder. He leaned into the microphone. "And if I'm not mistaken, you employ somewhere on the order of seventy-five thousand employees."

"The figures are correct, Mr. Chairman, but I disagree with the conclusion."

"Leaving me in a quandary over your opening statement, sir. Would you care to enlighten the committee or should we consider taking a second look at next year's budget proposal?" the chairman said. "I see you've brought along your attorney. You may wish to concur with her before responding."

The secretary smiled, and then scanned the legion of congressmen. "We're happy to allow the tenets of our budget to stand on its own merit as submitted, Mr. Chairman. However, we do see a need for change."

"As you seem to find this line of discussion amusing, perhaps you could expand on your last comment," the chairman said.

"Respectfully, sir, I must concede that the Department of Health & Human Services operates under a strict legal code set forth by Congress. The previous decades provide clear evidence, beginning with the policies of President Johnson. We operate under the shackles of an unmanageable bureaucracy, a virtual ball and chain, if I may be so bold."

"We've heard this rhetoric before, Mr. Secretary."

"They're called mandates, Mr. Chairman. The well-intentioned employees of HHS are not free to explore creative solutions to our national healthcare crisis," Baker said.

"We damn near send a blank check to your department, so I hardly see how you expect this committee to raise a brow when it comes to complying with rules and regulations." The chairman took a moment to confer with his colleagues, confirming that most agreed.

"I mean no disrespect, but perhaps you shouldn't," Baker said. He lifted his chin toward a nearby C-SPAN camera. "The

American people deserve more from these programs. My top priority should be to break the back of this national crisis, not by rationing failed healthcare policies, but by encouraging broader care through new delivery systems and drugs. Once we do so, the budget will take care of itself."

"Yes, I see. A noble spirit, indeed, Mr. Secretary," the chairman said. "Perhaps you would like to offer this committee something tangible. For once, give us something executable . . . just one example of how you intend to address this crisis."

The room fell silent again as one of Baker's staff passed a document down the line to the center of the table. Baker scanned it, and then set it down, returning to the microphone. "The current crisis cannot be averted by a single solution. We believe this approach will only heighten risk—"

"Specifics, Mr. Secretary," the chairman interrupted. He presented a stern profile for the camera. "We're bored to tears with rhetoric. The American people demand tangible evidence."

Baker paused for the chairman's diatribe to have its effect, scanning the suits in the loft where a majority sat cross-armed with faces of flint.

"The American people are best served by the government partnering with industry in this healthcare crisis," Baker said. "The underlying American economy is resilient and vibrant, a marvel to the world. The ingenuity and creative spirits of our citizens are the resources that will slay this dragon. By shifting our focus from mind-numbing bureaucracy to empowering government to lead solution-driven initiatives, the tide can be turned on our current failures—"

The chairman banged his gavel until Baker was silenced. "We're all familiar with your ideology."

"For example," Baker said with a raised voice. He shook his head, allowing the camera to take a sweep of the room. "By reforming policies surrounding pharmaceutical development and approval, the FDA can partner with companies to expedite lifesaving drugs into the marketplace. Emerging biotechnologies have tremendous potential to alleviate thousands of costly medical procedures in this country, each and every year."

"Do you have an estimate of the dollar impact?"

"The figure isn't precise, but I'd say one hundred billion."

"Let the record show . . . a hundred billion," the chairman said. "Spread over how many years?"

"You misunderstand, Mr. Chairman. This is an annual figure."

The congressmen squirmed in their seats. Some appeared to be straining at their leashes, frustrated that the chairman had yet to yield the floor. The chairman rapped the gavel once again.

"No one understands better than you that there are millions who require government assistance, even for basic care," the chairman said.

"Yes, I believe the Bible states that the poor will always be among us," Baker said. "However, we cannot underestimate the American people when it comes to charity. The members of this committee may have seen the administration's endorsement of the Rx Freedom Project—"

"That's strictly an overseas initiative," a congressman blurted out.

The chairman pounded the gavel.

"The congressman has just confirmed my belief that this institution has a bias for looking back, never forward. My point is, similar initiatives could assist the needs of the indigent population in our nation. Take a moment to consider what this would mean to HHS budget proposals in the coming years. All I'm asking is that we are allowed more autonomy in leveraging industry solutions, a partnership between big government and big business," Baker said.

"For someone steeped in capitalist solutions, I'm puzzled by your analogy," the chairman shot back. "Are you aware of the potential market fallout for our medical industries should they misinterpret your proposal?"

"I'm indeed surprised to hear this committee acknowledge that the fox is in the henhouse, Mr. Chairman," Baker said. "Of course, I embrace the healthcare industries and their promise for the future. They possess enormous potential, not only to serve their own interests, but to help HHS solve the current crisis. For the record, industry supports the Rx Freedom Project, and I am confident they will embrace a domestic effort as well. But to address your concern, the financial markets will take care of themselves if we move forward with conviction."

The chairman looked down at Baker. "Is there anything else you wish to say before I turn you over to my panel of distinguished colleagues?"

Baker looked over the chairman's shoulder, pausing as the camera zoomed in for a close-up.

"Yes, Mr. Chairman. It's time to slay this Goliath. The American people deserve a solution to this national crisis," Baker said.

"Secretary Baker, are you referring to yourself as a . . . David?"

"I'm suggesting we dispel with the partisanship, Mr. Chairman."

Chapter 40

**ATLANTA, GEORGIA
THURSDAY, SEPTEMBER 29
8 A.M. EDT**

Nicolai's image flickered across the screen as the transmission from Zurich delayed a few seconds, making his back and forth pacing look more like a game of hop-scotch. Avery and Jensen slipped into the Atlanta boardroom undetected, fighting hard not to laugh at his spastic movements. Nicolai sat down, and the video feed stabilized.

"Good morning, Nicolai," Avery said. He pushed aside a Danish and reached for his coffee. "We raided the Hotel Zuritech breakfast bar this morning."

"It's two o'clock on this side of the ocean, gentlemen. I trust you have good news," Nicolai said. He leaned back in the chair and folded his arms.

"Do you remember what I told you when we agreed to this collaboration?" Jensen said, staring directly into the screen.

Nicolai sat with a stoic expression on his face.

"We have excellent news," Avery said, jumping in. "The FDA has agreed to review the expedited submission."

Jensen leaned forward and slapped Avery on the back. He beamed up at the monitor.

"A review? I do not understand," Nicolai said, placing his palms down on the table.

"We won the argument," Avery said.

"But you said ZuriMax was to be expedited for approval," Nicolai said.

"I'm not believing this," Jensen said. His hand slid off of Avery's back. "We've just moved the FDA off the dime, and you're pissed?"

"Then forgive me. Please continue with your update so that I may join in your happiness," Nicolai said.

"We're moving forward with the data extraction on the restenosis patients," Avery said. "The biostatisticians will have the results in a couple of days. Once they're done, Dr. Jensen will be able to compare the data to his earlier research."

"When does the six month clock start ticking at the FDA?" Nicolai said.

"Upon receipt of the submission," Avery said.

"Then let's work around the clock to make it happen," Nicolai said.

"My team is already operating 24/7. We can't move any faster," Avery said.

"Do you have Dr. Jensen's data?"

"Hold on, Nicolai," Jensen said. "The comparative analysis is my responsibility."

"Dr. Jensen, this is a trivial matter. Please have the data sent to Avery immediately," Nicolai said.

"That's not going to happen," Jensen said. "I get first crack at the data, not to mention publishing rights."

"You will have your publishing credit, but let's not lose sight of the objective," Nicolai said.

"You don't understand. I own the data," Jensen said. "And I hold a copyright on the scientific paper."

"Avery?" Nicolai said.

"Albert, please calm down," Avery said. He leaned forward and picked up a carafe, pouring coffee into Jensen's cup. "We can work this out."

Jensen fired a look at Nicolai. "Let's hear it."

"We're already working under a non-disclosure agreement. There's no risk of anyone violating confidential information. Send the data to my team, and you'll retain the publishing rights. We'll even finish the paper for you," Avery said.

"This is insanity," Jensen said. "I've cut six months off your approval time, and you're beating me up over a few days to review data. I've got my integrity on the line here."

The men paused as Cal entered the boardroom and closed the door. Avery glanced up at the monitor and noticed Nicolai perking up.

"Calvin," Nicolai said. His arms opened wide. "It's so good to see you this morning."

"Sorry to interrupt, but I heard Dr. Jensen was in the building."

"But of course," Nicolai said. "Your colleagues have good news."

"I was at the meeting, Nick. How's the submission coming along?" Cal said, turning to Avery.

"The submission is fine," Nicolai said. "The wind is at our backs."

"I hope you're right," Cal said.

"You may wish to take a look at your healthcare czar's testimony before Congress yesterday," Nicolai said.

"If you're referring to Lawrence Baker, I saw him on the morning news," Cal said.

"His proposals bode well for the industry," Nicolai said.

"The timing is perfect," Jensen said.

"Precisely why we must file our ZuriMax submission while the political will is strong," Nicolai said.

"Send me a copy of Baker's testimony, Nick," Cal said. He stepped over next to Jensen. "And let me know when you have time to discuss the Academy agenda." Cal turned for the door. "Gentlemen, I'll leave you to the details."

The door closed.

"We have our window of opportunity," Nicolai said. He rose from his chair, pacing once again. "Get the application wrapped up or I will send someone over to handle it. What is the answer regarding your data, Dr. Jensen?"

"I'll amend our agreement, if it eases your mind," Avery said to Jensen.

Nicolai waited while Jensen studied the table.

"I own the intellectual property," Jensen said.

Nicolai hesitated, and then shifted his weight. "And I own you, Dr. Jensen."

Chapter 41

**ATLANTA, GEORGIA
FRIDAY, SEPTEMBER 30
7 A.M. EDT**

Cal pulled a cup out of the cabinet and poured from a steaming coffee pot that was sitting on the bar in the employee lounge. The cup clanked as he set it on a saucer and slid it across the counter.

"Do you see any painkillers back there?" Karl Spears said, cradling his forehead in one hand.

Cal checked the cabinet. "Tough day at the office?" he said, tossing a packet of Advil that landed next to the saucer.

"Yeah, let's call it that," Karl said. He tore open the Advil with his teeth. "I knocked off at four this morning, and I'm about to head back over."

A television hung over the bar, and Cal checked the time on the screen. "You're looking pretty good for only three hours of sleep."

"Try it for a week."

"What you need is a good woman," Cal said with a smile.

"A woman on top of this job would kill me." Karl popped the Advil and washed them down with coffee.

"I'm sure Avery appreciates the sacrifice."

"You would think," Karl said, checking over his shoulder.

"You've done these submissions before. It always comes down to the grind."

"No kidding," Karl said, toying with his cup.

Cal flipped off the television and leaned closer, facing Karl.

"Good morning, guys." Sheri said, waltzing in through the doorway. She was halfway across the room when she stopped and did a three-sixty. "What happened in here?"

"Decompression," Karl said.

"The ZuriMax team seems to have let down their collective hair last night," Cal said.

Sheri flipped a switch, and the lights flickered to life over in the seating area. Carnage was everywhere. Microwave popcorn bags, pizza boxes, and soda cans were strewn across the floor in front of the big screen TV.

"Damn," Sheri said, quickly slapping a hand to her mouth. "Sorry—it looks like a food fight broke out. I'll call housekeeping."

"Can I get you some coffee?" Cal said.

"No thanks, but I need to confirm next week's schedule. Darby and Gil arrive Monday morning, but I don't have them on your calendar."

"Start with a campus tour, and then they can set up their offices. I'll join them for lunch," Cal said.

"New employees?" Karl said.

"Darby Hopkins is our new vice president of marketing, and Gil Carter will be heading up sales," Cal said. "We're moving ZuriMax out to the launching pad."

"Cal, I wanted to speak to you about the files I mentioned last Sunday—"

"How about later?" Cal interrupted.

"I'm sorry. I didn't mean to barge in." Sheri turned on her heels.

"Let's do it Monday afternoon," Cal said, just as she disappeared out the door.

"Sheri's a keeper," Karl said. "She knows how to take care of business."

"Now that you mention it, she could do wonders for you," Cal said. "Should I drop a hint?"

Karl reached into a shirt pocket and extracted a pair of black-framed glasses. He fitted them to his nose, and then swatted a mop of hair hanging in his eyes. "We already tried."

"You look as if you have something on your mind."

"And this comes as a surprise to you?" Karl said, shaking his head.

"Would you like to discuss it?"

Karl leaned against the bar, reaching for his cup and saucer. They rattled, so he set them back on the counter. "What do you know about the attrition issue?"

"Only what was said in last month's meeting."

"That was hearsay," Karl said.

"There's more information now?"

"Have you ever felt like a voice crying out in the wilderness?" Karl's voice wavered.

"So what's the problem?"

"The original patient enrollment was three thousand, give or take. As it turns out, the final submission came in around twenty-five hundred."

"Wait a minute. Are you saying the attrition is linked to ZuriMax?" Cal said.

"The numbers confirm my suspicions," Karl said, looking up at Cal. His eyes were glassy. "But we'll never be able to prove it."

"Have you tried comparing the two data sets?"

"It's not possible."

"Listen, you know as well as I do, this is a controlled study. You're required to report all findings."

"Not if there's only one set of data," Karl said.

"Stop the nonsense, Karl. It's me you're talking to, not Avery. What are you getting at?"

"The original data was destroyed in the fire," Karl said. He adjusted his glasses and rubbed a patch of stubble on his chin.

"Then what makes you think it's attrition?"

"There were no reported deaths in the trial," Karl said. "Choose your poison."

"What else do we know?" Cal said.

"Both groups, ZuriMax and placebo, shrank proportionately."

"One for one?"

"On the money."

"Do you have a printout of the original patient list?" Cal said.

"Are you kidding? We've got more paper shredders in Beta Hut than test tubes."

"What about the FDA field personnel? Are they monitoring all of this?"

"They're grossly understaffed—you know that. The FDA relies on the honor system in most clinics."

"Then maybe it's time we put the question to Avery," Cal said.

"Not advised," Karl said. "I tried your so-called professional approach. After he chewed me out, he informed me that my job was to compile the submission with the data as reported from the clinics."

"What would you like me to do? Avery is responsible for the ZuriMax approval, but I'll help in any way I can."

Karl glanced at his watch, and then slid off the stool. He didn't bother to look at Cal. "I'd better get back to the lab." He took a couple of steps, and then stopped. "And I'd appreciate it if you didn't say anything to Avery, at least until I have time to study it a bit more."

* * *

Acorns popped beneath Karl's shoes as he descended the path to the recreation area. He stopped for a look back at the glowing strand of landscape lights that twisted up the hill to Alpha Hut. A little further ahead, he found solid footing on the wooden deck where halos floated around the lights mounted atop the railing. In a corner overhanging the river, he spotted Avery.

"Nothing like fresh air," Avery said as Karl approached.

"I've got a reservation at Hotel Zuritech, so don't even try to talk me into going back to work. Besides, it's Friday night. If I want to clear my head, I'll do it with a pitcher of beer over at Taco Mac."

"I'd prefer you stay focused," Avery said.

"That's why I'm going to bed. When everyone else in this town is sleeping in tomorrow, I'll be chipping away at the salt mines. What's on your mind?"

"You're a good man, Karl."

"Avery, it's late."

"Do you mind if I offer a bit of advice?"

"Last time I checked, I work for you."

Avery turned for a view of the river, but the darkness presented only flashes of whitewater. "I want you to back off the data issues."

"Listen, I don't—"

"Right now," Avery interrupted. "Give me your word."

Karl gripped the rail and said nothing.

"I was afraid of that," Avery said, dropping his chin. He turned to leave, but then stopped. "I want you to take a long look at the rapids out there. That's the reality you're facing, my friend." He paused to see if the comment would draw a reaction, but Karl remained silent. Avery hurried up the path.

Karl anchored his elbows on the railing and closed his eyes. Behind him, he heard footsteps and cocked his head sideways, fully expecting to see Avery standing there ready to have another go at him. A shadow entered his peripheral vision, but before he could turn, a pair of hands locked around his waist.

The attacker slammed Karl's body against the railing and knocked the wind out of him. He gasped for breath, but was immediately thrown to the deck. His consciousness fluttered into a dreamlike state as he felt himself lifted into the air and turned upside-down like a ragdoll. The sensation of rushing water surrounded him, overpowering his senses. And then everything went black.

Chapter 42

ATLANTA, GEORGIA
SATURDAY, OCTOBER 1
9 A.M. EDT

Kate dropped the bag of bagels. They missed the countertop and hit the floor as she froze in place with her mouth hanging open. Cal descended the companionway steps to find her in a state of shock. With one look at the salon, he went into motion, first checking the aft cabin.

"Holly!" Cal called out.

Kate didn't move a muscle as the forward cabin door inched open, and Holly stepped out.

"Hi guys," Holly said with a grin on her face.

"Don't scare me like that," Kate said. She placed a hand over her heart.

"Sorry, I was getting dressed."

"What happened in here?" Cal said.

The salon looked as if a piñata had burst. Clothes, shoes, books, and kitchenware were everywhere.

"We thought someone had broken in," Kate said, picking up a couple of tumblers. She reached over and deposited them in the galley sink.

"Bad habit—sorry," Holly said. She scrunched her nose and started picking up. "I've got coffee on the stove, if anyone is interested."

Cal took another look inside the aft cabin as Sheri and Singh Lee came clamoring down the steps.

"The bad habit is in there, too," Cal said, backing out of the doorway.

Sheri dropped a grocery sack on the counter. "Isn't there a law that requires sunshine at the lake on Saturdays," she said, turning in time to spot Holly pulling a thong off the door handle. Raising her eyebrows, she elbowed Cal. "What's going on?"

Singh Lee caught a glimpse of the scene and clung to the bottom step, like she was deciding whether to leave or not.

"Don't jab me," Cal said, grabbing his side. "Talk to her."

Kate picked up a pair of jeans and tossed them aside, only to uncover more underwear. "It's not Cal's fault," Kate said to Sheri. "He doesn't wear thongs."

Sheri's eye's popped as she turned to Singh Lee, who slapped a hand over her mouth.

"That's right, poke fun at the man," Cal said, stepping out of Kate's way. She dropped silverware into the sink. "I'm probably the only person on this boat that doesn't wear them."

"I'm so sorry," Holly said. Her face turned red.

Kate hitched a hand on her hip. "Care to explain how you know that?" she said to Cal.

Cal's iPhone rang. "No, I do not. But I will have coffee." He climbed the steps and disappeared up top.

When Cal returned, the women were sitting around the table with coffee and bagels. He poured himself a cup and slid in next to Kate on the settee. "I checked the weather, and I'm afraid sailing's out for today. It's probably best, anyway. We have a lot of ground to cover." He checked his watch. "And we're waiting for one more person."

"What's *her* name?" Kate said. She bit down on her lip to keep from laughing.

"Hey, is it my fault I'm surrounded by gorgeous women?" Cal said. He grabbed Kate and kissed her forehead. "But it's not a bad way to spend a Saturday. If the sun comes out, it's going to look like spring break up on deck."

"Yeah, well if I see a bikini today, someone's going to walk the plank," Kate said.

"Kate, don't threaten our guests," Cal said.

"I was referring to you, Captain Hunter."

"Woo-hoo," the women all chimed in unison.

"Ahoy," a voice called from outside. Everyone piped down. "Anybody home?"

"Sit tight," Cal said, sliding out of his seat.

Cal returned with Tony Harkins and made introductions. Afterwards, he gathered the group around the salon table, just as Sheri cracked a joke about Harkins's suit.

Cal waited for the humor to pass, and then said, "Okay, listen up. It's critical that nothing said here leaves the premises. As the saying goes, 'loose lips sink ships'." He eyed each person, one by one. "Now, I've asked Tony to brief us on what he has learned about ZuriMax so far."

"Sorry, I wasn't advised of the dress code," Harkins said. He lifted the lapel of his jacket. "As Cal mentioned, I am an attorney in Los Angeles. I first contacted him about a client named Roberto Perez who came to see me regarding a medical problem, shall we say. When I attempted to conduct a follow-up with the client, I was unable to locate him. After several attempts, I decided to pay a visit to his apartment in Anaheim. The place was locked up tight, so I spoke to the manager. With a little help from Andrew Jackson, the manager admitted that he had moved out. Only thing is, he said two guys in a van emptied the apartment, not Roberto."

"So he still hasn't attempted to contact you?" Cal said.

"That's right—and the reason for my suspicion. But there's one more thing that's odd. The manager showed me Roberto's car in the parking lot. Evidently, he moved so fast that he forgot to take it with him."

"Wait a minute," Holly said. "Are you the one who went to Jana's apartment?"

"That's right, darling. I haven't established a connection, but you make a good point. Jana's place was tossed pretty good," Harkins said. He reached inside his jacket and pulled out a cigarette.

"Not on my boat," Kate said.

Harkins took one look at Kate and put the cigarette away.

"Anyway, we've got two people missing and an attempted kidnapping," Cal said, looking over at Holly.

"Not to mention, people are dead," Harkins said.

The cabin grew silent.

"Is there something you haven't told me?" Kate said, eyeing Cal.

"Who's dead?" Holly said.

"Holly, he's not referring to Jana. Tony has a theory about two deaths in California linked to ZuriMax," Cal said.

"That's right, they both took the drug," Harkins said.

"Just a minute. Let's not jump to conclusions. It was a medication resembling ZuriMax," Cal said. "It's entirely possible that someone created a knock-off using the same actives. After all, the APIs were invented by a third party. And legally speaking, only patients enrolled in the clinical trial had access to ZuriMax. Sheri checked the patient list, and neither of the deceased was enrolled."

"Any chance the ZuriMax was stolen?" Singh Lee said.

"Now, that's what I'm thinking," Harkins said. "There's an underground market for prescription drugs, and it's quite large."

"Supplies are closely monitored during a trial," Cal said. "Besides, there were no reported deaths from the thousands legally using ZuriMax."

"What about the names Jana sent?" Holly said. "Didn't she suspect patients were being dropped from the clinical trial?"

"Good point," Cal said, turning to Harkins. "I've got more names for you to research."

"That's what I'm here for," Harkins said.

"Which brings us to something I've learned just this week . . . one of our scientists believes there has been a high rate of attrition in the trial. If he were able to prove it, it might corroborate Jana's story. Problem is, he doesn't have any tangible evidence," Cal said.

"Interesting," Harkins said. "Can I talk to this guy?"

"I'm not ready for that, yet. Give me your questions, and I'll see what I can do," Cal said. "I've also got a former Zuritech employee that needs checking out."

"I can help, Mr. Harkins," Holly said. "And no charge this time."

"You're a good sport," Harkins said. He rolled his head for a look at Singh Lee. "What's your story, darling?"

The cabin fell silent once again. There was steady clanking topside as a breeze unsettled the rigging.

"I told you, she works for me," Cal said. "Let's leave it at that for now."

"Are you from California?" Harkins said, still staring.

"Yes, how did you know?" Singh Lee said. Her eyes darted to Cal. "Did you? . . . I need a word with you in the forward cabin."

Chapter 43

**ATLANTA, GEORGIA
SUNDAY, OCTOBER 2
6 A.M. EDT**

Cal checked up and down the hallway, and then punched the keypad until it beeped. He eased the door open, giving the room a once-over as light spilled in from the hall. There was a distinct hum in the bowels of the darkness, but no signs of life as he motioned for Singh Lee to follow him inside. She slipped through the opening, closing the door behind her.

Rows of overhead lights clicked on in sequence as motion detectors sensed their presence. Once fully lit, Cal and Singh Lee stood in front of a five foot high rack of computer equipment that spanned the width of the room. Cool air jetted up through tiny holes in the raised panel flooring beneath their feet.

"The server is behind that rack," Cal said.

"What about the security code you just used?" Singh Lee said. "Won't they know it was you?"

"It's not mine," Cal said. "Sheri gave it to me and told me not to ask questions."

They rounded one end of the rack and started down a gap between it and the back wall. Cal's pace quickened.

"This is it," he said, reaching into his pocket. He studied a computer sitting on the floor as he pulled out a pair of surgical gloves. It had a black cover and was only about four inches high and fifteen inches in length.

"I don't know, Cal. It looks pretty bad to me," Singh Lee said. She stooped down and reached out with her hand.

"Don't touch it," Cal said in a low voice. "Use the gloves. I don't want fingerprints on the box."

"What if it sets off an alarm when we open it?" Singh Lee said. "My friend in Zurich says they install only the best technology."

"The guy you bribed?" Cal said. He tugged on a glove and let go. It popped against his wrist.

"Sort of—we went out a couple of times when I was over training with Martin. And you're a fine one to comment. What about this Harkins guy? He gives me the creeps."

"For the last time, I didn't ask him to check you out," Cal said. "You convinced me you were telling the truth, remember?"

"Totally," Singh Lee said. "But let him snoop around, if it makes you feel better."

"Did this boyfriend warn you about alarms in the system?"

"He never used the word *alarm*. Of course, most of the time I didn't know what he was talking about. He did mention something about audit trails." Singh Lee pulled on a pair of gloves.

Cal took out his iPhone, inserted a pair of earbuds and dialed. "I'm calling our IT contractor," he said to Singh Lee.

"Hi Cal, your running behind schedule," Chase said. "Are you in?"

"We're standing in front of the server now, Chase."

"How's she looking?"

"Like a toasted marshmallow," Cal said. He sat down on the floor. "Singh Lee was just asking if the server might be wired into security."

"Let's play it safe and take a look to see if there are any wires connected," Chase said.

Cal turned the server around for a better look. Then he checked the wall for outlets, but found nothing except a bundle of cables snaking out of the floor a few feet away. He glanced over at the computer rack where the cables were plugged in to a square box.

"No connections, Chase," Cal said.

"Awesome. Now, see if you can locate a name or model number on the front panel."

"Right there," Singh Lee said, pointing. She got down on her knees.

"Yeah, but it's charbroiled," Cal said. "Here, I'll hold it up for you."

Cal lifted the front edge of the server, angling it upwards. Singh Lee rubbed a finger back and forth, revealing a silver plate.

"PowerBlade T9000," Singh Lee said.

"Did you hear that?" Cal said to Chase.

"PowerBlade T9000—got it," Chase said. "That's good news. Do you have a screwdriver?"

Reaching into his back pocket, Cal said, "Go."

"There are screws at each of the front corners. Remove them and tell me when you're done."

Cal suddenly froze.

"What is it?" Singh Lee said.

Footsteps drifted in from the hallway and stopped outside the door, followed by a muffled conversation. Without warning, the door rattled, and Singh Lee jumped. She clamped a hand over her mouth as she heard laughter, and then the footsteps proceeding down the hall.

"What's next, Chase?" Cal said. He motioned for Singh Lee to hold the box in place while he worked with the screwdriver.

"The front panel should snap out," Chase said, pausing. "Tell me what you see."

Cal set the panel aside, exposing a maze of circuit boards and wires.

"It appears to be in better shape inside, but the wires are melted together in places," Cal said.

"Okay, in the front left corner you'll see a metal box with a green power display. That's the disk drive. A pair of spring clips will be holding it in place."

"Land ho," Cal said.

"What?" Chase said.

"Sailing term, sorry," Cal said. He set down the screwdriver and tried to grip the drive. "My fingers are too big to get around it. You try."

Cal held the outside of the server while Singh Lee slipped her fingers around the edges of the drive. She gave a tug. And then another.

"It's stuck," Singh Lee said. She pulled again, this time with her full body weight, but it didn't budge.

"The clips are melted in place," Cal said, leaning for a look inside. "I'm not sure this is going to work, Chase."

"Okay, let's stay focused," Chase said. "The T9000 is top of the line. With the outside case intact, I'd be blown away if that drive is damaged. Cal, take the screwdriver, and see if you can pry the clips free from the casing."

Cal grabbed the screwdriver as Singh Lee secured the server once again. He inserted it between the clip and casing, and then used the palm of his hand to pound it in. There was a pop. Pulling the screwdriver free, Cal inserted it on the opposite side and repeated the process. When he was done, he signaled for Singh Lee to try again.

With another tug, the disk drive broke free from the clips. Singh Lee removed the drive from the casing and turned it over to reveal a pair of wires tethered to the box. She found a plastic connector at the base, but it wouldn't give.

"The wires inside the plug are melted to the casing," Cal said.

"The wires are expendable," Chase said. "Do you have a pair of needle-nose pliers?"

"Check," Cal said.

"Use the pliers to cut the wires."

"Cut them—where?" Cal said.

"Anywhere. It doesn't matter," Chase said.

There was a snip, and Singh Lee hoisted the drive up in the air. "Land ho," she said, smiling at Cal.

"Mission accomplished, Chase. We're done," Cal said.

"Not so fast," Chase said. "I want you to reattach the front plate and position the server box just as you found it. Computer techs are trained to notice details, so let's play it safe."

"We'll finish up, and I'll have Sheri deliver the disk drive to you," Cal said.

"Have her bring it to my house," Chase said.

Cal hung up and reassembled the server. When he was done, Singh Lee helped him off the floor and headed for the door. Cal was about to follow after her when he remembered the cables. He looked back at the hole in the floor. "Hold on," he said, turning around.

As he drew closer, Cal noticed that a floor panel had been removed. He felt a surge of air coming from the opening as his eyes traced the wires to the server rack. He walked over and squatted down to study a label. It read: *Universal Power Supply*.

"What's wrong?" Singh Lee said.

Cal pivoted, dropping to his hands and knees for a look beneath the floor. His head disappeared inside the hole.

"These cables are feeding into something," Cal said, lifting his head out. "What's on the other side of the wall?"

"I don't know," Singh Lee said. She frowned like she didn't understand.

"They're attached to that power supply," Cal said, pointing to the server rack. "I'm no expert, but that's a lot of juice being piped somewhere."

Cal hopped to his feet, inching further along the wall past the cables. When he reached the back corner, he noticed a thin groove in an otherwise solid wall. He ran a finger down the line, stopping about waist high.

Singh Lee hurried over. "This place is starting to give me the creeps."

"Singh Lee, do you see what I see?" Cal focused on the outline of a large rectangle. He retraced the line until he felt a raised spot. "And look at this."

Singh Lee squeezed in. "It is a keypad. Only it's built into the wall so you barely notice it." She reached out.

Cal grabbed her hand, but then turned loose and made his way back to the hole, dropping to his knees. He stretched his arm underneath the floor and gave a punch. The floor panel next to the cables popped out.

"What are you doing?" Singh Lee said.

"Finding out what's on the other side of this wall."

Chapter 44

ATLANTA, GEORGIA
SUNDAY, OCTOBER 2
7 A.M. EDT

Lighting the display on his phone, Cal lowered it into the opening and buried his head beneath the floor panels.

"First you're going to try the keypad, right?" Singh Lee said, now standing over him.

"I don't see light on the other side," Cal said. He pulled his head out of the hole.

"Cal, are you listening to me?"

"It's too risky," Cal said. "I have an idea."

"What about Sheri's secret code?"

Cal remained on the floor. "I don't think so. That keypad looks like the one on our dishwasher."

"What is that supposed to mean?"

"I always push the wrong buttons," Cal said. "Kate doesn't let me operate it, anymore."

Singh Lee threw up her hands. "Tell me you're just screwing with me."

"I'm going under the floor to see what's back there. You let me know if you hear anything out here." Cal slid into the opening, headfirst. Once his waist disappeared, he suddenly stopped. Seconds later, he came wiggling out.

"You're just going to leave me out here, alone?" Singh Lee said.

Cal shook his head. "Change of plan. You're going under the wall."

"Wait . . . what? I'm not crawling around down there."

"Spare me the drama. You slipped Ecstasy into Martin's drink when you were in Zurich," Cal said. "This is no riskier."

"He was already drunk when I got to his office." Singh Lee said, eyeing the cables. "Anyway, I could be electrocuted by one of those wires."

"The studs in the wall extend beneath the floor. My shoulders are too wide to fit between them," Cal said. "Think of it as a wine cellar."

"Can I try the keypad first?"

Cal handed her the phone. "Use it for light."

Singh Lee swapped the disk drive for the iPhone and dropped to her knees, first lowering her head into the darkness, then her shoulders. "Hold me up so I can turn over on my back," she called out.

Cal reached down and cradled his hands around her waist while she rolled. Then he gently lowered her until only her feet were sticking out. He watched as the phone display lit up the darkness.

"Okay, push on my feet while I squeeze through," Singh Lee said.

Cal nudged her along until she was out of reach. "Don't touch anything without first talking to me," he said, sticking his head below the floor again.

"The cables are going up into another room," Singh Lee said. "I'm removing a floor panel." She let out a couple of grunts. "The lights are coming on."

Her words grew fainter as panels rattled on the other side of the wall.

"Singh Lee," Cal called out. He heard footsteps, but no response.

"You're not going to believe this," Singh Lee finally said.

"I'm listening," Cal said.

"There's a bank of security monitors on the wall. I can see live feeds from the employee lounge, the boardroom, your office and—oh, my God."

"What is it?" Cal said.

"It's Hotel Zuritech—room seven. And get this. One of the scientists is asleep in the bed. He's—he's—wearing SpongeBob Square Pants boxers."

"Forget about the boxers. Anything else?" Cal said.

"Hold on. I just noticed a second monitor wired into your office."

"There are two cameras in my office?"

"Are you sitting down?"

"My head's in the hole. What do you see?"

"The label under the monitor says it's your office at home." Singh Lee heard a bump on Cal's side. "What was that?"

"I hit my head," Cal said. "Take another look around to make sure you didn't miss anything."

He waited for what seemed like eternity.

"Cal, there are more monitors in Alpha Hut and Beta Hut. One is inside the computer room. I can see your backside sticking out of the hole," Singh Lee said, giggling.

"Come on . . . what else?"

"I see boat docks on four of the monitors, and then there's another that's displaying what looks like a warehouse," Singh Lee said. "Oh, and in the corner, listening equipment. Don't hold me to it, but it looks like they've bugged your house."

"Can you find a pen and write all this down?" Cal said.

"I've already checked. There's nothing."

"Okay, try this. Do you know how to use the camera on my phone?"

"Seriously?"

"Just do it."

Ten minutes later, the phone appeared, and then Singh Lee's head popped out of the opening. "This wasn't exactly in the job description when I hired on," she said, shaking her head like a dog. "Do I have anything on me?"

Cal leaned over and swatted her hair a couple of times. "There's nothing wrong with an honest day's work." He took the phone and grabbed her hand, helping her up.

Singh Lee brushed off her jeans as Cal dropped the floor panel back into place. After a final inspection of the area, Cal led the way out. Passing down the hall and through the lobby, they headed for Cal's car.

Once inside the Range Rover, Cal slid the disk drive under the seat, and then scrolled through the pictures on the phone.

"What are these guys doing?" Cal said.

"Whatever it is, it doesn't look good," Singh Lee said. "Some of the cameras are in strange places."

"Maybe we should lay out the photos for a better look," Cal said. "I can load them on my computer."

"But not in either of your offices."

"Good point," Cal said. He started the engine. "I just realized the lab doesn't adjoin the computer room."

"What do you mean?"

"Security claimed that chemicals from the lab destroyed the server. That doesn't make sense based on what we just found on the other side of that wall. Besides, nothing else in the computer room was damaged."

"No arguments here," Singh Lee said, lifting up off the seat. "One more thing." Reaching around, she pulled out a DVD case and handed it to Cal.

"What's this?" He popped it open.

"The video of Hotel Zuritech from two Thursdays ago—room seven."

Chapter 45

ATLANTA, GEORGIA
MONDAY, OCTOBER 3
9 A.M. EDT

Lightning flashed in the distance, and Cal counted in anticipation of the rumble in its wake. He stared out of the window at the gray morning, where water poured off the roof like Niagara Falls. The thunder boomed.

Getting up from his desk, Cal stepped out of his office to find Sheri hanging up the telephone.

"Don't leave," Sheri said. The color had drained from her face. "That was security. There's a detective on his way in to see you."

Cal stood silent at first, but then said, "Where's the disk drive?"

"Chase has it."

Returning to his office, Cal reappeared with the DVD case. "Take this to Singh Lee, and tell her to get it off campus. And warn her not to speak to anyone."

"Where are you going?"

"To meet the detective," Cal said. He headed down the hallway.

After introductions, Cal ushered the detective into the boardroom. Before he could speak, his iPhone rang. He glanced at the display—it was Sheri.

"Yes," he answered.

"Cal, there are two officers down by the river," Sheri said.

"Thanks." Cal hung up and offered the detective a seat. He mentally clicked through yesterday's operation, rehearsing.

"Dr. Hunter, I apologize for the imposition," the detective said.

Why are you inspecting the recreation area? Cal thought.

"Do you know Dr. Karl Spears?" the detective said.

"Karl, of course," Cal said.

"I'm afraid I have bad news. Dr. Spears was found dead yesterday evening at Stone Bridge Park."

Cal came out of his seat, clinging to the conference table for support. He exhaled. "What happened?"

"His body washed up on the bank. The coroner's preliminary examination indicates he was in the river all weekend."

"I just spoke to him on Friday," Cal said. He stepped away from the table.

"That's my understanding . . . Friday morning."

Cal cut his eyes.

"We spoke to Dr. Avery Messinger last night. He seems to recall that you and Dr. Spears had an argument in the employee lounge."

"An argument?" Cal said. He ran a hand through his hair, suddenly remembering the video monitors.

"He told us Dr. Spears arrived at work shaken up, apparently over an exchange between the two of you. What was it about?"

"I have no idea what he's talking about," Cal said. He sat back down. "Did he say anything else?"

The detective's walkie-talkie crackled, and then a voice paged him.

"Go ahead," the detective said into the walkie-talkie.

"The deck railing's broken next to the river. It's possible someone went into the water down here."

"Any evidence that might point to Dr. Spears?" the detective said.

"Negative. There's low visibility, and the rain's pounding us."

"Seal off the area, and head back in. We'll get photos when the rain stops," the detective said.

"I've only worked with Karl for about two months . . . since I came to work here," Cal said.

"Dr. Messinger says he's working on your new drug."

"That's right," Cal said. "But Karl works for Avery, not me."

"Dr. Messinger indicated that Dr. Spears didn't show up for his shift on Saturday or Sunday. The story confirms the coroner's time of death."

"He would be in a position to know."

"We checked the sign-in log for the building next door. It indicates that you and someone else entered on Sunday morning."

"That's right," Cal said.

"Were you looking for Dr. Spears?"

"Why would you think that?"

"What were you doing in the building, Dr. Hunter?"

"I'm CEO of the company."

"But why were you on campus yesterday—a Sunday?"

"Singh Lee and I came in to check on the project team. They've been working around the clock, so we stopped by for moral support," Cal said.

"Dr. Messinger asked around, and no one remembers seeing you."

"We went downstairs to the break room, but it was empty. We waited around for a while, and no one showed."

"Dr. Hunter, you were in the building for almost two hours," the detective said. The walkie-talkie came to life again.

"We've just entered the building, but the rain has stopped. We're headed back down," the voice on the walkie-talkie said.

"We camped out in one of the conference rooms," Cal said. "There was other business to discuss."

"And we've got dozens of scientists running around in the building and not a single one sees you."

Cal pushed back from the table and stood up. He pulled out a business card, handing it to the detective. "I'm going down to take a look at the river."

* * *

Cal climbed down the steps into the salon aboard *Coastal Confessions* where Holly was busy at a MacBook. "All right, talk to me," he said, sliding onto the settee next to her.

"You should check out the new iPhone," Holly said. "It's cool and has better resolution."

"Will do," Cal said.

"And I'm going to clean the cabin, so don't—"

"Holly."

"Okay, okay. Just chill, the pictures are right here. What do you want to see?"

A series of thumbnails appeared on the computer screen.

"That's great, right there. Let's start by labeling the photos. The first one is the *Alpha Hut Lobby*. Next is the *Boardroom*, then the *Employee Lounge*—"

"Slow down," Holly interrupted. She finished typing.

"*Cal's Office—Beta Hut Lobby—Beta Hut Conference Room—*"

"That's too long," Holly said. "I'll abbreviate."

"Suit yourself. *Avery's Office—Computer Room*. Can you enlarge that one?" Cal pointed.

"How's that?" Holly said.

"Looks great. Let's call it *Cal's Home Office*. The camera must be mounted on my bookcase. It's a perfect shot of the desk." Cal touched the screen.

Holly promptly slapped his finger away. "Don't smear my display."

"Unbelievable," Cal said, looking around the cabin. "And you're worried about a messy computer screen?"

"Personal—computer," Holly said, pointedly. Then she dropped her chin and gave Cal the cow eyes.

"Personal sailboat," Cal said, making a sweep of the salon with a hand. He laughed.

"Do you want me to clean up or finish with the pictures?"

"Five more," Cal said. "Enlarge the next one. Okay, these appear to be new monitors. See how they're tagged with sticky notes instead of plaques. Label the first one *Miami*. It looks like a marina. What are they monitoring in Miami?"

"More like the Port of Miami," Holly said. "Look at those cruise ships in the background."

"Sharp eyes," Cal said. "Then we have *New York—Los Angeles*—and *San Francisco*. They're all seaports."

"Wait a minute. Take a look at Miami again." Holly enlarged the photo, zooming in on a section. That sign says *American Dream*. Do you think it's important?"

"I don't know, but it's something to look into. Remind me to buy us both a new iPhone," Cal said. "Okay, label the last one *Newark*, and then zoom in on whatever that is on the wall."

"It's a banner. Here, let me blow it up some more." Holly clicked and scrolled. "It looks like *Rx Free*, but the end is cropped off."

"Check with Tony to see if any of this makes sense," Cal said. "And find out when he wants to meet again."

"He's scheduled to be here on Wednesday." Holly stopped typing and turned, facing Cal. "If he asks, please don't let him bunk on the boat."

"I thought you were freaking out over being aboard alone with Walker," Cal said.

"Yeah, but at least he's not a smoking sleazeball."

"Are you sure?"

"I'll clean the cabin and swab the decks," Holly said. She clasped her hands under her chin, prayer-like. "Please."

Cal stuffed a hand in his pocket and pulled out a Ziploc bag, dropping it on the table. "Put those away until Tony arrives."

"Glasses—why are they in a bag?"

"Google the name Karl Spears, and you'll find out. Tell Tony to do the same." Cal stood up. "You're still going to class, right?" He walked over to the companionway steps.

"Three days a week. And I'm taking the long route, just like we discussed."

"I'll work on the sleeping arrangements." Cal headed up top.

Chapter 46

**ATLANTA, GEORGIA
TUESDAY, OCTOBER 4
10 A.M. EDT**

Darby Hopkins was wrapping up a discussion with Cal when Gil Carter came scrambling down the hall with a briefcase slung over his shoulder. He blew past his own office and made a line for Darby's as Cal backed out of the doorway.

"Sorry I missed the meeting," Gil said, huffing.

Darby paused mid-sentence.

"I have five minutes. Let's step inside," Cal said.

"Our four year old pitched a tantrum this morning, right before an appointment with the real estate broker, which threw us into rush hour traffic and ticked off the sellers, and well, you get the picture," Gil said. He dropped the briefcase on Darby's conference table.

"Cal was just covering the short-term objectives," Darby said.

"Let's run through them quickly," Cal said. "Gil, I want you to take a look at the ZuriMax sales forecast that I e-mailed to both of you this morning. I need revised projections based on the assumption that we launch in six months with a restenosis indication."

"When will we begin promoting the broader claims?" Gil said.

"Assume fifteen months from now," Cal said. "And ramp the headcount accordingly."

"Cal's sending us the password for IMS access," Darby said.

"It won't be much help for restenosis, but we can review market trends for our projections," Gil said.

"Precisely," Cal said. "I've asked Darby to meet with Avery Messinger and Albert Jensen to work on the Academy presentations. While she's doing that, you can take a look at field force costs for the launch. Be sure to nail down estimates for product samples."

"Is there a preliminary budget?" Gil said.

"It's in the e-mail," Cal said. He opened the door. "Have Sheri send you my notes from last month's advisory panel."

"Are you free for lunch?" Darby said. "I'd like to drill into the details."

"I'm afraid not," Cal said. "Talk to Sheri about getting on my calendar." He disappeared through the doorway.

Three doors down, Cal turned into Singh Lee's office and closed the door behind him. Singh Lee was seated across the room at a conference table. "Are you sure it's okay to meet in here?"

"You know as much as I do," Cal said.

"I hope you don't mind, but I thought it best not to put together a presentation."

"Good thinking. Let's not take unnecessary risks. Now, you promised to explain Aviation and Trading."

Singh Lee swatted bangs out of her face. "Partially explain them," she said. "I managed to secure full administrative rights to the SAP system with the assistance of my friend—"

"About that," Cal interrupted. "Are you certain this guy won't sell you short?"

"I'd say he's more likely to burn down the Zurich headquarters than rat me out," Singh Lee said with a smile. "Anyway, let's start with Zuritech Aviation Corporation. The data suggests that cash flows into Aviation from Zuritech Trading Corporation."

"Good to know. Trading generates the cash," Cal said. "Was it currency hedging as you suspected?"

"Trading doesn't appear to sell or produce anything that would generate cash. But there are fund transfers into Trading from a UBS numbered account that belongs to a Swiss subsidiary of Zuritech AG."

"Nothing illegal, I take it?"

"Technically, no. But you may want to check with Nate," Singh Lee said. "There's one additional step. It seems the UBS account is funded by another numbered account in Grand Cayman, but the trail grows cold at that point."

"As a precaution, maybe you should extract the information out of the system—just in case we get cut off again." Cal eyed Singh Lee's computer on the desk.

"Uh, you're not going to like this. I don't have access."

Cal glared across at Singh Lee. "That's why I sent you to Zurich."

"I know, I know. But no one in the States has access to non-US data. My friend says he can't cover my tracks over here."

"Wait a minute . . ." Cal paused. "You told me Aviation and Trading are US subsidiaries."

"That's true, but as it turns out, they're also Grand Cayman chartered companies," Singh Lee said. "And don't ask me to explain."

"So the Grand Cayman bank account belongs to Trading?"

"There's no way to be certain. From what I've seen, it doesn't appear to belong to any of the subsidiaries. I managed to lift the Grand Cayman account number off an inbound wire to the UBS account. But when I searched the Zuritech treasury subsystem for the account, it wasn't there."

Cal sat silent for a moment.

"Nate said I shouldn't worry about US subsidiaries since I don't have signature rights."

Singh Lee made a face.

"What?" Cal said.

"That may be the legal opinion, but accountants don't look at it that way. In fact, the IRS will be much more aggressive if they decide to audit the books."

"Meaning, we're a couple of sitting ducks. But you raise a critical issue. Nate never mentioned that these were Grand Cayman corporations. Where has he been, anyway?" Cal leaned back in his chair, not waiting for a response. "You're positive you can't get into the system?"

"Only if I return to Zurich," Singh Lee said. "There's one more thing, Cal. When I spent those first weeks with Martin, he was working on a new US investment strategy."

"The investment strategy hasn't changed since I arrived."

"Well, you may want to check your stock options."

"Just a minute, there is a new option plan," Cal said. "I was the first to receive grants under it."

"Which means every employee before you is in a different plan," Singh Lee said. "I'm willing to bet that the company reserved the right to convert your options to a new class of US shares."

"Suggesting what?" Cal said. "They're positioning the US company for an IPO?"

"Martin told me that Nate's expertise is in initial public offerings—"

"Let's not get carried away. They've staked the future of Zuritech on the US," Cal said.

"Companies change strategies all the time," Singh Lee said.

"If what you're saying is true, he may be planning to take the money and run."

"I'm not sure I follow you."

"Martin could be setting up Zuritech Corporation as a short-term play. We launch ZuriMax while Zuritech AG pulls the trigger on an IPO and cashes out."

"But we both know that's crazy," Singh Lee said. "The real value in ZuriMax lies further down the road . . . after we hit full stride."

"And there's no apparent shortage of cash, especially when you realize Martin is engaged in offshore trading and acquiring corporate jets."

"Maybe we've overlooked the obvious—it's a tax maneuver."

"Or Martin wants us to think that," Cal said. "Tax strategies don't typically involve hidden video cameras. Has anything turned up on Nick?"

"Just a feeling," Singh Lee said. She slipped out of the chair and walked over to her desk where she unplugged a USB drive from the computer. "I've got eight gigs of electronic files from Zurich to comb through." She squeezed the drive in her hand, and then leaned over and pulled a DVD case out of her briefcase. "And I'd feel better if you did something with this." She rounded the desk.

"Let's get everything off campus," Cal said, taking the DVD. "Have Holly make a copy of the drive. She can help with the research."

"And the DVD?" Singh Lee said, reaching to retrieve it.

Cal gripped it tight. "Not a chance. This train wreck stays with me."

Singh Lee gave Cal a second look. "I hate to be the bearer of bad news, but Martin has a copy of the video."

"One more reason to find out what he's hiding," Cal said.

Chapter 47

**ATLANTA, GEORGIA
WEDNESDAY, OCTOBER 5
3 A.M. EDT**

The office was dark when Cal entered. He felt his way around a chair, and then dropped to his knees and slid a DVD recorder under the desk. With one hand, he grabbed the end of a cable, backing out far enough to raise up and settle into the chair. Swiveling around, he flipped on a lamp before turning to the desk again.

Wasting no time, Cal poked his head beneath the desk a second time and located a series of ports on the computer. He separated three connectors on the cable, but soon discovered there wasn't enough light to match the color-coding to the computer ports. Pulling out his phone, he lit the display and fumbled with the connectors until all three were plugged in. Next, he made sure there was a disc in the recorder and hit the power button.

Cal booted the computer and checked the time. He did a sweep of the room, and then hopped up to close the door before returning to his seat. When he returned, the computer display bathed the desktop in soft light. He grabbed the mouse and clicked an icon that launched a videoconferencing screen.

Images of Nate Friedman and Thomas Jacobs seated behind a table in Zurich appeared on the display. Nate's mouth was moving, but he couldn't hear the conversation. Cal leaned forward. "Good morning, gentlemen."

"Quite early in America, isn't it old man," Thomas said, after pressing a button on his remote. He turned to face the video cam. "How about a spot of coffee?" He held up a carafe.

"I have a pot brewing in the kitchen," Cal said. "And yes, it's three o'clock over here."

"But how often do you get to work from home in your pajamas?" Nate said.

Cal tugged on the front of his Kellogg sweatshirt with a smile. "I looked for you at the office yesterday, only to find out you're in Zurich."

"Sorry for the hour, but I'm operating on Swiss time this week," Nate said without further comment. "Tell me what's on your mind before Nicolai joins us."

"First, I wanted to thank you for finalizing Darby and Gil's employment contracts. I couldn't have managed without you." Cal reached beneath the desk and started the recorder.

"You can buy me lunch when I return," Nate said.

"I would like to get the option agreements out today. These guys are nervous," Cal said. "They walked away from a lot of money."

"No kidding," Thomas said. "I did it once and know exactly how that feels."

"I have the paperwork here, somewhere." Nate rifled through a stack of folders. "You're outside the firewall, so I'm afraid I can't send an e-mail. Do you mind a fax?"

Looking over his shoulder, Cal said, "Power's on. Fire away."

"We've finalized the number of options. I'll e-mail originals to your Zuritech office for signature," Nate said.

The fax whirred to life. Cal twisted and retrieved a couple of pages. "Just to be clear, the grants are tied to the publicly traded shares?" Cal said, scanning the top page.

"They're what we call C-class shares," Nate said, and then added, "per Martin."

"Why not common stock?" Cal said.

"I can answer that one," Thomas said. "Martin explained it at Nicolai's last staff meeting. Your new executives have US responsibilities. With so much at stake, Martin feels a special US series better aligns with capitalization initiatives."

"How does that work? Correct me if I'm wrong, only common stock is being traded. The C shares are clearly not marketable," Cal said.

"It's standard practice with international companies," Thomas said. "If you're concerned with valuations, I suggest you take it up with Martin."

"You're certain Martin created the C-class strictly for that purpose?" Cal said.

"Cal, you're a wholly-owned subsidiary," Nate said. "The arrangement supports our corporate strategy—a veil, more or less. Legally speaking, management is shielding the organization from US liability."

"In other words, you're ensuring that liability remains with me and the US board of directors," Cal said.

"Exactly," Nate said. "Anyway, you can see how the interests of the US company better align with those of your new executives."

"As long as you've explained it to Darby and Gil," Cal said.

The door to Cal's office parted, and a steaming cup of coffee slipped through the gap. He smiled and waved. Bumping the door wider, Kate stood in the opening. She gestured at her outfit and shook her head, mouthing, "I can't come over there."

Cal stood up, directing Kate over to the bookshelves where she wouldn't be seen. "Excuse me, gentlemen—technical difficulties," he said, leaning across the desk. When their hands touched, he stretched for a kiss. Kate smiled, and then tip-toed out. Cal returned to his seat.

"Cheers," Cal said, raising the cup to the monitor.

"Call me if there are questions about the options," Nate said. He checked his watch. "Let's get Nicolai in here before we miss the window." He left the room, returning moments later with Nicolai at his side.

Nicolai took a seat.

"Nothing but good news to report this morning, my dear Calvin," Nicolai said.

"Then the roosters will have something to crow about when they get up in a few hours," Cal said.

"Marvelous sense of humor," Nicolai said. "I hope the fortune you're about to make won't spoil you."

"Can't buy me love, Nick," Cal said. He cut his eyes to the door where Kate had departed moments earlier.

"Your American Academy of Cardiology is only a week and a half away," Nicolai said. "Avery and Dr. Jensen have rehearsed their presentations for us."

"I've asked Darby to provide marketing input," Cal said.

"ZuriMax must be on center stage for this meeting," Nicolai said.

"You've seen the plans for Sunday night. Dr. Jensen will speak after dinner, and then he'll present a scientific paper later in the week. The marketing booth is being shipped to the Grand Wailea, as we speak. Zuritech mementos have been arranged for the doctors."

"This I already know. But let's not forget, I intend for this to be a shot that is heard around the world," Nicolai said. "I trust everyone understands. There will be no shortcuts. We offer only the finest gifts for the doctors."

"Nick, the FDA sets limits on this sort of thing," Cal said. "We'll do everything we can."

"I'm sure you won't mind if we bring over a few perks for—"

"Hold on, Nick. That's precisely what I'm talking about," Cal said. "The FDA will—"

"Never know," Nicolai interrupted. "Thomas?"

"Cal, this goes back to our earlier discussion. As I explained, we've created legal separation between the companies. Zuritech AG has no official responsibility for your US marketing plans, so what Nicolai chooses to do on the Swiss books is of no concern to you. You didn't hear it from me, but we've also made arrangements to fly Dr. Jensen to Maui next Thursday. You and the FDA are none the wiser."

"Have you considered what happens if you make the FDA angry?" Cal said.

"What are they going to do, take our product off the market?" Nate said.

"How about a delayed approval?" Cal said.

"We realize our strategy is aggressive. But we've benchmarked best practices, and I must tell you, we are following proven methods," Nicolai said. "Our competitors are formidable, but we intend to be the first to attack."

"What do you mean?" Cal said.

Nicolai held up his hands, feigning indifference. "It means, Dr. Jensen will be presenting scientific evidence—"

"As a highly compensated spokesperson," Cal interrupted.

"Dr. Jensen is a respected researcher. He has every right to present scientific data to his colleagues," Nicolai said.

"But Avery's doing the work," Cal said.

Nicolai pushed back from the table and stood up. Looking down, he formed a pistol with his hand and elevated his chin. There was a moment of hesitation, and then he smiled as he pointed it at the camera. His thumb dropped like a hammer, and he walked out of the room.

"Dr. Jensen's research is solid," Nate said, breaking the silence. "You know how this works, Cal. Any of his colleagues will be happy to vouch for him. If he has contracted Avery to handle certain tasks, why make it an issue?"

"Fax over the agreement. I'd like to review it," Cal said.

"Cal, leave it alone," Nate said. He got up and left.

Chapter 48

ATLANTA, GEORGIA
THURSDAY, OCTOBER 6
9 A.M. EDT

Gil studied the river from his office. Orange and yellow leaves fluttered past the window, reminding him that the water was cold enough to turn skin blue. On the bank, he could just make out a section of deck that had been marked off with crime scene tape.

"I guess it was my turn to be late," Darby said, slipping through the door.

Gil turned as Darby strolled in carrying a leather notebook and Starbucks cup. He tapped the window. "I was thinking how awesome it would be to have WI-FI down at the river. I could send a photo of you and me working on the deck to my Pfizer friends, drinking coffee and analyzing data. How's that sound for eking out a living?"

"Like a man who wants to rub it in. This morning's headlines reported an Arctic blast in the Northeast last night," Darby said. She set the notebook on a conference table and joined Gil at the window.

"But you'll agree, it's not bragging if it's true."

Darby clutched her coffee, taking in the river until her eyes settled on the deck. "That's awful about the dead scientist.

According to Cal, the police think he fell in the river. I wonder what he was doing down there at night?"

"I know one thing he wasn't doing," Gil said.

"How's the hiring plan going?"

"I posted a dozen positions online last night, and my inbox already looks like afternoon gridlock. How am I going to screen nine hundred resumes?"

"Just keep living the dream," Darby said, laughing. "And put in a help desk call for that WI-FI. It looks like you may need it this weekend."

Gil eased over to the table and sat down in front of a computer. "Cal's supposed to drop off our stock options this afternoon. These guys are serious."

"Of course, they're serious."

"No, I mean they're investing ahead of the curve on this launch. They've even hired a spokesperson. I don't know if you ever met the guy, Dr. Albert Jensen. I made sales calls to his office during my early years at Pfizer. The man's on the bleeding-edge of medicine."

"I'm glad to see your sense of humor is intact," Darby said, pulling up a chair.

Gil leaned closer to Darby. "Did you hear about the jet? Cal got a brand-spanking-new Gulfstream when he signed on. The scuttle is, he jets all over the world any time he wants. He's taking it to Maui next week."

"Stop whining and take a look at this office," Darby said. "You've got it good, and you know it. Considering the stock options and company car, I'm fine with Delta Airlines." She rested her hands on the table. "Now, where are we?"

"I reviewed the regional data for torvastatin and found something interesting. There's a crater in the data like I've never seen before. I drilled into the details and discovered that prescriptions in the Southeast are plummeting like a SCUD missile."

"Torvastatin—that's LipidRx," Darby said. "What do you make of it?"

"The free-fall seems to be centered in Florida." Gil offered Darby a look at his display. "What would cause a top selling drug to take a hit like this?"

"There's certainly nothing new on the market, at least until ZuriMax launches," Darby said.

Gil moved the cursor across a color-coded map to California and clicked. A graph popped up on the screen. "There's also a blip in the Pacific region, but nothing material. The same is true for the Northeast."

"It could play to our advantage," Darby said. "If our competitors are losing market share, we may be able to exploit the weakness when we launch."

"The scripts typically grow this time of year in Florida. The snowbirds fly south. You don't think this is a new trend? Maybe the statins have peaked."

"Don't be silly. It's not like people are swearing off French fries all of a sudden."

"Yeah, I know. We'd better get moving on the forecast," Gil said. He stopped typing and slid out of his chair. "But first, let's see if there are any donuts left in the employee lounge."

* * *

Cal pulled the Range Rover up to the curb in front of a craftsman style house. The neighborhood was decades old, but clearly in the midst of a renaissance. A "For Sale" sign was posted on a lawn across the street beneath a row of sprawling oaks lining the sidewalk.

"I should bring Kate down for a look around," Cal said. "Those restaurants we passed a few blocks back looked interesting. Is the area safe?"

"It's called Little Five Points. And yes, you'll be fine," Sheri said, opening the car door. She led Cal up a driveway and around back of the house. In the rear, she climbed a flight of steps to a second floor landing and knocked.

"Hi guys," Chase said, opening the door. "Cal, it's nice to finally meet you."

Chase made eyes at Sheri as Cal stepped inside.

Cal looked around the apartment. From what he could see, it was tiny. The kitchen was more-or-less an extension of the living room. "Very nice."

Chase perked up. "Thanks."

"So you've finished up with the disk drive?" Sheri said. She dropped onto a vinyl sofa.

"Have a seat, Cal," Chase said, gesturing.

"Thanks, but I'll stand." A computer on the kitchen table caught Cal's eye.

"I'm afraid I have some bad news," Chase said. He stepped past the sofa into the kitchen. "Can I get either of you something to drink?"

"Nothing for me," Cal said. He headed for the table as Sheri came off the sofa.

"You told me the project was complete," Sheri said.

"Totally," Chase said, snapping a small black box off the table. He turned to Cal. "The drive was inoperable from the heat damage."

Cal glanced down at the object in Chase's hand.

"But you sounded so happy when you called," Sheri said, squeezing in next to Cal.

"Man, it's like you've never met me or something. That's because you agreed to hang out with me tonight," Chase said. He cut his eyes over to Cal, and then laughed hysterically.

Sheri spun around and stormed back to the sofa, where she flopped down with her arms crossed.

"So what are we doing here?" Cal said.

"I had nothing to do with it," Sheri said.

"Just chill, I'm only kidding," Chase said to Sheri. He handed the box to Cal.

"What's this?" Cal said.

"It's an external disk drive," Chase said, grabbing a cable off the table. "And there's no extra charge for the humor."

Cal took the cable by one end, letting it dangle like a snake.

"Don't be a geek," Sheri said.

"Come on, you've got to admit it's a little funny," Chase said.

"What do I do with this?" Cal said.

Chase watched Sheri out of the corner of his eye as he retrieved the box from Cal. "You plug the cable here. The other end connects to your computer. Once the computer detects the device, you'll have your data."

"So you were only kidding about the bad news?" Cal said.

"Actually, no. That new drive's going to set you back an extra seventy bucks."

Chapter 49

**ATLANTA, GEORGIA
FRIDAY, OCTOBER 7
8 A.M. EDT**

Cal knocked and entered the Beta Hut conference room, unannounced. The morning sun filtered in through the blinds, washing over the polished granite table like a reflecting pool. He glanced at the flat screen on the rear wall, and then to Avery and Albert Jensen who huddled next to a speakerphone.

"Dr. Patel, Cal Hunter has just joined us," Avery said.

"Please continue," Cal said, pulling up a chair next to Jensen.

"As I was saying, one of my staff came across a memo in our archives from a Dr. William Mallory," Dr. Patel said. "In it, he referenced an expanded access application. We were hoping you could shed some light on it."

"Dr. Mallory was my predecessor," Avery said. "I'm afraid his passing has left a gap in our files regarding the initial project plans."

"Dr. Mallory referenced a request to dispense ZuriMax in targeted patient groups while completing phase II of the clinicals," Dr. Patel said.

"To my knowledge, the program was never implemented," Avery said.

"What was the basis for the application?" Cal said.

"I can answer that one," Jensen said. "Bill felt the incidence of deaths brought on by patient non-compliance was avoidable with a combo therapy. As we all know, seniors aren't always consistent when it comes to taking meds. By making ZuriMax available to high risk cases prior to approval, he believed lives would be saved."

"That describes the type of scenario under which the FDA might allow controlled use of a non-approved drug. If we had data from the program, it could help your expedited review," Dr. Patel said.

"The actives in ZuriMax are derived from established drug classes," Avery said. "You should be able to draw correlations from existing treatments."

"Dr. Messinger, I'm sure you appreciate the complexities introduced by a combo therapy. It precludes the ability to make such direct comparisons. Would you agree, Dr. Jensen?" Dr. Patel said.

"You're forgetting, I'm satisfied with the clinical outcomes," Jensen said.

"And you're confident there are no safety issues?" Dr. Patel said.

"That's for the FDA to determine," Jensen said. "But if you're asking will this drug save lives, there's no doubt about it."

"Dr. Patel, I'm afraid Mallory's responsibilities fell to me," Avery said. "If such a program existed, I'd have been the first to come forward with it. I wish it were true."

"Have you reviewed Mallory's files?" Cal said.

"Thoroughly, but I'll have another look," Avery said.

"I see our time is up, gentlemen," Dr. Patel said.

"The ZuriMax application will be in your hands next week," Avery said.

"I trust you will be submitting an electronic filing?" Dr. Patel said.

"That's correct. Dumping a couple of tractor trailers full of paper on your doorstep isn't going to expedite anything," Avery said, laughing. "Have a good weekend, Dr. Patel."

Avery hung up.

"Who's buying the cigars?" Jensen said, coming out of his chair.

"The two most beautiful words in the world are ringing in my ears," Avery said. "Stock options."

Jensen raised his hands, spinning around disco-like before slapping Cal on the back.

"If you guys file the application before the Academy, I'll personally arrange the press conference," Cal said.

"A scholar and a gentleman," Jensen said, dropping back into his seat.

"I take it, the restenosis patient extraction went well," Cal said.

"Perfect," Avery said. "There were twenty-four patients with the gene. Nine were taking ZuriMax, and all showed statistical benefits versus the placebo group."

"That's strange," Cal said.

"What?" Avery said.

"You had more patients in the placebo group."

"It's called the law of probability," Avery said.

"What was the final patient count in the study?"

"Two thousand five hundred and thirty-eight," Avery said, standing up. He wandered over to the window. "What's on your mind?"

"Is the data fully validated?" Cal said.

"Twice," Avery said. "Bioscene did the initial validation, and then our biostatisticians repeated the process."

"And how did you handle the original data?" Cal said.

"What are you talking about?"

"The data destroyed by the fire," Cal said. "I take it, you found a way to compare the recovered data against the original? Surely, you kept a hardcopy?"

"We've already covered that," Avery said.

"Nate said we should make sure the application is buttoned up," Cal said. "I'm simply being thorough."

"Listen, if I had the original results, don't you think I would send them to the FDA. Bioscene independently entered the data, and they've assured me everything was handled according to protocol."

"And the restenosis patients confirmed my earlier findings," Jensen said. "The two sets of data generated identical results. Anyone in the industry would kill to have that type of validation."

"As long as you guys are comfortable," Cal said.

"I'd bet my company stock on this one," Avery said.

"We're sending them every piece of data we have," Jensen said. "That's as good as it gets."

"I rest my case," Cal said, sliding out of his chair. "What's the latest on Karl Spears?"

"So far, they're saying it was an accident," Avery said. "It looks like he lost his footing and went headfirst into the river." He returned to his seat and picked up a water bottle. "It's a tragedy."

"Let me know if you hear anything else," Cal said, turning for the door. He stopped. "And if you don't mind, I'd like a copy of the patient list." Cal stepped out and closed the door behind him.

Avery raised the bottle and heaved it across the room. It bounced off the flat screen and landed on the floor.

Chapter 50

**ATLANTA, GEORGIA
FRIDAY, OCTOBER 7
9 A.M. EDT**

As he was leaving Beta Hut, Cal heard someone behind him. When he turned, Singh Lee was facing him with a finger across her lips. Checking the walkway in both directions, she led Cal out to her car, directing him into the passenger seat.

Cal hopped in and sat quietly until they passed through the security gate. Singh Lee turned out of the Zuritech entrance and drove away from the main highway. As they picked up speed, Cal noticed that there was nothing but trees and brush down both sides of the road.

"Where are we going?" Cal said.

"Look under your seat."

Cal gave her a curious look, and then checked behind them. The Zuritech security gate had disappeared. He slid a foot aside and felt around with his hand. He pulled a laptop computer out and set it on his knees. Once he had it open, he hit the power button. "Sheri's expecting me any minute."

The computer beeped.

"I told her you would be with me," Singh Lee said, checking the rearview mirror. She held out a USB drive.

Cal upended the laptop and plugged in the USB, returning it to his lap. As he adjusted the display, a message popped up requesting a password.

"XLT3397F," Singh Lee said. Her eyes were bouncing between the computer and the road ahead.

Cal typed, but had to wait for the laptop to respond. Outside the car, the trees along the road had grown denser. Cal's iPhone rang, and he answered after checking the display.

"Hello, Nick," Cal said. He paused. "Yes, I received your e-mail . . . no hard feelings." They turned off the road next to a park sign. "Yes, I've reviewed a draft of Dr. Jensen's presentation, and it's fine . . . right . . . I'll do the introductions, and then turn the stage over to him . . . excellent . . . and thanks for the apology." He hung up.

"ZBA888GM," Singh Lee said. She steered past a pavilion to a gravel parking lot, pulling into a spot next to a van.

When Cal glanced down at the laptop, there was a second password request on the screen. He typed it in, and two files appeared. Clicking on the first one, he studied the river about thirty yards away as he waited for the file to open. On the driver's side of the car, the van blocked his view of the park entrance. A beep drew his eyes back to the screen.

"I knew you'd want to see this," Singh Lee said, reaching for the stereo. She flipped it on, just loud enough that they could still talk.

"It's a contract proposal between Zuritech and Albert Jensen," Cal said, commenting as he read. "Zuritech stock for services rendered."

"You'll notice that they're the common shares traded on the Swiss Exchange."

"Which reminds me, you were right about my stock options," Cal said, looking over at Singh Lee. She was scanning the river bank. "They have the right to convert my options to C-class shares." He returned to the document. "But this says they're giving Jensen a boatload of common shares. Fifty percent up front and the rest in the form of options to be deposited in a Swiss bank upon FDA approval of the restenosis claim. And look at the contract date. It was drafted before I joined Zuritech."

Singh Lee adjusted the volume on the stereo. "Check out the other one." she said, waiting for him to open the second file.

"It's an agreement with Dr. Raji Patel," Cal said, tightening his grip on the computer.

"The contract has the same terms as Jensen's, only with a later date."

"Where did you find these?" Cal said, continuing to scroll through the pages.

"In the Zurich office."

All at once, Cal stopped reading. "These are no good."

"What do you mean?"

"Look at the last page." Cal handed her the computer.

"What?" Singh Lee said, looking from Cal to the laptop. Then her voice lowered to a whisper. "The contracts . . . aren't signed."

"Which means we can't prove they were actually executed," Cal said. "Jensen's good at public relations. He'll easily shoot this down."

"At least it's a start."

"We'll run the documents past Tony. Did you find anything on Avery?"

"I have his employment contract, and he's got options, like yours," Singh Lee said. "But I've—"

"I need air," Cal interrupted. He got out of the car and slammed the door, heading down a path toward the river.

Singh Lee jumped out and sprinted after him, catching up as they neared the bank.

"Cal, I called my former boss at Kleiner Perkins."

"Have you lost your mind? He's probably in up to his neck with Martin," Cal said.

"I found a memo he'd written to Martin. It basically said—thanks for the opportunity to invest, but sorry we couldn't come to terms."

"Martin wanted Kleiner Perkins to fund the US startup? That means Zuritech needed capital."

"He told me Martin was pissed about the response," Singh Lee said. "The thing is, Martin knows venture capital, so he would have had a pretty good idea of what to expect before he asked. But get this. Kleiner Perkins felt Martin was playing the US business too conservatively."

"Meaning what? Martin doesn't believe ZuriMax is a blockbuster?"

"In their opinion, Martin was overly cautious about the launch. They felt maybe he was nervous about the FDA, but more specifically, US litigation."

"So Kleiner Perkins wanted a larger share of the company," Cal said. "Only now, we know Martin has reduced the risk by putting Dr. Patel on the payroll."

"Which makes the ZuriMax approval a shoe-in," Singh Lee said.

Cal crossed a stretch of grass, deep in thought. He stopped at the water's edge. "They found Karl's body somewhere in this area," he said, studying the river. He raised his palms to his forehead. "People are dead."

Singh Lee hooked an arm around Cal's waist and led him back to the path.

"Cal, I'm not comfortable discussing any of this at the office any longer."

"Where did he get the cash?"

"What?" Singh Lee said, facing Cal.

"Martin needed cash for the startup: the clinical trial, the buildings, the Gulfstream," Cal said. "Only he's not acting like a man with money problems. He found a way to fund the company without Kleiner Perkins."

"True, only there were no additional proposals in the files," Singh Lee said.

"But there is something going on in the Cayman Islands."

"You mean . . . the bank account?" Singh Lee said. Her mouth fell open in mid-sentence. Over Cal's shoulder, she spotted a man watching them from the van.

"Exactly," Cal said.

Singh Lee looked up, studying Cal's eyes. Then she stretched up on her toes and rested her cheek on his. Cal tried to pull back, but she locked her arms tight around him. When his resistance faded, she closed her eyes and kissed him.

Chapter 51

**ATLANTA, GEORGIA
SATURDAY, OCTOBER 8
1 P.M. EDT**

Peeking over the top of a menu, Tony Harkins took in the view from the Dockside Grill, checking out a houseboat as it glided up to the fuel dock. In the background motors revved and boat rigging clanked in the breeze.

"Business seems to be off for a Saturday," Harkins said, turning to Cal.

"The boating season is over," Cal said. "This isn't LA."

"Regardless, I could get used to this. Only I'm no sailor. I'd probably go for one of those big houseboat rigs."

A waitress came out to the deck area where they were seated and took their order, then disappeared inside.

"We're running out of time, and there's a lot of ground to cover," Cal said.

"Hey, you're the one who keeps saying to take it slow."

"The ZuriMax application will be filed next week. Seven days from now, I'm headed out to the Academy to host the top cardiologists in the country. Both events will attract national media."

"Impressive," Harkins said. "So why are we now in a hurry?"

"For one, my integrity is on the line. Negative press after the Academy carries a stiff price, especially for anyone tied to any of this."

"All right, so we both agree death and mayhem don't look good on the résumé," Harkins said.

"Where do you stand with the investigation?"

"We're making progress with Holly's list of vanishing patients. So far, four have been confirmed as deceased. The rest appear to be alive, but it'll take more legwork to determine their present condition."

"You're certain about the deaths?"

"I have positive ID from my buddy in San Diego. That makes six cases that we can pin to your miracle cure," Harkins said.

"But you need a cause of death."

"Listen, I've been doing some reading about how pharmaceutical companies are required to report adverse drug reactions to the FDA—ADRs, they call them. According to your own admission, Zuritech has reported nothing. Even patients with heart disease don't go from zero medical complications to six feet under without a good explanation."

The waitress slipped over to the table with a tray.

"I'll have a Blue Moon," Cal said, pausing for the waitress to finish up and leave. "How are you going to prove the deaths were caused by ZuriMax?"

"By demonstrating that all the cases had one variable in common—the drug. But we need more patients."

"You'll have five hundred names today."

Harkins cut his eyes at Cal. "Where did they come from?"

"We tapped into an old clinical database that was supposed to have been destroyed by a fire."

"A fire?" Do we have a copy of this database?" The waitress walked up and slid a frosted mug in front of Cal. "I'll have one of those, darling," Harkins said.

"We're reviewing the patient list now."

Harkins grabbed his sandwich and took a bite. "I'll tell my buddy we've got more names to run."

"What have you uncovered on William Mallory?"

"Spooky stuff," Harkins said. He looked around, and then wiped his mouth with a sleeve. "The crash investigators turned up an unidentified residue in the fuel tanks. They believe some type of contaminant caused the engines to stall. The problem is, they don't know what it is or why it didn't prevent the jet from taking off in Zurich."

"Are they still investigating?"

"The case is closed. It's one of those unsolved mysteries," Harkins said, as the waitress dropped off his beer. "And I would let it slide if it wasn't for this Dr. Karl Spears incident. What's his story?"

"He was one of our scientists. A week ago, he approached me with concerns about patient attrition."

"Meaning what?"

"He raised the flag on the number of patients dropping out of the clinical trial. He was the one person who could have shed light on the old database."

"Did you get anywhere with him?"

"He reported it to Avery, but was unable to prove anything since the data had been destroyed."

"And what does Avery say?"

Cal lifted his beer, and then set it back down. A horn blasted, and the smell of oily fumes drifted up to the table. He turned for a look at a houseboat tying up at the fuel dock.

"Basically, he sidestepped the issue," Cal said. "He told the police that Karl and I had an argument the day he drowned."

"And..."

"It's not true."

"Do tell," Harkins said. He pushed aside his plate and lit a cigarette.

"Avery's under pressure to complete the ZuriMax filing."

"But why would he lie?" Harkins said.

"There's a lot of money at stake—"

"Ahhh, now you're talking."

"He might be in over his head," Cal said.

"Well, I just heard a motive, but we'll have to connect the dots if we want to make a case of it."

"Even if he's involved, he's not in charge. Avery wasn't around when Mallory died. Your Perez client predates him as well." Cal raised a hand for the waitress. "Let's head back to the boat."

By the time they walked to the dock, Cal had briefed Harkins on the security cameras and stock options.

"As you've already figured out, we need signed contracts," Harkins said as they approached the boat slip. "We won't know who's responsible until we see an official signature. Let's take a look at the security shots and come up with a plan." He stopped in his tracks as they came alongside the boat.

"What do you mean it was a little nip?" Kate said. She stood in the cockpit of *Coastal Confessions* with a wench handle in her hand.

"Someone was following us," Singh Lee said.

"And why exactly did you take my husband to the river in the first place?"

Singh Lee stood clear of Kate's sweeping hands. "I said, I'm sorry—it was business."

"Business? As in giving Cal the business?"

"Kate, I was afraid. This guy carries a gun."

"Fair enough," Kate said, turning to Cal. "Did you see a gun?" Before Cal could respond, Kate cut him off, firing back at Singh Lee. "Who is he?"

Holly poked her head out of the companionway, took one look at the expression on Singh Lee's face and ducked below deck.

"He works on campus," Singh Lee said, looking to Cal for support. "I've seen him with Kurt, the security guy." Her eyes begged Cal to say something, but he only shook his head. Then she remembered. "Kurt Handle."

"I know Kurt," Sheri said, popping up in the cockpit. She nibbled on a piece of broccoli. "He's the one that helped with the Beta Hut fire."

"Is this the same fire that destroyed the database?" Harkins said.

"But I'm talking about the other guy. The one who drives a Jeep," Singh Lee said, ignoring Harkins.

"Oh yeah," Sheri said. "I've seen it on campus."

"His name is something like—Bos—Boswell—Broco . . ." Singh Lee said.

"You sure know how to pick 'em," Harkins said to Cal, rolling his eyes at Singh Lee.

Cal turned to Kate. "You know there's nothing to this."

Kate hesitated, taking a moment to eyeball Singh Lee, head to toe. "I want to see that video."

"Brasso—Baco . . ." Singh Lee continued.

"I thought we settled that?" Cal stepped forward and pulled himself up on deck.

"That was before this latest rendezvous. Besides, I'd like to see how she conducts business, as she calls it," Kate said.

"Bass—Boss—BOSCOE!" Singh Lee screamed.

"Boscoe?" Kate said, spinning around. "I thought the guy's name was Roscoe."

"What guy?" Cal said.

"The one who came to our house," Kate said.

"A guy with a gun came to our house?" Cal said.

"I didn't see a gun, but he hooked up the computer," Kate said.

"Chase handles our computer projects," Cal said, cutting his eyes over at Sheri. "What are they talking about?"

"Don't look at me, I love Chase," Sheri said.

"Wait a minute," Harkins said. Everyone paused as he pulled out a cigarette. "You're saying the Asian supermodel was making out with the doctor here?"

"Not now, Tony," Cal said.

"Mr. Harkins, are you suggesting my husband is doing this little tart behind my back?" Kate said, pointing the wench handle at Singh Lee.

"Did I say that?" Harkins said.

"Okay, that's enough," Cal said. "Everybody below deck. We've got work to do."

Chapter 52

MIAMI, FLORIDA
SUNDAY, OCTOBER 9
NOON EDT

Holly climbed a flight of stairs up to the second floor of the MerSea Hotel with Tony in tow. On the landing at the top, they stepped over a garbage bag, noticing that the wall behind it had been patched with fresh stucco. The carpet had a pastel sheen, a sure sign they were in the Art Deco district. Cars honked on Ocean Drive nearby as they found their rooms.

An hour later, they caught a cab over to Dodge Island where they were dropped off in a parking area adjoining Port Boulevard.

"What's happened to this place?" Harkins said. He spotted a cruise ship towering above sleek buildings hugging the waterfront. "My brother used to take fishing trips down here. He never mentioned any of this stuff."

"Which century was that?" Holly said.

"The one before Brazilian bikinis and twenty dollar martinis."

"Did you ever consider the possibility that he wasn't actually fishing when he came to Miami?"

"Archie delivers mail on Long Island. He wears wool shorts and knee socks."

"Ooh-la-la," Holly said. "Those are the worst kind."

"Yeah, yeah," Harkins said. "Now, how're we going to find this boat? What's the name again?" He patted his pockets, searching for something.

"It's called the *American Dream*," Holly said, distracted. "It's so beautiful down here."

Harkins pulled out a pack of cigarettes and thumped one out as they crossed the street. The cigarette crumbled between his fingers, and he slammed the pack into a trash can on the corner. They walked for another twenty minutes.

"How about over there?" Holly said, pointing between two buildings.

They headed around back to a parking area that opened up to a sweeping view of turquoise water. Walking to the opposite end, they found a sign for the *American Dream*. There was a gangway over to a dock, but no ship anywhere. As they approached, a guard stepped out of a security shack.

"The next departure's at three o'clock," the guard said. He broadened his stance, barricade-like.

"Have you got a cigarette?" Harkins said. The man's silhouette blocked out the sun, leaving Harkins standing in a pool of his shadow.

"Sir, there's no smoking in the area." The guard hitched his hands on a gun belt.

"Is it okay if we go across and take a look at the water?" Holly said, shading her eyes.

"You'll have to come back. I have to keep the area clear, ma'am."

"I don't see the boat." Holly pivoted, searching the horizon.

"You can't see her at the moment, but she's out there," the guard said.

"Do we need to buy a ticket or anything?" Holly said. She rocked her hips like a school girl.

"Just make sure your dad brings a valid prescription," he said, cutting his eyes over at Harkins. "And a driver's license or passport."

Holly turned to Harkins who was looking out to sea. He suddenly realized she was staring at him.

"I'm on several medications. Do you handle all of them?" Harkins said.

The guard stepped into the booth and hauled out a sandwich sign. He set it on the ground in full view.

"Any of these look familiar, Pops?" the guard said.

Harkins froze in place with a panicked expression on his face.

"Are you from out of town?" the guard said.

Harkins glanced over at Holly who was busy studying the list. "We're from Homestead. I brought the daughter along for a little dancing tonight." He worked his arms like he was doing the Twist.

Holly covered her mouth to stifle a laugh.

"But we'll be back," Harkins said to the guard, taking Holly by the arm. "What do you say we check out the beach?" They started for the parking lot.

"Hey, check out Fat Tuesday," the guard called after them.

"There's a security camera on top of the shack," Holly said to Harkins.

When they reached the parking area, a man in a Lincoln sat with his door propped open. He was devouring a sandwich, but somehow managed to speak as they walked by. "Missed the boat, huh?" A clump of lettuce fell into his lap. "These people are a godsend, I tell you."

"Are you waiting for the *American Dream*?" Harkins said.

"Yep," the man said before swallowing.

"Have you got a cigarette?" Harkins said.

"My wife's on the boat," the man said, shaking his head. "She's been going out ever since they started up this operation. Normally, I'd be aboard with her, but I had to see the cable company about a billing problem. Is this your first time?" He took another bite of sandwich.

"That's right," Harkins said.

"Did they tell you cash only?"

"We got the word," Harkins said, lying.

"Well, you've found the best spot in Florida to buy your prescriptions," the man said. "And they've got an incredible buffet."

"How long do they stay out there?" Harkins said.

"As long as it takes," the man said. "They hook up with the other boat, the *Rx Freedom*. Once they take care of everyone, they bring you back to port." He plucked the lettuce out of his lap and stuffed it back into the sandwich.

"Thanks for the information," Harkins said.

"Don't mention it," the man said, twisting around in his seat to watch them leave.

Chapter 53

**NEWARK, NEW JERSEY
SUNDAY, OCTOBER 9
2 P.M. EDT**

Cal slung a travel bag over his shoulder as he headed down the concourse. Singh Lee moved along next to him, struggling to keep pace as she pulled a suitcase on wheels. Spotting a sign for baggage claim, Cal followed the crowd to a bottleneck at the escalator. His iPhone rang halfway down. It was Tony.

"We're at the Newark airport," Cal said into the phone. "What do you have?" Announcements blared from the public address system, and he pressed the phone to his ear as they stepped off the escalator.

Singh Lee took the lead and wheeled her bag as Cal followed along. Near the Hertz counter, Cal stepped out of the foot traffic and listened.

"Don't risk it . . . go to the airport and take the next flight out," Cal said to Harkins. "And keep an eye on Holly." He hung up and joined Singh Lee at the rental counter.

"They've located the dock, but didn't see much," Cal said. "It sounds like they're transporting patients out to sea and selling them cheap drugs."

"At sea?"

"Harkins says it's a nice setup," Cal said, looking around to make sure no one was listening. "They're conducting business out in international waters."

"What's that got to do with ZuriMax?"

"He isn't sure, but Holly got a look at the available drugs. They're all top selling cholesterol and hypertension products."

"Wait a minute," Singh Lee said. "Zuritech has security cameras trained on these guys. They must be spying on the competition."

Cal grabbed Singh Lee's suitcase and rolled it aside once they finished up at the counter. "I think they're running the operation," Cal said. "Holly spotted a camera on top of a guard shack, right out in the open. With Zuritech monitoring back in Atlanta, I was afraid someone might spot them, so I told Harkins to head home."

"Cal, why would Zuritech sell drugs for the competition? It's irrational."

"Maybe even illegal," Cal said.

After dropping their bags at the hotel, Cal and Singh Lee found the Rx Freedom Project facility near the airport. The warehouse was discreet, housed in an office park where all the buildings looked the same. As they pulled into the parking lot, the sound of jet engines filled the air, cutting into their conversation.

"I see cars down at the next building, but no sign of life here," Cal said. He shifted the car into park.

"You're not afraid someone's watching?" Singh Lee said.

"The camera is inside, remember?"

They waited half an hour, and then eased the car around the building for a closer look. Out back, they found loading docks, but no workers. The exterior was metal and painted gray. A tractor trailer rig was backed up to one of the docks.

Cal and Singh Lee returned to the hotel, and then drove back to the Rx Freedom Project facility after dinner. With the parking lot now dark, Cal pulled into a spot that was a safe distance from the building.

Sliding out of the car, he stuffed a flashlight into his jacket. Singh Lee joined him, slipping a small notebook into her jeans. They walked slowly toward the building, monitoring the parking pad as they progressed. Clearing the front of the tractor trailer, Singh Lee spotted an entrance atop a set of concrete stairs as Cal climbed up on the truck. He checked the cab door, and it was unlocked. Then they proceeded to the stairway.

The door to the building was secure, and from the looks of it, solid steel. Cal thought for a minute, and then reached inside his jacket and pulled out the flashlight. He pounded it against the door.

"What are you doing?" Singh Lee rasped.

"Stand back in case someone answers," Cal said.

A few seconds later, he descended the steps.

"Warn me next time you intend to do something stupid," Singh Lee said.

Cal motioned for Singh Lee to follow. Back at the truck, he pulled himself up and popped open the door, hopping into the cab.

"There's a berth in back," Cal said, twisting around in the driver's seat.

Singh Lee climbed up and stuck her head inside.

"Try these," Cal said. He tossed down a key ring.

A second trip to the entrance brought Singh Lee back shaking her head. "No luck," she said, mounting the truck again. Cal took the keys and inserted one into the ignition. "You're not thinking of crashing through the loading dock, are you?"

"I'm not that crazy," Cal said, pulling the key out. He shoved it into the lock on the glove compartment and opened it. After a bit of fumbling, he found a remote.

"What's that?" Singh Lee said.

Cal pushed a button, and they heard rattling followed by a series of squeaks. Singh Lee lifted an ear in the air. He hit the button again, and the sound stopped.

"It operates the loading dock door," Singh Lee said, now looking at the building.

Leaning out of the cab, Cal followed her line of sight to an oversized garage-like door. He could just make out a two foot gap at the bottom. He hopped down and sprinted to the back of the truck, squeezing in next to the building. After a quick look, he climbed up onto the loading dock, sliding the bottom half of his body under the door. He motioned Singh Lee over, taking her by the hands.

"I can't see," Singh Lee whispered, once inside.

Cal sat up on the floor, waiting for his eyes to adjust. He spotted an exit sign over the door where they had tried to enter earlier. To the left, he noticed light shining from a hallway, and above it, something white on the wall. He felt Singh Lee press up against him.

"That's the banner we saw in the security photo," Singh Lee said.

"Which means the camera is somewhere down there," Cal said, pointing to the far end of the building. "Let's stay close to the wall and work our way around. I'll cover our heads for added measure." He got to his feet and helped Singh Lee up. She was barely visible in the darkness. Pulling his jacket over their heads, he held onto Singh Lee's hand and started around the periphery of the warehouse.

Fifty feet inside, Singh Lee stopped. "What is this stuff?" she said. Pulling away, she ran her hand down a wall of shrink-wrapped boxes.

Cal inched toward her and sat down, pulling her to the floor. "This row of pallets should protect us from the camera, but keep your head low." Pulling out the flashlight, he pointed it at the boxes.

There was a second level of pallets stacked on top of the first, running twenty yards and standing eight feet high. Whatever was inside, it was well-secured. Cal stood up and aimed the flashlight down the row and back to where Singh Lee sat on the floor.

"Rx Freedom Project has plenty of inventory," Cal said. He pulled out a car key. "Let's see what's inside." He stabbed the shrink-wrap, peeling away plastic as he went.

"Look, a label," Singh Lee said, giving a tug. "It's LipidRx."

"Let's try another one." Cal stepped across the aisle, slicing into more plastic. "It's the same."

They sampled pallets until they reached the end of the row.

"They're all hypertension and cholesterol drugs," Singh Lee finally said. "They must specialize in those therapeutic categories." She looked over at Cal propping himself against the boxes, just as he flicked off the light.

"Apparently so," Cal said. "And for some reason, Zuritech is involved."

"So it's just like Miami . . . they're spying, right?"

Cal thought for a minute. "But what if they aren't?"

"Look around you, it's obvious."

"Is it?" Cal said.

"The warehouse belongs to the Rx Freedom Project and—"

"They're supposed to be shipping donations overseas," Cal interrupted. "Every drug we've identified in this warehouse is listed for sale on the *American Dream* in Miami."

"You think these are bound for South Florida?"

"I'm not sure, but I've got a hunch they aren't headed abroad," Cal said. "Think about it. The monitoring room back at the office also has cameras in New York, Los Angeles, and San Francisco. The supply ship off the coast of Miami is called *Rx Freedom*. If I had to guess, I'd say they're diverting product."

"*We* are diverting product," Singh Lee said. "But why?"

"I can't say at the moment." Cal's eyes arched over to the unexplored hallway. He pushed off the pallet. "Let's see what other dirty little secrets are hiding in this building."

Chapter 54

**NEWARK, NEW JERSEY
SUNDAY, OCTOBER 9
11 P.M. EDT**

What Cal had first thought to be a hallway turned out to be a stairwell entrance. He and Singh Lee hurried inside with their heads covered, counting on the poor lighting to avoid detection by the security camera. There was a clipboard hanging on the wall, and beyond it, the stairway made a steep climb. Cal grabbed the clipboard and mounted the stairs with Singh Lee close behind him.

Up top, the steps ended at a closed door. With only a hint of light drifting up from downstairs, Cal turned to Singh Lee for reassurance and instantly wished he hadn't. The look on her face said it all. He groped for the doorknob in near darkness, surprised to find the door unlocked. In a matter of seconds, they were inside but not quite sure where. Cal felt his way along a wall, bumping into something only two steps in. He pulled out the flashlight and flipped it on.

A four drawer file cabinet blocked his path. He held the flashlight overhead and waved it in an arc, illuminating what appeared to be an office area. To his right along a back wall, he noticed a table and bulletin board. Beyond the file cabinet was a metal desk and chair. A plate glass window covered most of the wall behind the desk. He scanned the room a second time, and then slipped around the file cabinet to the window. Down below, he spotted the exit sign at the rear entrance, realizing the office overlooked the warehouse operations.

Cal dropped the clipboard on the desk and used the flashlight to orient himself to the surroundings.

"Over here," Singh Lee said, hurrying over to the table. She waited for Cal to catch up with the light, and then sat down in front of a computer and powered up, reaching for a binder propped against the monitor. "It looks like a manual."

"I feel trapped in here," Cal said, checking over his shoulder. There's only one way out. We'd better work fast. I'll check the desk while you work here." He returned to the desk, where the wheels on the chair squeaked as he sat down.

"Cal, this is a new computer," Singh Lee said. "And there's just one document on the hard drive."

Cal began his search, rattling desk drawers. "They're all locked."

There was a bang, and Singh Lee jerked around. "Shhhh."

Setting down the flashlight, Cal unclipped a handful of sheets from the clipboard. "Talk to me," he called out to Singh Lee.

Singh Lee flipped through the binder, holding it next to the monitor for light. "There are a number of dividers: *Product*, *Logistics*, *Inventory* . . . hello." She turned the notebook at an angle. "Cal, the next tabs are labeled: *Miami*, *New York*, *Los Angeles*, and *San Francisco*. But there's nothing behind them."

"I've got a stack of shipping manifests over here. The cities you just read off have all received shipments, but most of the goods have gone to Miami." Cal continued to scan the documents. "Everything that's been distributed so far looks like the products we saw downstairs."

Singh Lee slipped out of her chair and joined Cal at the desk with the binder. She leaned over the clipboard.

"Take a look at this. The paperwork for this shipment indicates that the product is bound for Miami, but the FedEx manifest shows it was air-freighted to Iraq," Cal said, handing the document to Singh Lee. "And here's another."

"We should make copies," Singh Lee said, twisting around. "There's no copy machine." She opened the binder. "The last tab in this manual is labeled *banking*. And there's a letter from . . ."

Cal stopped what he was doing to see what was wrong.

"It's from a Grand Cayman bank and addressed to someone named Christopher Smith. Does that ring a bell?" Singh Lee said.

"Never heard of him. What does it say?"

"It's a confirmation notice for a new account. Hang on." Singh Lee pulled the notebook out of her pocket and opened it up next to the binder. "The account number matches."

"The account matches what?" Cal said.

"The one I secured from the Zuritech system," Singh Lee said, stopping abruptly.

A series of clicking sounds echoed up from the warehouse. Outside the window, lights buzzed to life, one row at the time. Cal dropped to the floor, crawling around the desk to where Singh Lee now sat with the binder in her lap.

Cal remembered the flashlight and switched it off, but the room remained lit by the lights shining in through the plate glass. Returning to the window, he spotted a man in a suit entering the warehouse from the front of the building. He stopped in his tracks and dropped a bag that was in his hand. His eyes were glued to the loading dock, and then his head cocked upwards to the window. Cal hit the floor just as the sound of pounding heels hastened across the floor below.

Rounding the desk on his hands and knees, Cal scooted past Singh Lee who was scribbling furiously in her notebook. He hopped to his feet and sprinted for the door. Twisting the door lock, he studied the file cabinet until he heard footsteps in the stairwell. Cal grabbed the corners of the cabinet and shoved. It slid easily enough, but with a fingernails-on-chalkboard squeal as he jammed it against the door. It wasn't much of a barrier, but it would have to do. The sound seemed to hasten the pace of the footsteps.

Cal spun around to Singh Lee.

"What now?" she said.

"Help me with the desk." Cal hurried over, and they each grabbed a corner, dragging the desk away from the window. Keys jangled outside followed by shouts.

"Stand back," Cal said, letting go. He stepped forward and clutched the backrest of the desk chair in his hands. Hoisting it shoulder high, he drew the chair back, but the weight threw him off balance. The wheeled pedestal landed on the desktop as he struggled for a better grip. Singh Lee moved in to help, but he waved her off.

A key jiggled in the door lock.

Cal lifted the chair a second time and swung. The pedestal struck the window which exploded into thousands of chards that blew outward into the warehouse. The momentum ripped the chair from his hands as it disappeared amidst the tempest of glass.

Cal sprang forward and pulled out the flashlight, raking it across the window seal. Bits of glass continued to shatter as he leaned out for a look into the warehouse. Without hesitating, he leaped out onto a stack of pallets just outside the window.

Inside the office, the door sprung open and slammed against the file cabinet. Cal seemed unfazed as he stomped on his perch, testing to see if it would hold. He called out to Singh

Lee and turned, but she was already barreling feet-first across the desk. She attempted to slow herself with an outstretched hand, but came up with a fistful of papers. As her feet dropped off the desk, her knees slammed into the window seal, thrusting her headfirst out the window. Cal threw himself in her path, using his body to slow her momentum.

There was a resounding thunderclap in the office as the door struck the file cabinet a second time, knocking it to the floor. Dropping to one knee, Cal held tight to Singh Lee's arms in an effort to keep her from dropping over the side. As his weight shifted, the pallets tipped. Cal and Singh Lee, along with the boxes, plunged to the concrete floor eight feet below. As they bounced and tumbled atop the mass of shrink-wrap, Cal wrapped his arms around Singh Lee just before hitting the floor.

Rolling to a stop, Cal staggered to his feet still clinging to Singh Lee's arm. She let out a moan and stumbled, nearly taking them both down before finding her footing. Out of the corner of an eye, she spotted the man up in the window.

"Cal," she yelled.

They made a dash for the loading dock. When they were within striking distance, Cal dropped to the floor, dragging Singh Lee along with him. The force of their weight carried them under the dock door, and then into a free fall onto the asphalt outside. Cal landed first, letting out a sound that resembled a punch to the stomach. Then Singh Lee came down, knocking the remaining breath out of him.

When Singh Lee opened her eyes, she was sprawled facedown on top of Cal. She lifted her head, fearing the impact might have knocked him unconscious. But then she heard a groan and sprang to her feet, taking charge. She managed to get Cal upright and limp past the semi into the parking area. Halfway across, she heard the man yelling behind them, but didn't slow down. Once they reached the car, Singh Lee shoved Cal in and scrambled around to the driver's side. She jumped in and locked the doors, turning to find Cal doubled over in the seat. As Singh Lee reached out to him, she looked down at her shaking hand. It was still clinging to the papers.

Chapter 55

SAVANNAH, GEORGIA
TUESDAY, OCTOBER 11
11 A.M. EDT

The crisp Atlanta morning had given way to a coastal stickiness as Cal descended the jet's stairs with his shirt clinging. He stepped down onto the tarmac where the pilot and co-pilot had already deplaned. "Thanks for the lift," he said, raising his voice above the whine of jet engines.

"She's your bird," the pilot said.

Cal adjusted a pair of sunglasses as he continued past them. "Gentlemen, I'll give you a call when I'm headed back to the airport."

A driver awaited him, opening the door of a black Lincoln. Cal lifted his sunglasses for a look at the Gulfstream. A pair of sleek stripes ran the full length to the tail as the glossy white exterior basked in the Savannah sunshine. He hopped in the car.

Half a block off Bay Street, Cal got out of the limo, checking up and down the street before slipping into an alley. He sniffed the air, just as he caught sight of Jonathon Browning pacing next to a trellised seating area.

"I was afraid I'd made a wrong turn," Cal said. He walked up and extended a hand, only to be grabbed around the shoulders, bear-hug fashion. Cal slapped Jon on the back.

"Does Kate know you jumped the fence?" Jon said.

"What do you think?" Cal said, surveying the alley. "Is this the back of the Moon River Brewery?"

An alley door swung open, and a man sporting a salt-and-pepper beard strutted out, wheeling a trash can.

"They've added the Beer Garden since you were here," Jon said, stepping out of harm's way. "Sanky, I'd like you to meet a friend of mine, Cal Hunter."

Sanky's smile lit up as he raised a hand, but quickly withdrew it, wiping it on an apron instead. "Nice meeting you, Mr. Hunter."

"Sanky works part-time for the Brewery, but mostly for Captain over at the Seafarer Mission," Jon said.

"How is Captain?" Cal said, noticing Sanky's smile widening.

"Stubborn as ever," Jon said. "I know you're on a tight schedule, so what do you say to an early lunch?"

Cal and Jon ventured inside, pulling up barstools at a bistro table. They ordered burgers after the waiter served them a round of draft beer.

"It's been a while," Cal said, sampling the beer.

"Yes, too long. You'll be happy to know that the kids have settled in nicely at the beach, and there's a new someone I'd like you and Kate to meet. Now that the Baineses have moved out, I'm looking into restoring the beach house."

"Which reminds me, thanks for the sextant," Cal said. "You have an open invitation to come up for a sail, anytime."

"I'll take you up on it, but only after you visit us on Tybee. I'm sure Kate will love it," Jon said. "No offense, but you look like you could use a little R&R."

Cal ran a hand down his face. "I flew in from Newark last night. This was sort of a last minute junket."

"At least you're doing it in style," Jon said.

"The Gulfstream . . . right. It was due for servicing, so I managed to catch a ride," Cal said. "And I appreciate your flexibility."

"Don't mention it. What's on your mind?" Jon smiled, leaning back with his beer.

"I'm interested in a merger you worked on a few years ago. I don't recall the company's name, but at the time you had concerns about stock that was being issued overseas."

"That's right. It was a European biotech that wanted to compensate key individuals in the US with company stock."

"I was hoping you could explain how that works."

"I'm afraid, I'm under a confidentiality agreement," Jon said. He sipped beer before setting down his mug.

"I'm not after the specifics, just the legalities of US citizens receiving stock in foreign corporations."

"That I can do. Just remember, the devil's in the details. But in our case, the company wanted to issue shares listed on the London Exchange to physicians involved in a US-based clinical trial."

"That's the one."

"First of all, the FDA frowns upon physicians owning equity in companies that have hired them to provide unbiased clinical observations. It's a conflict of interest."

"Meaning—it's illegal?"

"Not if they hold only a few shares. A mutual fund or retirement plan is fine, but when there's real money involved, it requires disclosure."

"What if the stock remains outside the US?" Cal said.

"Yes, an added temptation," Jon said. "It's much harder for the FDA to police foreign equity transactions. That's why the regulations have disclosure provisions. They even require physicians to report free rounds of golf nowadays, but you know that."

"Are there tax consequences?" Cal said.

"Typically, once compensation is reported in the States, it is considered taxable income."

"But is it okay to keep the income outside the US?"

"One might find a loophole to avoid US taxes, but there are still FDA policies to contend with."

Cal turned around to the bartender and held up two fingers.

"How about FDA officials?" Cal said.

"That's an entirely different matter. The law prohibits FDA employees from owning stock in companies that are filing for new drug approvals."

"But if the stock trades overseas, you're faced with the same dilemma."

"That's right. Unfortunately, it's one reason more corporations are operating offshore," Jon said. "Cal, you're not involved in an FDA scandal, are you?"

The bartender served burgers, and then brought out more beer.

"Just bear with me," Cal said. "If you were a foreign biotech expanding into the US, are there reasons you might want to sell a business that's just launched a hot new product?"

"Maybe for growth capital," Jon said.

"Through an initial public offering?"

"An IPO is feasible, but you could also sell the business outright or merge it with an existing company."

"But let's say you've got sufficient capital? Why would you sell if the product is likely to be a blockbuster?"

Jon looked up at the ceiling before giving Cal the eye. "It's a stretch, but one possibility is to avoid liability. The US is relatively tort-happy compared to the rest of the world."

"But someone in the industry would know that up front."

"If they're smart," Jon said. He lifted his beer, and then set it back down. "This may sound crazy, but there are times when it makes sense to sell highly profitable businesses. Sometimes it's the best strategy for extracting a premium on an investment."

Cal pulled back from the table. "Maybe for a business that has peaked, but not one that's about to take off like a rocket."

"I'm only suggesting—"

"Think about a twenty billion dollar annuity with patent protection. The cash flow is off the charts."

"Fair enough, but plans go askew and companies have to make mid-course corrections. Call it . . . an emergency landing."

"Wouldn't that require SEC disclosures?" Cal said. "You can't sell on inside knowledge."

"Precisely. Does ZuriMax have any competition on the horizon?"

"Not for years," Cal said, shaking his head.

"Cal, let me repeat myself. Are you involved in an FDA scandal?"

"I've already told you more than you want to know," Cal said. "But to ease your mind, I have more personal concerns at the moment."

"Anything I can do to help? I can recommend a good attorney."

"I'm okay in that department," Cal said. He toyed with his mug, eyeing a tourist who had just pulled up at the bar. "What I need is serious protection."

Jon leaned closer. "In that case, I have just the person for you."

Chapter 56

CHULA VISTA, CALIFORNIA
WEDNESDAY, OCTOBER 12
10 A.M. PDT

Cal and Tony argued as they weaved down the hallway, squeezing past a steady stream of police officers hurrying in and out of doorways. They turned a corner, and Tony gestured to a windowed office, ushering Cal inside. A plaque on the door indicated that it belonged to a detective for the Chula Vista PD.

"This better be good," Cal said.

"He's running late," Harkins said.

"I haven't slept in my bed—"

"Just relax," Harkins said, motioning to a chair in front of a metal desk. "You think I've been living the life of a Maytag repairman?"

Cal parted the blinds, looking out. "I'm on a plane for Hawaii in three days."

"You're breaking my heart," Harkins said. "You sound like that poor little rich boy in the comics."

"Not now," Cal said.

"How about I have you arrested and put you out of your misery?"

An officer entered the room. "Gentlemen, I have five minutes," he said, dropping behind the desk. He opened a drawer and tossed out a Ziploc bag.

"Look familiar?" Harkins said to Cal, digging a tablet out of his shirt pocket. He set it next to the bag. "It's a perfect match, except for the scoring."

"Where did you get this?" Cal said.

The detective responded by sliding a paper across the desk. "The lab reports that both tablets contain the same ingredients. Tony tells me this is your drug."

Cal ran his finger down the page. "It doesn't match. The actives are twice the concentration of ZuriMax."

"What the hell's an active?" Harkins said.

"I've already told you. They're the ingredients that make a drug effective. In the case of ZuriMax, the actives lower cholesterol and blood pressure," Cal said, sinking back into his chair.

"I'll leave it to the two of you to hash over, but I've got this." The detective adjusted a computer monitor. "I took the list you faxed over earlier and ran a few names through the database. So far, we've got thirty-seven hits."

"Hits on what?" Cal said.

"People who are dead," Harkins said. "And brace yourself. Rodriguez and Perez are both on the list."

"So these are the names from the disk drive?" Cal said.

"And my ticket to a class action suit," Harkins said.

"Not so fast," the detective said. "We're just getting started, and a number of the names are from out of state. So far, we have Arizona, New Mexico, and Texas. Once I inquire across state lines, it's going to raise flags. The chief will get involved, and you know what happens then. But give the word, and I'll light it up." He gave Harkins a look, and then got up and headed for the door. "Have a good day, gentlemen."

"Son-of-a . . ." Harkins shot out of his chair like he was going after him, but then thought better. "You said a hundred stiffs would be a compelling argument?"

"That's right. A three percent mortality rate from the clinical study would be statistically significant," Cal said. "What's the problem?"

Harkins planted himself on top of the desk. "If he files a report, the allegation goes public. There'll be lawyers crawling all over this place."

"That's your problem," Cal said, standing up.

"How about giving me a leg up on the competition?"

"I'm supposed to feel sorry for you?" Cal checked the time on his phone. "I've got an appointment in Los Angeles."

"Let's not forget, people are dead."

"What is it you need?"

"I'm not sure, but the fact that Dr. Messinger sicced the cops on you is troubling, not to mention the two dead scientists."

"And I'm indemnified, right?"

"The detective knows you're cooperating."

"You've got until Friday," Cal said. He motioned Harkins into the hallway.

"There you go rushing me again."

"The Academy kicks off on Sunday. I warned you that Zuritech intends to make a big splash."

"So what are you saying?"

"Just file the suit," Cal said.

* * *

Umm Qasr, Iraq

Captain Robert Fine sat with his crew in the café, deep in thought. The table wobbled just enough to be irritating, grinding every few seconds on the cement floor. Fine picked up a wrap and slammed it down on his plate.

"What is that, anyway?" he said, cutting loose on Lenny.

"You don't want to know, Captain," Lenny said.

"Seven loads," Fine said. He dug inside his bomber jacket and came out with a flask.

Lenny grabbed a Coke can and poured into three coffee cups. Fine topped them off with bourbon.

Harris stuck a finger in his cup and stirred, then tasted it. "Man, that's flat."

"It can't be worse than the food," Lenny said.

"That's a ton of pharmaceuticals bound for somewhere," Fine said.

"To America," Lenny said in a mock accent. "Christoph can kiss my—"

"What does the manifest say this time?" Harris said.

"Who cares?" Lenny picked up his wrap, dunked it in the cup and bit off a mouthful.

"The locals don't seem to know these characters," Fine said, looking over his shoulder to the servers behind a counter.

"It must be one of those kiss and don't tell arrangements," Lenny said. "A few *dinars* under the table, if you know what I mean."

"I did a little research," Fine said. "These drugs are like gold."

"How much?" Harris said.

"At retail, one bottle is a hundred and fifty bucks," Fine said. "And we're hauling it in by the thousands."

"But how much?" Harris said.

"Millions," Fine said, cutting his eyes over to the window. It was dark outside, and he could see lights twinkling down at the docks. "Anybody catch a last name for one of these clowns?"

"*Nein*," Harris said.

"But that's not a bad idea," Lenny said. He reached inside his jacket and stood up.

"What are you thinking?" Fine said, tracking Lenny to the exit.

Rustling papers, Lenny propped himself against the door. "I'm going to find Christoph and have him sign the manifest. Then we'll know his full name."

Fine snapped back to the window. There were two vehicles with flashing lights racing down to the docks.

Just then, the door popped open, and Lenny fell backwards. A man caught him by the arm and broke his fall as a second man stepped in, helping corral Lenny back into the café.

Lenny pulled loose and straightened his jacket, giving them a look. Both men wore navy caps and protective eyewear. They fanned out, checking the area. When they were done, they circled back to the table.

"Name, rank, and serial number," Harris whispered into Fine's ear.

"Good evening, gentlemen," Fine said.

The men stepped closer, one of them nudging the bill of his cap. It had gold embossed letters.

"We'd like to talk to you guys about the ship down at the dock," one of them said.

"You go first," Fine said, rising out of his chair. "And you can start by telling us why the FBI is interested."

* * *

Los Angeles, CA

The ICU at Ronald Reagan UCLA Medical Center looked like rush hour. Cal checked in at the reception desk, and then slipped into a corridor lined with glass-sliding doors. Medical teams scurried in every direction as overhead speakers broadcast a steady stream of pages that echoed off the tile floors.

Cal continued down the hallway until he spotted a physician in one of the rooms, jotting on an electronic clipboard. He stepped inside.

Dr. Jason Tidwell checked his watch and walked over. "Cal, sorry to keep you," he said. "It's been a busy morning." He placed an arm around Cal's shoulder. "How about a cup of coffee?"

A short elevator ride later, Cal and Tidwell stood next to a floor-to-ceiling window overlooking a garden. Tidwell held a cup of coffee in his hand.

"I haven't seen you since you took the new job," Tidwell said.

"Is it always like this around here?"

Tidwell shrugged, and then smiled. "UCLA could use a man like you."

"Don't start that again."

"You have a standing invitation, but no pressure. Anyway, that's not why I called." Tidwell propped a shoulder against the glass. "I've been reading about the ZuriMax clinical trial, and I came across something interesting."

"The trial has just wrapped up."

"I know, but I wouldn't have asked you to drop by unless I thought it was important." Tidwell drew a slip of paper from his lab coat.

Cal took it and read. "It's an admission form."

"That's right. Do you notice anything peculiar?"

"I recognize the name, if that's what you mean. How did you come across this?" Cal said.

"I was on call the night she arrived. We tried everything possible, but her number was up. And I never thought anything of it until I reviewed the information on your clinical trial."

"So you think she was on ZuriMax?" Cal said.

"It's right there on the admission form. Her son filled it out."

"And the cause of death?"

"We didn't perform an autopsy, at least not at UCLA. But the symptoms indicated myocardial infarction."

"You seem certain," Cal said.

"As certain as one can be under the circumstances. I'd give it a ninety-five percent probability."

"So we've got an elderly woman with coronary disease that died at UCLA Medical Center. I'd say that's a daily occurrence around here." Cal looked out the window.

Tidwell leaned in closer to Cal, lowering his voice. "Either you've changed or you're playing a dangerous game, my friend."

Cal looked directly into Tidwell's eyes and studied them for a moment. "So which is it, Jason?"

"I pronounced Maria Perez dead, so let's not do this. We both know she died with ZuriMax in her system before Zuritech launched the clinical trial."

Chapter 57

**ATLANTA, GEORGIA
THURSDAY, OCTOBER 13
7 A.M. EDT**

Sheri grabbed Cal as he was passing through her office. She held on tight, managing to steer him over to the desk. Once there, she checked the hallway to make sure no one else was around.

"Cal, I've got people coming out of the woodwork looking for you." Sheri's eyes were bloodshot, like she hadn't slept. "And I'm running out of excuses."

"I'm here now," Cal said, prying her hands free.

"Avery's already bit my head off."

"I'm headed over to see him."

"Chase says the clinical data is going to be transmitted to the FDA tonight," Sheri said, reaching out again.

"You're not talking to Chase on your office phone, are you?"

"I don't have to. He's been over in Beta Hut all week."

"The data is Avery's problem," Cal said. "What's Chase doing on campus?"

"Avery hired him to produce an electronic file for the FDA. Chase has been promised a bonus if he completes the project by midnight. He's asking me what he should do."

"Schedule a meeting in a safe place. Where is he right now?"

"In the computer room."

"Under no circumstances is he to transmit before we meet." Cal patted Sheri's hand. "What else?"

"Singh Lee is coming unraveled. She hasn't left the office in two days."

"Tell her I'll stop by later," Cal said. "What are my travel arrangements for Maui?"

"Dr. Jensen is en route on the Gulfstream, but it returns to Atlanta on Saturday evening to pick you up around nine."

"Did you notify Avery?"

"Nick is flying in tomorrow for the weekly ZuriMax update, and Avery plans to catch a ride with him."

"We were supposed to travel together so we could finalize the agenda."

"He changed his mind this morning," Sheri said.

"Have we heard from Nick?"

Sheri started rubbing her temples. "No, he's been quiet as a mouse."

"Good," Cal said, hooking a finger under Sheri's chin. "Remember, I'm depending on you."

"One more thing," Sheri said, feigning a smile. "Darby and Gil have been begging to get on your calendar, but they left for the Academy yesterday. I thought you might want to know."

"What did they need?"

"They had concerns about the IMS data . . . something about a drop in prescriptions. They talked to Singh Lee, and she said to let you know as soon as you returned."

"Thanks," Cal said, pulling out his iPhone. He studied the screen. "Okay, listen. I have to call Holly, but I need you on standby. Clear my schedule for the rest of the day, and I'll find you when I'm done with Avery."

* * *

After checking Avery's office, Cal climbed the stairs to the Beta Hut main level. As he stepped into the hallway, he spotted Avery leaving the computer room, but in the opposite direction. When he reached the ZuriMax lab, Avery swiped his security badge and slammed the door behind him.

Cal passed the computer room and thought about stopping off to see Chase, but decided to stick to his original plan. Next door, he noticed a keypad on the clinical file room like the one at the entrance to the computer room. Moving to the end of the hall, Cal swiped his badge and entered the lab.

Standing in the open doorway, Cal scanned the room. There were rows of laboratory benches running across the room. Each had mounds of equipment, all covered with Pyrex beakers. Laminar flow hoods on the back wall produced mechanical humming that made it difficult to hear.

A door slammed down the hall, prompting Cal to ease the lab door shut. He glanced out a narrow vision panel above the doorknob and spotted Kurt Handle with his arms wrapped around the damaged server. Then a second man matching Boscoe's description barreled out of the computer room. Boscoe leaned forward to check the lock, exposing a pistol beneath his jacket. When he was done, both men hurried to an exit at the far end of the hallway.

Pulling away from the glass, Cal made a half-turn and nearly ran head-on into Avery. He stumbled, and then sidestepped Cal for a look out the panel. The hallway was empty.

"What are you doing here?" Avery said, barely audible as he collapsed against the door.

"Easy there," Cal said, reaching out to steady him. Avery straightened up and squeezed his eyes shut. "Sheri said you wanted to see me."

"I have news on the ZuriMax data," Avery said. He dropped onto a nearby stool. "It's fully validated."

"I thought—"

"Let me finish. You were hell-bent on protocols, so I convinced Nicolai that we should compare the recovered data to the original. I hope you're satisfied now." Avery slid off the stool and rounded the first bench. "Billions of dollars are waiting in the wings, and you're playing check-the-box. You take chances in this industry or you die."

"Calculated risks, not blind ones."

"There's blood in the water, and the sharks are circling. It's called survival of the fittest. Those are the corporate rules."

"What did the analysis tell you?" Cal said.

"The data is identical. It's like the fire never happened. You're about to be a rich man, Dr. Hunter. The industry and the media are going to make you famous all over again, so step back and let me finish my job."

* * *

An hour later, Cal climbed into the Range Rover, dialing as he pulled out of the parking lot. "Sheri, Singh Lee is waiting in her office," he said. "I want you to book her on tonight's flight to Zurich . . . shhhh . . . just listen. She'll give you the details. Have Chase and Holly meet me at six o'clock at that pizza dive you frequent . . . yes . . . you should come. And tell Chase to make sure no one follows him."

Chapter 58

**ATLANTA, GEORGIA
FRIDAY, OCTOBER 14
9 A.M. EDT**

Beta Hut was in full party mode when Cal arrived. Festive music sambaed over the multimedia system, fireworks exploded on the flat screen, and confetti covered the conference table as scientists shuffled in and out carrying plastic champagne flutes.

"The inmates have taken over the asylum," Cal said to Avery as he squeezed through the doorway.

"You are witnessing a milestone in medical history," Avery said, hoisting a champagne bottle in celebration. "As of eleven-fifty last night, the ZuriMax submission has been officially filed with the FDA."

"And from the looks of things, you've been celebrating all—"

"Congratulations," Nate interrupted. He slapped Avery on the back and stepped around Cal, wasting no time in getting out the door.

"Dr. Summers," Avery shouted, snagging her by the arm. "We need to wrap up the celebration. Take the champagne cart down to the break room."

"You're a party dweeb," Dr. Summers said. She rolled her eyes, taking hold of the cart to wheel it away.

"There's nothing worse than a bunch of needy scientists," Avery said to Cal, turning back to Summers. "You win. I'm declaring today a holiday. Have lunch brought in for everyone." Avery used the remote to switch off the fireworks and music.

It took a while, but the crowd finally cleared out, and Cal spotted Nicolai sitting alone at the far end of the table.

"Nick, congratulations," Cal said, making his way across the room.

"My dear, Calvin," Nicolai said, standing and spreading his arms. "It is a momentous occasion."

"Cheers, partner," a voice announced over a speakerphone on the table.

"Who's that?" Cal said.

"The miracle man, himself," Avery said, closing the door.

"Live from Maui," Jensen said.

"It's five o'clock in the morning out there," Cal said.

"I'm putting the final touches on a press release, and then heading over for eighteen holes on the Gold Course. The rumor is Phil Mickelson will be making an appearance. Then if anybody's looking for me this afternoon, I'll be sunning on the deck of the *Aloha Mama*," Jensen said.

"Have a seat, Cal," Avery said, dropping into a chair. "Albert, I faxed the contract revisions to the front desk. Call me before your golf outing, and we'll finalize them."

"Someone give that man a cigar," Jensen said.

"We'll celebrate with cigars and cognac when I arrive," Nicolai said.

"What's the latest on the draft?" Avery said.

"*The American Journal of Cardiology* has accepted it for immediate publication," Jensen said. "The editor's bringing the agreement to our golf match. Hold on to your hats 'cause there's gonna be plenty of horn-tooting this week, gentlemen."

"And you deserve much of the credit," Cal said, leaning back in his seat.

"The Academy will be ours," Nicolai said.

"It was touch and go last night, but that computer geek Sheri recommended knows how to make things happen," Avery said.

"There will be plenty of time to celebrate," Nicolai said. "We must not forget there is work to be done. Dr. Jensen, have you been briefed on the media talking points?"

"Does your momma have a son?" Jensen said. "I'm about to dazzle them with so much glitter they're going to think it's New Year's."

"I'm counting on perfection," Nicolai said.

"What's the plan if the FDA doesn't approve the application?" Cal said.

"What the . . . I don't believe what I'm hearing," Jensen said.

"It's called contingency planning," Cal said.

"Nonsense, Calvin. Zuritech has taken every precaution," Nicolai said.

"And there'll be hell to pay if the FDA attempts a delay," Jensen said. "Especially, after our media blitz."

"Which begs the question: how's your presentation coming, Cal?" Avery said. "Do you need help with your remarks for Sunday's dinner?"

"I'll have to tweak them based on this morning's news," Cal said. "But like you said, this is medical history."

"Just don't screw it up," Jensen said.

"Very well, gentlemen. We have an agenda," Nicolai said.

"I've got to run, boys," Jensen said.

"See you tomorrow," Nicolai said.

"Aloha," Jensen said.

* * *

Cal switched ears, pressing the phone tight as he paced in Singh Lee's office. "Okay, repeat the wiring instructions," Cal said. "That's right . . . and the sequence is . . . Panama-Switzerland-Grand Cayman." Cal heard a knock. "Hold on."

Sheri's head appeared in the doorway. She slipped in and closed the door behind her.

"The flight has been booked for Saturday morning. It's Zurich to Maui with a stopover in Los Angeles," Sheri said.

"The arrangements are set," Cal said into the phone. "Do you have the hotel fax number?" He paused. "Great. And remember, I want you in and out of there. Don't take any unnecessary risks . . . good luck . . . I'll see you in Maui."

"Change of plans," Sheri said as Cal hung up. "Avery gave his staff the afternoon off. They'll be celebrating all night, but they're required to come in for an administrative day tomorrow."

"So what does that do to us?" Cal said.

"You'll have to wait until tomorrow evening to go in, which means it'll be a mad dash to catch your flight."

"Are you helping with the project wrap-up?"

"Where else would I be?" Sheri said, walking over to the window. "What time should I expect you?"

"That's not a good idea," Cal said. "I want you off campus when this goes down."

"Cal," Sheri said, waiting for him to look at her. "Karl Spears said something really crazy after the Beta Hut fire. I thought he was joking at the time, but now I'm wondering if he was serious."

"What was it?" Cal said.

"Well, you know how he liked to kid around, but sometimes he used humor to defuse stressful situations," Sheri said. "Anyway, he told me that if anything ever happened to him, he was leaving you his bowling gear. And then he gave me the combination to his locker in the Zuritech bowling alley."

Chapter 59

ZURICH, SWITZERLAND
FRIDAY, OCTOBER 14
9 P.M. CEST

Singh Lee's cheeks were flushed as she struggled to break free from Martin's grasp. He had her pinned to the bed, and all she could manage was a side to side twist of her head. She felt pressure on her neck, and then burning as he drew blood to the surface with his mouth. She squirmed, and finally managed to wedge her arms between their bodies and pry him loose. He sat up with his legs straddling her.

"Dammit, Martin," Singh Lee said, pushing hair out of her face. She cut her eyes at him and twisted, reaching for a nightstand. As soon as her fingers made contact, she felt herself being drawn back to the center of the bed.

Martin used his weight to restrain her, this time starting on her blouse. The tiny buttons were a problem, so he reached for her collar and yanked. Buttons showered everywhere.

Singh Lee tried to sit up, but it only angered him. He slapped her, and then went for her slacks, loosening them enough to expose skin.

"Now, the moment of truth," Martin said.

"Martin, wait. I'm sorry," Singh Lee said, somehow managing to prop up on an elbow. She moved slowly, allowing the blouse to slip off her shoulder. "I want to make it up to you."

His eyes darted, finally locking in on her face, which appeared inviting now. He helped her, pulling the blouse free before tossing it to the floor. Then he kissed her, smiling as he felt a tug on his shirt. Closing his eyes, he unbuttoned it.

Singh Lee took his shirt and pitched it aside, reaching for the nightstand. This time she snagged the stem of a wineglass. Drawing it beneath Martin's nose, she teased him with the sweet bouquet.

"One more taste?"

"You didn't bring me to your room for this—swill," Martin said. He swung an arm that knocked a bottle off of the nightstand. It landed on the bed, soaking the sheets.

"Give me an honest opinion for once, and then we'll get to what's on your mind," Singh Lee said, holding the glass steady.

"So now you're a mind reader?" Martin said.

Singh Lee smiled and pressed the glass to Martin's lips. This time, he took it and drained the wine.

"Now, isn't that better?" Singh Lee said, starting to massage Martin's shoulders. She continued until he closed his eyes.

Martin said something, but the words came out slurred.

Singh Lee rolled him onto his side, fluffing a pillow under his head. After he was settled, she poked him to see if he would respond.

Reaching down, Singh Lee grabbed the security badge on his belt and snapped it loose. When she looked up, Martin's face was as peaceful as an angel.

* * *

Thirty minutes later, Singh Lee slammed a desk drawer as she dug out her cell phone and dialed. Just when she was about to hang up, Cal answered.

"I'm in Martin's office," Singh Lee said.

"Where is he?"

"He's in my hotel room," Singh Lee said. She sat down in front of a computer and started typing.

"What's he doing there?"

"Not now," Singh Lee said, pulling a notebook from her pocket. She transferred two series of numbers from the notebook to a pair of boxes on the screen. "I'm in the account now. The balance is one-fifty-seven."

"That's all?"

"One hundred and fifty-seven million," Singh Lee said, as she spun around. "I'm sending the fax."

"Were we right?"

"Let's just say, you're about to find out how good I really am."

"Instruct the hotel to hold the fax until I arrive on Sunday."

Singh Lee punched in a telephone number before turning back to the computer. "We're even now, okay?" She typed some more.

"Stick to the plan," Cal said.

"I want a clear conscience," Singh Lee said.

Chapter 60

ATLANTA, GEORGIA
SATURDAY, OCTOBER 15
11 P.M. EDT

Cal wasted little time after discovering that Avery's desk was locked. A trip to the Range Rover for a tire iron had quickly overcome the setback. Now rummaging through the drawers, he found documents crammed in every nook and cranny, many predating Avery's employment. As he proceeded, he kept an eye on the door.

There was a buzz, and Cal paused, reaching into his pocket for his phone. "Make it fast," he said.

"Cal, I just received a call from the pilot, and there's a problem at Briscoe Field."

"Go on," Cal said. He dropped a folder on the desktop and climbed into Avery's chair.

"The maintenance crew reported two suspicious-looking men attempting to board the Gulfstream. They claimed they were contracted to prep the flight for Maui. The pilot is en route to Briscoe, but says he knows nothing about the arrangement. His crew has managed to keep them off the plane, but they're not sure they can contain the situation."

"Who hired them?"

"They're not saying, but apparently they offered the regular crew a bribe to step aside," Sheri said. "Hang on, he's calling again."

Cal heard a click on the line, just as a door opened and closed somewhere down the hall. He scooted out of the chair and dropped to his knees behind the desk.

A second click.

"Here's the update," Sheri said. "The pilot just pulled up to the hangar and spotted an unmarked van. When he approached the driver, he said they were from the corporate flight department in Zurich and will be in charge of maintenance from now on. But he isn't buying it."

"How does he want to handle this?" Cal said.

"He recommends canceling the flight until things are sorted out."

"That's no good," Cal said. "There's too much riding on tonight."

"He's waiting for his co-pilot to arrive before making a final decision."

"When's that?"

"Within the next half hour," Sheri said.

"Okay, here's the plan—"

"Cal, I read the article about Mallory going down in a plane crash."

"Sheri, listen up. Have the pilot stall them. He can tell them he has to take a test flight when the co-pilot arrives, and then do a hop-over to DeKalb Peachtree Airport. Call Kate and tell her to meet me at the Atlantic Aviation hangar."

"What if they won't allow him to take off?"

Cal read off a telephone number. "Call the number and request assistance at Briscoe Field. Make sure they know which hangar, and then notify the pilot that help is on the way.

Whatever it takes, tell him to get the plane in the air. Anything else?"

"What about Karl's message?" Sheri said.

"I thought about it and nearly convinced myself it was one of his antics," Cal said. "I liked the guy, but he could be off the wall sometimes."

"So you didn't check out the locker?"

"Actually, I did," Cal said. "But I had trouble with the lock."

"But you got it open, right?"

"There was a bag with all of his bowling gear and a copy of an e-mail," Cal said. "I should have listened to him."

"What was in the e-mail?"

"It was from Mallory to Nick and dated only days before his death. Mallory had discovered that the ZuriMax formulation was toxic and wanted to abort the phase II work."

"What was Nick's response?" Sheri said.

"Well, there was a plane crash."

"This isn't happening," Sheri said. "Cal, get out of there."

"They've got to be stopped. Call me with any news." Cal hung up and climbed back into the chair. The folder in front of him contained medical journal extracts of Mallory's research. At the back, he found notes in Avery's handwriting. After scanning them, he stuffed the folder in a backpack and headed for the door.

Taking a stairwell, Cal climbed to the main level, checking the area before slipping into the hallway. There were few sounds as he made his way past the computer room and down to the ZuriMax lab door. He peeked through the vision panel, making sure no one was inside. Then he doubled back to the file room and punched in a code.

Once he was behind closed doors, Cal pulled out a flashlight and oriented himself, noticing a row of file cabinets about five feet high in the center of the room. He checked the tag on one of the cabinets, and then worked his way around to a second row against the back wall. When he finally located the cabinet he was looking for, it was locked, prompting him to pull out the tire iron again. He wedged it in and heaved. The metal groaned just before something popped loose inside. He tugged open the drawer and started the search.

Within minutes, Cal found the files he needed and transferred them from the cabinet to the backpack. As he was finishing up, the tire iron slipped out of his hand and hit the floor. Before he could make a move, someone was outside the door.

Dropping to one knee, Cal turned off the flashlight. He heard keypad tones, and then was blinded as the door swung open. Hitting the floor, he crawled over to the center row of cabinets and sat up with his back against them. Footsteps started across the floor, moving slowly into the room.

He heard breathing, and then felt the cabinets give, as if someone was tugging on a drawer. Cal pressed with his back to test the weight. The movement on the other side stopped.

Cal rose up into a crouching position and heaved into one of the cabinets. Top heavy, it tipped instantly, and he heard a scream. The cabinet bounced, and then crashed to the floor only feet away. A drawer popped open, and folders scattered like a deck of cards into the hallway.

The man lay facedown, and Cal put his shoulder into a second cabinet, sending it down on top of him. This time, he made no sounds. Cal stepped forward, studying the limp body before sliding the cabinet off. It was Kurt Handle.

When Cal looked up, the silhouette of a man stood in the doorway. The backlighting masked his face, but Cal had no doubt that it was Boscoe. Without a word, Boscoe reached for his pistol, and Cal dove. Compressed air sounds, like an air rifle, zipped over his head, sending Sheetrock crumbling down behind him. Cal tried to roll to one side, but a file cabinet came down on him.

The pain was sharp and brought on a nauseous feeling as Cal attempted to free himself. His vision clouded, making him think he was blacking out. But then the air grew thick, and he coughed, smelling fumes. With another try, he managed to pry himself loose. As he raised up, he saw smoke, and then fire spreading rapidly toward him. Five feet away, Kurt lay unconscious on the floor.

Cal scrambled over to Kurt and grabbed him by the hands, dragging him to the back wall. Returning to the cabinets, he retrieved the backpack and made his way back. He glanced up at the ceiling, wondering why the sprinklers hadn't activated, but there was no time to wait.

A copy machine sat in the corner. Cal ripped the electrical cord free and whirled the copier around, pointing it toward the wall. He lined it up, and then thrust forward. It smashed into the wall, and a section caved in, exposing studs. He wheeled the copier back and shoved it again, bringing down more rubble. This time glass shattered to the floor on the other side of the wall. Cal heaved the copier aside and looked into the lab at his makeshift escape route.

A cloud of dust hung in the air, and Cal gagged, turning to check on the encroaching inferno. The heat was intense and the doorway no longer visible as flames leaped higher, fueled by the trail of files scattered across the floor. Cal took Kurt by the hands and dragged him into the lab. He then secured a cart and loaded Kurt and the backpack on top, wheeling it through the door and down the hallway to the lobby.

The security guard wasn't at his station, so Cal continued out the entrance and down the walkway to Alpha Hut. When he looked back, a tongue of fire shot into the air over Beta Hut, illuminating the canopy of darkness. He let go of the cart just as rapid-fire shots whizzed past his ear, blowing away pieces of siding. With no idea of where the shots had come from, Cal grabbed the backpack and dove to the ground.

More shots fired overhead as he crawled into the brush next to the walk, then got to his feet. At once, he spotted Kurt on the move, scrambling off into the shadows. Doing an about-face, Cal reached into his pocket and pressed his key fob. Then he ran like hell for the Range Rover.

Chapter 61

**ATLANTA, GEORGIA
SATURDAY, OCTOBER 15
MIDNIGHT EDT**

The Range Rover peeled out of the parking lot and accelerated toward the security gate. Halfway up the drive, Cal slammed on the brakes as he rounded a curve, blinded by a pair of fog lights bearing down on him. He shifted into reverse and ran up on a median, spraying plants and woodchips into the air as he gunned the SUV back toward Alpha Hut.

Before reaching the parking lot, Cal swung the Range Rover off the drive and veered into the woods next to the building. When he looked into the rearview mirror, he spotted a Jeep in pursuit. The Range Rover bucked on the terrain as it started a rapid descent toward the river. There was a twang, and he ducked reflexively as a bullet ricocheted off the car. He spun the steering wheel hard to the left, and the Range Rover careened like it was going to flip over. But it leveled out, taking him on a new course parallel to the river, now running about fifty yards below him.

A glance in the mirror confirmed that the maneuver had done little to faze his pursuer. As the lights rapidly closed in, Cal was able to make out a roll bar and knobby tires, features well suited for off-roading. He heard bullets zip past, and then his outside mirror exploded. Fearing the worst, Cal jerked the steering wheel back and forth, sending the Range Rover into a zigzag pattern that took him closer to the river. The car's shocks bottomed out as it landed in a pair of ruts barely noticeable in the blanket of leaves. Cal fought the wheel until the vehicle straightened out, now certain he had found an old logging road.

Up ahead, the road disappeared beneath a canopy of saplings, and then without warning the car went airborne, clearing a ridge as it bounced like a bronco before starting down an embankment. Near the bottom, Cal spotted water, but only after it was too late to change course. The Range Rover plunged in, sending a tidal wave across the hood and windshield. He felt the wheels hydroplane, sensing he was about to lose control. Blind to his surroundings, Cal felt the car starting to tip just as it came out of a spin. With the change in momentum, the vehicle's weight shifted, and the driver's side wheels splashed down with the engine idling as it rocked from side to side.

The fog lights crested the ridge and swerved at the last second to avoid crashing into the Range Rover. There was a splash, and the Jeep's engine screamed to a deafening pitch, a sign that the wheels had failed to get a hold. As Cal flipped on the wipers, he realized he was sitting in the middle of a stream that crossed the road. It disappeared to his right over a ridge, making its way to the river below. He slammed the accelerator and felt the four-wheel drive engage, chewing through mud and water until he reached the bank, where he was able to make out the road again.

At the top of the next hill, the fog lights reappeared. The road opened up into a straightaway, and Cal gunned the engine until he was forced to brake for a bend in the ruts ahead. Behind him, the Jeep was closing in. Taking the curve a bit too fast, the Range Rover fishtailed on the leaves as it entered a clearing. Cal managed to stay on the road and pressed harder, even as the Jeep shot around the curve, maintaining the gap.

The speedometer leveled off at sixty, and Cal spotted a sharp turn up ahead that rose up and away from the river. With no time to think, he locked down on the brakes and spun the wheels. The tires plowed into the earth, trying to get a toehold as he begged: *Turn, turn, turn!* They responded at the last second, skirting a collision with an oak tree. The Range Rover's four-wheel drive dug in, chewing into the hill as it lurched forward.

When Cal looked over his shoulder, the Jeep was in trouble. The engine roared as the driver downshifted to slow for the turn. He watched as the fog lights set a direct course for the oak. The vehicle veered a second too late and clipped the side of the tree, sending it into a roll before plunging into darkness.

Ten minutes later, Cal crashed through a security fence and pulled onto a paved road. His cell phone rang, and he reached for the dashboard, activating the Bluetooth speaker.

"Where have you been?" a voice said.

"Tony?" Cal said. The rear tires caught on the pavement and squealed.

"You were supposed to call yesterday."

"Hold on," Cal said. He checked the rearview mirror. "Okay, go ahead."

"I filed the lawsuit," Harkins said. "Only I was counting on more evidence."

Cal exhaled, trying to catch his breath.

"Are you in the middle of something?" Tony said.

"I'm on my way to Maui."

"I guess you're having caviar about now."

"Right, and the waitress is a cute blonde—"

"You rich people are—"

"On the brink of extinction," Cal interrupted. "I have some news."

"Fire away," Harkins said.

"My life just flashed before my eyes."

"As in, someone tried to kill you?"

"I have your evidence," Cal said. "So round up your clients." He hung up and dialed Sheri.

"Cal, Beta Hut—"

"I know, it's on fire," Cal said, sensing Sheri's panic. "I want you to call Paula Ritchie and give her a heads-up on the story. Tell her to get a crew out to Zuritech, and make sure she catches a flight for Maui tonight."

"Tonight?"

"Tell her I'm picking up the tab, and we'll meet tomorrow afternoon at the hotel."

* * *

The Range Rover skidded to a stop in front of the Atlantic Aviation terminal. Mud dripped on the tarmac as Cal swung open the door. The Gulfstream sat in the night air with its blinking lights awaiting his arrival. Lifting the backpack off the seat, he hopped out and spotted Kate bounding down the jet's stairway.

Chapter 62

MAUI, HAWAII
SUNDAY, OCTOBER 16
8 P.M. HAST

Cardiologists and VIPs sat around circular tables in the Grand Wailea ballroom. The crowd was festive as waiters dressed in traditional Hawaiian costumes roamed about, serving coffee and slices of pineapple cheesecake. Cal dropped his napkin in the chair and excused himself, weaving among tables toward the front of the room, where a raised podium had remained unattended throughout dinner. Out of the corner of an eye, he spotted Darby Hopkins waving and turned her way.

As Cal walked over, Gil Carter rose from the seat next to Darby and greeted him. Cal stepped closer, checking a nearby exit over his shoulder.

"Would you care to explain what's going on?" Darby said, pushing back in her chair to stand up.

"At the moment—no," Cal said.

"You said you would stop by the booth this afternoon. Nicolai found time."

"My apologies," Cal said. "I was in a meeting."

"And weren't you supposed to be seated at Nicolai's table?" Darby said, gesturing to the center of the ballroom.

Cal didn't respond, but glanced over to catch Nicolai staring back at him.

"I understand you're not taking the podium tonight?" Darby said.

Cal's head snapped around.

"Nick said that?"

"Honestly, I didn't expect to see you here."

Cal pulled out his iPhone and checked messages, replacing it in his jacket. He turned to a man in a dark suit at the exit and gave a nod. "Do me a favor, and don't hold this against me."

"Are you getting fired?" Darby said.

"I'll explain later," Cal said. He buttoned his jacket and headed up front to the podium.

"Good evening, ladies and gentlemen," Cal said. "On behalf of Zuritech, I would like to welcome each of you to the thirty-fifth annual meeting of the American Academy of Cardiology. More importantly, I would like to thank you for joining us on this historic occasion and for the opportunity to dine with fifty of the finest cardiac surgeons in the nation."

The crowd applauded.

"My name is Dr. Calvin Hunter, president and CEO of Zuritech Corporation. As I look out over the crowd, I see so many faces—familiar faces that have been instrumental in the fight to revolutionize healthcare, making it an honor to be among such an esteemed group of professionals."

Cal paused for more applause, checking Nicolai's table again. He held a napkin to his mouth, leaning over to speak to Albert Jensen. Avery was in the seat beside Jensen. Cal gripped the podium as their eyes collectively seared into him.

"As many of you know, I have spent the better part of my career in the industry. I am sure you're also aware that I was part of a team at VistaBio that launched a product that changed so many lives. That experience, more than any other, has taught me to be a team player. And I have to tell you, I like playing on winning teams. After my fifteen minutes of fame at VistaBio, I refused to believe that my best days were behind me. You see, winning is not about egos. It's staying the course. It's about results. And for some of us, and I know I run the risk of being labeled old fashioned, it's how you play the game. Of course, the true measure in this industry reflects something much deeper. In the end, it's about hope, the families we touch, and the lives we save."

There was more applause, and Cal took a sip of water.

"With that said, tonight isn't about me. In fact, when you wake up tomorrow morning and reflect on these moments, please don't think of me or the wonderful team we've built in Atlanta. Think of the millions of patients who benefit from our mission as professionals. And when you do, I trust you will renew your own commitment to that calling.

"Tonight is about two special individuals among us. First of all, I would like to recognize Dr. Nicolai von Weir." Cal held out a hand, and Nicolai stood for a bow. "Nicolai is president and CEO of Zuritech AG, our Swiss parent corporation. He is also the architect of the product that will soon be known to the world as ZuriMax. If you are looking for a name responsible for the story unfolding at this Academy, look no further than the name of Dr. Nicolai von Weir." Cal looked across the crowd. "Here's to you, Nick."

Applause filled the ballroom.

"Also, there is a man who needs no introduction. Most of you recognize him for his work at Johns Hopkins University. He is a businessman, a surgeon, a statesman, and Zuritech's spokesperson—Dr. Albert Jensen."

Jensen popped out of his seat and waved to applause.

"Dr. Jensen is noted for his acumen in the industry. He has been vocal in the fight against the insurance giants, outspoken about the need for medical reform in our country, and a man of much influence. I recently visited Dr. Jensen in his office, admiring the photo of a beautiful Marlin he had hooked off the coast of St. Martin. As I studied the photograph, I later realized there was more than one big fish in the picture. Standing next to Dr. Jensen on the stern of his cruiser was none other than Dr. Lawrence Baker, Secretary of Health and Human Services. This man knows how to land the big ones."

Cal paused for the applause.

"The brilliance in taking ZuriMax beyond what you or I might have dreamed possible belongs to one person, and that person is Dr. Albert Jensen. I'm sure Dr. von Weir will agree. He is the kind of partner that is critical to Zuritech's corporate strategy. So without further delay, please welcome Dr. Albert Jensen."

Cal hurried off the podium, making his way to Nicolai's table. As he approached, Nicolai postured himself for a photo-op with the audience looking on. Cal reached inside his jacket and extracted an envelope, slapping it into Nicolai's hand to the flash of cameras.

"What is this?" Nicolai said, looking down.

"My salvation, Nick," Cal said. He turned and headed for the exit. The man in the suit opened the door for Cal and slipped out behind him.

Chapter 63

**MAUI, HAWAII
SUNDAY, OCTOBER 16
9 P.M. HAST**

Outside the ballroom, Cal's footsteps echoed off the marble walkway as he rounded a corner of the building, mounting a narrow flight of stairs. Fiery sconces illuminated the stairwell which was sandwiched between two buildings, hidden from the encroaching nightfall. He heard someone behind him, but continued on his course without looking back.

At the top of the stairs, he stepped out onto a stone breezeway adjoining a string of shops on one side and a brass rail on the other that opened into the night.

"Dr. Hunter, nice to see you," T-Rex said, falling into step alongside of him. He reached beneath Cal's tux and clipped a device to his belt. "Don't think I'm trying to get into your pants or anything." He struggled to keep pace, stretching a wire from the device to Cal's lapel.

Cal only smiled.

"Give me thirty seconds, and we'll do a sound check," T-Rex said, taking off.

Up ahead, the walkway connected to a terrace where a warm Pacific breeze washed in. Beyond the rail, the tops of lighted palms swayed like hula girls on the lawn below. Hotel guests strolled along in flowered shirts and sundresses as he descended a second set of steps.

"Looking gnarly, Cal," Jamie said, meeting him halfway down.

"Nice of you to notice," Cal said.

She stepped into Cal's path, coming just short of a collision. When Cal stopped, she pressed her palms against his cheeks, staring into his eyes as a breeze played with her hair.

"I'll bet your wife gets lost in those baby blues."

"I'm a lucky man, Jamie."

"Hey, someone told me the beach is good for . . . what do you call it?"

"Hypertension?" Cal said.

"Yeah, that's it," Jamie said. "Man, I can't mess with this." She fanned her hands away from his cheeks, running her fingers through his hair.

"Then let's do this," Cal said as he started down the steps.

At the bottom, the terrace spilled into the Grand Wailea's open air lobby, complete with sparkling canals winding through tropical plants and palm trees. In the distance, soothing piano notes drifted into the air as birds squawked in the trees, drawing Cal's attention to a view of the night sky. When he lowered his eyes, a burst of light hit him, and he headed directly into it, stopping only feet from a railing at the rear of the lobby. A gust lifted his hair as he turned to greet Paula Ritchie. T-Rex was standing next to her.

"That's a wrap on the sound check," T-Rex said. "Ten seconds, and we're live."

Paula reached down and squeezed Cal's hand, releasing it as the cameras started rolling.

"Good evening. I'm WNGA reporter, Paula Ritchie, coming to you with breaking news. I'm live tonight at the American Academy of Cardiology underway here at the posh Grand

Wailea hotel on Maui. Several weeks ago we reported on biopharmaceutical startup, Zuritech Corporation. As you may recall, the company is a subsidiary of Swiss-based, Zuritech AG, and currently considered by analysts to be one of the hottest biotech startups in the US. I have with me tonight the CEO of Zuritech Corporation, Dr. Calvin Hunter. Dr. Hunter, what can you tell us about these latest developments?"

"Thank you, Paula. Just one correction before we begin. I am the former CEO of Zuritech Corporation. As of about five minutes ago, I have resigned my position with the company."

"Perhaps you'd like to begin by explaining your actions?"

Cal took a deep breath as he looked over at the man in the suit who had followed him from the ballroom, standing with his arms crossed in front of a marble statue.

"Early last evening, I came into possession of documents that revealed troubling details surrounding Zuritech's breakthrough drug known as ZuriMax."

"Troubling how, Dr. Hunter?"

"Zuritech set out to obtain FDA approval for its new drug, just like any other pharmaceutical company, only a few years ago they ran into problems. In phase II of the clinical trials, the company discovered that the drug was unsuited for human use."

"Dr. Hunter, I realize professionals in the industry may understand, but can you explain what you've just said in layman's terms?"

"Tests revealed that the drug's composition was toxic in humans," Cal said, looking squarely into the camera. "At the time, Zuritech had received approval for an expanded access program, which allows controlled quantities of unapproved drugs to be dispensed to the public. Typically, this is done out of compassion for high risk patients. But to be clear, the company discovered the toxicity prior to implementing expanded access."

"So you're saying they took the proper actions?" Paula said.

"No, I said they discovered the problem. Tragically, Zuritech continued to test the drug on patients off the record. You see, they were proceeding on a trial-and-error basis, attempting to resolve the formulation's toxicity."

"Dr. Hunter, I've always understood that the Food and Drug Administration closely monitors the approval process."

"Paula, FDA programs frequently operate on the honor system. There just aren't enough FDA personnel to provide oversight. In Zuritech's case, the company found a way to leverage the resource constraints by engaging in unethical activities. The evidence I uncovered last night suggests that ZuriMax has long-term side effects and is responsible for numerous deaths. I want the public to be aware that the drug has been submitted to the FDA for approval with the same toxic formulation, but using a lower dosage."

"You're suggesting they cut corners?" Paula said.

"Yes, to fast-track the approval. Time is gold in the pharmaceutical industry. Once the drug is on the market, Zuritech knows it will take time for the adverse effects to surface from the milder formulation."

"But you said patients are already dead?"

"That's correct. There are deaths that have resulted from unapproved use of the drug, and the company has managed to cover them up. The statistics are incomplete at the moment, but I would estimate fatalities to be in the hundreds," Cal said. "Many more will die if the drug is commercialized."

"If what you're saying is true, why has no one come forward?"

Cal's cut his eyes to the man at the statue, who gave him a nod.

"The initial patients treated with ZuriMax are individuals who illegally entered the United States."

"Wait," Paula said, placing a hand on Cal's shoulder to steady herself. "Am I hearing you correctly? They tested the drug on illegal immigrants?"

"That's correct. Zuritech operated under the radar by using illegals as nothing more than laboratory rats. The victims were compensated for their services, but clearly had no idea of the risks involved. I believe this may prove to be the most catastrophic event in the history of the pharmaceutical industry."

"And what is your role in all of this?" Paula said.

"I was hired to launch ZuriMax in the United States, once it received FDA approval. Shortly after I arrived at the company I began to sense things were not right. This led me to investigate certain activities within the company that have resulted in tonight's story."

"Can you tell us more?" Paula said.

"I prefer not to comment since there are legal charges being filed as we speak."

"Do those charges include arrests?"

"Before I answer, first let me say I have assembled a team of professionals in Atlanta who have nothing to do with these activities. However, I do believe there are Zuritech executives and contractors, possibly government officials, who have broken the law."

"And the charges?"

"Violation of FDA regulations, money laundering, kidnapping, and possibly murder. I'd like to add, we currently have missing people who we believe were entrapped by these events. I would appreciate the media's cooperation in helping officials to bring them home safely."

"Dr. Hunter, these are serious allegations. What is law enforcement's response, and what do you plan to do now that you have resigned from Zuritech?"

"I'll answer the second part, first. As you know, I am a physician by training. For some time now, I have believed that my abilities lie in seeking out medical discoveries that will benefit mankind. That mission is unchanged. My wife and I plan to take a little time to ourselves, and then I'll get on with the next phase of my career."

"Do you feel that you have failed in this case?"

"Just the opposite, Paula. This experience has tested my character, integrity, and values. I intend to place it in the win column."

"You're saying it's been a success?"

"Lives will be saved . . . and at the end of the day that's what matters most."

"I'm sure we all agree," Paula said with a smile. "And I'm counting on an exclusive follow-up when you land your next assignment."

"As for the law enforcement question, let's go straight to the source," Cal said, raising a hand toward the statue. "I'd like to introduce Detective Charles Rhodes with the FBI."

Chapter 64

**ANAHEIM, CALIFORNIA
SUNDAY, OCTOBER 16
8 P.M. PDT**

Tony Harkins kicked back at his desk with his scuffed oxfords propped up on a stack of files that were ready to topple. A cigar stuck out of his mouth, still sealed in the cellophane wrapper. There was a thunderous noise outside, prompting him to switch the telephone to the other ear. As he shifted, he lifted a foot and kicked a portable television that was having reception problems.

"That was brilliant," Harkins said. The cellophane crackled as he spoke.

"So you're okay with what I said, legally speaking?" Cal said.

"It was priceless. Where are you, anyway?"

"Climbing on a barstool. Hold on," Cal said. "I'll have a draft . . . yeah, the tall one."

"And I'm sitting here watching palm trees sway behind this gorgeous Ritchie woman, wondering why I'm still in Anaheim," Harkins said.

"About sixty feet over her left shoulder, I'm kicking back with a Lavaman Red Ale."

"I know your type. You're one of those who like to rub a guy's nose in it," Harkins said. He bit down on the cigar and pierced the cellophane, unleashing a rash of spitting sounds on his end. "Hey, where's the blonde stewardess that flew over with you?"

"She's up in my room," Cal said. The bartender set down a beer.

"You son-of-a-beer-sipping rich boy," Harkins said. "Don't let Kate find out. That woman's like a cruise missile."

Cal heard banging sounds over the line, followed by the shrill of cats. He pulled the phone away from his ear.

"I thought you were in the office?"

"Those are cats fighting over scraps of Chinese takeout around back. I gotta get out of this dump. Hey, take a look at the tube."

Cal glanced over at the real Paula Ritchie and Charles Rhodes in front of the camera, and then up at a television over the bar. The scene switched from the Grand Wailea to a reporter standing at a port facility.

"Paula, we have breaking news from Umm Qsar on the southern coast of Iraq," a reporter announced. "Fox News has just learned that FBI agents are engaged in a sting operation to cut off an illegal network that is diverting pharmaceuticals bound for Iraq."

The reporter turned to a ship in the background.

"From what we have learned, the cargo liner you see docked here in the Persian Gulf is loaded with pharmaceuticals that were intended for humanitarian efforts. It has not been confirmed, but we are told that the ship is loaded with drugs produced and sold by some of America's largest pharmaceutical companies.

"We have also learned that these drugs were flown into Al Basrah on a Federal Express jet that departed yesterday from

Newark, New Jersey. Although Federal Express has not been charged with any wrongdoing, unconfirmed sources tell us that thousands of bottles of drugs confiscated by the FBI were shipped by a US nonprofit organization to Iraq. We also understand that the workers loading this ship are not Americans."

The reporter started walking with a camera in tow, offering a shot of the administration building. "FBI agents are questioning a Federal Express flight crew, as well as individuals from the cargo ship inside this building. An industry insider told us that the retail value of drug shipments of this magnitude is estimated to be in the millions of dollars. It is not known at this point how long the operation has been underway, but a spokesperson for US drug giant, VistaBio, has reported disruptions in the sales for one of their leading drugs. They have asked authorities to look into a possible connection. Fox News will be standing by on location for further updates. Paula, back to you."

"And the story continues to unfold," Paula said. Her image reappeared on the TV with Charles Rhodes by her side. "Detective Rhodes, while we were listening to developments in Iraq, WNGA learned that the FBI has made arrests at Briscoe Field in Atlanta. Reporters on the ground there said that two men have been taken into custody after a van they were driving was found to be loaded with materials believed to be explosives. It is unconfirmed, but we now understand that the van was parked at a hangar leased by Zuritech Corporation. It is also believed that the jet housed in that hangar is the one that flew Dr. Calvin Hunter, who spoke to us only moments ago, to Maui for this meeting. Would you like to comment?"

"Paula, this is an ongoing investigation, and we cannot disclose details at this time," Rhodes said.

"Did you hear that?" Harkins blurted out.

"Listen up, Tony. Did you file the breach of contract suit?" Cal said.

"Signed, sealed, and delivered. I don't have to tell you, but this is turning into one mother of a lawsuit. Which reminds me, you promised more files."

"I overnighted them to your office," Cal said. "The FBI has a copy as well."

"And they're ironclad?"

"Singh Lee recovered copies of the stock agreements with Albert Jensen and Dr. Patel in Zurich. The documents are signed by Nick—"

"Call them bribes," Harkins interrupted. He stuck the cigar back into his mouth. "It sounds better, especially when we get in front of a judge."

"I also have an e-mail from Dr. William Mallory that confirms he knew about the toxic effects of ZuriMax while he was working on phase II. He raised the flag shortly before his death."

"In a jet explosion, no less. I'll make sure the FBI compares the residue from Mallory's crash to the explosives they uncovered in Atlanta," Harkins said. "You're going to be one rich man, Dr. Hunter. That is, if Zuritech doesn't go bankrupt before we sue their Buster Browns off."

"I want you to make sure the employees are taken care of," Cal said.

"How about your buddy, Dr. Messinger?"

"Let's say he's innocent until proven guilty."

"Now about that Grand Cayman operation," Harkins said, striking a match. "You mentioned money laund—"

"Sorry, I've got to go."

"Wait, we're not done," Harkins said, hunching over the TV.

"I'm afraid so. There's a champagne blonde at one o'clock, and she's headed my way," Cal said.

Chapter 65

MAUI, HAWAII
MONDAY, OCTOBER 17
9 A.M. HAST

The elevator doors opened on the top floor of the Grand Wailiea's Napua Tower. Cal stepped out with Charles Rhodes, who checked his watch, and then motioned for Cal to follow. They walked up to a set of double mahogany doors baring a Hawaiian name plaque, and Rhodes tapped twice, twisting the handle and making way for Cal to pass by into a marble foyer.

"Call me before you leave town," Rhodes said, closing the door.

The foyer flowed into a formal living room where a baby grand piano sat in a corner. Grass cloth walls were covered with watercolors of local island scenes, and to the left and right, doorways led to bedrooms. To the rear, louvered doors had been folded back to frame a view of blue sky and ocean stretching to the horizon.

Cal slipped over to the piano, running a hand across the polished surface as he made his way out to the patio. Just outside, a sous-chef worked in front of a portable grill. The pan he was holding sizzled over leaping flames. To his left, Cal spotted his host seated at a table, fussing over an omelet. Cal crossed the patio to a brass rail and cast his eyes seaward, inhaling the million dollar view. Silver clattered against china behind him.

"Dr. Hunter," the man said, lifting his fork in the air. "I don't believe I've had the honor."

Cal thumped the rail and listened to the brassy report. Then he leaned out, resting his hands on top.

"Would you like breakfast, maybe some coffee?" the man said, stuffing the fork into his mouth.

Cal studied the grounds below where a reflecting pool stretched from the base of the hotel toward the ocean. At the far end, he noticed crystal blue fountains spewing among statues of dolphins dancing on the water. Palm trees lined the lawn to either side of the pool, and in the distance, he spotted Wailea Beach basking in the swells of the Pacific. The soothing sounds of the fountains and crashing waves were briefly pierced by din drifting in from the beach. Pushing off the rail, Cal cut his eyes to the chef, and then pulled up a chair next to his host.

"I saw last night's interview, and I must applaud your media savvy. You're a man who chooses his words carefully," the man said. He brushed at the air with his hand, and the chef stepped inside.

"It's your meeting, Mr. Secretary," Cal said. "What's on your mind?"

Lawrence Baker rested his fork and pushed back in the chair, crossing his legs. "In response, I was compelled to issue a press release regarding the Zuritech scandal. It seems you've managed to level suspicions at one of our officials."

"They're called indictments," Cal said.

"Don't get me wrong. Dr. Patel must pay for any wrongdoing on his part, but I wish to point out an inconsistency that you may have overlooked. This morning, our FDA biostatisticians reviewed the ZuriMax submission. It seems all the patients are there, even the ones with adverse drug reactions."

"If you're suggesting Patel was a victim in this crime, you may want to take a look at the rest of the evidence."

"My point is . . . the patient list is complete, even the ones who died from the drug," Baker said. "Your own accusations suggest that the operation was designed to conceal information from the FDA."

"It's quite simple. When crooks conspire to illegal activities, every once in a while Mother Justice finds a way." A smile brushed the corners of Cal's mouth.

"Dr. Patel would never be crazy enough to take a bribe, and then allow self-incriminating evidence inside the administration. It would be suicide."

"Let's face it, the man's a bureaucratic whore, and in my opinion, not exactly in a position to be calling the shots," Cal said, looking over at Baker. "But if you ask me, he got what he deserved."

"Of course, you realize ZuriMax will never be approved, at least not under Zuritech ownership. The press coverage alone will make it politically impossible."

"I should think not, Mr. Secretary. People are dead," Cal said.

Baker looked off into the ocean. "Dr. Hunter, about Albert Jensen. He is a dear friend, but I will not stand by him in this matter."

"In other words, you intend to deny any responsibility in all of this?"

Baker winced, as if he had been stung. "May I speak off the record?"

"I didn't come here to compromise," Cal said.

"Very well, I simply request that you defer the media to me. After all, you have no direct knowledge of discussions I may have had with Albert," Baker said. "He introduced me to Nicolai von Weir. At the time, they extolled the merits of ZuriMax and how it could impact our national healthcare crisis by lowering drug costs. He went on to say it would reduce the number of surgeries over time. It sounded like a winner."

"So you're saying you did have discussions about ZuriMax."

"Only for moral support. At the time, they characterized it as a medical breakthrough. At least, that was their claim."

"And what was your interest?" Cal said.

"We are at war, Dr. Hunter."

"You want me to believe that you had no influence over Dr. Patel's judgment?"

"I simply asked him to review the data for expedited approval, nothing more."

"Then I'm sure it will come out in the investigation," Cal said. "And I don't blame you for standing down when it comes to Dr. Jensen, especially since your aspirations seem to be much loftier than your present cabinet position."

"Thank you for your understanding."

"As for the future, Mr. Secretary, there is a price to pay for defying the public trust."

"Well spoken, Dr. Hunter. You're not thinking of running for office, are you?"

Cal rose from his seat. "I once took an oath to do no harm to the patients who put their lives in my hands. And for better or worse, the American people have placed their faith in you." Cal paused for a view of the Pacific. "But for the record, your presence here personifies everything that is wrong in Washington." Cal disappeared through the doorway.

"So noted, Dr. Hunter," Baker said under his breath.

Secretary of Health & Human Services, Lawrence Baker, Announces Investigations

WASHINGTON, DC - Lawrence Baker announced today that the FBI has opened an investigation into possible illegal activities conducted by an official within the US Food & Drug Administration. Dr. Raji Patel is alleged to have taken bribes from drug maker, Zuritech AG, which is currently seeking approval for its cardiovascular drug, ZuriMax. According to industry sources, the drug once widely considered to be the next major breakthrough in the treatment of heart disease, is now believed to be linked to a number of deaths previously undetected in the illegal immigrant population residing within the United States. Dr. Calvin Hunter, former CEO of Zuritech Inc. of Atlanta, Georgia, referred to the patients as "little more than laboratory rats" in a press conference from Maui, Hawaii.

In the same announcement, Secretary Baker condemned the actions of a US nonprofit organization, the Rx Freedom Project. The organization is believed to be responsible for diverting millions of dollars in donated pharmaceutical products back into United States that were originally earmarked for charitable distribution in developing countries. Baker stated that recent efforts by the FBI to locate the founder of the Newark, New Jersey based nonprofit agency have proven unsuccessful. It is believed that he may have used false credentials to legitimize the charity in the eyes of pharmaceutical executives and regulatory officials. Rumors suggest that a number of US pharmaceutical companies may be filing charges against the Rx Freedom Project and its founder, Christopher Smith. It is not clear from the announcement whether Secretary Baker believes the activities of the Rx Freedom Project are related to allegations leveled at Zuritech AG. Mr. Baker did indicate that all collaboration between the Rx Freedom Project and government agencies will be discontinued indefinitely, pending an FBI investigation.

Chapter 66

MAUI, HAWAII
MONDAY, OCTOBER 17
11 A.M. HAST

A humpback whale broke the water's surface in front of a mass of rock that seemed to be floating on the surface of the Pacific. There were several screams as beachcombers reacted, pausing to point and stare. The tail arched skyward, and more tourists leaped from their chairs for a better view. Cal raised a hand to shade his eyes, searching a sandy area beneath a grove of palm trees.

"Dr. Hunter," a voice called out.

Cal spotted a guy waving and standing next to a lounge chair with two girls. He marched over. "T-Rex," Cal said. "Are you ready for some fun in the sun?"

"Thomas Rexall," he said, extending a hand.

Cal reached out. "Excuse me?"

"Thomas Rexall—like the drugstore name," T-Rex said, diverting his eyes to Holly.

"Hello ladies . . . Holly, Jamie," Cal said.

"Nice swimsuit, Cal," Jamie said, giving him the once-over. "Kate's got a new one, too."

Cal looked from Jamie to Holly, and then to Kate sitting in the lounge chair.

"It was a gift from Kate," Cal said. "She's got a thing for palm trees."

"If it isn't the talk of the town, my adorable husband," Kate said, lowering a newspaper. "Did you read this?" She held the paper for Cal to see.

"I'll be signing autographs in the gift shop later today," Cal said with a smile.

The others huddled around Kate's chair for a look.

"I'd say Lawrence Baker is neck-deep in alligators," Kate said.

"Funny one, Kate," Jamie said, draping herself over Kate's shoulder.

Cal caught a glimpse of Jamie's tattoo and dropped his sunglasses on his nose, stepping back.

"Good news, Holly," Cal said. "The FBI has agreed to a plea bargain with Boscoe. Jana and Roberto are being held in Mexico, but they're okay."

"Awesome," Holly said, dancing in place. "Maybe I can invite her for a weekend on *Coastal Confessions* when she gets back?"

"I'll call Tony, and you guys can make it a pajama party," Cal said.

T-Rex shot him a look.

"It's an inside joke, Thomas," Cal said.

"Where've you been, love of my life?" Kate said.

"In a meeting," Cal said. "Why did we choose this beach instead of the one behind the hotel?"

"In case you haven't noticed, it's—I don't know—like paradise down here. But why don't you ask the kids?" Kate said.

Cal looked to Thomas and the girls.

"We're heading over to Little Beach," Jamie said. "It's past the rocks over there. You want to come?" She pointed as

Thomas and Holly took off. In the distance, a cliff jutted down to the water's edge.

"Let's do it," Cal said, reaching down and grabbing Kate's hand.

Kate held fast and yanked him down, sending Cal sprawling onto the foot of her chair.

"Hold your little palm trees right there," Kate said.

"What's gotten into you?" Cal said, looking from her to the others as he sat up.

The trio stared back blankly. Kate brushed them away with her hand as she leaned back.

"I'll explain it later," Kate said. "What's the word from Atlanta?"

Cal raised a finger to Kate, and then cupped his hands around his mouth.

"Sunset cruise on the boat when we get back home," he called out. "Where's Paula?"

Jamie did a three-sixty. Her hands and shoulders were raised, not missing a step as the group moved on down the beach.

"Sheri cleaned out my office, and Beta Hut is an ash heap. Chase is now a national hero," Cal said to Kate.

"Chase, the computer geek?"

"He added the old clinical patient data to the FDA submission," Cal said. "And Tony's agreed to represent the victims and their families. With the latest developments, I'm afraid Nick may have trouble leaving the country." Cal's smile went sour as he rolled his head for a look at Kate. "What?"

"I received a call from Singh Lee," Kate said.

"How's the little tart doing?"

"She hooked up with a doctor at the Academy this morning, Dr. Timothy Warren. Evidently, he went to school with her at Stanford, and quite a hunk. I think she's smitten with the guy."

"And you're telling me this, why?"

"Because he's good looking and has connections. I understand he's a medical researcher at the University of Rochester. After last night's reality show, he informed Singh Lee that he holds the original patents on the ZuriMax compounds and has been trying to contact you. He claims that Zuritech's sustained release mechanism is what screwed up the formulation. Not only that, but he believes he knows how to remove the toxicity. And get this, according to his contract all rights revert back to him if Zuritech fails to commercialize the product."

"So Singh Lee calls just to make chit-chat?" Cal said.

"They need a CEO for the new company."

"Not interested."

"Can I finish?" Kate said. "She asked if I was okay with her talking to you about the job."

"She didn't."

"Only problem is, they need fifty million in seed capital to get things rolling," Kate said. "They thought you might know how to get your hands on that kind of cash."

Cal hopped up, taking Kate by the hand.

"Starting right now, and for as long as I can spot a palm tree, we're on vacation." Cal pulled her out of the chair.

They strolled to the water's edge and paused to let the Pacific wash over their feet as Kate toyed with her bikini wrap.

"I have a present for you." Cal pulled a DVD out of his pocket and pressed it into Kate's hand.

"What's this?"

"You said you wanted to see it."

"And you believed me?" Kate looked down, turning the disc over in her hand.

"It's my way of saying . . . you're the only one I want swinging in my palm tree."

"In that case, have I got a surprise for you? No, make that two surprises," Kate said. She took a half-step forward, drawing the DVD back like a Frisbee. She tossed it into the air, and the disc sailed over the tops of the waves, lifting on the breeze. The wind nudged it higher, gaining altitude like it was climbing invisible steps. A gust flipped the DVD on edge, and the sun sparkled on its polished surface, just before Kamohoalii summoned it to the sea.

Kate shielded her eyes, smiling up at Cal. He leaned over and kissed her, and then took her by the hand and started down the beach.

"Did I ever tell you the crazy dream I had about Chinese takeout?" Cal said.

"I'm listening." Kate wrapped an arm around Cal's waist.

"It starts out on top of my credenza in a passion fit only for a buffet. There's fried rice, broccoli, and almond chicken showering all over the floor."

"In your office?" Kate said. "You're awful."

"We have rice and vegetables stuck to our clothes, and just as the little black dress is about to be sacrificed to the gods, I see my reflection in the window. There's a piece of chicken stuck right—here." Cal raised a finger to his forehead.

"Wait—wait—wait," Kate said. "I don't own a black dress."

Cal dropped the finger. "Kate, it was a dream."

"But you never said I was in it."

"Why would I tell you my dream if—"

"What color was her hair?" Kate interrupted.

"It must have been blonde because she looked like one satisfied woman to me."

"Uh-huh. And it was Chinese takeout? It better not have been that oriental Barbie Doll."

"Just a minute," Cal said, stopping in place. He reached out and rested his hands on Kate's shoulders. The wind flirted with her hair.

"So was it her?" Kate said.

"You said you had two surprises."

Kate smiled and took Cal's hand. "All this talk, and you haven't said a word about my new swimsuit."

Cal looked down, resting his eyes on a skimpy navy top covered in neon butterflies.

"Now that is reason enough to be on vacation," Cal said.

Pressing her fingertips to Cal's chest, she pushed him away and stepped back. Kate reached down and loosened the wrap and tossed it across a shoulder. Then she turned and looked back, lifting her sunglasses in anticipation of Cal's reaction. His eyes casually drifted to her hips.

"Holy . . . you're wearing—"

"Malibu Strings," Kate said, brushing a ribbon of hair behind her ear.

Cal looked around as tourists strolled by.

"Is that thing legal?"

"Don't point, dear." Kate took Cal by the hand and led him down the beach away from the beachcombers.

"So what's the deal with Little Beach?" Cal said.

"Cal, forget about Little Beach. I have other plans."

"And I have no say in the matter?"

"You tell me," Kate said. She let go of his hand and dropped the wrap, dashing for a stand of coconut palms.

"Hey wait," Cal called out. "I'm in."

Dennis Carr lives in Atlanta where he and his wife, Cheryl, enjoy sailing in their spare time. His writing delves into the private lives of corporate executives, where egos and bottom lines make for great mystery. *Corporate Rules* is his second novel.

Follow Dennis on Facebook

Made in the USA
Coppell, TX
27 November 2023